Cradle to Grave

Also by Aline Templeton

MARJORY FLEMING SERIES

Cold in the Earth
The Darkness and the Deep
Lying Dead
Lamb to the Slaughter
Dead in the Water

STAND-ALONE NOVELS

Traitor
Death is My Neighbour
Last Act of All
Past Praying For
The Trumpet Shall Sound
Night and Silence
Shades of Death

Cradle to Grave

A Marjory Fleming Thriller

ALINE TEMPLETON

WITNESS
IMPULSE
An Imprint of HarperCollinsPublishers

This book was originally published in 2011 by Hodder & Stoughton Ltd., an Hachette UK Company.

EPub Edition MAY 2014 ISBN: 9780062301819

Print Edition ISBN: 9780062301826

10 9 8 7 6 5 4 3 2 1

To the memory of Robbie Robertson: a good man

Chapter One

Wednesday, 19 July

SHE HAD NO idea how long she had been walking, though such light as there was had begun fading into an ominous twilight. Her flimsy trainers, caked with mud, were squelching and she had lost count of the number of times she had slipped and almost fallen. There was a bloody bruise on her ankle and a deep graze on one hand where she had clutched at a boulder to save herself.

But Beth was unaware of her injuries, unaware of anything, really, except the depth of her wretchedness. She'd always hated rain, ever since that dreadful night two years ago. That dreadful night . . .

The garden had looked strange and unearthly in the cold blue light from the street lamps. The trees were dripping and there were wet leaves on the path, slippery under her hurrying feet. And the trees dripped, dripped, dripped, on and on through the horror of her dreams afterwards. Oh, she hated rain.

Now the downpour that had drenched her hair and soaked right through her inadequate parka seemed as much a part of her as the tears she had shed.

The rocky track, starting at the cove, where a few cottages huddled into the shelter of the low cliff behind, led right round the headland, then circled back, following the rising ground to the top of the bluff itself, from which a precipitous path dropped down to the cove again. The viewpoint there had often been Beth's refuge, a place where no one could come upon you unawares, where sitting on the old wooden bench, you could be alone with the sky and the sea, and look out to the limitless horizon, dreaming of freedom from the cage of your circumstances. That had been Lee's promise to her – freedom.

Today, as she walked following the line of the coast, there was no horizon. Sullen sea and leaden sky merged in an indeterminate, lightless grey. The colour of despair.

She had been angry when she left the tiny house. 'Red angry', she called it: when rage possessed her so that she could hardly think, or breathe, even. She had yelled at him so much that her throat still hurt.

She wasn't angry now, though. The relentless pounding of the rain had doused the spark of fury and the greyness had seeped through her, through the pores in her skin, through into the core of her being.

The path had begun to rise sharply and she realised with a sense of shock that she was almost back at the bluff above the cove, a circuit of several miles, and the surge of adrenaline that had driven her to this fierce, pointless activity was long gone. She must have been walking for hours: her leg muscles were starting to twitch and she was breathless with exertion and stress. It was almost completely dark now too; the street lights outside the cottages had come on.

Suddenly she was very, very tired. Too tired to scramble down the path to the cove. Too tired to deal with what awaited her below. Later, she would have to. Just not yet.

The bench, 'her' bench, stood only yards from the edge, where a ramshackle fence with sagging wires and a weathered, barely legible notice warned against intrusion on to the eroding ground. Not even pausing to brush off the water collected on the seat, she sat down heavily and put her head in her hands. The hiss of the rain and the low moaning of the sea below seemed almost a cry from her own spirit.

It was cold, though, now that she'd stopped moving. The rain was heavier than ever, coming down in silver rods to flay her defenceless body. It would soon be too dark to see her way down. She would be forced to go back—

The noise assaulted her without warning, the air round about her reverberating with a sound like a clap of thunder directly overhead. But it went on and on, not overhead but beneath her feet. The ground was shaking, shifting, and the terrifying groaning grew and grew.

Screaming, she leaped up and fled back the way she had come, in a stumbling run, until the ground felt stable under her feet once more. She turned and saw that the bench where a moment earlier she had been sitting was slipping away from her, faster and faster, until it disappeared, along with the edge of the cliff, in a final apocalyptic roar.

'WHAT'S SHE LIKE, then?' The woman who spoke was perching on the edge of a table in the CID room in the Galloway Constabulary

Headquarters in Kirkluce. She was in her late thirties, neat and competent-looking, with a no-nonsense bob and make-up that suggested that when she expended time and thought, it wasn't on her appearance. Her grey trousers and wrap-top were smart but unobtrusive.

There were only three of them in the room. A demonstration was taking place outside the council offices to protest about the summer floods which had devastated houses in several areas, and the officers not on crowd control had gone along to hold a watching brief.

She had addressed DS Tam MacNee, but he didn't reply immediately. His swarthy, acne-pitted face took on a jaundiced look; he sucked in air through the gap between his front teeth, then said briefly, 'Just don't mess her about. That's all.'

'Big Marge,' DC Kim Kershaw persisted, reflecting on the nickname commonly in use for DI Marjory Fleming. 'Hunky with it, is she?'

MacNee rose to his full five foot seven – well, six and a bit, but when it came to MacNee, no one was counting. Not out loud, anyway.

'She's all right. And as of tomorrow she's back as my superior officer as well as yours. So keep a civil tongue in your head.'

He picked up the black leather jacket hanging on the back of his chair and shrugged himself into it, then with his hands stuck into his jeans pockets went out, leaving an awkward silence behind him. Kershaw looked after him uncomfortably.

DS Andy Macdonald, who was in his early thirties, tall, dark, with a buzz cut and an instinct for self-preservation, had wisely kept out of it. He took pity on her now. 'It's like the Cheshire Cat's grin. The atmosphere lingers long after Tam's left the room. You'll get used to it.'

'Can't get it right with him, can I? Oh, probably I will get used to him, or he'll have to get used to me. One or the other, or preferably both. We don't have to like each other – this is a place of work, not a dating agency.'

She saw that Macdonald's brown eyes were looking at her doubtfully. 'Oh, I don't mean I want to cause trouble, just the opposite. I want a good professional relationship, but with him it doesn't seem to work. I daresay we'll rub along. "Yes, Sarge," when it's an order – I can manage that. But for God's sake tell me what I need to know before I go putting my size sixes in it again. Pals, are they, him and the boss?'

Macdonald hesitated. 'It's a bit complicated. They go back a long way. He was her sarge when she was a rookie, but he never wanted promotion to a job that would mean more time at his desk. Not exactly a details man, our Tam. They work together pretty closely – worked together,' he corrected himself. 'She's clever – brilliant at reading the evidence – and he's got seriously good gut reactions. Great combination. But the suspension . . .' He sighed. 'Let's put it this way. He was on the side of the authorities. He thought she got it wrong. Big time.'

'Someone died, didn't they?'

'Someone died. Let's leave it at that. It was a misjudgement and media politics were involved. We all get our calls wrong sometimes and it's over now. If the tribunal's decision had gone the other way, I'd have handed in my badge.'

'Seriously?' Kershaw raised a deeply sceptical eyebrow.

Macdonald met her look squarely. 'I'm not kidding. Oh, not as some sort of loyalist support. I just wouldn't trust them. If it was her today, it could be me tomorrow.

'She was the first woman in Galloway to make promotion to DI, and if there were people who thought that was a man's job, they don't think it now. She's honest and she's fair-minded, and she's a good officer. She'll back you to the hilt unless she thinks you're not trying.'

Kershaw pulled a face. 'Very touching, Sarge. Has she got the place bugged, then?'

'Too smart. She's not interested in what we say about her behind her back. She's clever enough to know that's a good safety valve. Watch what you say to her face, though.'

'Thanks, Andy. That's useful. I always like to have a dossier on the boss. But to go back to the original question – what's she like, Big Marge?'

Macdonald grinned. 'Oh, like Tam said, don't mess.'

DARKNESS WAS THICK about Beth and it was still raining, though less heavily now. There was no track to follow, only miles of rough grass and moorland, and she was struggling through heather and stumbling over hidden rocks. Then boggy ground would suck at her feet until she thought she would be dragged down, down, down, and though there was no one to hear her, she screamed out loud as she fought herself free.

It was the dark of the moon, and with the heavy cloud cover there wasn't even a star showing through. Screwing up her eyes to make out what lay ahead in the murk, Beth sometimes wasn't sure she was going in the right direction. Her only guide was the sound of the sea – keeping it to her left meant that she had to be heading back along the peninsula and sooner or later would strike the road – but it was hard to make herself take the risk of going close enough to the edge to hear it.

After the landslip, it had all gone deathly quiet. Beth had listened for sounds of distress and heard none, but she had been too scared to go near enough to look down. She knew what she'd see, anyway – the cottages obliterated under tons of earth and rocks. She had reluctantly lived for a month in the one she'd inherited from her grandmother and there were three others in the little row: one empty, one belonging to a woman she'd taken care to avoid and one a holiday let. At least there was no need to consider Lee, but she'd seen a young couple there this week, with their baby – oh dear God, the baby! Bile rose in her throat and she retched, feeling acid burn her gullet. The baby, and the rain . . .

Then it had been London rain, though, just dreary, persistent, depressing. It was her night off and she'd been going out with a friend to have a few drinks, cheer themselves up. Only she wasn't, because they'd changed their plans and she was stuck in the house, angry and resentful and not feeling patient. It would all have been different if they hadn't gone out . . .

Beth jerked her mind away from that obsessive thought, which ran on a loop in her brain, only needing the slightest trigger to set it running. Her present situation was bad enough without dredging up the past.

She had fumbled for her mobile phone, in the pocket of her parka with her purse and a comb – all she had left in the world now, presumably – in the hope that up here on the headland she might pick up a signal, but it was obstinately dead. There was nothing to do but stumble on.

Every movement was painful now. She was black and blue all over from her frequent falls. Once, when she had blundered across a grouse, which had whirred up into her face with an unearthly cry, she'd thought she would die of fright. Her tired muscles were screaming for relief, but if she lay down and fell asleep here in this rain, she would die of exposure. She had reason to know that, all too well.

There would be no rescue parties setting out unless she summoned them herself. She was the only one who knew what had happened there at the end of the road, which led nowhere, except to Rosscarron Cottages.

Beth heard the dogs barking before she saw the keeper's house. They had heard her first, obviously, and were working themselves up into a state. Fear seized her: she wasn't used to country life and she had no idea whether they were caged or running free – or even whether their master would come out with a shotgun to defend his isolated homestead against strangers appearing out of the darkness.

Even so, she headed towards the sound and saw a square of light appear, as if floating on the darkness. Another light came on immediately below it. A moment later one was switched on outside too, revealing a house, some outbuildings and, as a door opened, a man with a shotgun. The dogs' barking rose to a frenzy and he switched on a torch, its rays probing the darkness.

Beth stopped, her heart pounding. But what was the alternative? To stagger on blindly to certain death, once her legs literally couldn't carry her any more and she collapsed? Plucking up her courage, she screamed at the top of her voice, 'Help! Help!'

Somehow, he heard her above the din. She could see his surprise. He swung the torch until the beam found her and she stood exposed and helpless. Then, to her intense relief, she saw him break his gun and come towards her with a halting gait.

'Quiet!' he snapped at the dogs, and, as obedient silence fell, shouted, 'Who's there? What's wrong?'

Sobbing with thankfulness, she blundered across the last few yards towards a five-bar gate, opened it and fell on her knees.

He hurried across to her, looking shaken. 'What the hell are you doing here? I could've killed you, for God's sake! Thought it was the fox after the chickens again. Well, I suppose you'd better come inside.'

She didn't notice the grudging response. He helped her to her feet and, stumbling and sobbing, she crossed the yard past the gundogs to Keeper's Cottage.

From their runs, two spaniels and a black lab watched, then, the entertainment over, went back into their kennels.

'THE PHONE'S DEAD. The lines must be down.' Maidie Buchan, her dark, wiry hair tousled from sleep, came back into the kitchen.

It was a gloomy room with a small window covered by thin faded curtains that barely met. An elderly Calor gas cooker stood in one corner, and the only storage was provided by a press and by cupboards under a Formica sink unit. A range on the end wall was cold and dead, and the plastic chairs round the kitchen table, also blue Formica, were unmatched, as if they had been picked up in sales here and there. It was immaculately, almost painfully clean, though, with patches scrubbed away on the old vinyl floor. On one of the shelves on the back wall there was a display of cheap, bright glass ornaments and plates in cheerful colours.

Maidie was in her thirties, thin and tired-looking, wrapped in a tartan wool dressing gown that had seen better days. She cast an anxious glance at her husband as she broke the news.

'That's all we need!' he snarled, looking unenthusiastically at the crumpled figure sitting slumped over the kitchen table. 'Where do we go from here? The woman's not making sense.'

Alick Buchan was almost twenty years older than his wife. An accident with his gun during his time with the army in Northern Ireland had left him with a limp and confirmation of his earlier conviction that the world was against him.

'She's in shock. She's freezing cold too.'

Maidie went to put an arm round her unexpected guest. Her hands were rough and work-hardened, but her touch and her voice were gentle. 'Look, I know you're shattered, but you're needing out of those clothes before you catch your death. I've switched on the immersion and there should be enough hot water for a bath. If you come through the house, I'll get you some clothes and a towel.'

She managed to coax the girl to her feet, though Beth was moving like an old woman and needed Maidie's support to cross the kitchen. 'She'll want a cup of tea when we get back,' she said to her husband. 'Can you put on the kettle?'

Alick grunted, then complied with a bad grace. It wasn't his job to go making cups of tea for strangers in the middle of the night when a working man should be in his bed. A landslide, the lassie had said, and her name, Beth Brown, but what with the way she was carrying on, and her teeth chattering, he hadn't been able to make out anything more.

Maybe the emergency services were dealing with it already, but with the lines down and this area being a dead spot for mobile phones, they couldn't find out. He could only hope Maidie would get Beth sorted so she could tell them what had happened. She was very young – not much past twenty, by the looks of her – so it was all just hysterical nonsense, probably, and then he could get back to his bed. He yawned, went to a cupboard and took out a bottle of whisky and a glass.

When the women returned, Beth was wearing a thick pair of flannelette pyjamas with a woolly sweater over the top, and sheep-skin slippers. She had a little colour in her cheeks, and at least the violent shivering had stopped. She sat down at the table again and began rubbing her hair with a towel, rather ineffectually, as if she weren't quite sure what she was doing. Her hair was very dark, in contrast to her fair skin, and she had a rather heavy face, with light blue eyes. He noticed that there was something strange about them, though he couldn't quite work out what it was.

Maidie was looking almost as pale as Beth. 'She managed to tell me. It's the Rosscarron Cottages, Alick. You know there's a wee sort of cliff up behind them? She was up there and saw half of it fall on the top of them. She was only feet away when the ground just disappeared.'

This wasn't what he had hoped to hear. 'Anyone there at the time?'

'She doesn't know. She says her partner's away, but there's a woman lives in one of the other cottages, and maybe a young couple on holiday with a baby. Alick, you'll need to get over there, see what's going on.'

'Why does this sort of thing always happen to me?' he grumbled. 'Oh, all right, all right. I'll have to go up and change.' He was wearing a Barber jacket and wellington boots over his pyjamas; he threw back the rest of the whisky in his glass and went upstairs.

Maidie made tea, then, after listening anxiously to check that he wasn't coming back, poured a slug of whisky into each mug. It would do Beth good to talk, and in her experience a drop of the craitur had considerable power to loosen tongues.

'I was scared, so scared,' Beth was saying when Alick returned fully dressed. 'I didn't know what to do. I just walked and walked. I couldn't see where I was going.'

His eye lit on the bottle of whisky, standing where he had left it, and unsuspecting, he returned it to the cupboard.

'Don't know when I'll be back,' he said. 'I'll maybe need to go to the big house, but I'd better check it out before I disturb Himself in the middle of the night.'

Maidie agreed. Gillis Crozier, her husband's boss, had quite an intimidating presence at the best of times and you wouldn't want to get him out of his bed for anything less than a full-scale emergency.

Alick went outside. The rain had stopped, though the clouds were still heavy overhead and he reckoned it wouldn't be long before it started again. He jumped into the elderly jeep and turned the key in the ignition.

It coughed, sputtered and stopped. He tried again. And again. He grabbed a rag, jumped out and dried everything he could think of. Then, swearing, he tried it again. And again . . .

Quarter of an hour later Alick came back into the kitchen. 'It's waterlogged. Can't get the bloody thing started at all. I've pushed it under cover in the barn – see how it is by morning.'

Maidie looked at him in dismay. 'So what do we do now?'

'What the hell do you expect me to do? Grope my way two miles along to Rosscarron House in the dark? And then another two to the cottages, maybe, and tunnel through the landfall with my bare hands? They could have the lines fixed by morning and then the people who're paid to do it can sort it out, instead of me. I'm away to get some sleep, that's what I'm doing.' He walked out.

'Beth—' Maidie turned to speak to the girl, to find that she had fallen asleep across the table. Maidie sighed, then shook her gently.

Beth came to with a start. 'What . . . ? Where . . .?'

'You're all right,' Maidie soothed her. 'There's a sofa in Alick's office you can sleep on tonight, and we'll sort things out in the morning.'

Thursday, 20 July

THE HENS MIGHT be birdbrains, but they knew enough to keep out of the rain, taking it as usual as a personal insult. The mash in the trough was a persuasive argument, but even so they emerged from the henhouse with muted, discontented mutterings. Even Gordon, the rooster, was too dispirited to make much of a job of hailing the morning. He was a downtrodden creature anyway: since his predecessor, Tony, had sinisterly disappeared leaving only a ring of feathers, the alpha hen, Cherie, had bullied him unmercifully.

Had there ever been a worse July? Marjory Fleming watched them, her tall figure huddled into a hooded oilskin jacket, but even so her hair, chestnut brown with the odd streak of grey, was soaking wet. Usually her chookies had an instantly soothing effect, but this morning their low spirits seemed to be infectious.

She should be feeling elated, instead of having a knot of nerves in the pit of her stomach. The tribunal yesterday had reinstated her, with immediate effect, and today she would be back at the job she loved. She had been totally cleared of the charge of racism, but there was a reprimand now on a record that before had contained only commendations. It would, she kept telling herself, feel just as it had before once she was back, but somehow she wasn't altogether convinced.

What had changed was her confidence in herself. Vanity had led her into a disastrous mistake, and in future when it was a judgement call – as in her work it so often was – there would be a small voice inside whispering, 'Are you sure?'

For the first weeks of her suspension, Marjory had kept herself busy. She had returned to a fitness regime, which had slipped badly of late, and then begun a relentless programme of purging neglected cupboards and tackling overdue decorating projects, which had left her family begging for mercy. She had been thinking, though, in terms of weeks, not months: her superintendent, Donald Bailey, had assured her that the chief constable would pull strings to get her back on duty as soon as possible – and perhaps he had. Sometimes officers were suspended for years.

But as a month had slipped into two and her projects were completed, the pointlessness of her daily life began to weigh her down. She had set up an efficient domestic support system, geared to her hectic working life, and it had left her with nothing to do. Marjory had always felt there weren't enough hours in the day; now she couldn't believe how slowly the hands of the clock crept round.

As each interminable day crawled past, she doubted herself more and more. She'd always accepted light-heartedly that as a homemaker she was a failure, but if she was no good as a police officer either . . .

Worried, bored and quite desperately unhappy, she became short-tempered. Her long-suffering husband Bill took to spending more time than usual on his work around the farm; she was snappish with her children, Catriona and Cameron. After having her head bitten off when she offered sympathy, Cat had withdrawn, and Cammie, who still had not quite forgiven Marjory for not being a mother first, last and all the time, had reverted to grunting as a means of communication. It was something he did rather well – international standard certainly, and possibly even world class.

Eventually, it seemed futile to make the usual early start to her day. It only meant more hours to fill, and Bill could easily let the hens out and make his own breakfast – he always complained that Marjory's porridge was lumpy anyway. She had slept later and later, yet felt exhausted all the time. Her fitness programme lapsed; she just hadn't the energy for it, but she resisted with scorn Bill's suggestion that she should see a doctor. There was absolutely nothing wrong with her. It was just that she had been working flat out for years and a rest was exactly what she needed.

Her brittle defensiveness only shattered when Cammie, in a clumsy effort to help, dropped a casserole, which shattered on the floor. She heard her own voice screaming at him, saw his white, miserable face and burst into tears.

She couldn't stop. She was entirely unaware of Cat and Cammie exchanging stricken glances and sliding out of the room. It seemed quite a long time later, when she had sobbed herself to a standstill, that she heard Bill's voice saying quietly, 'Finished?'

Marjory looked up blearily. He was holding out a handkerchief and she took it, shamefacedly mopping her eyes.

'You needed that,' Bill said calmly. 'You need a drink too. Come on.'

'Cammie . . .' she said, as she got to her feet.

'Never mind Cammie for the moment. He's OK; you're not.'

Marjory allowed him to lead her through to the sitting room which had seen so many of their long conversations over the years. She sat down in her shabby armchair and Meg the collie, who had followed them through, came to press herself against her mistress's legs in silent sympathy.

Stroking the silky head, she laughed shakily. 'I'm sorry about that, Bill. I don't know what came over me.'

Bill brought her a heavy crystal glass with a generous slug of Bladnoch, the local single malt.

'*I* know,' he said. 'Been there, done that. You're starting to get depressed.'

She glanced up. She remembered the foot-and-mouth epidemic, when the killing squads had wiped out his healthy sheep as a precaution; the wound, clearly, still hadn't quite healed.

Yet somehow his understanding annoyed her. 'Of course I'm depressed. In my position if I wasn't depressed, I'd have failed to understand the situation.'

'Yes, I know, love. But when you start not wanting to get out of bed, and bursting into tears over nothing, you can't pretend you're just being logical.'

Feeling crosser than ever about having the rug pulled from under her, Marjory muttered rebelliously, 'Maybe I can.'

Bill had a smile lurking at the corners of his mouth. 'Getting annoyed about nothing at all – that's another symptom.'

'Oh, you!' She glared at him, then picked up a cushion and hurled it. He caught it effortlessly, trying not to laugh.

Her own laughter was close to tears, and her lip wobbled. 'Don't laugh at me, Bill.'

He came across to her. 'Move up,' he said, and squeezed into the chair beside her, putting his arms round her and dropping a kiss on her forehead. 'I'm not laughing at you. I'm trying to make you laugh with me. Nothing better for getting things in perspective. But I'm serious – go on like this and you'll spiral down into real depression, where you can't see the sun even when it's shining in the sky. I know what you're doing. You're telling yourself a story that isn't true – that somehow without your work, you're nothing – and sooner or later you'll start to believe it and fall apart.'

Majory's voice was muffled as she snuggled into his shoulder. 'It's pretty much true, though, isn't it? I'm hopeless at my other role.'

'As a farmer's wife, you mean? This farmer's perfectly satisfied. I didn't marry you to get a housekeeper – and *that*'s a mercy.'

He was trying to make her laugh again and she managed a watery smile, sitting up and twisting round to face him.

'But, Bill, I've no idea how long this will go on. Some people can be on "gardening leave" for years – and I don't like gardening. I've got to do something.'

Bill got up, stretched his cramped arm and fetched the Bladnoch to refill their glasses, then sat down in his own chair opposite.

'You have to make it something you've got to do. Set yourself a target and stick to it. What is there you're interested in but never had time to do – yoga, flower-arranging?'

Majory gave him a quelling look, but she was thinking. 'They sent me on a short psychology course last year. That was fascinating. Maybe I might pursue that, get a reading list. View it as professional development . . .'

The next morning she had got up with a sense of purpose, and though the worries and frustration certainly remained, her programme of study meant that she felt in control of her life once more. The fitness regime had been reinstated and her household, finding her recognisable again as the woman they knew, had breathed a collective sigh of relief.

And then yesterday the tribunal had cleared her name. Now all she had to do, she told herself firmly as she checked for eggs and collected up the pails, was to get on with the job and live down the humiliation. And rebuild her bridges with Tam MacNee, who apart from the most stiff and formal expressions of regret, had been a stranger to her over these interminable four months.

She felt another nervous twinge in her stomach as she squelched back to the farmhouse.

Chapter Two

ALICK BUCHAN WAS making no attempt to hurry his breakfast. He supped his porridge and drank his tea with maddening deliberation, while his wife, casting anxious looks but saying nothing, bustled about him as if her own busyness might nudge him into action.

Beth Brown, aching in every limb and feeling now the bruises and cuts she had been too shocked to notice last night, sat gripping her mug of tea so tightly that her knuckles showed white. Her brown hair straggled round her pale face, and her eyes were red-rimmed and puffy. Her fitful sleep had been punctuated by hideous dreams: she was in prison again; now she was standing in the dock; the court was rising; the judge had terrible flashing eyes; then the roof fell and she was buried alive under tons of earth . . . She had forced herself awake at last and, too afraid to go back to sleep, had sat up shivering in the cold, grey dawn.

It was barely light outside even now, with a leaden sky. When she had heard sounds of movement, Beth had dragged herself to her feet and got dressed in the jeans and sweater she'd found lying on a chair beside her. The jeans were a bit tight, but she could get into them if she left the waist fastening undone. She sipped at the tea as if even swallowing was an effort.

Eventually, able to bear it no longer, Maidie said to her husband, 'Why don't you try and start the jeep while I make your toast? You'll have to go – the phone's still out, and dear knows when they'll get it mended.'

Grudgingly, Alick got to his feet and went outside. Maidie peered out of the rain-streaked kitchen window, reporting on his progress. 'He's shut the bonnet now. Oh, and wiped his hands on the back of his jeans. That's good. Oily marks to get out in the next wash.'

Just as she spoke there was a loud wail from upstairs. Maidie pulled a face. 'That's Calum. I'll have to get to him before he wakes up Gran. Can you make the toast for Alick, Beth? If it's ready for him, he maybe won't sit down again.'

Stiffly, Beth got up. It hurt to move, but if there was something she could do to be useful, she didn't mind the pain. It had been all too clear last night that, however kind Maidie might be, Beth was an unwarranted intrusion as far as Alick was concerned. A small spark of anger flickered; she didn't want to be here, any more than he wanted to have her. It wouldn't cost him much to pretend to be civilised about it.

As she toasted the bread under the grill of the old cooker, she heard the engine of the jeep catch and then start running smoothly. It stopped and started again a couple of times without a problem, and glancing out of the window she saw Alick jumping down and hurrying across the yard to the house, his hair flattened to his head by the teeming rain.

As he opened the back door, he saw Beth alone and stopped.

'Maidie not here?'

'Your son was crying. She said you'd to have some toast. Here – I've buttered it.'

He took the plate from her without thanks, dug his knife into a pot of raspberry jam and spread both slices thickly. 'I'll take them with me. Might as well get on with it, if I have to.'

Beth's parka was drying on the old-fashioned pulley overhead. She went to pull it down, but Alick frowned.

'You're not coming with me,' he said flatly. Then he paused. 'Unless you want to be dropped off somewhere. With family, maybe?'

Beth could hear the hope of getting rid of her in his voice. 'No,' she said coolly. 'I've no one. Just the cottage. I thought maybe the police would want to speak to me.'

Disappointed, Alick was dismissive. 'What can you tell them they can't see for themselves? And the emergency services won't want people like you getting in the way.'

Beth nodded with apparent submission. She'd learned that trick long ago.

'A night out with a friend? Oh, that's all right, then. You can go another time – have an extra night off. Not this week, though – we've a lot on. Next week, probably. All right?'

She'd agreed, because it was the best-paid job she'd ever had and the result of saying no could be losing it, even though she was at the end of her tether after a difficult day and the promised extra night would never materialise.

Alick seemed satisfied with her practised response. He was on his way out when his wife appeared with a small child on her hip. He looked about eighteen months old, curly-haired and with big, dark eyes, and he was grizzling quietly.

Alick, his mouth full of toast and with the other slice in his hand, said thickly, 'I'll call in and tell Himself what's happened – maybe the phones are all right there. We'll sort her out later.' He jerked his head ungraciously at Beth and left.

Perhaps to cover her embarrassment, Maidie went to get a tissue to wipe her son's tears and his runny nose. 'I think he's getting another cold. He was a right little b yesterday and no doubt he's planning—'

A peremptory voice interrupted her, from upstairs somewhere. 'Maidie! Maidie! Where are you? What's going on?'

'Oh damn! It's wakened Gran. I'd hoped for another hour's peace.' Maidie sighed. 'I'd better go to her.'

'Leave Calum with me,' Beth said quickly. 'I'll look after him.' Maidie hesitated. 'He's not very good with strangers, but. . . .'

Beth held out her arms, smiling, and to his mother's surprise the toddler stopped crying and after taking a long, appraising glance, reached out to her. Beth gathered him to her hungrily.

'You're a lovely boy, aren't you, pet?' she said. 'And no one could be happy with a horrible cold, could they?'

She spotted a small chest of toys in a corner of the kitchen and went to pick up a toy car. 'Look, Calum – it's going to run along here and run along and—Oops, crash! It's fallen off.'

The toddler gave a gurgle of amusement. As Maidie watched, smiling, another shout of 'Maidie! Did you hear me?' came from upstairs.

She sighed again. 'I'll have to go to her.' Then she paused at the door. 'You're awfully good with children, aren't you?'

'I've always loved kids.'

And as Maidie disappeared upstairs, the phrase echoed in Beth's head like the slam of an iron door.

It was another hot day in the airless London summer and the sun was streaming through the great windows. The atmosphere was damp with the breath and the sweat of spectators packed into the public seats. In the crowded press box, hacks with notepads sat scribbling, scribbling.

There had been some dull technical stuff from a defence witness and a somnolent hush had fallen. Despite the chilling majesty of the Old Bailey courtroom, she had felt heavy-eyed herself. Below her on a ledge, a bluebottle on its back spun round and round, buzzing and buzzing in a frenzy of helplessness. She knew just how it felt.

When the next witness was called, the atmosphere changed as if a breeze had blown through. Suddenly there was a hum of talk and the reporters were sitting up.

Her grandmother looked very tiny as she took her place in the witness stand, thin and frail, but with her pain-racked body fiercely erect and her chin tilted. Her flame-red hair looked almost like a flag of defiance.

But compared to the loud, confident tones of the barrister, her soft Scottish voice sounded hesitant as she said, 'But she's always loved the bairns.'

'I CAN'T TELL you how good it is to have you back, Marjory.'

There was no mistaking Superintendent Donald Bailey's sincerity. Even his bald pate was rippling as he gave her a beaming smile. 'We had a couple of shocking substitutes wished on us – shocking.' His plump face clouded as he detailed a few of the inadequacies of Fleming's temporary replacements. 'But we have to put all that behind us now.'

'Absolutely, Donald.' There would be no one happier to put it all behind her than DI Fleming herself. But she suspected

Bailey, whose inadequacies when he was an inspector she had exposed in her most recent case, was no longer as supportive of her as he had once been; her suspicions were confirmed as he went on.

'There's something I have to say to you, though – not official, you understand, just a word to the wise. For your own sake, Marjory, be very careful for the next bit. There were mutterings in high places about the adverse publicity all this generated. So cover your back – everything by the book, all "i"s dotted, "t"s crossed. Keep your head down, that's my advice.'

She had worked that out for herself, but it didn't feel good to have it spelled out. 'Thanks for the warning, Donald,' she said, a little stiffly. 'I certainly intend to.'

'Of course you do!' His voice was slightly too hearty. 'Excellent, excellent. The matter's closed now as far as I'm concerned. Now, to business . . .'

There was a considerable backlog, both operational and administrative, for Bailey to go through with her. Fleming's head was spinning by the time he shuffled the papers together on his desk and said, 'That about covers it.'

Fleming flipped shut her notebook, keen to get going. She wouldn't be out of here before midnight, by the looks of things.

'Thanks, Donald. That's been enormously helpful. Anything else?'

'Our most immediate problem at the moment is the flooding. There was a demonstration yesterday afternoon – you heard about it?'

Fleming nodded. 'There's a lot of sympathy in the town. It's all in places where houses should never have been built. For instance, the Carron – I can remember myself seeing flooding at the mouth there years ago, so why the council allowed the project to go ahead without proper flood defences being in place . . .'

Bailey snorted. 'Absolutely ridiculous! They've been talking about defences for years and done nothing about it – there should never have been planning permission. And after all this rain, every river and burn is in spate, of course. I can tell you, Mr Crozier isn't a popular man at the moment.'

Gillis Crozier was a local lad who had done well out of the pop music he had been promoting since the late seventies in London, then a few years ago had reappeared to buy Rosscarron House, a former shooting lodge on the Rosscarron headland, as a second home. He had a finger in a lot of pies, though, and this latest property venture, right on his own doorstep, looked to have been ill judged.

'And of course,' Bailey went on, 'this pop festival has been a flashpoint too.'

Fleming smiled. 'I've two teenagers planning to go. They seem to see a three-day mudbath as a pleasurable activity, though I suppose for Cammie, as a rugby player, mud's more or less his natural element. I'd have thought Cat might have been more delicate about it, but apparently someone called Joshua who's coming from the States is not to be missed. With a band called Destruction – big in retro disco, she tells me.'

Bailey looked pained. 'If you say so. But the point is, we have two problems. The householders there who are flooded out were upset already over "the invasion of the Great Unwashed", to quote the gentleman who insisted on seeing me personally to complain.'

'It's bringing much-needed casual work to the locality,' Fleming pointed out. 'Ushering, catering, rubbish collection – these events are good business. And the shops will get a boost too.'

'Yes, yes,' Bailey said tetchily, 'that's all well and good. But there are a couple of problems it's thrown up and I'd like you to look into them as a matter of urgency. In the first place, Crozier's filed a complaint about vandalism. Cables that were laid out last week to be connected have disappeared – massively expensive, it seems. Then yesterday he saw that someone had written in weed-killer in the camping field, "No raves here." Or, to be strictly accurate, since the wet weather had made the weedkiller spread, what it actually said was, "No Daves here," but you get the gist.'

Fleming couldn't suppress a choke of laughter. Bailey looked surprised, then grinned himself. Sometimes, if only sometimes, the humour showed, which leavened his pomposity.

'Oh, I suppose . . . But really, Marjory, it isn't funny. Crozier is quite worked up about it, and he's worried about what they might do, with a lot of high-voltage equipment coming in.

'The other problem is the report from Traffic about that bridge over to the headland.'

Fleming shook her head. 'Haven't been there for years. I can't remember what it's like.'

'It was only built for the shooting estate. You're talking about hundreds arriving over the next few days – indeed, a handful of them have apparently arrived already. The Carron's high, of course, and Donaldson, the new man in Traffic . . . Well, between these four walls, Marjory, I think he's a bit of a fusspot. He's say-ing he's not sure about the bridge with that level of traffic.'

Fleming was startled. 'But surely to get insurance they must have done a proper risk assessment?'

'Of course. So this is a complete bolt from the blue.' Bailey's expression indicated that in a properly ordered society this sort of upset would not happen. 'So what I want you to do is go out and see Crozier, try to get a handle on the vandalism and make your own assessment of the bridge. I can't bear to think of the trouble it's going to cause if it has to be cancelled – all those disappointed fans with nowhere to stay and nothing to do.' He shuddered.

'Right,' Fleming said, getting up quickly before he could think of anything else to add to her workload.

As she went to the door, Bailey said, 'We really don't want to encourage Donaldson to be overcautious. If we all went down that route, we'd end up afraid to get out of bed in the morning.'

The obvious implication was that real chaps laughed at Danger, snapping their fingers in her face. Fleming felt rather differently, aware that her precious children, along with the precious children of hundreds of other parents, would be crossing this dubious bridge. She decided to go and talk to Donaldson before she left.

Before that, she had to go to the CID room and see her officers for the morning briefing. The team she liked to work with most closely was depleted: Tansy Kerr had resigned and gone off on a belated gap year while she thought about her future, so that left Andy Macdonald, Ewan Campbell and Tam MacNee.

Oh, yes. Tam MacNee. The knot of nerves in her stomach, which had dissipated slightly while she talked to Bailey, gave another twinge.

MUSIC WITH A heavy beat was, as always, playing when Alick Buchan opened the door to Gillis Crozier's office, having been kept waiting in the kitchen by the Filipino who always came up from London with Crozier, and in Buchan's eyes looked down on the peasants who were outdoor staff.

The office had stark white décor, furnished in the minimalist style with a lot of glass and steel, which quarrelled with the original Victorian features. Buchan always felt uncomfortable in this room and it wasn't entirely due to the way his boss affected him.

'The Rosscarron Cottages?' Crozier, unshaven and showing signs of having dressed hastily, looked stunned as he was told what had happened. He was a big, powerfully built man running a little to fat, with dark hair gone grey, and a long face seamed with lines, which gave him a saturnine appearance. 'That – that was where my parents stayed, where I grew up! Who's living there now?'

'Kind of hard to tell. The girl was in shock. She says there's a woman stays in one and maybe a couple and their baby in a holi-day let.'

'No time to waste, then. Let's get things moving.' He went over to his desk, picked up the handset, listened, then frowned. 'It's out – no Internet either, then. OK, you get down there and check it out, Alick. I'll send someone into Kirkcudbright to alert the police and rescue services. Then I'll be right behind you.'

'Yes, sir.' Buchan went out, resentfully experiencing the slight easing of tension he always felt on leaving. He'd no reason for it: Crozier was a good employer, paying a fair wage and not making unreasonable demands – even ready to say thanks for a job well done. But Buchan liked to think he tugged his forelock to no one, yet somehow here he was doing it: 'Yes, sir. No, sir. Three bags full, sir!'

They'd been in the army together, though the other man had gained a commission. Crozier hadn't had any more advantages than Buchan had himself, growing up in the Rosscarron Cottages out there at the end of 'the road to nowhere', as the locals called it. Maybe it wouldn't be so galling if he'd relied on privilege to get him where he was now, rolling in money – though Buchan had resented the toffee-nosed bastards who'd had it all handed to them on a plate too.

Up here on the headland, the bruise-coloured clouds seemed to wrap him like a shawl. With the wipers going at double speed, Buchan pressed on down the narrow road, which ran for a mile across bleak, featureless moorland, ducking into a passing place as a large silver Mercedes drove up towards him. Oh, he knew his place! But there'd be some fun when people started arriving for the festival.

Lower down, the visibility was better, but all he could see was drifts of rain sweeping in from the sea, below on the left there, a sheet of gun-metal grey. On that side, a smaller road – barely more than a tarmac track – led down a slope, then along the river to where the flooded houses had so mistakenly been built. Straight ahead was the Carron itself.

The bridge that crossed it was a wide, sturdy structure set on wooden struts embedded in concrete piers with elaborate wrought-iron railings and a tarmac surface laid across the wood and metal of the bridge itself. It was a version of the bridges built on estates all across Scotland by Victorians for their posh shooting parties and the lorry loads of slaughtered birds being ferried south.

With steeper, shelving banks here topped by low bushes, the river was contained and the bridge was still well above even its present high level, but even so Buchan cast an anxious glance at it as he drove across. The flood water was gushing angrily along, frothing and bubbling, with small rafts of branches and debris collecting round the base of the piers.

Standing water splashed around the wheels of the jeep as he drove the mile and a bit from the bridge down the other side of the river to connect with the road running along the shore of the Solway Firth – the road to nowhere, which finished at the Rosscarron Cottages. Near its mouth, the river had overflowed its banks, but it was much worse on the far side, where the smart houses with their sea views were awash, the cars parked outside engulfed in water and mud. They'd have to shell out a fine premium for their insurance next year! But then, they could afford it, jammy beggars.

From here, it was less than a mile or so to the cottages and his foot unconsciously slackened on the accelerator. There was no telling what he'd find: people distressed, injured, dead, even. He'd had experience of that serving with the army, but at least there you always had back-up. He kept glancing in the rear-view mirror, hoping to see Crozier's huge black Discovery, but the road behind him remained obstinately empty.

Buchan turned a corner into the short straight before the cottages and found himself suddenly feet away from a wall of earth, rocks and rubble. He swore, slamming on his brakes, and brought the jeep to a shuddering standstill, its nose into soft earth.

His first thought was to back up and inspect the damage, mercifully slight, his second to go back and warn his boss before the Discovery came barrelling into the back of his jeep – Crozier was famous for his lack of respect for local road conditions.

The landslip was blocking the road and the foreshore, right down into the sea. He listened, but all he could hear was the sound of the waves and the steady hissing of the rain, not voices or screams or anything. A good sign or a bad sign? He wasn't sure, but anyway, here was the boss now. He flagged him down, pleased that the responsibility for dealing with this was his no longer.

'WELCOME BACK, MA'AM!'

When DI Fleming arrived for the morning briefing, DS Andy Macdonald came forward to shake her hand and there was a smattering of applause.

Fleming coloured. It was kind of him, but it made the moment of getting back to business as usual more difficult. 'Thanks. Glad you're pleased to see me,' she said, then went on briskly, 'I only hope the mood lasts once I've finished tasking you.'

She went through a list of reports she wanted and the priorities for the day, then, after the meeting, dealt with individual queries. Perhaps she was being oversensitive in noticing that Tam MacNee had positioned himself on the outer edge of the group, but she worked her way towards him anyway.

'Tam! Good to see you.'

He took her outstretched hand, not quite meeting her eyes. 'Boss.'

'How's Bunty?' she persisted. 'Haven't seen her for a while.'

His eyes flickered as she mentioned his wife. Then he said flatly, 'She's fine.'

Fleming nodded and turned away, feeling chilled. A woman she didn't recognise was standing patiently, waiting to speak to her – Tansy Kerr's replacement, presumably. She came forward as Fleming looked towards her.

'DC Kim Kershaw, ma'am.'

Fleming looked at her appraisingly. Neat, competent-looking, smartly dressed in neutrals – quite a change from Tansy Kerr, whose style had been adventurous, to say the very least. She realised that she herself was being given a similarly cool, measuring look. Interesting. She smiled.

'Are you fairly new here?' How she hated needing to ask that question!

'A month, ma'am. I've been in the CID for a couple of weeks now, so I'm still finding my feet. I was a detective in Glasgow before, but I asked for a transfer.'

She didn't have a Glasgow accent – east coast, from the sound of it – but Fleming said lightly, 'You and DS MacNee will have a lot in common, then.'

There was a fractional pause, before Kershaw said, 'Absolutely,' with such total lack of emphasis that she might just as well have said, 'You have to be joking!'

It would have been more tactful to ignore that, but Fleming was inclined to believe that in many situations tact was an overrated virtue. 'You don't share Tam's enthusiasm for Glasgow?'

Kershaw clearly shared her views on tact. She said, with some force, 'No. I don't. And the place my daughter was at in inner-city Glasgow was a disaster.'

'What age is she?'

'Nine.' Kershaw's lips twitched in a half-smile, though Fleming thought it looked as if she didn't smile readily.

'Settled in all right?'

'Brilliantly!' This time the smile was wholehearted. 'Debbie's a different child already.'

'That's good. Now, we ought to have a talk. Come up to my office – in half an hour, say?'

As Fleming moved away, she heard a guffaw and turning her head saw MacNee in conversation with one of the brasher young detectives, about whom she'd had some doubts before her suspension. From the direction of their eyes, and the swift looking away as they saw she had noticed, it was clear the joke had been about Kershaw.

She could imagine MacNee resenting the slighting of his beloved Glasgow, which he'd left only at the insistence of his wife, who came from Dumfries, but this was totally unacceptable. She took it head on.

'MacNee, I'd like to see you. My office, ten minutes, all right?'

It was an order, not a question. MacNee said, 'Boss,' again.

After she left, there was a brief silence, then the hum of artificial conversation. MacNee, his colour heightened, busied himself at a desk, then exactly nine minutes later went out.

As the door shut behind him, a voice said, 'Stand back from the windows. They might come in at any moment.'

ANGER HAD CARRIED Fleming out of the room and along the corridor, but as she climbed the stairs, it began to change to concern. That was utterly unlike Tam. What the hell was wrong with him?

She let herself into her office on the fourth floor of the Galloway Constabulary Headquarters and went to the window. She had always like the outlook over the roofs of the canny market town of Kirkluce, out through the canopy of leaves on the plane trees along the High Street. Those leaves were sodden today, flattened and dripping from the ceaseless rain. She turned away.

Once as familiar to her as a second skin, her office felt strange. If she had been an imaginative woman, she reflected, she might almost have felt it was hostile, as if it had resented its violation by strangers. It was lucky she wasn't an imaginative woman.

She sat down at the desk which, apart from the pile in the in-tray, was most unfamiliarly tidy. She'd more to do than consider the psychology of inanimate objects when there were animate objects needing urgent consideration. There were two problems – Tam's attitude to her and his attitude to the new detective.

MacNee had thought Fleming's suspension was justified. He wasn't wrong: much of her own agony over the past months had arisen from her knowing that it was. But surely by now . . .

She couldn't afford to feel hurt. They weren't in the playground now, best friends falling out. This was a professional relationship with her most effective officer, and it was her job to make it work. They had a shared past and a dedication to the job, which she believed to have bred a certain loyalty – and growing up in one of the rougher areas of Glasgow had left Tam with a positively tribal sense of being true to your pals, overdeveloped, even.

Was that it, right there? Had his reaction to her been guilt, not hostility? Did he assume she would despise him for having, as he would see it, gone over to the enemy? Perhaps she was overanalysing, with her recent reading in psychology making her look for deeper meanings where none existed. But it would fit.

The problem with Kershaw was more immediate. According to Bailey, things had slipped during Fleming's absence and it certainly looked as if they had. This was, quite simply, a disciplinary matter, and before she started understanding Tam, she had to knock him back into line. She wasn't looking forward to it, though.

MacNee's body language was expressing deep discomfort as he came in. His head was lowered, and when he looked towards her, it was at an angle so that their eyes could not connect.

Fleming had no intention of making it easier for him. She didn't ask him to sit down and, after a brief acknowledgement, allowed a pause to develop until she saw him shift from foot to foot.

'I presume you know what this is about.' Her tone was cold.

'Sorry,' he said, addressing the remark to the surface of her desk. 'I made a stupid joke, that's all.'

'I'll go along with the first part of that last statement. I want you to think about the second part.'

He didn't speak, and nor did she. At last MacNee burst out, 'I know I shouldn't have done that. It just gets to me, the way she goes on about Glasgow – always rubbishing it. And anyway . . .'

'And what?' She waited, but when he said nothing, went on, 'Not a very professional way to behave – not even a very adult way to behave, really. And from the way she spoke when I made that remark about you having a lot in common, I don't think it's an isolated incident, is it?'

MacNee studied the floor.

'Let me spell it out. You're a senior officer. That's harassment, if she chose to pursue it. But let's not be technical, let's be blunt. It's just plain bullying. For heaven's sake! You're not a bully, Tam – you've always been the one who stood up for the underdog. What the hell's wrong with you?'

Fleming saw the shaft go home. MacNee rubbed his hand down his face. 'Sorry. I didn't think about it – she's well able to stand up for herself, and . . . It's just . . . Things have been difficult lately. Sorry, like I said.'

'Sit down, Tam.' Her voice had changed. 'What's the problem?'

He sat down, but all he said was, 'Oh, just this and that. I'll sort it out, and you won't have to warn me again.'

She could see that he wasn't going to confide. She tried not to think that before, if he had a problem, he'd share it with her. It might not even be true, but it still hurt.

'Right. I accept your assurance and I'm sure Kershaw will accept your apology when you make it to her.'

CRADLE TO GRAVE 35

MacNee nodded and got up. 'Is that it?'

Fleming sighed. 'No, sit down again. I want to clear the air. I'll freely admit I was hurt that you didn't contact me these last months, but I can understand that you thought I'd brought it on myself.'

For the first time he met her eyes. 'Yes. I've always stood by my friends, but . . .'

So her instinct had been right. 'You're a very loyal person, Tam, but loyalty doesn't mean saying wrong's right, and I was wrong. I know that. I got what I deserved. We don't disagree. I didn't expect anything from you except perhaps sympathy. We all make mistakes—'

He interrupted eagerly. 'Oh, you'd my sympathy, all right. Bunty wanted me to go and see you, but I couldn't lie and say you were right. I thought you'd be disappointed, angry, even—'

Now Fleming cut him short. 'Enough said – let's move on from there. We've a job to do, and what I want more than anything else is to be able to get on with it as usual. All right?'

'Sure,' MacNee said, though the response was almost offhand and he still seemed subdued as he left.

Perhaps she'd forced the pace. But the sooner she could put those miserable months behind her, reset the clock to where it had been . . .

Studying psychology was a mixed blessing. It made you realise that you couldn't set back the clock, that experience shaped you, and that both she and Tam – and all their colleagues – were to varying degrees different now.

Even so, you could choose not to look back. There was plenty in her own past that Fleming had no wish to remember and she'd found ignoring it was as good a way of managing the present as any.

She would, she decided, arrange that he came with her to see Crozier. It was a long drive and maybe in the course of it some of the awkwardness would disappear.

CROZIER GUNNED THE motor boat along the line of the coast. It had taken him only moments to realise the impracticality of clambering over the landslip, and shouting proved pointless too, with the wall of soft earth and rubble deadening the sound. His boat, kept moored at the mouth of the Carron for rough fishing, was close by, and he had Buchan and a couple of other estate workers with him. They'd brought spades in case digging was needed, and a couple of hatchets too. You never knew what you were going to find.

He took a deep drag on his cigarette. His was a complicated history where the Rosscarron Cottages were concerned, and revisiting it was painful.

Unbidden, a picture came to his mind of his younger self, halfway up the cliff that had now fallen: aged ten, perhaps, with more ambition than skill, stuck and terrified, with his handhold crumbling. If it hadn't been for Kenna – a bit older, neat and agile, a better climber than he would ever be – he'd have fallen to his death. He could almost see the red flame of her hair as she appeared below him, hear her contemptuous voice saying, 'Move your foot to the right, you gomeril – there's a rock ledge.'

Kenna . . . His throat tightened. She was all he remembered of his teen years: the ecstasy, the pain and ultimately the despair. Then life had happened to them both elsewhere, until—

He scowled. He didn't want to go back to the cottages. He'd even taken to heading out in the opposite direction in the boat when he left the moorings, to avoid coming this way. But she was dead now; his parents, dead too, had long since sold up and he had no more connection with this place.

They were starting to run through mud in the sea, a dirty red-brown stain spreading out as far as the eye could see. In a moment, when the boat rounded the curve, they'd be looking at what had happened. No one said anything, but Crozier could sense the tension matching his own. He took a last drag on his cigarette and threw it into the water, where it died with a tiny hiss.

There was the bay. Crozier caught his breath. They all did. There was a gaping, jagged scar in the bluff behind, and below was devastation.

The neat terrace of two-up-two-downs, built of red sandstone, had taken the full impact of the landslide. Number 1 Rosscarron Cottages – the one that had long ago belonged to his parents – was almost completely buried. Number 2, next door, had been engulfed in the torrent of earth and water that had swept through the house, forcing its front door open and half off its hinges, and there was a gaping hole in its roof. The two nearest the end of the road, numbers 3 and 4, were less badly affected, though there were a couple of smashed windows and the mud had invaded the ground floor, then spread out, sticky and smelly, a foot deep, across the road and the shore in front of them.

At the sound of the boat's engine, a young man appeared from number 4, shouting and waving his arms frantically. He was dishevelled and filthy with mud, and he had a bloody bruise on one side of his face.

'Thank God someone's come!' he exclaimed, as the boat was beached and the men got out, moving gingerly to keep their footing. 'We couldn't phone for help or – or do anything!'

He was, Crozier realised, very young – hardly more than a boy, with his prominent Adam's apple bobbing up and down in his distress. Behind him a slight, fair-haired girl appeared, carrying a sleeping baby; she was sobbing.

'I was so scared!' she wailed. 'I thought the mud would just come higher and higher, and all the lights went and it was that dark . . .'

She reminded him of his own daughter. Crozier went over and put a reassuring arm round her. 'It's all right. Everything's all right now.' He looked at the boy. 'Any casualties?'

'Just Jan – she's the lady who was next door to us – but we took her in with us last night. I think she's broken her leg.'

Crozier turned to look at the two most damaged cottages. 'No one in there?'

'That one's empty.' He pointed to the buried house and shuddered. 'Just as well. There's a couple has the other one, and I went over last night after it happened. Couldn't get in and it was too dark to see much, but I shouted and there was no reply. Jan said she thought they'd gone out.'

Crozier jerked his head at Buchan. 'Better make sure.'

The man plodded off through the mud as Crozier said, 'I'll come and speak to the lady. We've sent someone to alert the emergency services, so they'll be here before long to get you out. Did you have a car?'

The lad pointed to the heap of earth. 'That was the parking area. The cars are under all that.' Whatever was there wasn't going to be recognisable as a car when they got it out.

'Hope everyone was insured,' Crozier was saying when he realised that Buchan had come back and was standing looking at him meaningfully. Oh God! Since Ballymena, even the thought of a dead body turned him queasy.

'You go back in,' he urged the young pair. 'Look out what you need to take with you. I'll see you in a minute.'

As they walked across to their cottage, the other men, quick to pick up the significance, stood as if frozen in a live tableau. Once the couple were safely inside, Crozier walked towards number 2.

Through the damaged door he could see the stairs, and daylight above, where a huge stone had come through the roof. But Buchan was mutely indicating the left-hand window, surprisingly still intact, and with a gesture Crozier indicated that he should check out whatever was in there.

The inner door was wedged by mud. Buchan had to fetch a hatchet, and with a few blows broke through it and disappeared inside. Probably they didn't all hold their breath until he came out again, but it felt as if they did.

Buchan reappeared and limped over to him. 'There's a body. Man lying under rubble in the sitting room, bad head injury.'

'Definitely dead?'

Buchan gave a sour grimace. 'Oh, aye. Definitely dead.'

Chapter Three

KIM KERSHAW ARRANGED her face in an expression of intelligent interest as DI Fleming explained her general philosophy of policing in the community. There was nothing wrong with it: good, standard ethical stuff that she'd heard often enough before, but she'd had bosses who talked the talk quite eloquently while their gait in walking the walk was uneven to say the least. She didn't have a trusting nature – not now – and what she'd seen of both the police and the criminal fraternity had only deepened her cynicism.

Fleming's hazel eyes were penetrating, though, and Kershaw was careful not to let these thoughts register on her face. She answered the questions Fleming posed about her professional life fully, about her personal life briefly: she was divorced; she had one child; she was renting a perfectly satisfactory ground-floor flat in Newton Stewart.

Despite sex-discrimination rules, she had suffered interrogation in the past about her childcare arrangements, but this time, when she didn't elaborate on her circumstances, Fleming didn't probe. Kershaw did catch a look on the inspector's face, though, which suggested that this reticence might have been filed away as interesting information.

Fleming was winding up the meeting now. 'Sorry I can't give you longer, Kim, but as you can imagine, I'm up to my eyes this morning. Looking forward to working with you, though.'

While you'd never describe Big Marge as good-looking, her smile lit up her face in a very engaging way and Kershaw found herself smiling back.

'Thanks, boss. I'll do my best.'

'Good. That's all from my point of view. Any questions?'

Kershaw had been hoping for an opportunity. 'Not a question, ma'am, but may I say something?'

'Of course.'

The tone was cordial enough, but she sensed that the other woman was on her guard. She took a deep breath.

'DS MacNee has just apologised to me. I appreciate your concern for me as a newcomer, but I don't need you to fight my battles. I'm perfectly able to deal with him myself and it won't help to have an awkward relationship made worse by him getting grief from you.'

There was a pause, during which Kershaw remembered Andy Macdonald's warning and began to wish she'd taken it to heart.

Then Fleming said calmly, 'I admire your capacity to be direct – and I don't mean that in a sarcastic way. I'm all for straight talking. On the other hand, I don't think you quite appreciate what I was doing. Your relationship with MacNee is your own business. You'll have to sort things out between you. My business is the good discipline of my officers. A divided team is an ineffective team, and I don't tolerate any behaviour that affects our standards of professionalism. My intervention was on that basis. Do you understand now?'

Wrong-footed, Kershaw muttered that she did.

'Good. I'm sure you'll be a valuable addition. Thanks, Kim.'

Kershaw left, reflecting on the interview. There had been no aggression, no animosity; Fleming had merely been as blunt as she had been herself in spelling out her position. Why, then, did she feel like saying, 'Phew!' as she shut the door behind her?

'AND THIS BLUE one on top. Now, what shall we do? Oh dear, over it goes!'

Beth Brown laughed as the toddler gleefully knocked the tower of bricks to the floor.

'Do it again? Here we are – green one, red one . . .'

From her seat in the corner of her son's sitting room next to the mottled brown thirties fireplace, Ina McClintock Buchan watched Beth like a spider assessing the potential of an unfamiliar species of fly.

A lifelong habit of discontent had etched itself on Ina's features, producing eyes narrowed by suspicion and harsh lines between her brows. Even when she smiled, usually in triumph at some barb that had found its mark, there was still a sour downturn to her thin-lipped mouth.

Now she said, 'You'll be wanting away, to get back to your family, no doubt.'

Beth, placing a yellow brick on top of the green and the red, didn't look up. 'Not really.'

Ina frowned. '"Not really"? What kind of answer is that?'

Beth gave her a sidelong look, then shrugged.

The thin lips tightened. 'If that's your idea of manners, it's no wonder if your family don't want anything to do with you.'

Goaded, the girl retorted, 'I never said that! I've none to go to, that's all.'

'Funny thing, that – no family,' Ina mused artlessly.

'I'm an only child and my mother's dead, all right?' Beth snapped. 'If it's any of your business.'

'What about your partner, then? Maidie said you'd a partner – apparently that's what you call it these days when you're a bidie-in.'

'He's – he's away.'

Beth was biting her lip and she put the brick in her hand on to the tower so clumsily that it collapsed. Calum crowed and clapped his hands.

'Away where?' Ina persisted. 'You'll be wanting to let him know what's happened before he sees it on the telly and gets a fright.'

'Well, I can't, can I? Phone's not working.'

With malevolent glee, Ina heard real anger there. The girl was glaring at her, and there was something curious about her eyes. What was it, now?

As Beth looked away to say something to the child, Ina realised there was a gap between the bottom of the iris and the lower lid. It made her eyes look as round as marbles and oddly staring.

'Funny eyes you've got. Not natural, that, is it?' Ina was saying when the door opened and her daughter-in-law came in with mugs and a plate of biscuits on a tray.

'For goodness' sake, Gran, you can't go saying things like that!' Maidie protested. 'Beth, don't pay any attention. You've got very pretty eyes – lovely colour, and quite unusual with your dark hair.'

Ina pursed her lips in annoyance. Maidie's unrelenting cheerfulness and imperviousness to insult had always been a source of frustration.

'I'll say what I like and you'll not stop me,' she said, but the moment had passed. Her victim was on her feet, persuading Calum to help put the bricks in the box before he got his juice.

'Good boy, Calum! Now sit down nicely so you don't spill.' Beth scooped up the child with practised ease and settled him beside her on the sofa.

'You're an absolute godsend!' Maidie handed Beth a mug. 'I've got a dozen things done this morning that I haven't had time to do for weeks, and there's a cake in the oven for tea. That'll be nice, won't it, Gran?'

Gran's face indicated merely irritation at this attempt at good cheer, and Maidie went on, 'Calum's been a wee angel for you, Beth. I barely recognise him! You must have worked with children – or have you young brothers and sisters?'

It was an innocent remark. So why should Beth's face have gone scarlet? Ina wondered. Something odd there. 'She's an only child,' Ina put in – purely in a spirit of helpfulness, of course.

'I've – I've never worked with children,' Beth stammered. 'I – I did other things.'

It was so clearly untrue that Maidie in her turn became flustered. 'Sorry, I – I didn't mean to pry.'

'She's lying, obviously,' Ina said in a conversational tone. 'What's she lying for?'

Beth jumped to her feet, startling the toddler, who bawled in fright. She went to the door and wrenched it open.

'I'm going out.'

'Beth, it's pouring!' Maidie protested in distress. 'There's no need—'

The girl turned in the doorway. 'Oh, yes, there is. I'm leaving before I do something I'll regret to that evil old bat!'

The door slammed behind her.

'Well! Nice manners, I *don't* think!' Ina tittered.

For once provoked beyond bearing, Maidie picked up the sobbing Calum and carried him out, saying over her shoulder, 'She's absolutely right. I should have called you that more often, instead of just thinking it.'

The door was slammed again, leaving Ina McClintock Buchan alone, with an unpleasant smirk of satisfaction on her face.

BETH FELT SICK, sick and frightened as she half-ran past the kennels. They hadn't believed her; she'd never been a good liar.

'You were angry, weren't you, when you had to give up your evening out?'

The man in the wig hadn't moved his eyes off her face since the questioning began. She felt as if he had flayed away the skin, as if now he was paring the flesh off her bones.

She hesitated. 'I said I didn't mind.'

She knew it sounded feeble. He let a pause develop. Then, 'You said you didn't mind.' He gave the word intense significance. 'Said it. But you didn't mean it, did you?'

And she hadn't known how to reply.

What was going to happen now? She didn't dare to think.

'THE SUPER'S RIGHT – Donaldson is a bit of an old woman,' Fleming said, as she drove towards Kirkcudbright with MacNee. 'But that isn't to say he hasn't got a point. After all, the Carron's burst its banks already and this rain's showing no sign of letting up. The bridge was still clear when he checked it yesterday, but the level wasn't falling. And apart altogether from the question of

the strain on the bridge with the river in spate, you have to consider that you could have hundreds of fans stranded if it rises
any more. There'd be absolutely no way of getting them off the
headland that wouldn't involve helicopters or a flotilla of boats,
and I'm not sure how much of the Dunkirk spirit survives in
Kirkcudbright.'

MacNee grunted. 'Good excuse to cancel the whole thing. A
lot less hassle – traffic control, undercover drugs surveillance . . .'

Fleming gave him a look of exasperation. She'd been prepared
for awkwardness, ready to work towards their old easy relationship, but he was just being bloody-minded. 'For heaven's sake,
Tam, we were all young once! At least I certainly was, and I'm
prepared to give you the benefit of the doubt.'

'If it's cancelled, we'll still get the morons arriving anyway,
just ettling to cause trouble.' MacNee was determinedly morose.
'Damned if we do, damned if we don't.'

'You're a right little ray of sunshine today, aren't you? Maybe
the rain will stop and the river will go down.'

She had hoped he might respond in kind, but MacNee only
pointed through the windscreen where, beyond the frenetic
wiper activity, all that could be seen were banks of purple-grey
cloud.

For Fleming, patience had never been one of the easier virtues.
Be like that, she thought and, switching to professional mode,
said, 'Anyway, do you have any background on Gillis Crozier?'

MacNee shrugged. 'Not a lot. He comes and goes to London.
We've certainly not got anything on file. I took a wee look after I'd
a call from my pal Sheughie in the Glasgow Force a while back,
saying the name Rosscarron had come up and asking if one of the
big boys on his patch was hanging round here.'

Fleming raised her brows. 'And was he?'

'If he was, he wasn't selling tickets. But there's maybe more to Crozier than meets the eye. Suddenly he's in the building trade – makes you wonder . . .'

'Indeed it does. And this new pop festival too – it's pretty low key, and he can't be expecting to make big money from it. But that's another perfect way to launder cash, with all the casual payments. Let's put some feelers out. We've a few CHISes around who might know something, haven't we?'

'If we're allowed to speak to them any more, with all these new regulations,' MacNee said with some bitterness. 'In the old days I could have picked my pub, bought one of the grasses a wee quiet bevvy and found out everything I needed to know.'

'Covert human intelligence sources, not grasses. That's an offensive term.' Fleming was getting tired of MacNee's attitude. 'You know damn well that cosying up to villains led to money changing hands in the wrong direction – there were far too many scandals that way. In any case, nowadays in some circles getting hold of a gun's not a lot more difficult than buying a pint of milk and CHISes need serious protection.'

'Cloak-and-dagger stuff,' MacNee sneered. 'Just a word over a pint would be less obvious. Here! I wonder where they're away to in such a hurry?'

They were just coming past the end of the road to Kirkcudbright Police Station when a badged car, lights flashing, pulled out ahead of them.

'Will I check in and find out?' MacNee leaned forward to the radio, but Fleming groaned.

'Oh, for goodness' sake, don't go looking for trouble! If we're really needed they'll call us in, but if we're not, I don't want to feel obliged to offer support. I've enough to do today without anything extra.'

'Fine,' MacNee said, elaborately moving his hands back. 'You're the boss.'

The words 'Too right I am' sprang to her lips, but Fleming managed not to say them.

The police car sped off and vanished, while Fleming drove at a more sedate pace along the road south, watching for the unmarked side road leading to Rosscarron.

'It's one of these places you're not meant to go to unless you know where it is,' she was complaining, when she saw the first AA temporary sign saying, 'Rosscarron Music Festival.'

'Maybe if we took it down, they'd all give up and go home.' MacNee earned another exasperated glance from his boss as she turned off again at the next sign.

This road, even narrower, ran along the line of the river and Fleming gasped as she saw the extent of the flooding on the farther, lower side.

'That's a disaster! Those houses weren't cheap and it'll cost a fortune to sort them out once the water goes down.'

The smart executive homes were indeed a sorry sight. Filthy water was lapping two feet above ground-floor level and outside, three or four vehicles were engulfed in a sea of sludge. Even with the car windows shut, the officers could smell the stench from the drains.

'You'd think that must be a serious health risk,' Fleming said. 'Do you know if everyone's moved out?'

'They were evacuating them a couple of days ago, but one or two were pretty reluctant to leave and we can't force them. There's

one in particular kicking up. He's aye greeting about something –
even came all the way to Kirkluce to speak to the super in person.'

'Donald did just mention that.'

'Jamieson's his name. He's been raging about the festival for
weeks now till the local lads are sick fed up – maybe he'll be happy
now he's really got something to complain about. Wants officers
round the clock to guard against looting, seemingly. Looting,
down here, for any favour! And of course we're to arrest Crozier.
Jamieson seemed kinda hazy about grounds for a charge, but dead
sure he should be in jail.'

'I see. I can feel for him, of course, but let's hope he's seen sense
and cleared out by now.'

The road had a film of water covering it at first, but as it rose
towards the bridge, the banks of the river, dark and dirty with
mud, rose too and here the water was still contained, though deep
and gushing down with considerable force. As she drove across,
Fleming peered anxiously at the level, though so far at least the
bridge was still three or four feet clear.

'From what Donaldson told me, I'd say it hasn't risen much
since yesterday. And it looks a solid enough structure. The fore-
cast isn't great, but most of the headwater will have come through
by now. I'll get out and have a good look around to appease Donaldson on the way back, but I can't see a real problem.'

'Fine,' MacNee said, but he was looking over his shoulder
towards the smaller road on the right.

'Something caught your eye?'

He turned round again. 'There was a man walking down there
to the houses, so someone must still be staying there.'

'Jamieson?'

'Don't know what he looks like. It was just he looked round, and when he saw the car, he walked faster. Maybe we should . . .'

'It's an unmarked car, so why should that be suspicious? He probably just thought of something he meant to do,' Fleming said dismissively. 'Anyway, we're not on patrol, Tam. We've a job to do, and the sooner it's done, the sooner I can get back to my in-tray. I could swear that when I left, the legs of the desk were beginning to buckle.'

THE EIGHT-YEAR-OLD BOY, wearing premium jeans and a Diesel top, was sitting on a high stool at the breakfast bar in the clinically white kitchen of Rosscarron House. He had fair, curly hair, worn long, and he was rhythmically kicking the counter.

'Don't do that, Nico.' Cris Pilapil glanced across the room with ill-concealed irritation. He was chopping onions at the stainless-steel-topped island unit, and in a pan on the range-style cooker spices were roasting, filling the air with their sharp fragrance.

Nico went on kicking. 'You didn't say please.'

'Please, then.'

'But I don't want to stop. And I don't have to do what you say.'

'Fine.' Cris took the pan off the heat, then went back to chopping the onions with neat, economical movements.

'I want my breakfast.'

The demand was ignored. Suddenly Nico jumped down, pushing the stool over with a crash. He shouted in the man's ear, 'I want my breakfast!'

Cris finished the onions and picked up a red pepper. 'You didn't say please.'

'I don't have to say please. You're my servant.'

'I'm your granddad's servant. Let's go and see what he thinks, shall we?'

Nico took a step back, considering. Involving his grandfather in situations like this was seldom a good idea.

'Please,' he threw over his shoulder, then picked up the stool and climbed on to it again.

Cris put down his knife. 'What do you want?'

'Bacon roll.'

As the man went to the huge American fridge to fetch the bacon, Nico began kicking again.

'CAN'T RAISE THE boss,' DS Andy Macdonald said to DC Ewan Campbell. 'She's not in the car and her phone's off.'

'Out at Rosscarron. No signal there.' Campbell, a red-headed Highlander from Oban, tended to speak as if dictating an old-fashioned telegram with a charge per word.

Macdonald looked at him with respect. 'You don't say a lot, but you always know what's going on, don't you?'

'I listen,' Campbell said simply.

Macdonald grinned. 'OK, I talk too much. We'd better head on down there, anyway. This is going to be an all-hands-on-decksituation. Does Your Omniscience know where Kim is?'

'Late shift,' Campbell obliged.

'Just lost her morning off, then, hasn't she? You've got her mobile number, no doubt.'

Campbell looked at him coolly. 'Lazy bastard. Get it yourself.'

'That's hurtful, you know, really hurtful. And insubordinate. Anyway, I've just remembered I've got it on speed dial, so I won't put you on a charge just this once.'

KIM KERSHAW LEANED over the child in the wheelchair, holding out a brightly coloured toy bird.

'Look at this, Debbie!' She jiggled it invitingly and after a moment the girl stretched out an uncertain hand and touched it.

Kim's face brightened. 'Well done, honey! Now, if we press this, it sings – listen!'

At the sound of the little tinny song, the blank eyes flickered with some sort of interest and a carer passing by stopped with a sympathetic smile.

Kim turned eagerly. 'She actually reached out for this. That's definitely a step forward.'

'Debbie's in a good mood today,' the woman said. 'Got a smile from her this morning, didn't I, Debbie?'

'Did you?' Kim looked wistfully at the child's expressionless face, sighed, then said, 'She's so much better here. I can see real improvements. It was so awful in that other place – nobody cared. They didn't talk to her like you do. You couldn't expect her to make progress there.'

'We-ell,' the carer said uncomfortably. Talking couldn't make any difference to Debbie Kershaw and it was heart-breaking if her mother thought it would.

'I wish I could have her at home,' Kim said, 'but . . .'

'She needs more care than you can give her,' the woman said firmly. 'Don't go beating yourself up about it. And if there's an emergency . . .'

Kim shuddered at the recollection of previous emergencies, before she had been persuaded to put Debbie into residential care, occasions when she had thought that thanks to her lack of skill she might lose Debbie altogether.

She smoothed back the dark hair from Debbie's face. The brown eyes were dull again, and Kim looked in the bag at her feet. 'Now, let's see what we have here. The musical box – you liked that yesterday.'

Kim was winding up the gaily decorated toy when her mobile phone rang. She fetched it out of her bag, glanced at the caller number and grimaced.

'Yes? . . . Oh, all right. Be there as soon as I can.'

She put the toys back in the bag and, taking the thin, fragile hand, bent to kiss her daughter's forehead. 'Bye, sweetheart. I'll be back soon.'

The carer watched her go. Some people truly had it tough. She'd just been brooding about the fuss at breakfast over her own ten-year-old wanting her ears pierced. Put it all in perspective, really.

IN A HOUSE the size of Rosscarron, it was only to be expected that there would be staff – a local wifie, perhaps, drafted in when the owner was in residence. But Fleming was definitely taken aback when the front door was opened by an exotic-looking young man with dark brown eyes and skin the colour of *café au lait*. He smiled politely at the officers.

They showed their warrant cards. 'Is Mr Crozier in?' Fleming asked. 'We were hoping for a word with him.'

'He's just got back – upstairs changing. It was all pretty messy, as you can imagine. I'll tell him you're here. If you'd come with me . . .'

Exchanging puzzled glances, Fleming and MacNee followed him across the hall. Its architectural style was high Victorian, but it had been painted glossy white with one dramatically purple wall. A couple of white chairs with purple upholstery stood against the back wall on either side of a narrow white table, but otherwise it was echoingly empty.

The room Pilapil showed them into was also shiny white and, Fleming supposed, minimalist. It was bare, certainly, with no signs of the casual detritus of normal family life, and the only decoration was two of what were probably called *objets* in stainless steel on a glass table, and a huge abstract consisting of black and orange stripes. But this looked perfunctory, somehow, as if it had been painted to order to match the sofas and chairs, which were solid blocks of black and orange leather. These were placed at uncomfortable distances from one another, which confirmed the impression of indifference. The only signs of personal taste were a huge plasma-screen TV and speakers in all four corners of the room.

'Brr!' MacNee said, sitting down. 'Makes you feel cold, just coming in here.'

'Wouldn't choose it, myself. What was all that about?'

'Seemed to be expecting us, didn't he? Sounds as if something's happened. Maybe that's what the lads in Kirkcudbright were going off to.'

With some irritation, she could hear him thinking, We should have checked. 'OK, we should have checked. I was wrong. Satisfied?' Aware that she had let her annoyance show, she went on, more temperately, 'Still, sounds as if we're going to find out now.'

Fleming walked over to the window. The room was towards the back of the side of the house, and beyond a characterless garden, consisting mainly of roughly mown grass, some shrubs and a sort of copse of low trees and bushes, she could see a structure at the top of the rising ground behind.

'That must be the stage,' she said. 'And there are some caravans beside it – for staff, presumably – and then a few small tents lower down. Some of the fans must have started arriving already. Why would anyone choose to spend an extra night camping in weather like this? They must be mad!'

From somewhere in the house, someone began to play an electric guitar. It sounded as if it was directly overhead, and MacNee winced.

'Someone practising for the gig, I daresay,' Fleming said, her mouth twitching at her sergeant's expression. 'Sounds pretty good, actually.'

'Hmph. Loud, anyway. Just so long as no one expects me to listen to a performance, that's all.'

'You'd probably be expected to pay, from the sound of it,' Fleming was saying dryly when Gillis Crozier came into the room. They both got to their feet.

He had just a look of Clark Gable's Rhett Butler, Fleming thought, only an older, sadder, wiser Rhett, and clean-shaven, of course. The seamed lines on his face suggested the same whiff of brimstone, and she guessed that to groupies in the music world he would have been powerfully attractive when he was younger. Now, though, that face suggested that life had not just been a giddy round of glamorous parties with willing young women.

He didn't greet them formally. 'Dreadful thing, this,' he said heavily. 'Dreadful.'

The officers looked at him blankly. 'I'm sorry, sir, I'm afraid this is something we haven't heard about,' Fleming said. 'We came to discuss the problems with vandalism.'

'Oh, yes, that.' He dismissed it with a wave of his hand. 'I thought you'd come about the landslide at the Rosscarron Cottages down below there. A man dead, a woman injured, homes destroyed . . .'

The guitar had just stopped and there was an appalled silence, before Fleming said, 'That's terrible news. I think, if you'll excuse us, we'll leave the other matter for the moment.' She took her mobile out of her pocket and squinted at it. 'No signal. If I might just use your phone . . .'

'No point. Lines must be down somewhere – they've been out since last night.'

'Then we'd better get on over there.'

Just then the sitting-room door opened and a man came in behind them, a very tall, slim man with a mane of iron-grey hair swept back from his face – an interesting face, with a slightly crooked nose and grey eyes so light they were almost silver. The black jeans and black granddad shirt he wore made him look taller still.

'Oh, sorry, Gil!' He had a faint American accent. 'Am I interrupting something, or—' He broke off. Stared. Then said, 'Good God – *Madge!*'

Slowly, Fleming turned her head and for a moment time slipped. She could hear the thump, thump, thump of the heavy bass, taste the astringent burn of smoke in her throat. The air was thick with it, blue-grey wisps floating in the beam of the rigged-up spotlight. There was a sickly-sweet, decadent edge to it too, as well as the rawer smell of beer and sweat and youth itself in the cramped back room of the pub. The band was coming to the raucous end of the last number now, its signature tune, 'And the Walls Came Tumbling Down', and for a moment she had almost thought they would.

'Joss? But – but you're in America!' she said stupidly.

'Evidently not.' He smiled sardonically. 'So, how's it been, these last twenty-odd years?'

Chapter Four

With Calum on her hip, Maidie Buchan was stirring the soup for lunch when her husband came in. He was wet, dirty and visibly shaken.

He said nothing, only crossing to the cupboard where the whisky was kept and collecting the bottle and a large tumbler, then sitting down heavily at the kitchen table and filling the glass to the top.

'What's – what's wrong?' Maidie faltered.

Alick swallowed, grimaced, then said, 'Where is she?'

'Beth? She's . . . out.' It wasn't the moment to tell him it was his mother who had driven her out. Not that he'd care, anyway: Ina was smart enough to treat her son with wary respect, and the money she paid for her keep was more important to him than whatever burden it might place on his wife.

'You know she said her partner wasn't there? Well, he was.'

Maidie's eyes widened. 'Dead?'

'Dead. Could barely see him for plaster and rubble. But who was it had to go in there and check he's really dead, with the house ready to come down any minute?' A shudder ran through him. 'Not Himself, that's for sure – wouldn't sully his hands. Like last time. Oh, he's still got me doing his dirty work, even though I'm not under orders now. One day I'll tell him what he can do with this lousy job.'

That was a threat so familiar that Maidie barely heard it. 'Oh, poor, poor Beth! Was there anyone else? What's actually happened?'

'There's a young couple with a bairn – they were all right – and a woman that's hurt her leg. The end cottages weren't so bad. The other two are wrecks, basically – hers is one of them. Roof's stoved in, stairs smashed. The police were there, won't let anyone move the body out till they've done their stuff. And what's bugging me is, where's the girl going to go? Has she family or that?'

Maidie said stiffly, 'No, I'm pretty sure she doesn't. She'll have to stay here till she gets something sorted out, Alick.'

He glared at her. 'That's what I was afraid of. We end up having to pick up the pieces. Why does it always happen to me? She couldn't have gone to the big house, where another mouth to feed wouldn't even be noticed – oh, no! Stumbles in here in the middle of the night, so there's no way—'

Maidie cut across him, horrified by his attitude. 'Apart from anything else, she's well worth her keep for the help she's giving me with Calum.'

The whisky was starting to take effect. 'What're you needing help with Calum for?' he said belligerently. 'Should be able to take care of your own child.'

Today, for the first time, Maidie had told her mother-in-law what she thought of her, and it had been a heady, liberating experience. Instead of meekly backing off, as she would normally have done, she said, 'If it was just Calum, aye, I could. But your mother deliberately makes work for me and I'm getting fed up of it. She's perfectly fit to live on her own – she's not seventy yet, for heaven's sake, and she doesn't need waiting on hand and foot, like she expects here. Having help from Beth'll stop me telling her she can leave right now and take her money with her.'

Alick blinked at her in owlish astonishment. He'd never known Maidie answer back before.

And she didn't wait for his response. 'What's worrying me is how on earth we're to break it to Beth.'

Alick drained the tumbler and got up, a little unsteadily. 'That's your problem. I'm away to have a bath and get the smell of death off my hands.' He topped up his glass and went to the door.

'She was so sure her partner wasn't there,' Maidie said, almost to herself. 'She wasn't worried at all.'

Alick swung round. 'Aye, and that's a funny thing, if you ask me. People that go out sometimes come back unexpectedly.' He paused, and his eyes darkened as if he was reliving a bad experience. 'And he did. Poor bugger.'

BETH WAS TIRED of bloody walking. She'd walked more recently than she had done in the whole of the rest of her life put together. If you could bank exercise, the last month would mean she could go back to London and never take another step that wasn't on concrete. Back to London – if only!

London. Beth had lived there all her life until— Well, afterwards she hadn't. She'd been too scared to stay, but with what she knew now, she'd have been better to try to lose herself among the millions of people who lived where nature came in neat little packets called parks. Nature there knew its place; it didn't threaten you, like it did here.

She was on a little track now, skirting a sort of thicket of scrubby bushes, dripping dankly. She didn't know where it was leading, but it was off the road, where she might meet people. She wasn't sure how long she'd been out, either. She wasn't wearing a watch, and time had gone weird since yesterday. Then again, in her world, things had been going weird for a long, long time.

Beth had hated moving house. At first it had been a relief just to settle at all, here in the odd, dark little cottage that had been Granny Kenna's, even though it meant putting her head in the crocodile's mouth. She'd been prepared to take that risk; it was better than going on looking over her shoulder, feeling her heart pound at a footstep behind her on a quiet street for the rest of her life. And she'd believed Lee Morrissey totally and utterly—

And how clever had that been? What had Beth done with her brain the day she'd met him in the little corner shop?

She'd been afraid to go out these last few weeks. Women had lined up to scream and spit as she was driven away from the court, and the press had orchestrated a frenzy of anger.

The little ground-floor flat that had been home to her until her mother died, and after that somewhere to stay, was up for sale. She was exhausted and terrified by the constant ringing of the doorbell and banging on the windows and the assault of a battery of flashlights if she stepped outside. Even once she wasn't a story any more, she had the permanent feeling of being spied on, followed, though when she turned her head, all she could ever see was the usual thronged London pavement, with indifferent people busy about their indifferent lives.

She was permanently afraid of being recognised. She never shopped twice in the same place so no one would be interested enough to look at her closely.

She was queuing with her chicken tikka and pint of milk in a tiny, cluttered corner shop which smelled of curry when he joined the queue behind her and said, glancing at her basket, 'My favourite too.'

She looked round. He was fit, he was smiling, and she'd barely spoken to anyone for days. His casual friendliness was like a blink of sunshine in a long, dark day.

She smiled back. 'Everyone's favourite, probably.'

He nodded, paused, then said, 'Do you come here often? Oh, I know it's a cheesy chat-up line, but it was all I could think of.'

It made her laugh, and when he said, 'Fancy a beer before that?' she agreed.

She was flattered, hungry for company, desperate to talk to someone – anyone. She hadn't meant to tell him what had happened, but she found herself pouring it all out.

He was sympathetic. He took her hand in both of his. 'That's tough, babe! You've had a bum deal. Now, how do we fix it?'

It was a new experience – a man who cared. She allowed herself to believe that there and then, over a beer in a squalid little pub, he was appointing himself to do battle for her, relieving her of the fear that stalked her daily life.

Lies, lies, lies! Her whole life she had been surrounded with lies. Even her own mother hadn't been straight with her – you would think you'd recognise a lie when you heard it by now. But how dumb could you be? How stupid, how pig-stupid? He hadn't meant any of it. He'd been playing some sort of game, though Beth still didn't understand quite what it was.

Would there be any money left at all in the joint bank account she'd been besotted enough to agree to? Or would she have nothing left, except a house buried under several tons of earth?

Even being totally cleaned out wasn't the greatest of her worries. Now, once again, she was afraid. Now she knew Lee's prom-
ises had been false, she was back where she had been, only worse.
In the wrong place – in entirely the wrong place. She felt a chill
down her spine and looked over her shoulder. Did they know she
was here? Were they watching her, even now?

AT THE DISASTER scene, the emergency services had swung into
action. A JCB with earth-moving equipment was attacking the
pile of mud and rubble, and behind it the approach road was
clogged with police cars, two fire engines with cutting gear and
an ambulance on standby. A coastguard cutter was acting as a
ferry to take necessary personnel on the two-minute trip round to
the cottages until there was a clear way through.

By the time DS Macdonald and DC Campbell were dropped at
the site, there wasn't much for them to do. They'd been planning
to take witness statements, but the inhabitants had been airlifted
out already. Inspector Michie from Kirkcudbright was busily in
charge, at the moment speaking into a radio phone; it looked as if
he had mounted a textbook operation, with blue-and-white tape
round the cottage where the body had been found and a constable
logging their names as the officers came on shore.

Feeling surplus to requirements, the detectives stood awkwardly on the area in front of the cottages, while men in yellow
jackets, with shovels and stiff brushes, attempted to clear the
treacherous sludge from underfoot.

Suddenly Campbell declaimed, "'If seven maids with seven
mops swept it for half a year, Do you suppose,' the Walrus said,
'that they could get it clear?'" Then, encountering an astonished

look from his colleague, he mumbled, 'Sorry. Lewis Carroll. Alice – you know. Just came into my mind.'

'You're weird, frankly,' Macdonald said. '*Alice*? Oh, forget it. Here's the inspector now.'

Michie nodded a greeting. 'Nasty situation here, right enough. Is DI Fleming on her way?'

'Haven't been able to reach her. What's the position?'

'They've put in props to stop the building collapsing, and the photographer and the pathologist came in by chopper. The latest estimate is that the road'll be open in ten minutes or thereabouts, so once the doc's done his bit, we can get the body moved out and start clearing up. I'd have liked to get DI Fleming's OK before we did that, though.'

'I've left a message on her mobile,' Macdonald said, 'but we think she's up at Rosscarron House with no signal, and the lines seem to be down.'

Michie nodded. 'They haven't found where the fault is as yet. Could be anywhere – apparently the flooding can loosen poles so they topple.'

As they were speaking, a grey-haired man in white overalls and boots came out of the cottage, bending his head to get under the temporary steel beam fixed above the door and stripping off a pair of rubber gloves. He came over to the officers.

'That's me finished. With the state of things in there, I can't make any proper examination till you can get him out. He's got an obvious head wound from a beam, but that wasn't what killed him – internal injuries, at a guess. Anyway, the photographer's done his stuff, so you can get him shifted now.'

'Thanks, Doc. The cutter's waiting to take you back.'

When Michie returned from seeing him off, Macdonald asked about the age of the victim.

The inspector pulled a face. 'Couldn't really tell you. There was a lot of dust and plaster. They'll need to clean him up to get an ID, poor sod.'

'Do we know who he was?'

'The witnesses had gone by the time I arrived, but one of the coastguard lads said there was a girl living there too, but she was out at the time.' He hesitated. 'At least, they thought she was. I just hope to God there's not any nasty surprises when we start clearing the rubble.'

'The witnesses – where are they?' Campbell asked.

'They took them all to the hospital in Dumfries. There's an older lady has a suspected broken leg, and the couple with the baby were in shock.'

'Best turn Kim Kershaw back, get her to go there.' Campbell nodded towards the radio phone in the inspector's hand.

'Good thinking,' Macdonald acknowledged, and delivered the message. 'We'd better get back ourselves, anyway. Nothing for us to do round here, until we can find out what's happened to the girl and talk to her.'

'That's the JCB breaking through now, look,' Michie said suddenly, and hurried off.

'Good,' Campbell said. 'Don't like boats. I get sick.'

'In two minutes?' Macdonald said bracingly. 'You can't possibly.' Then, as Campbell said nothing, he shrugged. 'You're not normal, that's your problem.'

'I JUST WANT to check very briefly on the campsite before we go down to the cottages,' Fleming said, as they drove away from

Rosscarron House, the radio chattering in the background. 'I'd like to see the situation there first hand.' Her voice was higher-pitched than usual and she was talking fast. You'd almost think there was some subject she was trying to avoid.

'Fine,' MacNee said shortly. He'd been deliberately resisting Fleming's attempts to put things back on their old footing. She'd given him an official flea in his ear, and however right she was, and however childish his own reaction might be, he'd planned to stand on what he saw as his professional dignity for a bit longer. This, however – this was altogether too good to miss. He'd never been hot on dignity, anyway.

'*Madge*,' MacNee said, lingering lovingly on the name. 'You know, I always kinda wondered where Madonna got the idea from.'

Fleming coloured. 'Oh, yes, laugh away.'

'Oh, aye, I'll do that all right.'

'But if you so much as breathe a word of it around the lads, I'll . . .' She paused to consider her options.

'Have my guts for garters?' MacNee suggested helpfully.

She gave him a quelling look, then with triumphant recollection went on, 'I shall see to it that it gets around what happened when you tried to arrest Annie Maclehose for soliciting.'

MacNee looked thoughtful for a moment, then said, 'Fair enough.' He couldn't resist returning to the topic, though. 'You didn't know he was coming?'

'Wasn't it obvious? Cat had said something about Joshua and a band called Destruction, but when I knew him, he was Joss and the band was Electric Earthquake. Then he went off to the States and I thought he'd sunk without trace, like most pop bands do.'

'You didn't exactly hang around for long talking about "Auld Lang Syne", though, did you?'

Fleming looked uncomfortable. 'Well, you know his nose is crooked? Bill did that.'

'*Bill?* Here! Are we talking about the same guy – the "hardy son of rustic toil", good-natured to a fault?'

'Well, there were . . . reasons.' Fleming's colour deepened further.

'Reasons?' MacNee knew the value of persistence in interrogation, and when Fleming sighed, he reckoned she was cracking. To encourage her, he said, 'And if I knew the story, I'd not be so likely to find myself speculating to Andy Mac, just accidentally, mind.'

Fleming acknowledged defeat. 'There's no time just at this moment. I'll tell you on the journey back. Now, not an ideal site, this, is it? They don't seem to have given much thought to what it would be like in weather like this.'

The rough field up at the back of Rosscarron House was on a slope and near the bottom it was marshy already, with visible streams trickling down. Although only half-a-dozen vehicles had arrived, the ground had been churned up by the lorries bringing in equipment to the upper field, and it was hard to see how the numbers arriving later could be catered for.

There was a gate with a Portakabin beside it, presumably for security staff, though there was none in evidence. When they drove through, though, a youth with a row of rings in both ears appeared in the doorway and shouted, 'Hey! You need to show your tickets.'

Fleming drew up and produced identity, looking round. 'Haven't much here to stop gatecrashers, have you?'

'Team's coming this afternoon. Just a couple of us at the moment. Not much doing anyway, weather like this.' He shot back inside.

'The security's rubbish,' Fleming said, as she coaxed the big Vauxhall up the slope. 'Asking for trouble, frankly. And I'd have taken the four-wheel drive this morning if I'd known about these conditions. I tell you, Tam, I'm worried.' She parked beside an elderly camper van, which seemed to be the hub of activity.

It was brightly painted with amateurish flowers, and its sliding door was open. From it, a canopy had been rigged up as protection from the rain and a dozen people were huddled under it, laughing and talking. From a speaker Mick Jagger was belting out 'Satisfaction', and inside a bulky woman was dispensing tea from a huge teapot, and a large grey-haired man, similarly middle-aged, had a crate of beer at his feet, which seemed also to be for sharing. They must have been a good twenty years older than the next oldest in the group but for the moment at least were the life and soul of the party.

The man was in conversation with a young man with unnaturally blond hair and a petulant expression, but as Fleming and MacNee got out of the car, he broke off to call out to them, 'Come one, come all! Beer or tea – beer from yours truly, and tea, if you fancy it, from my good lady Angela.'

Then, as they approached, he frowned. 'Not really dressed for it, are you, my loves?' he said, looking askance at Fleming's walking shoes and MacNee's trainers. 'You'll learn that the first rule is to come equipped, when you have as many battle honours as we have.' He indicated, with some pride, the stickers that almost obliterated the back windows of the van. 'Glastonbury 1970, that one there. Day after Jimi Hendrix died – we were all in mourning.'

The blond man gave them a narrow stare. 'Something tells me they're not your average punters. Cops?'

Interesting, MacNee thought, watching him as he and Fleming took out their warrant cards and she explained that they were just checking out the site. Admittedly, they looked out of place, but people who instantly thought of cops usually had reason to know. He looked around the others too, with the trained observation that had long ago become instinctive.

'Any problems?' Fleming was asking.

There were two girls who looked about sixteen. One of them asked, 'Do you know when the catering's coming? We didn't, like, bring any food or stuff – thought they'd be here by now.' Then she giggled, looking up under her eyelashes at the spiky-haired young man beside her. 'We're, like, starving – I'd do *anything* for a burger.'

'Don't you worry, my love,' the large grey-haired man said. 'We won't see you go hungry, will we, Angela? We've learned enough to know the catering always lets you down and we prepare accordingly.'

He turned to Fleming. 'Bob and Angela Lawton. Not much impressed with this, to tell you the truth. The Portaloos are all right – the toilets are always the first things we check, aren't they, love?' Angela nodded confirmation, and he went on, 'But the ground here's shocking for these poor kids. High water table, see – they'll all be sleeping in waterbeds if it doesn't stop raining. I suppose that's Scotland for you, isn't it? But we love the Scotties, don't we, Angela, so we keep right on coming to these festivals, all the way from Dorset.'

He beamed patronisingly, and MacNee felt Fleming's eyes boring a hole in him. In a contrary spirit, he said, 'Good to hear it, sir. Hope you enjoy the music.'

As they turned away, he noticed the blond man have a brief, low-voiced conversation with another young man, before heading off down the slope towards the house. Not a camper, then.

'All the business stuff seems to be in the upper field, beside the stage,' Fleming said, as she started the engine. 'The lower field seems to be all there is for tents – it's not exactly T in the Park, but it's going to be ridiculously cramped if they get any sort of gate.

'Anyway, what do you make of the groupings among that lot? The blond man – staying at the house, I'd guess. The two girls together, though if I was their mother, I'm not sure I'd let them out. Three obvious couples, and then the two young men – the short guy with spiky hair, and the taller one with sideburns. The guy with the spiky hair seemed to be with the girls, but the other one didn't seem to be with anyone. Wouldn't have thought many people came to things like this on their own, would you? And the couple with the caravan – too good to be true?'

'Check,' MacNee agreed. 'The guy, though – probably just came hoping to pull.'

'That would figure. But I'm not happy about this whole thing – the organisation seems far too casual. I don't know how many they'll get, out here in weather like this, but it could be a disaster waiting to happen. The Kirkcudbright lads will have to keep an eye on it once the numbers start building up.

'I'm going to have a close look at the bridge on the way back and see if we can find a reason to declare it unsafe. If much more water starts coming through and the headland's cut off, there'll be a major logistics problem with food supplies, for a start. And we've enough trouble down at the Rosscarron Cottages without looking for more.'

DC KIM KERSHAW looked with considerable pity at the pair in front of her, as they sat together in a patients' sitting room in the Dumfries and Galloway Royal Infirmary. They barely looked old enough to be parents, and their six-week-old girl, yelling lustily, looked as if she didn't find them convincing in that role either. Her mother who, Kershaw reckoned, couldn't be more than eighteen herself, jiggled the baby helplessly for a bit, then thrust her at her partner, in tears herself.

'You take her, Craig. I don't know what to do with her and I've just – just had enough! Holiday! Some holiday! OK, it was cheap, but you never said there'd be, like, nothing to do. Then the weather, frigging rain all week, and now this!'

Craig put the baby to his shoulder, patting her ineffectually. 'Not my fault, was it?' he said, aggrieved. 'I nearly got killed too, remember. But we didn't, right, so what are you greeting for, Donna? That's probably what set her off greeting too.'

As Donna opened her mouth indignantly, Kershaw stepped in, raising her voice above the noise.

'I was wanting to ask you about last night.'

It was no use. She could barely make herself heard over the din and the distracted parents weren't listening anyway. Kershaw went out into the corridor and looked hopefully up and down. Spotting a nursing auxiliary, a middle-aged, competent-looking woman, she hailed her.

'Look, have you a minute? I'm a police officer, trying to get a statement from the young couple in there, but their baby's bawling so I can't hear myself think, let alone speak. Any chance you could take it out of earshot for a bit? I won't be long, I promise.'

The woman gave her a good-natured grin. 'I'll see what I can do. I've had three of my own, so I know what it's like. Ten minutes is all, though – I've to be somewhere after that.'

With order restored, Kershaw produced her notebook, took down personal details and repeated her question.

'There was this kinda . . . well, just noise, really, like, loud,' Craig said. 'We were upstairs with the baby, ken.'

'Do you know what time it was?' Kershaw asked, but he shook his head.

'Just – it was pretty dark. All the lights went and the house was, like, shaking like it was an earthquake, sort of. And Donna was screaming and yelling. It was like we were in a horror movie, only, well, real.' He shuddered. 'I grabbed the bairn and went to the door – bashed my face on a sharp edge . . .'

He fingered a scratch on his cheek, and Donna put in, 'Nearly dropped the baby too.'

He glared at her. 'That was with you hanging on to me and yelling we'd all be killed. Didn't help.'

Hastily, Kershaw interjected, 'And then?'

'It was the water downstairs,' Donna said, shuddering. 'I was, like, going mental. It was all slimy and muddy with sort of stuff in it and you couldn't see and it was up to our knees – I'll be waking up screaming the rest of my life.'

Craig's expression suggested that he did not relish the prospect. He went on, 'Then we got out, and Jan next door was calling help or something. She'd hurt her leg. She'd a big torch by her door so that was better, and she kinda hobbled out with a stick. But the road was blocked so there was nowhere to go and it was that wet and cold.'

'Thought we'd die out there,' Donna put in. 'So I go, "If we're going to die anyway, might as well die out of the rain, right?" And Jan goes, "If I don't sit down, I'll fall down." So we went back in and found somewhere we could sit. But it was, like, horrific. I'm scared to go to sleep – I'll wake up screaming—'

'Yeah, you said,' Craig said unsympathetically, and she put out her tongue at him.

'The other house, where the man was killed,' Kershaw began, then stopped when she saw the looks on their faces. 'Sorry – you didn't know?'

'Oh. My. God!' Donna said, eyes wide. 'Someone was, like, dead – right there beside us?'

'I saw them all round the cottage with their tape and stuff, but I sort of thought it was because it was falling down.' Craig's face had turned white.

'Did you look last night?' Kershaw asked.

He shifted in his seat. 'Kind of. But it was really dark, ken, and Jan said they were both out. And there wasn't a noise, like anyone . . . well, groaning or stuff.'

'I think he was probably killed outright,' Kershaw said. She had no idea whether that was true or not, but she was sorry for the boy. Craig looked relieved.

The sound of a wail approaching down the corridor, suggesting that for all her experience the nurse had failed in her mission to pacify, brought Kershaw to her feet. She closed her notebook.

'That's all I need from you. I'll get this typed up into statements for you to sign, but there's no rush. Thanks for your help.'

As she went out, passing the baby on her way in, Craig's envious voice said, 'It's all right for some,' and she heard Donna's shrill reply, 'You're just rubbish, you know that?' The odds on their being together to celebrate their daughter's first birthday weren't good.

MAIDIE GLANCED ANXIOUSLY at the kitchen clock. Beth had been out for a long time now. The rain had gone off, but the sky was still threatening, and with the girl getting so chilled last night, it wouldn't do her any good to get soaked through again.

It crossed her mind to wonder if she had actually gone for good. That would please Alick, but Beth had said she'd nowhere else to go, and Maidie couldn't bear her to think that shelter wouldn't be gladly offered in such a dreadful situation.

Alick's attitude had left her profoundly shocked. Oh, she knew he was mean, of course, and she'd grown so used to his complaints about the unfairness of life that she barely heard them any more. As a crofter's daughter, she was accustomed to the harsh realities of rural poverty and they'd rubbed along well enough. She'd had no high expectations when she married him: she wasn't bonny, and there'd been no other offers. And without Alick there wouldn't have been Calum, the light of her life.

A big issue like this hadn't cropped up before, though. Today, the sheer nastiness of the Buchans, mother and son, had aroused something in her she hadn't known was there. Beth had come to them in desperate need, and now she was both homeless and bereaved, she needed protection. The girl was barely more than a child herself, and Maidie's maternal instinct was strong.

There was Beth now. From the kitchen window she could see her trudging towards the house. Maidie carried Calum through to the sitting room and put him down on the floor.

'There you are, wee man,' she said. 'Gran will play with you.' She didn't look at Ina, so was spared the look of indignation on her mother-in-law's face as she looked up from her *People's Friend*.

Beth was opening the outside door as Maidie came back into the kitchen. She hesitated on the threshold, giving the other woman a sideways glance.

'Sorry,' she muttered. 'I was out of order.'

'It was Gran who was out of order,' Maidie said firmly. 'It's sort of a hobby with her. Come away in and sit down. Are you very wet?'

'Just my jacket,' Beth said, taking off her parka and draping it on the overhead pulley to dry. She sat down at the table obediently, saying nothing, just studying her hands.

'Beth,' Maidie said, her stomach fluttering with nerves, 'I've – I've – I'm afraid I've got some bad news for you.'

'The cottage,' Beth said. 'It's wrecked, isn't it? I knew it would be.' Her voice was flat, emotionless.

'Well, yes, but it's – it's worse than that.' Maidie gave a nervous little cough. 'You know you said your partner wasn't there? I'm afraid you were wrong. He was.'

'No, he wasn't,' Beth said flatly.

It was even harder than Maidie had thought it might be. 'He must have come back, Beth. They found him in your house, dead.'

'Dead? Lee? I – I don't know what to say.' She was oddly calm.

Shock, Maidie decided. It affected different people different ways. 'I know it's hard to take it in. It'll hit you later. Grief's like that.'

Beth looked at her coolly. 'Grief?' She gave a short laugh. 'We'd quarrelled. I found him out, you see. He was a bastard, a total bastard. I threw him out.'

Gran was right: there was something funny about Beth's eyes. Maidie couldn't think of anything useful to say, and could only take refuge in the familiar.

'I'll make us a cup of tea anyway, shall I? It's meant to be good for shock.'

And if Beth wasn't shocked, she certainly was.

A HEAVY LORRY was rumbling up the road towards Rosscarron House as Fleming and MacNee left the camping site on their way down to the Rosscarron Cottages. Fleming pulled in to one side to let it pass.

'I wonder if that's catering for the starving masses,' she said. 'Probably half of them come planning to survive the weekend on nothing but junk food.'

'And beer – they'll have plenty of that, all right. And dope, no doubt, though the dealers'll be out in force as well. Rare healthy pastime for the young. Don't know what the parents are thinking about, these days. Shouldn't be parents, the half of them.'

Fleming gave him an anxious glance. MacNee had always, of course, been a cynic, but there was a sort of sourness about the way he spoke that wasn't normal.

'Oh, come on!' she said, half laughing to try to make light of it. 'My own kids are coming tomorrow. There's plenty of decent, sensible kids, and good parents too.'

'And plenty of the other kind. See Kershaw? Asked her how she managed the job with her kid and she said she's in a boarding school. What kind of parent is that? Why have kids at all?'

'Tam!' she protested. 'There's plenty parents scrimp and save to send their kids to boarding school where they reckon they'd get a better chance. Cammie's got rugby pals who love it – fantastic facilities, and more time and great coaching. He'd be off tomorrow given half a chance.

'Anyway, people's circumstances change. Kim's divorced with her living to earn, and her daughter's probably far better at boarding school with chums and lots of activities than having a patchwork of babysitters who could let her down at any time.'

His face was mutinous and she knew she could have saved her breath. Still, it had given her an insight into Tam's antagon-ism towards the new detective: Bunty's childlessness had always been a great grief to her, and though Fleming suspected that Tam himself could have lived with it, he cared deeply for the sake of his adored wife.

They were driving down towards the bridge over the Carron now and Fleming, happy to change the subject, said, 'I think we should both take a serious look at the bridge, Tam. I'll park on the further side where there's a bit more space and then we can have a good poke around.'

She drove on to it slowly, looking over the side. 'Do you think the level's down at all from this morning? It could be—'

Suddenly everything was slipping sideways, out of her control. The bridge was tipping. With a tearing sound the Vauxhall crashed through the metal barriers at the driver's side and plunged nose first into the river.

Chapter Five

INDIE MUSIC WAS pounding from the speakers in the white sitting room at Rosscarron House, but the two men with beers in their hands seemed inured to the level of sound.

'Cigarette?' Gillis Crozier leaned forward to hold out a packet to his guest. He had been virtually chain-smoking for the last half-hour.

'Got my own, thanks.' Joss Hepburn took out a packet of Marlboros and lit one, leaning back in an unyielding black chair and reflecting with a sort of desperate boredom that at least it gave him something to do. Sitting here while Crozier twitched wasn't his idea of entertainment, though admittedly, trying to arrange a pop festival without Internet or even phone would make anyone twitch.

But then, it had been a crazy idea in the first place, and he'd been crazy to allow them to twist his arm. He was regretting it now, though it had almost been worth it just to see Madge Laird's face. A copper – who'd have thought it!

'So, you've absolutely no idea what time the rest of the band are arriving?'

'No,' Hepburn said for the fourth time. 'The arrangement was, they'd call when they landed. Never crossed my mind this would be a dead spot. I guess they'll have your landline on a schedule somewhere, though that's not exactly a whole heap of use at the moment.'

'It's a right bugger, this entire thing.' Crozier crushed out his half-smoked cigarette into an overflowing ashtray. 'Someone trying to tell me something, do you think? I can't get confirmation of times of arrival for equipment or supplies or the other first-day groups – I don't know where anyone is and they can't tell me. Alex was taking time off from his legal duties in London to do a job for me and was to report back, but he's obviously been delayed and can't let me know, and the bands we're expecting can't warn me if there's a problem. If I'm honest, I'm not sure how we're going to cope, given the weather. Never seen rain like it at this time of year.'

'Not just a huge amount you can do about it now, is there – artists on their way, kids starting to party out there already. But—'

The door opened and a woman came in. She was small and slight, in her mid-thirties perhaps, with a cloud of fair hair and unhealthy-looking skin with a hectic flush. She was clearly distracted.

'Have you seen Declan? I need him urgently.' Her words were slightly thickened and she licked her lips as if her mouth was dry.

Hepburn, after a swift glance at her eyes, drooping and red-rimmed, dropped his own and made a business of stubbing out his cigarette.

Crozier's voice was strained. 'Gone up the hill to the campsite to see how many people have arrived, I think.' She left before he finished his sentence.

He lit another cigarette and inhaled deeply. 'My daughter, Cara,' he said, then as Hepburn made a noncommittal noise, burst out, 'I know, I know. You don't have kids, do you?'

'No. I never go looking for trouble.'

'Wise man!' Crozier said with feeling. 'I found her stash yesterday and I got rid of it. Pointless, probably – she'll get it from somewhere else. My adored only child and I'm helpless. I've tried everything – keeping her short of money, bribing her, threatening her – but she's not interested in kicking it. All she says is, "I can handle it, Dad," and then she gets upset with me. I may have to do something drastic, or she's going to kill herself.' He shrugged. 'Before, I knew she maybe dabbled a bit, but recently . . . After all that's happened to her, I can understand why she tries to blot it out.'

With a sinking feeling, Hepburn finished his beer. Agony uncle really wasn't his scene; there was nothing bored him more than other people's personal problems, but he couldn't exactly say, 'Sure, sure,' and walk out.

He continued the discussion reluctantly. 'Well, hard for kids, growing up in our kind of world. You can't stop them meeting guys who'll put the stuff their way.'

'Like her husband,' Crozier said grimly.

'Declan? Oh, he's not so bad. I've had a bit to do with him, off and on.'

'He doesn't do drugs himself, but she makes him get them for her.'

It likely wouldn't be tactful to say, 'Oh well, keeps it in the family.' Instead, he gave a discouraging, 'Mmm.'

Crozier barely heard him. 'After the baby, of course.'

'Of course.'

Something in the way he spoke must have betrayed his ignorance. Crozier looked at him sharply. 'Don't you know about the baby? Didn't Declan tell you?'

'We didn't have that sort of relationship.'

Crozier got up and walked to the window, turning his head away. 'And I suppose it didn't make the news in the States, like it did here. That was part of the hell of the whole thing.'

Hepburn got to his feet too. 'Hold it right there, Gil – we can't have this sort of conversation without a glass in our hand. What you need is a Scotch. Where do you keep it?'

'Oh . . .' Crozier looked at him blankly for a second, then said, 'Cris – ask Cris. He'll get it for you.'

'Great!' Hepburn went out, rolling his eyes and groaning quietly as he shut the door.

The music had changed to a mordant Leonard Cohen number. Crozier stared blankly out of the window. He wasn't thinking about the baby. He was thinking about Kenna, when he had seen her that last time, after she had so terribly betrayed him: the burnished copper of her hair, still without a thread of grey, springing from her head as if its energy had drained the colour from her face and life from her wasted body. It should have been a time for love and grief, not for accusation and anger.

The door opened again behind him and Hepburn's head appeared round it.

'Gil, I'm sorry. I didn't want to break up our talk, but the boys will have landed by now and be trying to raise me. I figured that if I headed off towards Kirkcudbright, I could pick up a signal and get you an ETA. And I'm almost out of Marlboros too – don't know if they'll have heard of them out here in the boondocks, but I sure hate smoking anything else. Hold the thought, will you?'

'Of course,' Crozier said bleakly. He had been naïve to try to open up about his personal tragedy to Joss Hepburn, whose ruthless disregard for anything except his own interests was one of the secrets of his professional success. And anyway, talking didn't change anything.

DS ANDY MACDONALD knocked, a little hesitantly, on the door of Superintendent Bailey's office. On the few occasions when he had entered this sanctum he'd been summoned. He hadn't been the bearer of bad news either, and he certainly didn't trust the super not to shoot the messenger. In response to an impatient, 'Come!' he took a deep breath and opened the door.

Bailey scribbed a signature on a paper in front of him, then looked up. 'Macdonald?' He was clearly surprised.

'Sorry to disturb you, sir. It's DI Fleming.'

'Yes, Fleming! Where is the woman? I need to talk to her about a statement on the Rosscarron Cottages, but I can't get hold of her.'

'No, sir. We think she and DS MacNee went to Rosscarron House.'

'Yes. I sent her. Should have been in an ideal place to send back a report.'

'There's no signal there for mobiles, as you probably know.'

'Of course, of course.' Bailey was always reluctant to confess to ignorance. 'But she's got a radio, hasn't she?'

'That's just it, sir. The communications room has reported that DI Fleming's car radio has gone dead.'

'Gone dead? What on earth for? Oh, malfunction, I suppose.'

'We don't know, sir.'

'I need to speak to her.'

Bailey was chewing his lip. He was, Macdonald guessed, under pressure from somewhere; generally, he wasn't bad as supers went, but he tended to lose it when things went wrong.

He went on, 'Phone the man – what's-his-name – Crozier. Ask where she is.'

Macdonald shifted uneasily. 'The phone lines are down too, I'm afraid.'

'Oh, this is ridiculous!' Bailey slammed his fist hard on the desk. 'I don't know what Fleming thinks she's playing at. The press are getting very restless – how can I release a statement when I haven't had a report from her?'

Pleased that his guess had been accurate, Macdonald said helpfully, 'Well, I've been to the scene. Perhaps I could . . .

'For heaven's sake, man, why didn't you say so? Have you something down on file?'

'Not yet, sir.'

'Then *get* it down, Sergeant. You've got half an hour. Less, preferably. All right?'

'Sir.' Macdonald turned to go, then paused. 'And do you want someone to check on DI Fleming?'

'Oh, no doubt she'll turn up. It's too bad – there's been enough trouble over her already. I should have thought the least she could do is keep a low profile and get on with her job . . . What are you waiting for, Macdonald?'

MacNee's head was spinning. The scream of futile brakes, the crump of mangled metal, the explosive force of the airbags, the shock of icy water creeping up around him . . . and now a sudden, brutal silence. His eyes shut against the dizziness, he tried to make sense of it.

He opened his eyes as the airbags deflated. He was half suspended by his seat belt, with the Vauxhall at a nose-down angle. But he could move everything – he was all right. He took a deep breath.

'God!' he said with a shaky attempt at lightness. 'Donaldson wasn't such an old woman after all, was he?'

Fleming didn't respond.

'Marjory? Marjory?'

She was slumped against the steering wheel, facing towards him. Her side airbag had failed to inflate; her eyes were closed, and he could see a bruise on her temple.

He stretched awkwardly to feel for a pulse in her neck. The car rocked crazily at his movement and his stomach lurched with it. He still hadn't got a pulse.

He dared not lean further over. He reached cautiously for her limp hand and at last found the tiny node with its throb of life. Thank God for that!

But they had to get out of here. Water was beginning to build up, but if he dislodged the car, if it tipped, rolled over . . . MacNee could feel the cold sweat standing out on his brow.

There were no lights at all showing on the instrument panel and he was afraid even to try the radio; he was pretty sure it was dead anyway, and he could smell petrol. If the tank was breached, the tiniest electrical spark could turn the car into a fireball. He wasn't even going to think about other short circuits water might create.

He had to get out. Craning his neck, he took stock of the position: the bridge above him, tilted at a crazy angle with its metal railing broken and twisted; wooden spars and debris floating in the swirling water; the tail of the car resting halfway up the steep bank on the headland side.

The rain had come on again. In the diminished light, the river seemed colder, darker, more deadly than ever. And it was coming into the car, higher and higher; soon, if the weight shifted, it would dislodge the car anyway.

With another glance at his unconscious companion, MacNee tried, not hopefully, to open the door, but the force of the water was holding it shut, and though the window was just clear of the surface, it was electric. He dared not even try to operate it.

There was a heavy torch in the glovebox. It was under water, but bracing himself against the dashboard and moving with infinite caution, MacNee groped until his fingers grasped it. His first attempt to smash the window failed, but it shattered at the second blow. Clearing the remaining glass rubble from the window frame, he didn't even notice the dozen tiny cuts it made on his hands until he saw his blood in the water.

Fleming gave a faint groan and moved a little. The car swayed. Good that she was coming round, sure, but MacNee wasn't so crazy about the moving part.

He'd have to move himself, though. No alternative. He prised off his shoes and undid his seat belt, then hers. If the car ended up on its roof in the river, he didn't want to be fumbling with straps.

Gritting his teeth in a grimace of concentration, MacNee levered himself up and out through the window space, twisting painfully to get a grip on the roof for purchase, then eased himself out. For a terrifying moment the car rocked, but settled back.

He lowered himself into the fast-running river and, clinging to the edge of the window, tried to calculate the depth – five, six feet? The difference was crucial to a man of his height who couldn't swim.

It was mercilessly cold. There was debris from the bridge buffeting him, and the pull of the current was a shock. His feet didn't touch the bottom and for a second MacNee thought he would be swept away. But he grabbed on to the door handle then, kicking out with his feet for buoyancy, worked his way along to the one on the rear door. Beyond that, the tail of the car rose out of the water above him and he paused to catch his breath.

Seven feet, eight feet round below the unstable car to the river's edge – could he stay afloat that far, with the current against him? The car was shaking now: Fleming must be starting to come round. He didn't fancy being below it if it was dislodged.

With a sort of frenzied doggy-paddle, MacNee launched himself round the end and across the stretch of water. Greedily, the current snatched and tugged at him with almost animal force, but high on terror, he fought through and at last solid, if muddy ground was beneath his feet. His breath sobbing in his chest, he leaned against the bank. But there was no time to waste – Marjory next.

It was only then he realised that the car's tail, resting on a curve in the bank, was blocking his access to the driver's side. He simply hadn't thought that through. His teeth were chattering with cold, he was aching in every muscle, and now he would have to climb a steep, muddy bank, then come back down again. And quickly – anything could happen to the car. Swearing didn't do any good, but he carried on anyway.

The bank, eroded by the flood water, shelved in and MacNee, exhausted already, slipped back down again, and again, and again. Even when at last the tufty grass on the top of the bank was within his grasp, a clump came out in his hand and it took a contortionist effort to save himself from falling back to the bottom. He hauled his wet body over the lip of the bank and collapsed, his chest heaving with exertion. At least the effort had warmed him up a little.

But Fleming was still down there, still in imminent danger, starting to move, perhaps. If she moved too much . . . Groaning, he got up, walked round the curve to the other side of the car and dreeped down, lowering himself by his arms as far as he could, then dropping into the water. He had no idea how deep it was here; he could find himself slipping under and having to fight his way to the surface, or landing awkwardly on a rock and ending up a casualty himself.

At last, though, his luck seemed to have turned. He landed on soft ground, in the shallows, and he could wrench the driver's door open. A flood of water poured out at his feet.

'Marjory!' he said sharply. 'Marjory! Can you hear me?' He slapped at her hand.

Her eyes shot open. They looked ill focused; she screwed them up in an effort to see. 'Tam? What's – what's happened? Where . . . ? Can't move!' The words were slurred; her eyes closed again.

'Bridge collapsed. Move your hand, Marjory. Can you move your hand?'

She didn't seem to hear him. Fear grabbing at him again, he picked up her hand and slapped it. 'Move your hand, Marjory!'

At last, uncertainly, she moved her fingers.

'And your feet, Marjory – your feet!'

MacNee could see that at last she was coming to, and as she did, he saw panic appear in her face.

'My feet – yes. But Tam, I can't sit up! I can't sit up!' Her breath was ragged with terror.

'It's all right, it's all right. The car's nose down, that's all. Just don't make any sudden movements and we'll be fine,' MacNee said with a confidence he didn't really feel. 'Does anything hurt except your head? No? Now look, I'm going to put my shoulder below yours and lever you up, and then you'll see . . .'

Her mind was obviously clearing and she looked shame-faced when she realised that gravity, not injury, was the problem. 'Sorry. Not very impressive, that. I'm remembering now. The bridge – should have checked it before, not after.'

'You'll know another time. Now, we're needing to get you out of here before we die of cold.'

They were both shivering violently. The rain was lessening and a wicked little gusting breeze had sprung up, driving the clouds scudding across the sky and bringing greater wind chill, and Fleming's dismay showed as she realised her position.

Her face was alarmingly pale, apart from the bruising round her temple. Blood clots, depressed fractures . . . MacNee knew enough about head injuries to be afraid she might without warning drop at his feet, but it would hardly help if he started to panic now.

'Och, you're fine,' he said robustly. 'Now, slide towards me – that's right, good lassie! Put your arm round my shoulders and I'll pull you clear.'

Fleming gave a cry of fright as the car tipped, but MacNee, his strained muscles screaming, pulled her clear with a supreme effort and dragged her back through the shallows in case it fell. With a shudder, though, the car settled back.

She leaned against the bank, swaying a little, but with control of all her limbs and clear enough in her mind to start insisting that she was absolutely fine. Which plainly she wasn't, but at least it was a step in the right direction.

She was also grateful. 'I could have drowned in there. You saved my life, Tam. I don't know how you begin to thank someone for that.'

'Och, havers,' MacNee said gruffly. 'Buy me a pint sometime and we'll call it quits.'

He hadn't finished the job, though. How the hell was he to get her up the bank? MacNee was a small man, Fleming a tall woman; manhandling her out of the car had been hard enough, and he couldn't see her now doing much to help herself.

Fleming was looking at it despairingly. 'I can't get up there. You'll have to go for help.'

He didn't want to leave her. She was chilled to the bone already, her knees were buckling, and if he left her, he didn't think she could stand for any length of time; if she sat down in the water, hypothermia could have set in by the time he got back.

He looked around for inspiration, then realised that with the angle it was at, the open door of the car formed a sort of angled shelf. He wedged it firmly into the bank, which actually stabilised the car too. He should have thought of that sooner.

'Here,' he said. 'Rest on that and I'll scramble up there.'

Sitting down thankfully, Fleming eyed the bank above them. 'Give me a minute, Tam, then I could give you a leg-up.'

She didn't look as if she could stand up herself, far less take his weight. 'Och, no,' he said. 'Just give me a wee clap when I get to the top, eh?'

MacNee was eyeing it up without enthusiasm, looking for possible footholds, when a voice hailed them from above, an amused voice.

'Having fun down there, you guys?'

It was the man Fleming had called Joss. MacNee saw her look up sharply, but he couldn't quite make out her expression. It certainly didn't mirror the intense relief he was feeling himself.

JAN FORBES, SITTING up in bed in a side-ward with one of her sturdy legs in plaster and wearing a hospital nightgown, was looking remarkably chipper, DC Kershaw thought. She was certainly impressively calm by comparison to her fellow victims, with her iron-grey hair neatly brushed and her eyes bright with interest behind her spectacles.

Kershaw took her details. Jan was, she told her, Dr Forbes, 'but of course I'm not a medic. PhD in botany, specialising in heaths and heathers mainly, so don't start telling me about your bad back!' She laughed merrily.

She was a lecturer at Glasgow University and the cottage, it seemed, was mainly a study centre for her, bought some years before but inhabited only sporadically during vacations or when working on a project.

'Wonderful place, Rosscarron. So quiet, no phone, no TV and of course virgin territory for academic study, though I daresay that's not what you're interested in.

'Now, what can I tell you? Not much about last night, really. It wasn't that late – seven o'clock, perhaps, but with the weather it was very dark already and I'd had to put the lights on. Then there was this terrible crash, almost like an explosion, and a rumbling that went on and on and on, and of course the lights went out. I couldn't see much, just a torrent of water and mud pouring through, but I'd have been safe enough if I'd kept my head. I did in my leg by leaping to my feet and taking a header over the coffee table. Serves me right – I should have had more sense than to panic. Then, of course, that poor young couple had this old fool to deal with as well as a crying baby – and they're barely more than children themselves when all's said and done. I do trust they're all right?'

She looked an enquiry and Kershaw attempted to seize the initiative. 'Yes, fine. Dr Forbes—'

She was corrected. 'Jan. "Dr Forbes" makes me think of my father. Now, he *was* a medical doctor.'

Ruthlessness was called for. 'Jan, I have to ask you about the couple in the cottage on the other side. We don't know anything about them as yet. Can you help me?'

'I knew them hardly at all. I only came down here last week, you know. Bumped into her a couple of times and she was perfectly pleasant, but she wasn't disposed to be chatty. I didn't know their names or whether they were living there or just on holiday.'

'Can I press you further on this? What were they like? What was their relationship?'

Jan's nose wrinkled in distaste. 'Are you asking me for gossip? I don't like it. I talk, but I don't gossip – I've seen the havoc it can wreak in university departments.'

'It would be very helpful – give us a fuller picture.'

'I see. Very well, then.' For the first time Jan paused, clearly ordering her thoughts. 'The girl had a very pale skin and very dark hair – tinted, I would guess – and she was around my own height, five foot four or five. Aged twenty, perhaps. I couldn't tell you about the man. With the weather we've had, we all just rush to our cars with our hoods over our heads.

'I saw her once on the single sunny afternoon we've had in this last week, sitting on the seat on the top of the cliff – when it was a cliff.' Alarm showed suddenly in Jan's face. 'Oh my goodness! Do you know where she is? She wasn't up there when it happened, was she? I saw her going past my door, out along the headland, but my desk is in the window and I was working there all afternoon.

I'd definitely have seen her coming back, so I was pretty sure she wasn't at home. But I never thought . . . Oh dear!'

'Is there no other way round?' Kershaw asked.

'Across the moors, then on to the road on the Rosscarron estate. She could have done that, I suppose, but with the weather . . .'

'She may well have been located by now. There's certainly absolutely no reason to think she's been caught up in this,' Kershaw said soothingly. 'But tell me about him. You said he was out too?'

'Yes, yes, I did. I saw him leaving earlier in the day.' Jan fell uncharacteristically silent.

'You mentioned gossip,' Kershaw prompted at last. 'What you've told me couldn't be classed as gossip and I think there's something you're not telling me.'

'Oh dear!' Jan sighed again. 'Is it really necessary to muck-rake? I can't see what it can achieve.'

In the face of such determined reluctance, Kershaw could see that disclosure was the only way forward. 'I think perhaps you may not know that his body was found in the house next door to yours.'

She encountered a very sharp look. 'And you couldn't have told me that at the outset, Constable Kershaw?'

Feeling uncomfortable, Kershaw considered saying she thought Jan knew. Under that stern gaze, though, honesty seemed wiser. 'Sometimes withholding information is a tactical decision.'

'Indeed?' There was a chilly pause. Then Jan said heavily, 'Poor young man. Oh well! There was a quarrel, you know, and she threw him out. There was a lot of screaming – he seemed to be refusing to go at one point. I suppose it was around three o'clock or thereabouts. Eventually he appeared outside wearing a parka and carrying a suitcase, heading for the car park. I couldn't see her, but the door slammed afterwards so she must have been watching him go.'

'And was it then she walked past your window?'

Jan thought for a moment. 'Yes, I think so – or was it a little later? I certainly couldn't swear to it. I was absorbed in my work, and I try anyway not to pry.'

'But he must have returned. Did you hear nothing?'

'The houses are – *were* quite solidly built. I only heard their row because they were having it at the front door. I put on some music after that, I remember, quite loud music – I'm a Wagner buff. Good gracious, I believe I was listening to *Götterdämmer-ung*! Quite sinisterly appropriate! But—' Jan stopped, struck by an unpleasant thought. 'If I hadn't assumed he was out . . .'

'Wouldn't have made any difference.' Kershaw was beginning to believe her own assertion. 'Were they in the habit of quarrelling?'

'I couldn't say. When I saw her, she looked . . . glum, I suppose is the word. If they were on holiday, she didn't look as if she was enjoying it much.'

'Who did the house belong to?'

'I don't know that either – oh dear, I'm not much use, am I? It was empty when I bought number three, but a while ago there was a woman living there when I came for a break. I spoke to her a couple of times, but she was clearly very ill and I heard she had died. I guess the house was sold – it was empty any other time I was here.'

Kershaw closed her notebook. 'Right. I think that's all I wanted to ask at the moment. If there's anything you think of, here's the number to call.' She gave Jan a card. 'Thanks – I appreciate your help. How long will you be in here?'

'Oh, they're turfing me out today. I'm going to friends who run a little hotel just on the coast beyond Gatehouse-of-Fleet. They're prepared to take on the halt and the lame, so I'll be well looked after till I can pick up speed on my crutches.'

As Kershaw left, Jan called after her, 'I keep thinking about the girl. I do trust she's all right – but if that's where she was living, has she somewhere to go? I'm sure they'd have her at Rowantrees, and of course, if money's a problem, I can take care of that. Let me know if I can help.'

A good Samaritan, Kershaw thought, returning to her car. Sometimes, in this job, you needed reminding that the world wasn't entirely populated by ratbags.

WHEN ALICK BUCHAN came downstairs again, he was quite obviously drunk. His wife was sitting at the kitchen table, which was set for lunch, with three places.

He looked around. 'Where is she?'

Maidie, her face troubled, said, 'She's gone out again. I told her the dinner was ready, but she wouldn't wait. I made her a sandwich.' She got up and went over to the stove. 'Sit down and I'll call your mother.'

'Has the girl left for good?'

'No, I don't think so, Alick. I told you, she's got nowhere to go.'

'Aye, has she! She'll go to the big house, and that's flat. He's plenty rooms and plenty food – about time he did his share. Puts everything on me – bastard! Bodies, even – he'd no right! I'm not taking it from him, I tell you that.' Alick lurched to the door. 'I'm away there now. Tell her . . . tell her it's where she's to go if she comes back.'

'Alick, you're not driving—' Maidie put her hand on his arm to restrain him, but he pushed her away so violently that she knocked against the wall.

'Mind the house, woman!'

Rubbing her bruised shoulder, Maidie looked helplessly after him as he walked unsteadily towards the jeep, climbed in and drove away.

There was a sudden yell from Calum in the other room and a moment later the kitchen door opened and Ina Buchan appeared with the purple-faced, screaming child in her arms. She thrust him at his mother.

'Whatever's the matter? What happened?' Maidie asked in alarm.

There were spots of colour in Ina's cheeks. 'He got a good skelp from me, that's what's the matter. He's a naughty boy and you can look after him yourself in future. Now, where's my dinner?'

BETH WAS WALKING, walking. She had taken the tarmac track this time, tired of struggling with uneven footing, but she had kept her hood up even though the rain had gone off and there were actually one or two breaks in the clouds. She was alone in the wild, silent landscape, but even so she kept looking about her with what was almost a nervous twitch. She was angry with herself for feeling nervous – and deeply, permanently angry with the man who had made fear her familiar companion.

She was so happy, happier than she'd ever been in her life, really, those first days after Lee moved in with her. Love, companionship, laughter – there hadn't been a lot of that in her life. He made her brave, unafraid to return to normality as they played house in the little flat. She even lost her feeling of being followed.

She knew about Crozier's threat, of course. Pay in blood, *he had said. The newspapers had made much of it and she had been really scared, but when she talked about it with Lee and he told her it didn't mean anything except that the man was hurting, she began to believe him and put it out of her mind.*

So when she switched on her mobile one morning and found the text message, it shattered her cosy idyll. She screamed; Lee, pouring boiling water into mugs for coffee, splashed himself and swore.

'What the hell did you do that for?' he demanded.

Tears sprang to her eyes at his tone. 'See for yourself!' she said, holding out her phone in a hand that trembled.

'You think I've forgotten? Never. You're alive, she's dead.' The message was stark.

Lee took it, frowning. 'Oh great! What a sod! They must have kept your number. But it doesn't matter. It's just bluster. Look – it's gone. We'll get you another phone. He doesn't know where you are.'

But he did know. The note on the mat a few days later told her that. 'Murderess,' it said. 'I'm watching you all the time, until I'm ready.'

She began sleeping badly again and having flashbacks when she did sleep – the tiny body, white and cold as stone . . .

'We have to move, now,' Lee said. 'The sale's gone through – we'd be moving in a couple of weeks anyway. You've got that house your granny left you.'

She had been happy here, briefly, and there was no way she was going to her granny's cottage – full of memories, right on Gillis Crozier's doorstep, if he was at Rosscarron House. But she agreed to move. What else could she do? There was no point in going to the police with the note; they'd made it clear enough where their sympathies lay.

So they moved away – and moved again, and again. But always, before long, he found her once more. She changed mobiles too, but always there would be a text message, a note – once, even, a little package on the doorstep containing a grotesque, grinning plastic skull.

'He's employing the best in the business, isn't he,' Lee said grimly.

Her nerves were shot to pieces. She tried not to irritate him, but he was getting impatient.

'I've had enough of this,' he said one night when, yet again, a note had found them. 'You said he went a lot to a house near your granny's? Let's go there and confront him.'

Kenna had died not long after the trial. Thinking of her grand-mother still hurt, and she felt guilty as well: she had been too afraid to travel to Scotland to say a proper goodbye. She tried one last protest.

'I don't want to go there. It'll make me sad, and I'd be scared to be so near him. He could easily get me up there, make it look like an accident.'

'So we carry on like this, with you going steadily mental? I don't think so,' he snarled.

Lee had been getting less and less understanding, and then she would lose her temper. They weren't happy now, like they had been, and sometimes she wondered why he stayed.

Worse, sometimes she thought she knew why. He'd given up whatever it was he did, and if it hadn't been for the money from the sale of the flat and her mum's insurance, they'd have real problems. It was disappearing at a frightening rate and when it was all gone, he'd probably be gone too. By then, anyway, she might be dead. Sometimes she thought she would just die of a heart attack, when one of the messages arrived.

Now, he was controlling his irritation with difficulty. 'We have to get real. He most likely doesn't want to kill you anyway or he'd have done it by now. It's like what he wants is to do in your head. So let's eyeball him. Your granny's house – Crozier would never think to look there. Once he's arrived, we'll go together, surprise him, just walk in and tell him it has to stop. Then we've got the rest of our lives together for happy ever after. All right?'

It wasn't all right. It made her feel sick just to think about it. But she'd been broken down by the endless, relentless pursuit, and when Lee said unpleasantly, 'If you've got a better idea, like moving house every five minutes and screaming in your sleep and twitching all the time, count me out,' the combination of carrot and stick – eternal bliss or the hell of loneliness – was enough to make her agree.

All this walking and the troubled thoughts that came to her in the silence were exhausting when she was so shattered anyway, but it was preferable to being in that little house, the atmosphere rank with undercurrents of unhappiness. She didn't know which was hardest to deal with, the old bat's hostility, Alick's resentment or Maidie's bewildered kindness.

And she was scared, very scared. She had nowhere to go, but the longer she stayed here, the more dangerous it would be and the greater, too, would be the chance of exposure. Since it all happened, she hadn't spent time in the company of other people, except Lee. She didn't want to go back to thinking about Lee – Lee, dead. It was easier to think about the practicalities.

She had to get out of here. Alick was her best bet. He was as keen to get rid of her as she was to go – she could tell from the way he looked at her. She could ask him to drive her into Kirkcudbright; there was a bank there and she could find out if she'd any money left. At least she had a credit card in the purse in her pocket.

Anyway, she was the victim of a disaster. She could go to the social services, and they'd have to find her somewhere to stay, wouldn't they? But that would mean the police. No, not the police.

But if she stayed here . . . She was between a rock and a hard place. Between the devil and the deep blue sea, as her granny would have said.

If Granny Kenna wasn't dead . . . Beth's eyes brimmed. Granny would have helped her, seen her through this crisis, as she'd seen her through the last. Now there was no one. No one at all.

She had been walking for a long time – aimlessly at first, then with purpose, almost as if she felt inexorably drawn. And there, as she rounded a corner, she could see a house – his house. It was crazy to go closer, and yet . . . The predator could never imagine being stalked by its prey.

There was no one about. With her hood pulled forward and her head down, she went off the track and climbed up to where, from the shelter of some scrubby bushes, she looked down at his house, hatred in her eyes.

Chapter Six

'WHAT THE . . . ?' The driver's jaw dropped as his green Ka turned a bend in the road and he saw the bridge ahead, leaning at a drunken angle amid shattered spars and debris. He swore, braking sharply.

His front-seat passenger gasped, and one of the girls in the back seat screamed.

'It's only frigging collapsed!' the man next to him said, stating the obvious. 'And hey, there's a car!'

They stared, appalled. 'Do you suppose there's, like, people inside?' one of the girls asked with a shudder.

'Have to take a look, don't we?' The driver released his seat belt. 'Come on, mate. You girls stay here.'

Clutching one another's hands, the girls waited. 'Oh, I can't watch!' one cried dramatically. 'Tell me it's OK!'

The two men turned, one giving the thumbs-up as they came back to the car. 'No panic. It's empty, and one of the doors is open. Scared, not hurt, I reckon – didn't have far to fall. But we'd better call the police.'

One of the girls had her mobile out already, then pulled a face. 'No signal. Have to go back to that town with the funny name. So, I guess that's wrecked the rave. Fancy a weekend camping by ourselves in the rain?'

DS TAM MACNEE darkly suspected the guy had been having a laugh, though Cris Pilapil's smooth-skinned brown face was perfectly solemn as he handed MacNee a pair of his own chinos and a shirt that was the sort of explosion of colour that made you want to cover your ears as well as your eyes, and took away MacNee's white T-shirt and dark jeans to be washed and dried. The trainers, at least, fitted, though the chinos were a bit too long and too tight. But that was the least of MacNee's discomforts.

He was in some pain from his abused muscles, the glass cuts on his hands were stinging, and he was smarting, too, over Joss Hepburn's efficiency as a rescuer. The man was a bloody giant, which gave him an unfair advantage – dropping down off the bank, giving Tam a leg-up, then hoisting Marjory on to his shoulders so that with Tam's help from above she made it to the top. Then Hepburn had got himself up, no sweat. And the bastard had thought it was funny.

Marjory had thankfully collapsed into the bed Pilapil had ushered her to, but MacNee was struggling with his duty of gratitude, despite being warm, dry and having a large Scotch at his elbow as he sat at the huge glass dining table in yet another white room in Rosscarron House. He could be struck by snow-blindness at any time, and there was rubbish music going on and on and on, though none of the other six round the table seemed even to be aware of it, far less listening.

He had his concerns too about Marjory. She ought to be in hospital even now, having a brain scan, but she'd been adamant that all she needed was rest. He just hoped she wouldn't wake up dead.

What MacNee hated more than anything was the feeling that he was trapped. There was no way out of this until a temporary bridge was in place, unless HQ decided they were so indispensable that they needed to be taken off by chopper. Aye, right!

He was simmering with frustration. He felt he ought to be doing something – anything – but Crozier, inviting him to have lunch with a sort of weary courtesy, had pointed out there wasn't anything they could do. MacNee had never been good at not doing anything.

So here he was, looking at the bowl in front of him, which held rice and some meat in a pale green sauce – that wasn't natural, for a start. Curry, they'd said, but it didn't look anything like the curry you got in the Indian on Kirkluce High Street.

Opposite him, a kid of about seven or eight was eating a pizza, or rather mucking about with a pizza, tearing off chunks and shoving them into his mouth. He saw MacNee's envious glance and began making faces, crossing his eyes and putting his fingers in the corners of his half-full mouth to pull it into a square shape.

'Nico!' Crozier said sharply. 'If you're going to eat like a pig, you're going to have to leave the table and eat on the floor.'

It was so predictable that MacNee almost groaned aloud. Grabbing his plate, Nico lay down on the floor and carried on eating with suitably disgusting animal sound effects.

Crozier looked at his daughter. 'Has he had his Ritalin today?' he asked.

Cara looked vague. 'I think so. I'm not sure.'

Crozier sighed, then shrugged. He looked, MacNee thought, a defeated man.

Cara had been polite when MacNee was introduced, smiling and even making a charmingly sympathetic remark, but she seemed somehow detached and MacNee didn't have any difficulty in working out why.

He hadn't taken to her husband, Declan Ryan, the blond man they had seen visiting at the campsite, the man so swift to identify plainclothes coppers. Ryan was ignoring his son's behaviour and now was having some sort of domestic discussion with Pilapil.

MacNee had been surprised to find the hired hand sitting down to eat with his employer. He'd have thought, given this sort of money, that the serfs would be kept in their place. He was even more surprised by the tone of the conversation.

'If you need loo paper and fresh towels in your bathroom, you know where to find them,' Pilapil was saying. 'The cleaner didn't appear today.'

'So?' Ryan said insolently.

Crozier intervened. 'Declan, I've told you before. Cris is here to organise my life and cook me the meals I like. He's not here as a personal slave to idle young men.'

Ryan's expression suggested that he would like to reply, but after a moment he said meekly, 'Sorry, Cris,' with a brief, false smile.

On the payroll too, was he? MacNee studied him covertly as he ate the surprisingly delicious food.

Declan Ryan was, MacNee conceded, quite good-looking if you went for the sulky, sissy-looking James Dean type. Women seemed to, though he couldn't see it himself. With a name like that you'd guess at Irish extraction, though his accent was pure

Estuary English. He certainly didn't appear to have much control over his son, who seemed to be spoiled by his mother and thoroughly out of hand. You'd have thought a pair like Declan and Cara, sunk in 'luxury's contagion, weak and vile', would be just the sort to buy some poor lassie to keep him out of their hair, but there didn't seem to be anyone around.

The other member of the party, Joss Hepburn, had said almost nothing. He and Crozier both lit up the moment they had finished their curry, and now Hepburn was leaning back in his chair sending out almost visible waves of boredom.

Finishing his cigarette, he got up. 'Just going to my room. Let me know when you get a signal that the outside world still exists.'

MacNee glanced at his watch, with a sudden start. He hadn't realised how the time was passing – it was three o'clock already. If they weren't back in some sort of communication by six, it was going to cause him problems, but there was nothing he could do about it, nothing.

Crozier was saying, 'I'll have to go up and tell the kids at the campsite that the party's off. Don't relish it, but it's got to be done. They need to be packed up – someone's bound to have reported it by now, so it shouldn't take too long to get them out.'

Cara, taking an interest in the conversation for the first time, said sharply, 'Declan, you go.'

Ryan looked at his wife for a long moment. 'Oh, right.' He didn't sound happy, but he said, 'Right,' again, and to his father-in-law, 'It's OK. If you don't want to do it, I will.'

It had been a significant exchange and MacNee saw Crozier look from one to the other, but he said only, 'Fine. I certainly wasn't looking forward to it. Tell them they'll get refunds, of course. And at least the rain's stopped, thank God!'

It had, indeed, and even some rays of watery sunshine were coming in the windows.

Crozier got up. 'I'll need to go and have a word with the contractors up in the top field. They'll all have to be paid off. This whole exercise is going to cost me a bomb.' He shook his head. 'Right, then, Declan – you'll take care of the campers? Thanks. I've a couple of things to do now, but I'll drop by and add my apologies on the way back from seeing the caterers. What about Nico? Will you take him with you?'

Nico, hearing his name, got up from the floor. 'I don't want to go,' he whined. 'It's boring.'

'You stay with me, angel,' Cara said dreamily. 'Watch a DVD – that'll be cool, won't it, sweetheart? Harry Potter?'

The boy gave his mother a look of contempt and left the room.

MacNee cleared his throat. 'I was thinking I'd come up the hill with you, Mr Ryan. Just to reassure the punters, ken?'

He thoroughly enjoyed the look of dismay that passed between husband and wife.

'Oh God! That's all we need!' Inspector Michie looked horrified. 'The bridge as well!'

The PC who had waylaid him in the corridor to give him the news said, 'I suppose it's just part of the same problem as the cottages. And at least no one seems actually to have been hurt, as far as we can tell.'

'Well, that's something. The rescue services are at full stretch – there's another river burst its banks over in the Machars. But get on to the telephone engineers and tell them to pull their fingers out so we can find out what's happened. Unless they've a problem needing immediate attention, they'll just have to wait till the army's got time to put across one of those Bailey bridge things.'

GILLIS CROZIER'S MIND was on his unwelcome guests as he went into the cloakroom to fetch his outdoor clothes. Police in the house, on top of everything else, was just about the last straw. He had almost heard the crackling of tension round the lunch table. And when could he hope they would go?

Problems seemed to be piling in on him, but it was the family problems that made him feel someone was twisting a knife in his stomach. He'd seen the exchange between Cara and her husband over lunch. Drugs, no doubt – but what could he do?

He'd adored Cara since they'd put his tiny daughter in his arms and he'd looked into those unfocused baby-blue eyes. He'd been possessed with a fierce desire to give her the perfect life – everything that money could buy, he had promised her. But he hadn't been thinking of heroin at the time, and now unfocused eyes were a sign of an unfolding tragedy.

Perhaps if his wife hadn't walked out, it might have been different. She'd been the disciplinarian, but he'd always been a lump of putty in his daughter's hands. What Cara wanted, Cara got, and an addiction problem was the result. There were days when he felt so burdened by guilt that it was an effort to stand up straight.

He'd thrown money at the problem, tried everything from coaxing to threats, and for a time she would cooperate in the latest fashionable rehab before she went back to it again. After the baby died, though, she was beyond reason. His fault, again.

He had no time for his son-in-law – sly, sycophantic little sod – but in a way he could understand why Declan kept Cara supplied.

Denied a fix, she would get that look of fury, hatred, even, and however much you told yourself it was the drug talking, it hurt. God, it hurt!

He'd been such a failure as a father, a failure as a husband too, and he was helpless to stop the disaster that was his grandson getting worse day by day. The only thing he seemed to be good at was making money – as if that mattered now. And he'd made it mainly in a way that meant police officers were extremely unwelcome guests. Crozier gave a sigh that was almost a groan.

As he pulled on his waterproof boots, the doorbell rang and he paused hopefully. A rescue party? He heard Pilapil going to answer it and then a brief conversation.

But when he called, 'In here!' and Pilapil appeared, he was pulling a face.

'Buchan,' Pilapil said, with a tremoring-hand gesture. 'Wants a word. Shall I get rid of him?'

Crozier considered. 'Tempting. God knows I've had enough today, without that. But I'd probably better see him. Find out what his problem is, will you?'

'I tried. Wouldn't tell me. Said he has to see you.'

'Right, right.' Crozier pulled on his other boot and went out into the hall.

'Alick! What can I do for you? Do you want to come into the office?'

'No. No need.'

The man, Crozier realised, was not just drunk but very drunk. It had been a difficult day, certainly, but even so . . .

'Look, Alick, the best thing you can do is go back to Maidie, have a cup of tea and a rest, and then come back later. You've had an upsetting day.'

'Upsetting! Aye, you could say! You've not had an upsetting day. You've not been ordered to go and – and deal with the corpse, just like before. I'm not – I'm not in the bloody army now under your bloody orders.'

It was a shock to realise that the incident, so long ago, had festered in the man's mind. 'Alick, we were all having to deal with bodies at Ballymena. I did too, and it haunts me, just like it haunts you.'

'Aye, but I'd to take the worst – the woman with her head . . .' Buchan began to shed drunken tears.

'Look, come in and sit down and we can talk about this. Cris'll bring us some *strong* coffee.'

Pilapil, hovering in the background, nodded and turned to go as Crozier attempted to take Buchan's arm and lead him through to the office, but Buchan shook him off. Pilapil stopped, eyeing the man.

'No!' Buchan shouted. 'I'm – I'm not wanting your talk. You're to take the girl.'

Baffled, Crozier said, 'What girl?'

'Landed on us. It'd be nothing to you – have her here. Costs money to feed folk, only you – you wouldn't know, with your big house and your fat wallet.'

As Crozier still looked blank, Pilapil prompted, 'I think he means the girl who came in last night and told him about the landslide.'

Buchan turned to look at him blearily. 'Aye, her. You've bedrooms here – rooms and rooms. It's not right.'

'No, we don't, actually.' Pilapil's voice was crisp with distaste.

'I think we may be talking money here.' Crozier reached into the hip pocket of his jeans. 'Alick, you perhaps don't know that the bridge over the Carron has collapsed and we've got two police officers here indefinitely. It's been very good of you to take in this girl and I don't want you to be out of pocket over it. I'll pay for her board and lodgings until she can leave. Here's a hundred pounds for a start.' He peeled off five twenties from a wad of notes.

With some difficulty, Buchan's eyes focused on the money. 'You – you think you can buy everything. Well, you can't. You can't buy Alick Buchan, you dirty, rotten bastard!'

Nevertheless, he snatched the notes from Crozier's hand. Pilapil moved swiftly to open the front door and Buchan lurched out of it. He spat on the doorstep, then headed uncertainly for the jeep, parked in the drive.

'He's going to drive!' Crozier said in alarm. 'He could be off the road at the first bend.'

Pilapil dangled a key. 'He was holding it when he came in and he didn't even notice when I took it off him. God knows how he got himself here. He's looking for the key now.'

From a window to one side of the front door, they could see Buchan digging in his pockets, then, shaking his head in bewilderment, going off with a limping stagger.

Crozier sighed. 'I'll go and talk to him once it's worn off a bit. That's all I need.'

NICO RYAN WAS bored. He'd seen Harry Potter too many times already, so there were no surprises, and his mother hadn't watched for very long before she drifted away. He wandered out of the house, kicking up stones in an aimless sort of way, then ducked in under the bank of rhododendrons opposite the front door. The purple blossoms were over now and all the dead petals were brown and soggy.

The shrubs grew thickly together and he had made himself a little den underneath, with a rug and some cushions he had taken from the house without anyone noticing. They were all damp and fusty with the rain, but that, mingled with the smell of sodden earth and rotting vegetation, was part of the mystery of his secret place.

Nico liked it because he could watch people coming and going without being seen. It made him feel very strong and powerful, and he enjoyed that. Once he was big and had lots of money and it was his house, not his grandfather's, he'd tell everyone what to do. He'd be mean to them if he liked and there wouldn't be anything they could do about it.

He saw his grandfather coming out of the house and crossing the drive, and he screwed his face up into an expression of hate. Granddad had told him off again today. He shouldn't do that. It made Nico angry just to think about it. He wanted to hit something, throw something . . .

There was a big stone embedded in the earth beside his rug, and when he picked it up, all sorts of little pale creatures started scurrying away in a panic. Diverted, he looked at them, then turned the stone on its edge and brought it down, again and again and again, squashing as many of them as he could.

THE ENCOUNTER WITH Buchan had upset Gillis Crozier. He liked to see himself as a decent employer, demanding but not unreasonable, and paying wages that were more than fair. The depth of resentment Alick Buchan had concealed all these years shocked him, and he didn't feel up to negotiating with the contractors yet who, quite reasonably, would try to drive a hard bargain.

The sun was shining strongly now and the sea, far below in front of the house, had silver sparkles so brilliant that it was almost painful to look at it. He headed towards it on a rough track, then stood at the end, lost in thought. A breeze was blowing and the air had a green, grassy freshness as the sodden ground began to steam gently in the warmth.

Perhaps he'd been wrong to give Buchan the keeper's job when he came back to Rosscarron three years ago. In the army, the man had always been one of the awkward squad, but there wasn't much employment around here and Crozier had felt sorry for his former comrade-in-arms, invalided out after a careless accident with his own rifle. Sooner or later you must pay for every good deed!

Ballymena, 1976. Crozier remembered the carnage all too well, though he had tried to put it out of his mind. He remembered, too, the sickeningly injured dying woman he had sent Buchan to deal with. But his own job was to bring order out of bloody chaos and there had been no time to consider individual sensibilities. Perhaps Buchan ought to have been sent for counselling, but it wasn't so fashionable in those days. You got on with the job, shut up about it and tried to forget.

It was probably too late to help Buchan now, and his drunken outburst had created a problem. He could only hope the man would backtrack once the drink stopped talking. Having to sack him would be deeply unpleasant.

Perhaps he'd just sell up here, find somewhere else. Crozier needed a headquarters outside London, but not necessarily here. Choosing Rosscarron had been a sentimental decision and they were rarely sound; it had been in part a desperate attempt to give Cara and her children a healthier lifestyle, but that had failed. Worse than failed.

Yet again Crozier's mind went back to Kenna Stewart. She had been haunting him all day since he had seen the cottage that had been hers, and the one he had grown up in himself, wiped out by the landslide.

She had been two years older than he was, small, with fine features, creamy pale skin, bright blue eyes and a personality as vivid as her flaming red hair. In that isolated place they were constantly thrown together; she had treated him like a younger brother, teasing and mocking, and from the age of thirteen he had worshipped her with a sort of bewildered adoration.

When he was seventeen, there had been a heady summer when she had almost taken him seriously. Almost. She was attracted to him, he knew that. She'd even let him kiss her a few times, but she'd only laughed when he talked of love and the future.

'You're still a wee boy, Gillie my lamb,' she had said. 'I'm a woman now. You've a lot of growing to do yet.'

And perhaps he had, but she could have waited instead of going off with a man whose face should have warned her he was no good. When Crozier heard through his parents that she was alone and pregnant in London, he had written to her with a quixotic offer of marriage. She'd stubbornly refused to take it seriously, and, his youthful pride wounded, he hadn't repeated it.

Then Crozier had joined the army, done well and forged friendships that had got him into the music business when he resigned his commission. He'd made his own mistake with Cara's mother, now the third wife of a French pop star. He'd long lost touch with Kenna and indeed by then she had taken on a romantic unreality in his mind.

Yet when he had heard on the local grapevine shortly after he bought Rosscarron House that Kenna Stewart had returned to the cottages, his heart had given a foolish leap. Could they be approaching the happy ending to two long, sad tales?

She was thinner than he remembered, and older of course – they were both that – but the hair and the eyes were still the same, eyes that lit with an inner glow when she saw him. He'd been feeling nervous about the meeting, even preparing in his head a suitable speech of welcome for a new neighbour, but it died on his lips when she said, 'Gillie! My God, how I've missed you!'

He had kissed her, on the lips but tentatively, and they had gone on to talk about youth and folly and pride.

'Still,' he said at last, taking her hand – such a thin, delicate thing – in his own great paw, 'we can start again. We've got a second chance.'

Kenna's eyes filled with tears. She had come home, she told him, to die within sight and sound of the sea. Six months, a year, perhaps a little more if she was lucky.

They were together almost constantly after that and she even went into remission for a spell. He was hardly ever in London, neglecting business to be with her. They talked endlessly, about the past and the present. The future was banned.

They both had family worries. Crozier's were about Cara, heavily pregnant now, after having produced a son with problems, which were never quite openly ascribed to her choice of lifestyle. Kenna was still grieving over the death of her daughter, a single mother, also from cancer, and she was worried about her granddaughter, Lisa, in London.

And from that had come the deadly, disastrous plan. Lisa was working in a day-nursery for a pittance; Crozier's grandson was being raised by irresponsible parents and an ever-changing succession of foreign girls who couldn't speak English. The answer seemed obvious.

'This is a marriage made in heaven,' he had claimed, laughing.

Hell, more like.

The last time he saw Kenna, death was at her shoulder. She had outlived prediction, but the bright blue eyes, which had sparkled with life and laughter, were dulled now by illness and grief, and huge in her gaunt face. In the small, dark front room she was wrapped up in a soft shawl and a fire was burning, though it was a warm summer's day.

Anger had deadened his feelings. 'You knew, Kenna! You knew she had a temper when you wished her on me.'

'Never with children.' Her voice might be weak, but she was unyielding. 'You saw the references she had from the nursery where she worked. You heard what your daughter's cleaner said in court.'

'Heard, of course I heard! But I also heard, *after* the trial, about the anger-management course she'd been put on when she was on remand. Do you think, if the jury had known that, they'd have brought in the same verdict? You knew she had a temper, Kenna – you betrayed me, you of all people. I can't forgive that.'

Kenna bowed her head and was quiet for a long moment. Then she said, 'You're angry with me now. It doesn't mean you're going to kill me, does it? The jury heard the relevant evidence and she was acquitted.'

'Oh, yes, I know she was *acquitted*!' He spat out the word. 'A clever lawyer, a cleaning woman who had a grudge against Nico because he's lively and not the easiest child.'

'Still, acquitted.'

Stubborn. She always had been, and what heartache they had both suffered as a result! Pain made him cruel.

'Your granddaughter is out there, alive. Free. Able to look to a future. Mine can't. Mine's in a little white coffin, rotting slowly.'

Kenna gasped, putting a hand to her throat. 'Gillie, don't. That's a terrible thing to allow to lodge in your mind. It's warping you. It will poison your life, if you let it.'

'She's poisoned my life already. And the life of my other grandchild.'

Her reply was sharp. 'And you threatened her, Gillie. You stood outside that court and said that you'd see to it that she paid in blood for what she'd done.'

Crozier couldn't meet her eyes. 'It was just – just words.'

'Words can poison too. She's living in fear.'

He knew he should give reassurance, but the knowledge that the girl too was suffering gave him a dark, secret joy.

'Actions have consequences,' he said.

Kenna looked at him and he saw pity in her eyes – pity, from a woman who had only days, hours, perhaps, to live.

'Gillie, my darling, if you don't forgive, it will hurt you more than anyone else.' She closed her eyes and sagged in her chair, and for a moment he caught his breath. But they opened again.

'I can't take any more. Can we say goodbye, with love?'

If he agreed, if he softened by even the smallest degree, he would fall apart. Clinging to his anger for support, he said harshly, 'No, I don't think so,' and, to his eternal shame, walked out.

It was the worst thing he had ever done, in a life that had been far from blameless. Kenna was right, of course: he had been tortured ever since by the memory. And now, sometimes, he even found himself looking at his grandson with dismay and wondering . . .

But he mustn't wonder. What was done was done, the past was past, and he had more than enough present problems to deal with.

The contractors would be waiting. He turned his back to the sea and headed towards the house, across the garden and up on the path through the little copse of trees towards the lower field.

THE POLICE CAR drew up beside the shattered bridge and the two officers got out to inspect it, and the car, nose down in the river, its open door wedged into the bank.

'Going to have fun getting this sorted out, Sarge,' the constable said.

'You could say. They were lucky they could walk away from it. Anyway, check out the number – find out who it belongs to.'

He read it out and walked over to inspect the wreckage while the other checked the computer, then came back giving a whistle of amazement.

'Know whose it is? DI Fleming's, that's who! That'll have everyone jumping like hens on a hot griddle!'

His senior officer turned. 'And I'll tell you something else, laddie. See that bridge strut sticking up out of the water? That's not broken – that's been sawed through.'

FLEMING STILL FELT very light-headed as she went carefully downstairs, holding the banister. But she had slept and showered and was even back in her own clothes, magically laundered to perfection and left in her room while she slept, thanks, presumably to the young man they seemed to call Chris. He'd fed her Nurofen before she went to sleep, too, and her headache was bearable. She was still frightened, though: knocks on the head were chancy things, and she'd have gone to see a doctor if there was one available. Since there wasn't, she'd just have to tell herself, along with everyone else, that she was all right.

The music, which they appeared to use in this house instead of wallpaper, had been switched off and without it the white hall echoed and the house felt curiously cold and empty. As she stood hesitating at the foot of the stairs, the silence seemed to gather about her and it wasn't comfortable; she had the fanciful thought there was something – or someone – nearby holding its breath. Nonsense, of course.

She walked briskly to a couple of doors, her shoes clicking loudly on the hard flooring, and knocked but got no answer. She didn't like to barge in and decided instead to go through the below-stairs door which presumably led to the domestic premises.

The kitchen, lined with high-gloss white cupboards and fitted out with a lot of stainless steel and the sort of high-tech equipment Fleming couldn't imagine ever needing, was clinically clean and bare of any clutter, utterly impersonal. It too was empty.

Noticing a phone on the wall, she picked it up hopefully, but it was still dead. She replaced it slowly, trying not to dwell on the uncomfortable fact that she couldn't just walk out of this strange house, no matter how much it was getting to her.

She returned to the hall. Where was MacNee? She could do with some support. Her head was swimming a bit, but surely it wasn't only that which made her feel it was all very odd.

The room Fleming had woken up in – all white too, though with a chalky distemper on the walls and splashes of blue and green in an abstract painting and some cushions – was like a bedroom in a luxury hotel, and the rest of the place didn't suggest the sort of holiday house where you could kick off your shoes and relax.

She was twitching about being out of touch with headquarters. Bailey would have been expecting her to go straight to the Ross-carron Cottages to direct operations there and wouldn't be pleased when she wasn't available to answer the questions the press would undoubtedly be asking. By now, of course, they would know what had happened to the bridge and would be having to deal with the problem of hundreds of disappointed youngsters, including her own. Bailey would love that too.

It couldn't have happened at a worse time. Bailey had spelled out that her suspension had raised question marks in her superiors' minds and what was needed now was a peaceful spell when she could win back trust with quiet efficiency. That wrecking the car wasn't her fault would be acknowledged, but the feeling that she had created more problems – including, blackest of sins, a budgetary one – would linger. She could almost hear Bailey's voice muttering, 'Blasted woman!'

She felt vulnerable in her work, and she felt vulnerable in this weird house where the white walls, which should have given the illusion of airy space, seemed aggressively restrictive. And where the hell was Tam?

Fleming looked about her uncertainly, then decided to go to the sitting room at the back of the house where they had been taken earlier to wait for Crozier. As she went towards it, she could hear the sound of raised voices, though the accompanying sound effects suggested that they were recorded rather than real. When she opened the door, this room too was empty, but the big plasma screen was showing Harry Potter in the customary encounter with some sinister being. Fleming entered the room, shut the door behind her and switched off the TV.

The sun was streaming through the window now and she went over to enjoy the first rays of summer warmth in what felt like weeks. Wisps of steamy vapour were wreathing the low trees and bushes of the scrubby spinney opposite.

As she watched, a rough-looking man came lurching out of it and down over the grass in front, then headed off away from the house. He was looking round about him blearily and Fleming's practised eye had no difficulty in recognising one, in the old phrase, 'having drink taken', though he looked as if he might suffer from a limp as well.

She was turning away from the window when the door opened behind her and a mocking voice said, 'Hey, hey! If it isn't the Great Detective!'

With a sinking heart she turned to face the man she had once believed would be the love of her life, Joss Hepburn.

Chapter Seven

DECLAN RYAN WAS simmering with frustration. What did he have to do to get rid of the bugger? His nerves were ragged enough already; he didn't need this.

God knows he'd tried to shake him off. He had disappeared upstairs after lunch, hoping he could slip out unnoticed, but Mac-Nee had staked out the hall, so eventually, with a bad grace, he'd had to come downstairs.

'Oh, there you are! I was just having a wee forty winks,' the man said, getting up from a chair by the hall table with an unpleasant smile. Lying bastard!

Ryan had led him up the path through the garden and they'd been at the campsite for the best part of an hour. MacNee showed no sign of leaving, clinging like one of the burrs you found in the undergrowth around here, which only hooked on more firmly when you tried to remove them. It was vital to get him away from here.

He'd switched on the charm with MacNee, leading him up the muddy path through the copse of trees at the side of the house, which came out at the top of the camping field by the Portaloos. Then he'd done the glad-handing bit, going round the happy campers individually, explaining at length about the problems, apologising and promising that Crozier would be coming up from the house soon to speak to the contractors in the top field and would have a word with them after that. Once he'd guaranteed refunds and possibly even compensation, there had been no unpleasantness, though that might have had something to do with the presence of the Law at his elbow, literally.

There'd been no chance of a quiet word with Bob Lawton, and Ryan's facial signals, made behind MacNee's back, were met with a blank stare – not unnaturally, with MacNee taking an unhealthy interest in their camper van. Now Angela was all ostentatious innocence, clucking over the officer's unfortunate experience and offering him a cup of tea, 'or a beer, since you're off duty?' She hoped!

Inspiration struck. Ryan broke in on Angela's hospitable offers. 'I'd better go down to the bridge and take a look at the destruction for myself. I'll see you back to the house, Sergeant.'

He hadn't really expected to get away with that, and he didn't.

'Och, no,' MacNee said. 'I'll chum you down – see what it looks like from dry land.'

It wasn't ideal, but anything was better than having him hanging around here. 'I'll pick up the Discovery at the house, then,' Ryan said, and they headed down the path together. He was probably only imagining that he heard a gusty sigh of relief coming from the Lawtons' direction.

'SHE'S DONE *WHAT*?' Superintendent Bailey demanded. 'Driven her car off a low bridge? I don't believe it – this is too bad!'

DS Macdonald quailed. 'I don't think she could help it, sir. The bridge seemed to have been—' he swallowed hard '—sabotaged.' He half shut his eyes, waiting for the blast.

With Bailey, irritation might be noisy but calamity was dumb. He sagged in his chair, staring at Macdonald in disbelief. There was a moment's silence before he said heavily, 'All right. Tell me what's happened.'

'Struts and props on the bridge seem to have been sawn through. The car's a write-off, but they could see the interior was intact and airbags had inflated – no sign of blood or anything. There was no one around when the officers reached the scene, but I think we can safely assume MacNee and Fleming either got themselves out or were rescued.'

At the mention of the wrecked car Bailey had winced, but he said only, 'Presumably if there was serious injury, it would have been possible for someone to get across the river to call in help?'

'I guess so, but it's running pretty high, so you wouldn't do it unless it was a serious emergency. Otherwise the headland's completely cut off. Should we try to raise a chopper to fetch them back?'

The superintendent considered. 'It's not urgent, is it, since we can be fairly sure they're all right? And everything has to be costed – that car's money down the drain too. Leave it for the moment, Andy – see if we can get someone else to pick up the bill. I'm more concerned about the notion of sabotage. What are we thinking here?'

Macdonald, unused to the concept of community of thought with his superintendent, said tentatively, 'There was a gentleman who was very unhappy about the idea of a pop festival being held at all, and then his house was flooded. He presumably has something of a grudge.'

Bailey's face brightened. 'Good thought, Andy, though I would quibble with your description of Jamieson as a gentleman. Bring him in and we'll see what he has to say for himself. All right?'

Up to a point, Superintendent, Macdonald thought, but he said only, 'I don't think anyone knows where he is at the moment, sir. Evacuated, presumably, but—'

'Then find out!' Bailey's voice rose again. 'And the kids arriving for the festival – what's happening about that?'

'Traffic are handling it, sir. They're stopping cars on the road down from Kirkcudbright.'

'Heading them off at the pass? Best we can do, I suppose. We just have to hope they don't decide to cause trouble – we've got enough of that already.'

MACNEE HAD BEEN disciplining himself not to look at his watch again until at least a quarter of an hour had gone past. As the time ticked by, it only made him feel worse. It must be almost five o'clock by now. His resolve broke.

It wasn't, quite. Ten to five: there was still time to get things sorted out if the phones were back on when they returned from the riverside. Or maybe when they reached it, there'd be someone on the other side – thwarted ravers, say – who could be given a message.

MacNee was twitching anyway. There was nasty stuff going on here, and he'd never liked closed spaces much. Maybe you couldn't describe acres of moorland as a closed space, but it felt pretty oppressive when you couldn't get away, and he was capable of feeling trapped in a cul-de-sac when he'd only to walk to the end of the road.

Still, he reminded himself, it had been an interesting after- noon. Since they had set out from the house, his driver had not once glanced in his direction or said a word. Oh, at the start Ryan had been all pally, falling over himself to be helpful, but the charm had worn thin as MacNee showed no sign of leaving him to get on with his purchases in peace, and it had vanished altogether as MacNee succeeded in his objective of getting under his skin. What he needed to decide was whether the vibes he was now getting from Ryan were annoyance or fear. He was without doubt under stress of some kind.

Likely both. The Lawtons, certainly, had been sweating. Without the camouflage of a whole pop festival, they were standing out like a sore thumb. Of course, that was their protection as well: nothing was going to happen while he was anywhere nearby, and now he wasn't, no doubt there would be expensive little packages being stashed all over the countryside. Still, he would put the word out to the Drug Squad and with any luck they'd be picked up next time.

Ryan was blatantly planning to lay in supplies for his wife before their handy doorstep delivery was moved off the site. MacNee had the distinct impression that Daddy didn't approve, and could be heavy-handed, so maybe it was tricky keeping the stuff around, or getting it locally.

Actually, he had the impression that there was quite a lot Daddy didn't approve of, starting with his son-in-law and going on to what went on in the Ryan household – like the way they brought up their son, who seemed almost disturbed. Perhaps the kid was just over-indulged, but with a mother who had Cara's problem it wouldn't be surprising if it was a bit more than that.

The kids up at the campsite had seemed clean enough, though – a bit of weed or E going around, no doubt, but he'd be surprised if it was more than that.

MacNee was still uncertain about the two young men he and Fleming had remarked on before. One, thickset, tall and uncommunicative, still seemed to be on his own, but the other, who introduced himself as Damien – in his mid-twenties, probably, and still a bit baby-faced with gelled brown hair – had stood with his arm familiarly round one of the teenage girls, who was all over him like a rash. If MacNee was her father, he wouldn't have been happy about it. Not happy at all.

Perhaps it was just as well he wasn't anyone's father, though Bunty wouldn't see it like that. He gave an unconscious sigh.

'Here we are!' Ryan pulled in at the side of the road. 'Frigging hell, that's some mess!' He jumped out and without waiting for MacNee went to stand on the bank of the river.

The Carron was still running high and strong, though definitely lower than it had been. Joining Ryan, MacNee looked hopefully across to the other side, but the road was empty. Given that the punters should be arriving in their hundreds by now, that suggested warnings had been posted, but there was certainly no sign of a rescue party.

'They're not going to put this right overnight, exactly. How long are we going to be trapped here, then? You're the police – how do they deal with a situation like this?'

MacNee felt sick, seeing now the full extent of the damage. 'Depends on how urgent they think it is. They could call in the army, get them to put up one of those Bailey bridges they use to get tanks across rivers – they'd have it sorted in half a morning – but it'll be at the bottom of the to-do list. If anything goes wrong in the Central Belt, they'll jump to it, but out here . . .' He shrugged. 'We're just meant to put up with it till they've sorted everything else.'

He was looking at the wreckage of the bridge as he spoke and suddenly he stiffened. 'Here! See that spar, sticking up? That's not broken – that's a clean edge. Someone's cut through it deliberately.'

Ryan followed his pointing finger. '*What!* Are you telling me someone's sabotaged it? You're kidding!'

'I wish I was. There's another spar the same, look – over there.'

'For God's sake! Who would do something like this? Someone could have been killed.'

'Someone almost was,' MacNee said grimly. 'And as soon as I get to a working phone, we'll start finding out. Come on – let's get back.'

He wasn't about to share them, but he had his own ideas. The man he had seen on the road going down to the flooded houses, the man he had guessed was Jamieson, who had an obsessional grudge against Gillis Crozier. His revenge? If so, he was dangerous, seriously dangerous.

Maybe the scale of destruction would have satisfied him, but maybe it was only the start, and how could you predict what someone clearly doolally would do next?

Of course, he might have left the headland before it happened. He could be anywhere, but he could also be right here, in one of the flooded houses, biding his time . . . Perhaps MacNee should go along and check, though he'd have preferred to do it once there was back-up available.

When they reached Rosscarron House, Ryan said, 'Maybe they've got the phones back on,' and jumped out, leaving MacNee to follow. Remembering his own problem, he glanced at his watch. Almost half past five – he hoped to God that they were back in touch with the outside world.

WITH HER BACK literally to the wall, Fleming felt like an animal at bay as Joss Hepburn advanced towards her with a teasing smile.

He was, if anything, a more attractive man now than he had been at twenty-five. Then, he had seemed an exotic creature in staid Kirkluce, glamorous and edgy; he was still that, but the hooded eyes and sardonic lines around the mouth gave him a more sophisticated gloss of cynical charm. Not for the first time, she thought how unfair it was that men aged so much better than women and she was conscious, too, that with the bruising to the side of her face she was hardly looking her best. Not that it mattered, of course.

Fleming forced a smile. 'Joss.'

'Struggling back on duty, in the best traditions of the Service? Are you sure you should be out of bed? How many fingers am I holding up?'

'Twelve,' she said sarcastically. 'I always thought the two extra ones were a bit creepy, myself.'

She almost had to push past him to reach one of the chairs, where she sat down with an assumption of ease as Hepburn threw back his head and laughed.

'There's no one quite like you, Madge – you know that? Can't think why I let you go.'

'You hadn't a choice,' she pointed out, with some asperity. 'I dumped you, remember?'

'Helped by your bucolic friend. Oh, I remember.' He sat down opposite her, fingering his crooked nose. 'Do tell me – did he hang on to his prize, or did you give him a courteous thank-you and move on to someone more . . . entertaining?'

Fleming felt her hackles rise. 'If by "entertaining" you mean the sort of person who thinks it's clever to put LSD in my drink, knowing the kind of reaction I had when I tried cannabis, I wouldn't agree with your definition.' She found she was still angry, though it was years now since she'd suffered from the hideous flashbacks.

Hepburn did, actually, look abashed. 'OK, I shouldn't have done that. But to be honest I reckoned the cannabis story was a cover for being scared in case your policeman father found out and shopped you.'

'*Scared!* It was nothing to do with being *scared*, except of what could happen if I tried it again.' Suddenly she was nineteen once more, easily goaded to unwisdom by the age-old taunt 'Scared, are you?'

She wasn't nineteen. She was a mature woman and a senior police officer and she had to do better than that. Sounding professionally po-faced, she said, 'Considering the mopping-up I have to do for people who didn't have a bad experience early on, I count myself lucky. I hope age has brought wisdom to you too – or are you still desperately in search of your youth with the wacky baccy?' She'd smelled its faint, sickly trace on him when he came into the room.

Hepburn looked amused at her acerbic tone. 'I think I should take the Fifth on that one, given who I'm talking to. You might whip out the handcuffs, though on second thoughts . . . ?' He raised his eyebrows suggestively.

She wasn't going there. Ignoring the provocation, Fleming firmly changed the subject.

'Joss, tell me what goes on here.'

To her surprise, she saw him go very still for a moment. Then he pulled out a pack of cigarettes and gestured towards her. 'Do you mind? I guess you don't indulge?'

Fleming shook her head. He lit the cigarette, but over the flame his eyes were watchful. 'What do you mean?'

'It doesn't strike me as anyone's ideal holiday home. I don't think I've ever been anywhere with a less relaxing and welcoming atmosphere.'

'Oh, I get it!' Hepburn laughed – surely not with relief?? 'It's because it's not really a holiday home. It's a combination of an office and a hotel – say, like a kind of conference centre. It's cheaper to have a headquarters outside London, and Gillis had this romantic idea of going back to his roots. Saw himself returning as the laird, I guess, and he can have business contacts here and give them the fishing and shooting bit as well.'

And did, Fleming wondered, the business contacts include the 'big boy' MacNee's pal Sheughie had been interested in? Once she got out of this place, she was definitely going to take a closer look at Mr Crozier's interests. 'What line is he in?' she asked, trying to make it sound like an idle question.

Hepburn matched her tone. 'Don't ask me! The pop scene, obviously, but that apart I guess he's an entrepreneur – a bit of this, a bit of that. Tell me about you, though. The police force – that was a bit of a shock. What happened to the crazy Madge I knew?'

He'd copied her own tactic for getting away from an unwelcome subject, but she wasn't about to let it get personal again. 'She grew up and found an interesting job. And you? You're based in the States now?'

'Based, yes. But I've done a lot of stuff in Europe as well. Not much over here – only since retro disco's taken off.'

'My daughter's a serious fan. She'll be gutted that the concert's off.' This was better. This was edging into the area of normal, boring small talk.

'I can give you a signed photo for her, if you think she'd like it.'

'I'm sure she'd be thrilled.'

'And I could write a bit on the back, about some of the things her mother got up to.'

The door opening was a welcome sound. Even more welcome was the sight of Tam MacNee. But . . .

'Tam!' she said in astonishment. 'What on *earth* are you wearing?'

MacNee flushed a dark red. 'My clothes are being dried,' he said gruffly. 'This was what they gave me.'

'Might be the start of a whole new look for you.' Fleming didn't try to hide her amusement.

'I see you got yours back a bit sooner than I did,' MacNee said sourly. 'Maybe the lad that took mine away could hurry along with them.'

'Cris?' Hepburn was enjoying himself too. 'Must have figured you needed a makeover. He's quite a guy – not a great talker, but I guess he's got a warped sense of humour. Tell you what, as a favour to a friend, I'll see if I can find him.'

He was just going out when a sudden blast of cacophonous sound came through the speakers. Fleming and MacNee both jumped.

Hepburn paused. 'Ah, that must be Gillis back.'

'What – what on earth is it?' Fleming said faintly.

'Metallica.' Hepburn was amused by their reaction. 'Used as torture at Guatánamo, I'm told.'

'How do we switch the bloody thing off?' MacNee growled.

Hepburn, still grinning, obliged. As he went out, MacNee looked at Fleming.

'Take it you're feeling all right, then, having wee jokes with your pal at other folks' expense. Well, get a load of this. The bridge collapsing wasn't an accident.'

Horrified, Fleming listened as he explained.

'And we're stuck here,' he finished. 'God knows how long it'll be before they get us out.'

'If we're stuck, and you're right about Jamieson, he could be stuck as well,' she said. 'Not a pleasant thought.'

'It had occurred to me,' MacNee said dryly.

'If he reckoned sabotaging the bridge was just a gesture, he's reckless at the very least. But then, we don't know that he did it, Tam. There's no way we could detain him. The most we could do is have a chat, and it might be better not to scare him off by letting him know we're on to him. Anyway, let's find a car and get down there to have a look.'

'Not before I get my own clothes back,' MacNee said firmly.

BETH BROWN HURRIED back to Keeper's Cottage. Her haste made her hot and sweaty, but it was only when she got within sight of the house that she risked putting her hood down.

Maidie Buchan, with Calum on her hip, was just closing the gate to the kennels, where the dogs were guzzling bowls of food. As Beth reached her, it was clear she had been crying.

The right thing to do was ask what was wrong, but that would only waste time. Living with Alick Buchan and the old witch was enough to make anyone cry and there wasn't a lot Beth could do about that, even if she wanted to. And at the moment all she wanted was to get away from here, slip back into her old anonymous life.

Calum, recognising a friend, beamed and held out his arms. Touched and flattered, Beth took him from his mother and gave him a hug.

'Have you been feeding the doggies?' Calum nodded solemnly. '*What* a clever boy!'

Maidie's tragic face brightened. 'He's been so good this afternoon, haven't you, my lambie?'

Calum, satisfied at having undivided attention, held out his arms to his mother again.

'You're just a wee rogue!' she said fondly, taking him back. 'Did you have a nice walk, Beth? Lovely now the sun's out.'

Beth ignored the polite enquiry. 'Maidie, I've been thinking. Thanks for everything, but I'd better go now. I thought Alick could maybe take me to Kirkcudbright. Then I'll be fine—'

'Alick!' Maidie's bitterness burst out. 'Alick'll not be taking anyone anywhere for a bit. He's sleeping it off. Got drunk and insulted his boss, and come tomorrow we'll probably have to be out of here, without a roof over our heads. Anyway, no one's going anywhere. The bridge is down, and God only knows when it'll be repaired.'

Preoccupied though she was with her own problems, Maidie did wonder about the look of horror on Beth's face as she said, 'You mean I'm trapped? Trapped here?'

'THE PHONE'S STILL off,' Declan Ryan said, as he came into the kitchen, where Cris Pilapil was preparing the evening meal.

Pilapil didn't look up. 'Yes, I believe so.'

'Gillis won't be pleased. What are we going to do about it?'

Pilapil brought the side of his knife down to crush a clove of garlic and shrugged.

Ryan raised his voice. 'I said, what are we going to do about it?'

'We could try shouting, I suppose, but short of that the answer's nothing.' His sidelong glance was contemptuous.

Clenching his fists, Ryan said coldly, 'I'm looking for Gillis, as it happens. Where is he?'

'In his office, I presume. I heard the music start not long ago.'

'He's not there. That was me. I can't find him.'

Pilapil was chopping lemongrass now. 'He said he was going up to see the contractors.'

'Yes, but he didn't. I drove up to the top field just now and the minute I arrived they pounced on me. Wanted to know what was happening, when they were going to be paid. Put me in an awkward position.'

'Bad luck.' Pilapil picked up a wok and set it on the stove. 'I saw him leave the house after lunch. That's all.'

'You've been your usual charming and helpful self.' Ryan went to the door. 'If you see him before I do, you might like to tell him that someone sabotaged the bridge, probably his little friend who likes writing messages with weedkiller. He could have killed someone. Let's just hope it hasn't given him a taste for it. We can't get away, and probably neither can he.'

MacNee had got his clothes back and returned the shirt and chinos with sarcastic thanks to Cris Pilapil, whose polite expression gave nothing away. He produced the keys for the staff runabout and MacNee, with more sincere thanks this time, collected Fleming and drove off towards the river and the flooded houses.

Fleming was shaken when she saw the evidence of deliberate destruction. 'That could have been kids, in a small car without the airbags we had to protect us – more or less,' she added, fingering her brow. 'I hadn't realised quite how bad it was. Tam, how long are we going to be stuck here?'

MacNee's only answer was a shrug. He was looking across the river. 'No one there,' he said, looking at the empty road, then at his watch. 'I'd been hoping . . .'

He'd looked at his watch several times, she realised, and he was definitely anxious. 'What's the matter, Tam? They obviously know what's happened and they're turning people back. That's good news.'

'Yes.' He sighed heavily, turning away. 'Not a lot we can do about it, I suppose. Do you want to drive along towards the houses or walk?'

Fleming stopped. 'Tam, there's something wrong. You've been twitching all the way down here. I want to know what it is.'

MacNee looked at her. Then he said, 'Och, it's just the animals. They get fed at six o'clock and it's past that now. I can't see when we're going to get back and my neighbour won't know to go in.'

'What about Bunty? Surely—'

'Bunty's away.'

Tam always hated being without her. It probably explained why he seemed out of sorts at the moment, though usually she'd have been deaved long before now with his complaints about looking after the selection of abandoned dogs and pathetic cats that Bunty always had under her motherly wing.

'Off at one of her sisters' again? But when she phones and can't get a reply, she'll call your neighbour, won't she? I wouldn't worry, Tam. It won't do the creatures any harm to wait for their tea. If the teas I've had from Bunty are anything to go by, they'll be overfed anyway.'

'Likely you're right. We'll walk, shall we?' He led the way down the side road to the flooded executive homes and Fleming followed.

The water level had definitely gone down since the last time they looked and they were able to walk to within twenty yards of the properties. Fleming, feeling rough anyway, found it hard not to gag at the stink of sludge and sewage, intensified by the warmth of the sun. The road was thick with mud and cluttered with debris – nasty enough, but further on, the houses were still sitting in a foot and a half of water. She paused, considering her footwear.

'We'd need waders,' Fleming said. 'Maybe they've got some at the house, or the water may have gone down more by tomorrow. I can't say I'm wild about getting my clothes soaking wet and filthy all over again for the sake of interviewing someone who might not even be there.'

'Certainly not,' MacNee said with deep feeling. 'Can you see anything to suggest someone's still around?'

They stood in silence scanning the half-dozen houses, one of which must be Jamieson's. There was no sign of life, no evidence of recent occupation.

'No,' she said, and feeling deflated and useless, they went back to the car. The sight of the bridge had emphasised their isolation and Fleming headed back to Rosscarron House with profound reluctance. Her headache had returned with force and she could only hope Cris hadn't run out of Nurofen.

'CHUM ME TO the toilet?' one of the teenage girls said to her friend, now entwined with Damien on a rather damp sleeping bag in front of their tent.

Damien looked up impatiently. 'Oh, for God's sake, Mel! You're not at school now! "Please, miss, can my friend come with me to the toilets?"' He mimicked her voice.

Melanie addressed herself to the girl. 'Come on, Stacey,' she whined. 'We're meant to be here together – you promised. And I don't like going away up there by myself. It's getting dark now.'

Stacey groaned. 'Oh, all right, if you're going to make a big thing of it.' She gave Damien another lingering kiss, disentangled herself and stood up. 'Don't go away, lover. Won't be long.'

Blowing him a kiss, she set off with her friend up the hill.

The nearer end of the long row of Portaloos was beside the spinney near Rosscarron House and the girls took the two end ones. It was Stacey who came out first and stood looking around her as she waited impatiently for her friend.

When Melanie emerged, Stacey was giggling, pointing towards the spinney, where shadows were gathering. 'There's a guy there, passed out. Must be drunk. Haven't seen him around, have you?'

Melanie peered into the dimness. 'He's, like, old.' She screwed up her nose. 'There's no one old here, except Bob and Ange. Must be from the house.'

'Why'd he be lying up here, then? Here, maybe he's not well. Should we check? I'll get Damien.'

'What for?' Melanie's tone was hostile. 'We can check ourselves, then get help if he's ill or something.'

The girls went to investigate. It was a man with iron-grey hair, and he was lying on his side with his head against a big stone. It was only as they got nearer that they saw the blood.

Their piercing screams echoed across the campsite. Damien jumped to his feet, but another man was faster up the slope. When he reached the girls, they ran to him, pointing.

'Is he – is he *dead*?' Stacey had begun to cry.

He went to look, picking up a flaccid hand, and he was feeling for a pulse when Damien arrived. Stacey, with a shriek, flung herself into his arms.

He called across her head, 'What's going on, mate?'

The other man straightened up. 'Yeah, he's dead. Poor beggar must have slipped and banged his head. Take the girls down and keep everyone else away, all right? I'll go and tell the police down at the house.'

Chapter Eight

'THAT'S IT, ISN'T it?' The telephone linesman came back to the little van, parked on the road towards Rosscarron House. 'We've checked everything else. It's a break in the line on the other side of the river.'

His colleague, looking weary, groaned. 'I've been on the job since six this morning. If you think I'm swimming across, you've another think coming. I'm knocking off.'

'Don't see what else we can do. Make a report to the police – tell them we need access before we can repair the fault.'

He got into the car and started the engine. 'Anyway, folk managed without the telephone for hundreds of years. Another day won't matter.'

'MAYBE THE SUPER'S gone home,' DC Kim Kershaw said in an attempt to cheer up her colleague.

DS Andy Macdonald grimaced. 'It might be better to get it over with now. His reaction's not going to be any different in the morning, is it?'

'No,' she admitted, 'but you might be feeling stronger.'

Kershaw, Macdonald and Ewan Campbell were reviewing the day in a corner of the CID room. It had been long, tiring and unsatisfying, with problems accumulating and no loose ends tied up.

'Maybe by tomorrow they'll have got the bridge repaired and then it's Big Marge's problem,' Kershaw went on with determined optimism.

'Can't see it.' Macdonald was sunk in gloom. 'All the solutions are expensive, and there's not much urgency, really. Could be late tomorrow or even the next day before it reaches the top of the priority list. I just wish there was some good news to tell him.'

'Haven't found the girl's body in the rubble at the Rosscarron Cottages,' Campbell offered. 'Has to be good.'

'We won't know for sure till we find her, and we haven't, any more than we've found Jamieson. Bailey will be fit to be tied when he hears no one has any idea where he is.'

'Maybe one of them will have turned up by tomorrow,' Kershaw suggested.

Macdonald gave her a darkling look. 'You're a right little ray of sunshine today. It can get quite irritating, you know.'

'One of my favourite films, *Pollyanna*,' she said demurely. 'You should try playing the glad game – you know, find something to be glad about in everything. For instance, Ewan and I can be glad we don't have to go and see the super. We can go to the pub instead. Fancy a jar, Ewan?'

Campbell got up. 'Wouldn't mind.'

'Join us later, Andy. Come and lick your wounds,' Kershaw said over her shoulder as she left.

Swearing under his breath, Macdonald went along to Bailey's office. There was no answer when he knocked.

He wasn't sure how he felt about that. He'd have been glad to get it over with, but on the other hand he was glad he could knock off now and go to the pub. Hey! Maybe there was something in Kim's glad game after all.

'I'LL GET THEM in,' Kershaw said. As Campbell went to a table by the window, she glanced around the pub, nodding to a couple of officers at the other end of the bar.

She liked the Salutation. It was an old-fashioned, no-nonsense pub, with wood floors that weren't designer beech and walls still yellowed by years of cigarette smoke. There were two rooms, divided by a fireplace open on both sides, and she liked it that when no fire was burning, it just held dead ashes, not an elaborate floral arrangement of fake flowers. It served good beer, the house wine didn't strip the skin off the roof of your mouth, and it was only a stagger across the road for an exhausted copper coming off duty. The cherry on the cake was that you were among friends: the local villains shunned the Salutation as if a dose of plague came along with the sandwiches.

The *spécialité de la maison* was cold sausages and she ordered two, then changed it to three. If Macdonald got bogged down, they could always eat it for him.

Kershaw was in a good mood today. She'd been heartened by seeing Debbie so well looked after in that cheerful, friendly atmosphere, Jan Forbes's decency and generosity had lifted her spirits, and above all she'd had a day without Tam MacNee's sharp comments and sourly disapproving silences. People kept telling her it wasn't like Tam, but as far as she was concerned the longer he was marooned at Rosscarron House, the happier she would be.

She carried over Campbell's pint and her own red wine, then went back for the sausages. 'One's for Andy,' she warned as she sat down. 'Cheers!'

Campbell raised his glass, but he didn't say anything. 'How's the baby?' she asked, trying to get a conversation going. She knew he had one, but she didn't know anything about it.

'Fine.' Campbell speared one of the sausages.

She was obviously doomed to ignorance. Kershaw took a sausage herself, and tried again. 'Where do you think that girl is, Ewan?'

Campbell considered for a moment. 'On the headland some-where. Has to be.'

'I suppose you're right,' Kershaw said slowly. 'The gamekeeper who raised the alarm – she would probably have taken shelter at his house. And Jamieson – if we can't find a trace of him over here, he could well be over there too.' She scowled. 'Oh great – that's where it's all happening, isn't it? MacNee and Big Marge aren't cut off from the action – we are!'

'Typical Tam.'

'So when can we expect to get across?' Kershaw had started fretting. 'Are we just going to have to twiddle our thumbs until they come back and tell everyone they've got it wrapped up?'

'Likely.'

Campbell really wasn't much fun to talk to. 'It's a bit of a bum-mer, but what can we do?'

'Be glad we don't have to explain a wrecked car to the super.'

The joke surprised her into laughter just as the door opened and Macdonald appeared, shaking his head in answer to her enquiring look.

'Went off to a meeting this afternoon and didn't check back in,' he said.

Kershaw got up. 'I'm buying. Pint? I got you a sausage already.'

As she spoke, her mobile phone rang. She fished it out of her bag and glanced at the caller's number. 'I'll have to take this.'

She moved a little bit away, but as she listened her face became sombre. 'OK,' she said tersely. 'Be right there.' Putting the phone back in her bag, she called, 'Sorry, got to go,' and hurried out, leaving the two men staring after her.

'What's that about?' Macdonald said.

'Her kid, probably. Think there are problems there.'

'How do you know that? Oh, don't tell me. You listen, right?'

'Right.' Campbell finished off his pint and accepted Macdonald's offer of another.

When Macdonald came back from the bar, he looked down at the empty plate on the table in front of Campbell. 'Here – thought Kim said she'd bought me a sausage?'

'Ate it.'

Macdonald glared. 'I'm trying to play the glad game, but I have to say I can't see an upside to that one.'

'It's no loss what a friend gets?' Campbell suggested, with a hopeful smile.

'Mum's awfully late tonight,' Catriona Fleming said, coming into the kitchen of the Mains of Craigie farmhouse, where her father was sitting at the table with a cup of coffee, a newspaper and Meg the collie, blissfully asleep by the Aga, for company. 'Her supper's going to be completely dried out. What's she doing?'

Bill Fleming looked up from the page of stock prices. He was a tall, solidly built man in his forties with fair hair, receding and greying a little now, blue eyes and an open, good-humoured face.

'Don't know – it's a bit odd. Her office phone is on voicemail and her mobile's been off all day, so I guess she's somewhere out of range. I'm beginning to think I might phone the station to see if they know what's going on.'

'It's probably the problems with the festival,' Cat said morosely.

She had already bent her father's ear about the unfairness of life at considerable length over supper, and he said hastily, 'Yes, of course. She'll have a lot on, with all that.'

'I think you should phone, though,' Cat said. 'You could find out if maybe the festival will go ahead if they get it sorted out. That would be really cool.'

'Why not?' he said, fetching the phone. Anything that might lift the cloud of gloom that had enveloped the house since his disgruntled daughter and son had discovered their weekend plans were in ruins was worth a try.

He listened to the information the duty sergeant was able to give him, then put the phone down looking a little stunned.

'They were a bit vague, but it seems she and Tam MacNee are over on the Rosscarron headland and the bridge has come down – that'll explain the problem with the festival. The phone lines are down too, apparently, and no one's sure when they'll be back on. Not tonight, certainly.'

Cat's blue eyes, so like her father's, widened. 'You mean, she's over there, probably, like, marooned along with *Joshua*, for days maybe? And she doesn't even like pop music! Oh, it's so *unfair*!'

She flung herself out of the room and Bill, with a sigh and a shake of his head, went back to the stock prices.

IN THE MEAGRE sitting room of Keeper's Cottage, Maidie Buchan sat wrapped in her misery. Alick hadn't come downstairs for his tea, but no doubt when he'd slept it off he would be demanding food, even if it was the middle of the night.

Not that he'd missed anything. There had been an unpleasant atmosphere, with Beth sitting silent at one side of the table and Ina making even more nasty sarcastic remarks about Maidie's cooking than usual while staring at Beth in a way that was just plain rude.

Eventually, Ina said, 'Your face is kind of familiar, with those funny eyes. I'm sure I've seen you somewhere before.'

Beth jumped up and left the room, without waiting for the rice pudding. Maidie had brought through a plate to the sitting room, where she'd taken refuge, but it had been refused.

Now Beth was huddled in one corner of the room, pretending to read a back issue of *People's Friend*. Ina was watching a gruesome medical programme; she always enjoyed those, the gorier the better. Maidie hated close-ups of blood and guts, but tonight it hardly mattered since she wasn't really seeing it anyway.

The only good thing was that when she'd got Alick into bed, she had found a wad of notes in his trouser pocket. She had no idea where it had come from, but there was a very good chance that when Alick woke he wouldn't remember anything about it. She had stashed it away as a tiny nest egg in case she and Calum found themselves out on the street one day.

Calum had really taken to Beth. She'd given him his bath tonight, and hearing the sounds of gleeful splashing from upstairs, Maidie had found herself smiling too as she made the tea. When Beth brought Calum back, beaming and glowing from his bath, she was looking happy as well. Maidie had never seen her like that; when she was laughing and smiling, she looked quite pretty.

Beth wasn't smiling now. Maidie noticed that she hadn't turned a page for half an hour and she was tearing at her nails. A bead of bright blood appeared as she tore off a strip of skin, but she only sucked her finger and went on staring blankly.

There was something badly wrong there. Maidie had tentatively asked her when they were on their own if she was very upset about her partner's death, but Beth hadn't confided, only saying that she just wanted to get away from here.

Well, they all had their problems. Maidie went back to contemplating her own.

WHEN THE SITTING-ROOM door opened every face turned expectantly to Cris Pilapil – Cara, Nico, Ryan, Hepburn, MacNee and Fleming. They had been watching some mindless quiz game of Nico's choosing, which was, at least, better than background pop music and a strained atmosphere. The air almost seemed thickened by tension; Fleming was starting to feel she needed extra-deep breaths to get enough oxygen.

It was Nico who spoke first. 'Can we have supper now, then? I'm starving!'

The burger he had demanded half an hour earlier was sitting half eaten on a coffee table, and Fleming was afraid that MacNee would disgrace her by falling on the remains if they had to wait much longer for Crozier to return. Pilapil had said he was dealing with some problem with his keeper – but why should it take so long? And why was Pilapil now looking like that?

'No,' he said to Nico, his voice very flat. 'Someone to see you, Sergeant. Or the inspector.'

MacNee jumped to his feet; Fleming followed more slowly. She had been feeling uneasy; his tone sent a shiver through her. She didn't want to have to confront whatever was out there. 'By the pricking of my thumbs, Something wicked this way comes . . .'

Now she was being ridiculous. MacNee certainly wasn't troubled. As the door shut behind them, he crowed, 'The rescue party at last – about time too!'

'Mmm.' Fleming could only wish she shared his optimism. As MacNee preceded them down the corridor leading to the hall, she asked Pilapil if someone had come from across the river.

'Not as far as I know.' His face was drawn and anxious, and she was sure his mind, like hers, had gone to the absent Gillis Crozier.

The man who stood in the hall was the single man with dark hair and sideburns whom they had seen up at the campsite. He was quite tall and athletic-looking, with broad shoulders, and there was something about the way he was standing . . .

MacNee, recognising him too, stopped dead. 'Oh – you.' There was a wealth of disappointment in his tone.

Fleming stepped forward. 'DI Fleming.'

'Ma'am.'

So she was right. She turned to Pilapil. 'Is there somewhere more private?'

'Of course.' He indicated one of the doors off the hall. Then he burst out, 'Is this – is this bad news?'

The man looked uncomfortably towards Fleming and she nodded.

'There's a grey-haired male had an accident up there by the campsite. Around six foot, late fifties probably. He seems to have fallen and hit his head. I'm afraid he's dead.'

The colour drained so quickly from Pilapil's face that Fleming moved forward instinctively to catch him if he fainted, but he spun round and with his hand to his mouth half ran across the hall and disappeared through the below-stairs door.

Fleming, looking grave, crossed the hall and the others followed her into another white, soulless space with the obligatory abstract above the fireplace, set up as a conference room with a long table and chairs. As MacNee shut the door she looked towards the other man.

'And you are . . . ?'

'DS Pete Hay. Drug Squad. Glasgow.'

'We might have guessed. What's the position?'

'Two girls found the man, lying on a path at the edge of that group of trees and bushes in the corner of the campsite near the toilets. Bashed his head on a big stone, as far as I could see. It's pretty muddy underfoot – just got unlucky, by the looks of it. They didn't know who it was and I haven't seen him before.'

'Gillis Crozier,' Fleming said heavily. 'He was expected back in the late afternoon and he didn't appear. They seemed to think he might have gone to see his gamekeeper about something unspecified, but I was beginning to wonder.'

At least it was an accident. It was almost a relief, after her initial fears. She'd allowed the atmosphere to get to her, that was all.

'What do we do now, ma'am?' Hay asked. 'Don't suppose—'

'No, the phone's still out. We'd better get up there and take a look. Tam, can you find Cris and ask him for torches and the keys to the Discovery? Oh, and see if there's a tarpaulin or something like that.'

MacNee had taken one of the chairs and was slumped forward over the table in an attitude of depression. He ran his hand down his face. 'Right,' he said dully, and went off.

Fleming and Hay went into the hall to wait for him. 'Tell me,' she said, 'what did you make of the older couple with the camper van who seemed to go to an improbable number of pop festivals?'

Hay pulled a face. 'Oh, dealing without a doubt. There seemed to be some negotiation going on with the blond guy who came up from the house. But they were on to me. I'd expected to be able to disappear into the crowd, but with so few people I was a bit obvious.'

'We noticed you too – a man on his own. They should have sent a woman officer as camouflage.'

'She was meant to be coming tomorrow – trying to save on the overtime budget as usual.'

'We all know about that,' Fleming was saying as MacNee returned, carrying a couple of powerful searchlight torches and a set of car keys, with a thick plastic sheet over his arm. Pilapil appeared behind him, shaking and tear-stained, and clearly finding it hard to control his sobs.

'Can I – can I come?' he faltered.

'I'm afraid not,' Fleming said. 'I'm so sorry. This is obviously very difficult for you, Cris. You're clearly very shaken, but you know the family well – would it be best if you broke the news, or do you want me to do that?'

That seemed to steady him. 'Oh, I'll do it,' Pilapil said, and there was bitterness in his voice. 'They won't care much. Cara would happily have sold him down the river to get her next fix, and Declan will find it hard not to smirk. I suppose you're sure it was an accident?'

Breaking the news to the family was a duty any police officer was happy to relinquish, but Fleming almost stepped in. He had gone down the passage to the sitting room already, though, and she didn't feel she could run after him and grab him to stop him. Anyway, her own observation of the family suggested that his assessment would prove hideously accurate.

IT WAS STILL not entirely dark. The sky was a deep, velvety blue, almost cloudless, and the pale thumbnail of the new moon had appeared, along with the brighter stars. Cool, damp air rose from the grass as Fleming, MacNee and Hay got out of the Discovery and walked over to the Lawtons' van. It looked as if all the campers had gathered there under the awning, in a pool of light from a couple of electric lanterns.

The side of the van was open and Angela, presiding again over a large teapot, was filling mugs and handing them out. Behind her, the two girls were sitting with their hands wrapped round mugs and blankets round their shoulders. In the dim light they looked very pale and shaken and much younger than the bouncy, confident teenagers they had been earlier.

Angela called over her shoulder, 'You all right, my loves?' and got wan smiles in response. Fleming would have been quite impressed with her motherly concern if she didn't suspect that Angela's normal habit was to supply more than tea and sympathy.

The murmur of hushed voices ceased as the officers stepped into the circle of light. Bob Lawton stepped forward.

'Am I glad to see you, Inspector! Let no one ever say there's never a policeman around when you need one. An appalling thing, this. Poor guy – I just can't believe it.' Indicating incredulity, he shook his head so hard that his jowls flapped.

'We're just going to drive up there to take a look,' Fleming said. 'I need to ask you all to stay away from the area. I understand the toilets are nearby, but please use the ones at the far end.'

In the van, Melanie shuddered. 'Wouldn't go near it if you paid me. When can we get home, that's what I want to know.' At her side, Stacey nodded vigorously.

'I'm afraid we don't know that as yet. We'll just have to be patient for the moment.'

From the back of the group, a belligerent-looking young man pushed forward. 'That's not very impressive, is it? My girlfriend's in a state, just wants to get out of here, and all you can say is, you don't know and we'll have to be patient?'

'I'm sorry,' Fleming said, showing, she felt, exemplary patience herself. 'I can fully appreciate your feelings, sir, and as you can imagine I'm unhappy about it as well. But at the moment, with no phone connection, there's nothing we can do. Now, if you'll excuse me . . .'

Ignoring the indignant 'That's just not good enough' and the muttered support from several others, the officers returned to the Discovery and drove up to the edge of the field. Fleming parked it so that the beam of the headlights illuminated the area, and carrying one of the torches, she got out. MacNee and Hay hung back as she went to investigate.

It was definitely Crozier. He lay only yards from the edge of the little wood of straggling trees, mainly stunted birches and elders, with a thick undergrowth of bushes and bracken. The light from the torch caught his wide-open, glassy eyes, giving them a macabre life, and Fleming hastily redirected its beam.

The stone his head was resting against – about a foot by nine inches in size, she estimated – lay on the grassy edge of the rough path leading down to the garden of Rosscarron House. The centre of the path was worn down and with the rain it was now treacherous, churned-up mud. It would be easy enough to slip, though he must have come down very hard to get an injury like that. Poor, unlucky bastard.

Fleming shone her torch back down the path, looking for the marks of slipping that would tell the story of his fall. He'd probably tried to save himself and come down heavily and awkwardly.

There were none that she could see. Frowning, she cast the beam back down the path, then played it along the verges. Still nothing, apart from a muddle of footprints in the mud.

Fleming stiffened. Oh God, surely not . . .

She returned to look at the injury. There was blood on the stone, certainly, but as she bent to look more closely at the mess of bone and brain material, it became clear that this wasn't the result of a single contact. There were three separate, though connecting, injuries, and when she played her torch on the undergrowth nearby, there was another smaller stone, also marked with blood.

For most of this interminable day, she had been struggling with pain and light-headedness. Now, a wave of dizziness and nausea overtook her and she had to grab at the trunk of a nearby sapling to steady herself. She dropped her head, taking deep breaths.

'Boss? Are you all right?' She heard MacNee's anxious voice and looked up to see him starting down the path towards her. Somehow, she managed to shout, 'No! Stay where you are. I'm coming up.'

The fewer people who went trampling around a murder scene, the better.

KIM KERSHAW STOOD at the front door of her ground-floor flat in Newton Stewart, trying to steady her shaking hands enough to fit the key into the lock.

Stupid! she scolded herself. It was all right now; she'd stayed until she'd seen Debbie comfortably asleep, and for a little longer while she breathed a thankful prayer.

It so nearly hadn't been all right. It had been one of Debbie's worst fits, and she knew from the strained expression on the doctor's face that he was worried too. But they'd brought her through, and now Debbie was all right.

All right, she told herself again, as she opened the door into the neat, silent flat. Until the next time.

MACNEE WAS FIGHTING to keep his eyes open. It was a long time since he'd been on watch through a night shift, and he'd had kind of a heavy day too, one way and another. His shoulders were sore, his back was sore, his arms were sore, and he wanted his bed.

He mustn't let himself sleep, though. He'd tried the car radio to keep him awake, but it was only tuned to channels playing rubbish music and he couldn't find any sport. At last he got out and took a walk around.

Even if it was July, it was pretty chilly at two in the morning and he huddled inside the borrowed Barber jacket he'd put on over his own leather one. It was very, very still. At the bottom of the field, where the tents were, there were no lights or sounds of voices. Bob Lawton had come up to the toilets about half an hour ago, but now everyone seemed to be asleep. Except him.

MacNee had never liked the country. Oh, it was bonny enough – he cast a disparaging look at the black night sky, with its galaxies of brilliant, wheeling stars – but there was something uncanny about silence in the country. It started pressing in on your ears until it almost hurt, and every rustle, every cracked twig made you jump, even though you knew it was only some night creature going about its business. He didn't like that thought – all these animals you couldn't even see. And an owl had gone by too, not long ago, looming without warning out of the darkness, silent on its muffled wings. MacNee didn't like owls either: unchancy creatures, owls, reminding him that his only human companion was lying still and silent, with the night-dew gathering on his plastic covering.

MacNee shuddered. Burns's words unhelpfully came to mind: 'That night, a child might understand, The de'il had business on his hand.'

Marjory Fleming had offered to spell him, but he'd refused to let her. She'd been deathly white and not even steady on her feet, and as he'd pointed out brutally, she'd be useless when she was needed in the morning if she didn't get some sleep now. It told him how bad she was feeling that she didn't overrule him.

He wouldn't have wanted her out here on her own anyway. Someone had all but killed them at the bridge this morning; someone actually had killed Gillis Crozier. The same someone? And did he have anything else in mind? It was an unnerving thought and had him looking nervously over his shoulder.

Still, rescue was close. Once the authorities heard what had happened, they would pull out all the stops and he ought to be back home by mid-morning at the latest. The pets might not be happy, but at least they wouldn't have starved.

DS Hay should be well on his way by now. It was fifteen miles to Kirkcudbright after you got yourself across the Carron, but Hay did that kind of thing for fun – triathlons, apparently. The river would be a lot lower by now, but even so MacNee, his mind on the tug of the current this morning, wouldn't have fancied it. These hearty types had their uses after all.

A louder crack, and a shuffling somewhere in the spinney, raised the hairs on the back of MacNee's neck. Then a low, sturdy shape appeared, its striped head swivelling as it sniffed the air.

MacNee retreated. He'd seen film of badgers, of course, but he hadn't realised they were as big as this. If it took against him, he'd a feeling it could do him a nasty mischief. He made shooing gestures and the animal scuttled back into the undergrowth.

Even so, he climbed into the Discovery again. Maybe he could find something a bit better on the radio. He pressed buttons and at last heard a song he recognised – Johnny Mathis singing 'Misty'. He caught his breath.

They'd played it the first time he met Bunty – there'd been a film, or something, and you heard it everywhere that summer. It had been at a disco on a blind date one of his pals had arranged. He'd held her close, she had snuggled up to him, and that had been it, really. 'Misty' had always been their song.

Bunty. She meant the world to him. He sat listening to the music, tears welling up and running down his cheeks.

FLEMING COULDN'T SLEEP. It had been a real struggle to get herself upstairs and into bed, but now she was wide awake. What made it worse was that it was her duty to sleep; as Tam had pointed out, she would be needed more in the morning. At this rate, she might as well be up the hill, taking her turn and giving Tam a rest, though realistically she knew she wasn't fit to do it.

Why couldn't she sleep, when she was so wretchedly tired? Painkillers had helped her headache, but her mind was doing its hamster-in-a-wheel act, going round and round and getting nowhere.

Fleming had never encountered a situation like this. It was one thing to investigate a murder in your official capacity and then go home to normality—

Home! Her mind skittered off to think about Bill: he'd have phoned the station to find out what had happened, probably.

He wouldn't be lying awake worrying about her, that was for sure. Bill didn't do lying awake.

Normality. Everything about this was weird – the isolation, the house, the dysfunctional family – and she was, quite possibly, under the same roof as a murderer.

However much she told herself that they had a suspect already in a man who'd nearly caused her own death, she kept going back to the way she had felt when Pilapil's summons came: she'd expected evil, and she had found it. She'd never been cursed with second sight; her premonition had been a reaction to the atmosphere in the room. So what did that tell her?

Fleming shivered and pulled the duvet more closely round her. She wasn't cold, though; she was just plain scared, there in the darkness, with only the line of light around the bedroom door from the corridor outside. She shut her eyes and tried to switch off her overactive brain.

Then there were footsteps outside, and she could hear a low-voiced conversation. Her eyes shot open and went to the door, which unusually for a private house – though not perhaps for an informal conference centre – had a proper locking device. She had made sure it was secured, but that was an illusion; there must be master keys. Did the handle turn, or had she only imagined it? She didn't know: her vulnerability was playing havoc with her thought processes. Murder as a professional challenge was one thing; having to live with it was quite another.

Who— But no, she must take a grip. If she started considering suspects and motives, sleep would never come. She needed to think of something else.

Like the problem of setting up a murder inquiry without resources. She knew all too well that this was the time, when memories were fresh, that statements should be being taken. Or what if something else dreadful happened overnight, when she should have been on watch in the house? She'd had to tell them all what had happened; then she'd instructed Cris to lock Crozier's study and bedroom and bring her the keys, which had taken her to the limit of her physical endurance – but how sympathetic would her superiors be to excuses if it was a botched investigation? In her current position, as Bailey had warned her, she needed to show she was on top of the job.

That wouldn't do either. She was getting herself more and more worked up. Fleming turned over on to her other side, but that left her with her back to the door. She turned round again.

And what if Joss were the killer? Joss, who could still make her question— But she wasn't going to go there either. It was bad enough that her connection with him would be a great story for the newspapers, and she wouldn't trust him not to tell them. She could see the headlines now—

Stop it! She raged at herself. Relax. Do deep breathing. Count sheep. Count backwards, in threes . . .

Bailey, oddly enough, had come into her bedroom. It seemed strange, but then she realised it wasn't her bedroom but his, and she had to explain that she had got things wrong . . .

At last, Marjory Fleming was asleep.

Chapter Nine

Friday, 21 July

IT WAS THE noise of a helicopter directly overhead that woke her. Marjory Fleming sat bolt upright in bed, somehow knowing instantly that she had overslept. Though a jolt of pain reminded her that sudden movement was still unwise, at least her head was clear. She looked at her watch – half past nine.

Half past nine! She could never sleep later than seven, even when she wanted to on an off-duty day. She sprang out of bed in a panic, though surely if there had been developments overnight someone would have called her?

From the small window in her bathroom, which looked towards the back of the house, she could see a Coastguard Sea King hovering above the hill, making to land in the camping field. That gave her, probably, ten minutes to get downstairs before they could arrive at the house.

But it was morning. She wasn't alone, in the dark, feeling threatened. Whatever happened today, the night was over.

She cringed as she looked in the bathroom mirror. The bruising had spread, taking on technicoloured hues, and without make-up of any kind there was nothing she could do about it. She employed the packaged toothbrush and comb so thoughtfully provided and, after the sketchiest of ablutions, flung on her clothes and hurried downstairs. She reached the hall just as Cris Pilapil opened the door to admit a helicopter pilot along with DCs Campbell and Kershaw. Pilapil gave no sign of the agitation that would suggest problems overnight. He acknowledged Fleming, then disappeared below stairs.

It was Kershaw who stepped forward. 'Are – are you all right, ma'am?' she asked, making a rather too obvious effort not to look shocked. Campbell, less tactfully, gaped.

'Looks worse than it is,' Fleming said briskly. 'What's happening?'

Half-a-dozen uniformed officers had been flown in, Kershaw explained, and DS Macdonald was up at the campsite field directing them while explaining to the unimpressed campers that they couldn't leave until they had all given their details and statements. Telephone engineers had come too and now seemed confident that they would be able to trace the fault.

'How's MacNee?' Fleming asked with a considerable feeling of guilt.

'Briefing Macdonald at the moment,' Kershaw said, 'but he wanted to know if he could go back with the chopper – problems at home, he said.'

'I know about that. Yes, of course – he must be dead on his feet.' Fleming turned to the pilot. 'Are you heading back immediately?'

'That's right. I'm to stand by for a request to return, always supposing the phone's back on. If not, I'm to come back in the afternoon anyway, though as I understand it, the army's been detailed to set up a Bailey bridge once the debris has been cleared.'

Fleming nodded. 'Right. I won't hold you up, then.'

As the pilot left, Campbell said, 'JCB's there now. Saw it as we flew in.'

'That's good news. Now, I need to be briefed on what's happening. There's a sort of conference room here.'

They were filing in when Pilapil appeared with a tray of coffee and muffins. He looked as if he hadn't slept, with great dark circles under his eyes, and his skin had a grey tinge.

'I thought you might like something to eat.' He set the tray down on the table.

Fleming's gratitude, as she took the mug of coffee from him, was heartfelt. Then she said, her voice very gentle and her hazel eyes full of sympathy, 'Cris, it must be hard for you. You were obviously very fond of your boss.'

Even the mention of Crozier distressed him. 'He was a good man. A good man, with a sad life. I owe everything to him.'

'Why don't you sit down and tell us about him?'

Pilapil hesitated for a second, then sat down.

'I'm not wanting coffee,' Campbell said. 'Here, take my mug.'

Absently, Pilapil accepted it, cupping his hands round it, though the room was warm enough. He took a sip, taking time to order his thoughts. At a nod from Fleming, Campbell got out a notebook.

'I was a rent boy,' he said at last. 'I was in a bar in London one night with a client and there was . . . a disagreement. He was a frightening man; he was hissing threats in my face and I was afraid. Then a man who had been sitting along the bar tapped him on the shoulder. I'll never forget what he said: "Leave the kid alone – you may be bigger than him, but I'm bigger than you." He was too, and he looked as if he knew how to handle himself. The other guy was easily scared – bullies usually are. He only said, "You're welcome. He's trash," and left.

'To be honest, I thought Gillis was just another punter, but at least he had a kind face. He bought me a drink and we talked. He wasn't trying to pick me up; he was prepared to help me. No one else has ever done that.

'He'd a mate who'd a Thai restaurant, and he said he'd get me work with him. I liked the job, and they let me do a bit of cooking. It's the first thing I've ever been good at – changed my life.

'Gillis is – was,' he corrected himself painfully, 'crazy about Thai food and eventually he asked if I'd like to be his personal assistant – cook for him, run the houses, do office stuff if he needed it. He even got me training, so I could. I've been with him ten years now and – and I don't know what I'll do, now he's gone.' Pilapil's eyes filled with tears again.

'I can understand how you feel,' Fleming said. 'Cris, you asked me last night if we were sure your boss's death was an accident. I don't know if you've heard already, but I'm afraid it wasn't. Gillis Crozier was murdered.'

From the look of shock on his face, it was clear he hadn't. '*Murdered?* I didn't mean . . . I didn't really think . . .'

'We've got an investigation running now. When did you last see Mr Crozier, and what did you do after that?'

After Crozier went out, Pilapil had gone to the kitchen to finish clearing up after lunch, then to his own private quarters further along the below-stairs corridor. He hadn't seen anyone until Declan Ryan came into the kitchen, where Pilapil had gone to prepare the evening meal, sometime after five.

'There was a problem with his gamekeeper, wasn't there?' Fleming prompted, and heard the story of the confrontation with Alick Buchan.

'What does he look like?' she asked with seeming inconsequence.

'Rough. Shaggy grey hair. Walks with a limp.'

'I see.' Interesting! But she went on, 'And there were problems with vandalism too, weren't there?'

'A man called Jamieson made a lot of threats,' Pilapil said. 'He was a very angry man, I think – angry about the festival, angry about his house flooding. He came here a lot, shouting. But . . .' He hesitated. 'I think his threats were all about getting the police, so . . . I don't know.'

'Any difficulties with anyone else?'

'Apart from Declan, you mean?' Pilapil's face flushed with anger. 'He's a bad man – a jackal following a lion. He wants to be a partner in the business, but Gillis doesn't rate him. Takes everything from Gillis, poisons his life in return. Cara has – problems. We all know that . . .' He looked towards Fleming uncertainly.

'Yes, we do,' she said.

'Gillis has been trying to get her into rehab, but she won't hear of it. Declan gets the stuff for her and it keeps her happy so she doesn't give him grief. I think Gillis was almost ready to give up. And after the tragedy, when he took a hard line with her, she would simply flip.'

'The tragedy?' Fleming and Kershaw spoke together.

Pilapil looked from one to the other in surprise. 'You mean you don't know? It was in all the papers for weeks – months, even. Their nanny killed the baby, then found herself a smart lawyer and got off.'

Fleming frowned, but Kershaw said at once, 'I remember! Of course – the Ryan baby! It was in London. What was her name? Lisa something . . .'

'Stewart,' Fleming supplied. 'I recall the headlines now, though I can't claim to have followed it closely. I certainly didn't realise there was a local connection. It was very sad—'

As she spoke, a phone rang. They all jumped: it seemed very loud and shrill in its unexpectedness. Fleming said, 'Thank goodness for that,' and Pilapil got up and hurried to answer it.

She turned to Campbell and Kershaw. 'Get most of that, Ewan? Food for thought there, certainly. Now, bring me up to date with the outside world.'

UP THE HILL, the murder site had been circled with official tape and under DS Macdonald's direction uniforms were taking statements while a photographer filmed the area and took shots of the body. A pathologist was standing by, ready to move in once the recording of the site was complete.

The Sea King had taken off again, bearing a groggy-looking DS MacNee back to civilisation. He hadn't appreciated it when Macdonald had asked him if he'd enjoyed his wee break.

'See the country?' he had said bitterly. 'Next time anyone's to go outside Kirkluce, it's you, not me, right?'

'Oh, and here's me thinking you'd be right at home on the banks and braes like your pal Rabbie.'

'I'll tell you this. If he'd been stuck out all night on a bank or a bloody brae, he'd have written something different.'

'I think that's heresy, isn't it?' Macdonald called after him, as MacNee, without deigning to turn his head, got into the chopper and was whirled away.

'SO WE'RE WAITING for the path report on the body at the Ross-carron Cottages,' DC Kershaw concluded her report.

Fleming looked slightly stunned at the thought of so much going on without her knowledge. 'And there's a girl still missing, then?'

'Thought you might know where she is,' DC Campbell suggested.

'Me?'

Kershaw waited for Campbell to elaborate, but she was learning the unwisdom of conversational expectation where he was concerned and stepped in. 'Ewan thought she could be at the game-keeper's cottage. Dr Forbes, who lived in the next-door cottage, saw her heading off on the path round the headland, and after the landslip there'd be no way back except across the moorland. And how otherwise did the keeper know what had happened and raise the alarm?'

'I didn't know he had,' Fleming said. 'But we need to get to him urgently anyway, after what Pilapil told us. I saw him coming out of the little wood yesterday late afternoon, so he's definitely in the frame. We need to get hold of Jamieson too. Tam and I went down to the houses, but they were still under water and we decided to leave it until the morning, when we could borrow waders.

'Ewan, get down there now and see if you can raise him. Cris will fix you up with boots. If you can each commandeer a car, you could get along to the gamekeeper's cottage to talk to the girl, Kim. I'd better make contact with the super and then sort things out here.'

With some surprise, Kershaw heard nervousness in Big Marge's voice. And when she thought about it, she really wouldn't like to be in the inspector's shoes if Bailey was in one of his more unreasonable moods.

BETH BROWN, TOO, had felt a lurch in her stomach when she heard the helicopter overhead. It was good in one way – at least she could get out of this dreadful situation – but it was bad in another. Things could go wrong, very wrong.

She was cramped and sore from sleeping on an old, tatty horsehair sofa in a back room, used more as a store than an office. Its slippery surface made blankets and pillow slide off when she turned over, and the dust from bags of animal feed kept making her sneeze. Anyway, she felt she could hardly breathe with the atmosphere in this miserable little house.

Alick Buchan had come down to breakfast hung-over and in a filthy temper. Seeing her at the table, he had given an odd sort of half-snarl, almost like one of his own dogs, but said nothing.

Beth was spared Ina's constant, unnerving scrutiny since she mercifully expected breakfast in bed, and while Maidie took the tray up to her, Beth helped Calum with his Rice Krispies. He was out of sorts this morning, with a runny nose and a cough, and he crossly pushed away a spoonful, which landed in her lap. She shook her head at him, smiling, as she went to get a cloth. Poor little chap – he was obviously miserable.

She sat down again and reached for a toy, which she suddenly popped up from behind her back. The child gave a gurgle of laughter and his father glared.

'Get that brat to shut up!' he demanded, and Beth, directing towards him such a look of cold loathing that he blinked, picked Calum out of his chair and took him over to the sink to wipe his face and hands.

The sun was shining, though a little uncertainly, and there would probably be rain later. Still, it was worth getting a soaking to escape from the house, and chatting to Calum as they walked would stop her brooding.

'Tell Maidie I've taken him for a walk,' she said, leaving Buchan to his headache.

IT WAS A glorious day now. From the rough road leading from Rosscarron House to Keeper's Cottage, there was a view to the sea below and the gannets were diving, white arrows piercing the deep blue. The sky was an innocent turquoise with puffy clouds, though a streak of silver grey far off on the horizon hinted at change to a darker mood.

DC Kershaw wasn't admiring it. She was frowning as she drove Alick Buchan's jeep, struggling to recollect all the details of the tragedy of the Ryan baby. She remembered it pretty well: like many another working mother who had to entrust her child to paid carers, it had sent a shiver down her spine.

Cara Ryan didn't seem to have been a good mother – or even a good-enough mother, which was all most women aspired to – but you could only pity her for what had happened.

The baby, a girl, as far as she remembered, was about three months old when she was discovered lying outside in the garden of the Ryans' smart house in Putney. It was a cold, wet autumn night and she'd been dead of hypothermia when they found her.

Kershaw remembered the nanny quite clearly: a red-haired girl, heavy-faced, with round blue eyes like marbles. She had been given a very rough ride by the press, who conducted a trial by media before the case ever came to court.

But Lisa had come across well, and the evidence given by the Ryans' cleaner had painted a vivid picture of the baby's brother as jealous, difficult and possibly even disturbed.

The jury was convinced, the police blatantly less so. They had taken Lisa's acquittal badly, describing the verdict as 'disappointing' and saying flatly that there would be no further investigation.

Even so, it had left the baby's brother stigmatised. That must have been a sickening blow for the Ryans, on top of the loss of their daughter, and it was no wonder poor Cara had chosen to deaden the pain.

At the time, Kershaw had on the whole been inclined to believe the nanny's story. There had been plenty of cases in the past that showed that while young children might not have a full understanding of their actions, the capacity for evil was definitely there.

But that was before the stories had started to leak out about the red-haired nanny's temper. There had been a backlash, and Kershaw remembered the grandfather uttering threats, which were certainly unpleasant, if understandable. That was Cris's ideal employer – well, there was always more than one side to a person's character. Hitler loved animals.

Crozier certainly hadn't been universally beloved – not by his son-in-law, not by his gamekeeper, who was now squarely in the frame for his murder, with a witness to testify to his drunken rage and DI Fleming, no less, seeing him emerge from the spinney, where the body was found.

Her orders were to get Buchan to agree to come in for questioning, since they didn't have evidence to arrest – not yet, anyway. She'd wait for Campbell to come to pick her up before she tried, but she did hope he wouldn't be too long.

IT WAS KIND of eerie, plodding in the mud around the deserted houses. DC Ewan Campbell, in thigh-length fishing waders that were a little too small for him, surveyed the depressing scene.

The water had receded, leaving a thick layer of silt behind, and the stench, wafted on a breeze from the sea, was disgusting. As Campbell walked round the stranded cars, he tried to work out the cost of all this – millions, certainly.

The doors to some of the houses had burst open under the force of the flood water; these he entered, working his way through a layer of sludge, negotiating the flotsam of furniture – a kitchen table upside down in an entrance hall, a sofa at an angle halfway up a staircase, a huge plasma-screen television face down in a doorway.

In one house where access to the staircase was clear, he went upstairs and somehow it was even weirder to see everything normal here. He found he was looking guiltily at the footprints his waders had left on the pristine cream carpet.

Other front doors were still locked, as their owners must have left them. One of these, Campbell noticed suddenly, had a nameplate saying, 'Jamieson' above an electric bell. He pressed it from force of habit then, feeling foolish, knocked on the door. There was no answer, no sound of responsive movement from inside.

He hesitated for only a moment before kicking in the door. In the general chaos here a search warrant seemed an unnecessary formality and damage to the door wouldn't even be noticed in the massive restoration. After a few well-placed kicks, the lock broke and he pushed the door open against the resistance of the mud, which was a full nine inches deep on the ground floor. He called, 'Hello! Police. Anyone there?'

There was no sound, beyond the glooping noise of the rippling mud disturbed by his entry. He looked about him.

Here there were signs that someone had done some clearing after the house had been flooded. Tables had been stacked on top of wrecked sofas, every upper surface was piled with belongings and, most telling of all, there were a lot of muddy footprints on the beige stair carpet. Was the owner of the footprints upstairs, refusing to answer, hiding somewhere? He could hardly be unaware of Campbell's presence.

It was an uncomfortable thought that someone might be up there, silently waiting for him. Moving cautiously now, Campbell took off the waders and parked them; then, in stockinged feet and on tiptoe, he climbed the stairs.

The upper floor here, like the one in the other house, had suffered no damage. The doors to a bathroom and three bedrooms, leading off a galleried upper hall, stood ajar, giving glimpses of neat, conventionally decorated rooms. He pushed the doors of the first two open with due caution, waited, then looked around. They were all empty.

It was a nice house, expensively fitted out and with good-sized rooms. The ones to the front had the sea view that would have been the property's greatest selling point. Yes, it was very nice; in fact, he could just see himself and Mairi here, with a good bedroom for the wee one, and a room for a little brother or sister as well, and then there wouldn't be a spare for visits from his mother-in-law.

The room at the far end was the master bedroom, the largest of them, with windows on two sides and a small en-suite shower room. And here there were definite signs of recent occupation: a kettle, a camping stove, jars and tins, packaging and rubbish in a bin.

Campbell touched the kettle. If it had been warm, that would have told him something. It wasn't.

The bed with its rose-patterned bedspread was neatly made, and there were no clothes lying around. In the bathroom, the basin and shower were dry, but again that didn't tell him anything. He had no idea how long it might take for drops of water to dry, but on balance the indications were that someone had been living here since the flood, but wasn't any longer.

Even so, it was again with some caution that he went to open the built-in wardrobes. They covered one wall and were quite big enough to provide a hiding place for someone who didn't want to be found. One proved to be empty; the other held only a man's clothes and shoes, including a pair of wellies caked in mud. But there was certainly no one hiding there, so it looked as if their quarry had fled, perhaps after seeing the results of his handiwork – if, indeed, it was his.

Campbell went back downstairs, put on the waders again, wincing a little at the tight fit, and left the house. He cast a speculative glance at the garage, but without a warrant any evidence found would be inadmissible in court, so a search would be pointless, or even counterproductive.

He ploughed through the mud back to Crozier's Discovery, which Pilapil had suggested he should use. Kim would be at Keeper's Cottage waiting for him to bring her, and with luck Alick Buchan too, back to Rosscarron House. He just hoped that she'd managed to sweet-talk him into coming quietly.

As THE SOUND of the car's engine died away, the small man with thinning grey hair, crouched in darkness and nine inches of mud at the back of the cupboard under the stairs, let out the breath he seemed to have been holding since he heard the engine of the car he guessed must be from the police arriving. He was trembling uncontrollably, partly with cold and partly with fear.

He groped his way to the door, fumbling for the handle, then tried to open it. It hadn't been easy to close it in the first place, and now the pressure of the mud was holding it shut. For a panic-stricken moment he thought he was trapped, but another frantic shove got it open wide enough for him to wriggle through.

He blinked in the daylight as his eyes adjusted. His lips tightened when he saw the damage to the door – but after all, what did it matter? The devastation round about him was only a reflection of the devastation of his own life.

He waded to the stairs. He hadn't even had time to put on his boots and now his socks and his trousers were filthy. He'd have to use some of the precious water remaining in the tank to clean his feet. He'd been sparing with it, but there couldn't be much left by now, and anyway the man he had seen was just the vanguard: soon, others would follow. The neighbours would return to assess the damage; the clean-up operation would begin. What would he do then?

He had no idea how it had come to this. After Margaret's illness and death, it had been like a sort of madness, when the anger he'd felt about the unfairness of her suffering, and his own, had spilled over into rage directed first at the intrusion of noise and strangers on his quiet mourning, then the destruction caused by another man's greed. And now his life was in terrifying chaos.

He'd had an alcoholic friend once, a professional man who had lost job, home and family, and had eventually died on a cold night, sleeping wrapped in rags under an archway in a Glasgow back-street. He and Margaret had marvelled sadly at how such a thing could happen. Yet here he was, in a worse position, even, than his friend, and he had been no more able to stop himself.

There were still some of Margaret's sleeping pills in the bathroom cabinet and he had a bottle of whisky he'd salvaged from the cocktail cabinet. He was still too scared to take that way out, but perhaps as he became forced to accept that there was no other escape, he'd find the courage from somewhere.

Chapter Ten

FLEMING HELD THE phone a little away from her ear, pulling a face as, after the most perfunctory enquiry about her state of health, Bailey demanded to know what on earth was going on, in tones which suggested that in finding herself at the scene of a murder Fleming was in some sense culpable.

The stickiest part came when they got on to actions taken last night after the discovery of the body.

'Yes, yes,' Bailey said. 'MacNee was policing the site, and Hay came to raise the alarm, but you haven't told me what you were doing, Marjory.'

She swallowed. 'I'm afraid I had to go to bed.'

There was an awful silence, then, '*To bed?*'

'I'm sorry. I had concussion when the car crashed and I was quite simply unfit to continue.'

Fleming could almost hear Bailey recalling the regulations about harassment. 'I – see. But Marjory, the golden hour, when we have our best chance of good evidence, wasted!'

'I agree, it was most unfortunate. But now I have officers in place . . .'

She went on to describe the tasks she had allocated and her own activities – background checks to be made on Crozier, interviews to be done with family – and talked bullishly about Alick Buchan as the prime suspect.

As always, Bailey liked the thought of a straightforward you're-nicked-sunshine. 'An early arrest and charge would certainly cover your back,' he conceded, 'but I have to say it's looking a bit exposed at the moment.'

Fleming didn't need him to tell her that. She rang off feeling depressed and with a hollow feeling in the pit of her stomach.

She had let herself into Crozier's study to have privacy for her phone call, and she looked around it now. There was a control deck for the house's sound system, but apart from that the white, impersonal room told her almost nothing about the tastes of the man himself. It was clinically tidy, with a desk that had only a computer, a tray of pens and two wire baskets on its glass surface.

Fleming wasn't used to desks that looked like that. Though she could always find what she was looking for, her own could only be described as deep litter and in her heart of hearts she suspected that those who were always putting things away either hadn't enough to do or had something to hide.

With a pop festival meant to be going on right at this moment, Crozier would have had plenty to do, yet there was nothing in his out-tray, and his in-tray held half-a-dozen invoices and a couple of business letters.

There was a huge cork board on one wall and here there were schedules, letters, lists and Post-it notes galore. Fleming squinted at a couple, one about a band called Zombie and the Living Dead with a technical specification that went over her head, another demanding plaintively what had happened to the running order for Saturday night. Certainly, they all related to the festival, but surely there should be more bumf than this?

There was a bank of filing cabinets on another wall and Fleming went over to look. There were two marked, 'Festival'; these were unlocked and she pulled them out, looking without much interest at files with labels like 'Bands', 'Accommodation' and 'Lighting'.

The drawers below were identified only by numbers and letters, and these, when she tugged experimentally at one or two, seemed to be locked. Pilapil, presumably, would have the keys, but she'd leave that until there was better-qualified manpower on hand to do an in-depth search. The computer would have to be checked out as well.

Fleming was just turning away when she noticed that one drawer in the end stack was not fully closed. It was almost an invitation and she went back to pull it open.

For a moment she stared at it, not quite understanding what she was seeing. Every file was empty, and the hangers had been put back so hurriedly that the drawer was unable to close properly. She pulled open others in that stack and the one next to it; they too were empty, though the sagging cardboard of the sides showed that they had not been unused.

She felt sick and cold. Pilapil had, as requested, locked the study and given her the key last night, but she had been feeling too ill to think clearly. She should have demanded every key, and while she slept someone – or more than one person – had come in and cleared out – what?

Something they didn't want the police to see, that was for sure, but she didn't know what it was, and now she couldn't see how she was going to find out. There had been plenty of opportunity to destroy anything that needed destroying while she slept.

KERSHAW LOOKED AROUND the meagre kitchen of the Buchans' cottage with a shock of pity. It was so bleak, so lacking in any sort of comfort! You were always hearing about poverty in the inner cities, but rural poverty was every bit as wretched and often unsupported by charities and the 'initiatives' beloved of governments looking for the popular vote. There weren't a lot of votes in country areas.

Maidie Buchan certainly looked as if her life held no joy, or even hope. She took the keys of the jeep listlessly and said that her husband was out dealing with a blocked drain.

That suited Kershaw perfectly. 'Perhaps I could have a word with you while I'm waiting?' she suggested.

'Yes, fine.' Maidie looked flustered by the request. 'You'd – you'd maybe better come through the house, then. Gran's there, but . . .'

In the sitting room, there was no sign of the missing girl, only an overweight elderly woman with a downturned mouth, squatting toad-like in a chair in the corner of the room.

'Who's this, then?' she asked rudely, eyeing Kershaw as if she had brought a bad smell with her into the room.

'It's the police, Gran.' She turned to Kershaw. 'My mother-in-law, Ina Buchan.'

She was immediately corrected. 'Ina *McClintock* Buchan. I'm one of the Dundrennan McClintocks.'

This conveyed nothing to Kershaw beyond the information that Ina was a snob – with, on the face of it, not much to be snobbish about. 'Can you tell me—'

Ina cut across her. 'What are you wanting here, anyway?'

Ignoring her, Kershaw said to Maidie, 'Mrs Buchan, we're looking for a girl who lived in the Rosscarron Cottages. Did she come here, the night of the landslip?'

There was a snort from Mrs Buchan senior. 'Oh aye, she came, all right. She's still here. We can't get rid of her.'

Maidie went red. 'We've been happy to give Beth shelter at a time like this,' she said with some dignity, adding, in response to Kershaw's raised eyebrows, 'Beth Brown. She arrived in the middle of the night in a terrible state. She'd been out a walk and she was up above the cottages, sitting on the seat there just a wee minute before the ground collapsed and it went over. She was that shocked!'

'And she's still here?'

'She's away out with my wee boy – she's awful good with him. She'll likely be back soon.'

'I'll wait for her, if you don't mind. Meanwhile, could I just ask you both what you were doing yesterday afternoon?'

Ina's eyes narrowed. 'What are you wanting to know that for?'

Kershaw didn't reply and Maidie said hastily, 'We were both here all afternoon. Gran doesn't get out much, and I'd a lot to do.'

'And Beth was with you?'

'Some of the time,' Maidie was saying when Ina again interrupted.

'She was out most of the afternoon. Sulking, most likely. She's got quite a temper, that girl – walks out the room if you so much as look at her. And never said a word at tea last night – just glared. That's not manners, is it? She was looking upset, mind you.'

'Beth's not wanting to stay here any more than you and Alick want to have her,' Maidie retorted. 'And it's natural she'd be upset, after all that's happened – her partner and everything.'

'She knows about that?' Kershaw asked.

Maidie nodded. 'It was Alick had to go into the house and he found the body. That was what set him off—' She stopped, biting her lip, as Ina impaled her with a stare.

Kershaw filed that away. 'What time did he get back from Ross-carron House?'

Maidie opened her mouth to speak, but Ina held up her hand imperiously. 'Stop! You're not saying another word till we're told what all this is about.'

They'd hear soon enough. Kershaw explained, and saw from Maidie's stricken expression that not only did she now under-stand the thrust of the questioning, she was afraid that her hus-band might have killed his boss.

Ina understood too. 'Ridiculous!' she snapped. 'When my son comes back, you'll talk to him yourself, no doubt, if you've no more sense than to think he might do a thing like that. But you'll not get anything out of us to trap him with.'

Kershaw was resigning herself to a silent wait when she heard someone coming into the house, and a child's fractious wail.

Maidie jumped to her feet. 'That'll be Beth with Calum,' she said, heading for the kitchen. Through the open door, Kershaw could hear a woman's voice saying, 'He's just miserable with his cold. Come on, Calum, I'll wipe your nose for you and give you a cuddle.'

The child's wailing stopped. Maidie said, 'There's a police-woman here wants a word with you, Beth.'

Beth's voice, when she spoke after a silence of several seconds, sounded suddenly flat. 'Right. I'll go on through, then.'

She appeared in the doorway, carrying a rosy-cheeked toddler with a pink nose and watering eyes, who was snuggling into her shoulder. She was a dark-haired girl who looked to be in her early twenties, with a sallow, rather pudgy face and light blue eyes – very round eyes, with a gap between the iris and the lower lid. Eyes as round as marbles . . .

Taken by surprise, Kershaw blurted out, 'I know you! You're Lisa Stewart, aren't you?'

The girl who had called herself Beth Brown shrank back as if she had been struck. There was a cry of triumph from Ina.

'I knew I recognised her! You know who this is, Maidie? You know who you've been trusting with my grandchild? She's the one who put that baby out in the rain to die, then got off with it. Get your murdering hands off that child this minute!'

Calum's mother's face registered shock and uncertainty. Kershaw could see Maidie fighting her immediate impulse to snatch her precious boy from the other woman's arms.

Beth – no, Lisa, saw it too. Blindly, she thrust Calum at Maidie and began to cry with great heaving sobs.

'I didn't do it – I would never hurt a child! Never, never!'

Calum, looking bewildered, began to wail again. It was to Kershaw's considerable relief that she saw through the window the Discovery drawing up outside.

DECLAN RYAN WAS, without a doubt, a nasty piece of work.

Fleming was working from the conference room, conducting the interviews she wanted to do before going back to headquarters.

She had started with Cara. She would be a pretty woman, Fleming thought, with her fair hair and baby-blue eyes, if it weren't for the bad skin – the result, no doubt, of whatever was cushioning her from reality.

She was tearful, admittedly, but she spoke in a gentle, emotion-less voice. 'I can't believe my father's gone. And who would kill him? He was a lovely man.'

The interview hadn't taken long. Cara couldn't think of an enemy he had in the world, and asking her about times proved equally futile: she vaguely thought that she and Nico had prob-ably watched a film together and agreed to the suggestion that it might have been Harry Potter, but that apparently was the limit of her recollection. When Fleming said the sitting room had been empty when she came downstairs, Cara frowned for a moment, then said they might have gone upstairs, but she couldn't really remember.

Ryan, in contrast, was totally on the ball. Below the floppy blond hair, his eyes, which were the merest fraction too close together, were sharply watchful, reminding her of Pilapil's description of him as a jackal. He came in wearing a cocky smirk, skinny jeans and a T-shirt bearing the legend 'I was Keith Richards's drug dealer.' He was definitely waiting for her to notice it.

Fleming looked at him coolly. 'Wind-up-the-pigs time, is it, Mr Ryan? Wasted on me, I'm afraid.'

With some satisfaction, she saw she had read his mind and it had thrown him. The smirk disappeared and his 'First thing that came to hand, actually' was definitely defensive.

Not tough enough, then, to say, 'Absolutely. So what?' Was the cockiness a cover for weakness? She thought it showed in his face. Following up her advantage, Fleming said, 'Since you've brought up the topic, where does your wife get her drug supply?'

He was prepared for that with a smart answer. 'From the phar-macy, actually. She suffers from depression. And don't worry about the "Mr Ryan" part. We were all chums together last night, Marjory.' He gave her a false smile as he sat down opposite.

She squirmed inwardly at the implication of intimacy; being a guest in the house had certainly diminished her effectiveness. She selected her next weapon with care.

'I prefer to keep this official, Mr Ryan. I gather you and your father-in-law didn't get on?'

'Who told you that? There was nothing wrong with our relationship.' Anger put an ugly twist on his mouth, but it gave way to petulance. 'Oh, you got that from dear little Cris, I suppose. Jealous as a cat, you know, because I'm family and he isn't. Always hoped his charms would persuade Gillis to make a will signing everything over to him, but my beloved pa-in-law wasn't that way inclined. It's a family business anyway.'

'And what, exactly, is that business?' Fleming waited for the reply with considerable interest.

Ryan pushed his chair away from the table and leaned back in it, stretching out his crossed legs and putting his thumbs in the pockets of his jeans. 'Oh, promotion, mainly, but Gillis had a finger in lots of pies. The venture into property wasn't his smartest move, though, and now the festival's completely doomed. He was losing his touch, frankly. Better as a Mr Fix-It, putting people together, you know? That sort of thing.'

Fleming didn't know, really, but what she did know was that the ostentatious relaxation of Ryan's position was completely at odds with the tension that came across in his voice, and the twitching of a muscle at his temple, too, suggested stress. The business would be checked out later, but meantime there was something else she wanted to know, if he would tell her – which was unlikely.

'Do you have a key to your father-in-law's study?'

He couldn't hold the casual pose. He sat up, and his voice when he said, 'A key? Cris has one. Do you want it?' was so innocent that she had not the slightest doubt that he knew why she had asked.

'No, I have that one. Are there others?'

'Oh, probably.' Ryan gave an elaborate shrug. 'Never needed one, actually. When it was just the family here, Gillis didn't bother to lock the door.'

He wasn't stupid. True or not true, it was a good answer. 'So you are saying you didn't go in there last night?'

'Last night? Look, I had Cara throwing fits, I had Nico high as a kite and refusing to sleep. What would I want to go to the study for?'

'I don't know, Mr Ryan. Perhaps you could tell me?' Fleming waited for a long moment, keeping her eyes on him. He shifted in his seat, but didn't respond. 'No? Then there are just a few other technical things I need to ask you.'

She discovered that there was a solicitor's office in Kirkcudbright that had handled the local interests, like the housing project and the organisation of the festival. She jotted down the details, then said, 'That's all I need. I won't detain you – you must have a lot to do.'

It took him by surprise. Ryan was looking uncertain as he got up, but he said in a silly, mocking voice, 'Aren't you going to do the whole bit about my whereabouts? Oh, Inspector, you are so mean! I was looking forward to that. I was going to say, "My alibi is Detective-Sergeant Tam MacNee. To break me you'll have to break him first!"' He struck a defiant pose.

'I know that already, Mr Ryan. Thank you for your cooperation.'

He paused in the doorway. 'I take it you will be arresting Buchan? It's a clear-cut case, and my wife will be distressed as long as her father's killer is still at large.'

It was almost comic the way his voice had suddenly taken on that middle-class, my-taxes-pay-your-wages tone.

'We prefer to have some evidence first,' Fleming told him, and saw his face grow dark before he left the room. As the door closed, she gave a small, involuntary shudder. She would have described herself as case-hardened, but she was deeply thankful that she would soon be in the Sea King being taken back. Weak men and nervous dogs were often the most dangerous and she was glad she wouldn't be spending another night under the same roof.

And she wasn't looking forward to her next interview either.

ALICK BUCHAN HAD, after all, proved to be a pussycat. When he got back to the house and Kershaw told him what had happened, his weather-beaten face paled so that the broken veins in his cheeks showed as bright red patches. She didn't ask any questions, only invited him to come with them to the police station, and he agreed immediately, despite the shrill protestations of his mother. His wife, holding her son close, watched in dumb despair as he climbed into the Discovery.

Lisa Stewart was in the back already, studiously facing away from him and staring out of the window. After her tearful outburst she had regained control with steely determination, answering Kershaw's questions with brief, factual answers. She had been up on the bluff when the landslip took place; she had walked through the night to get help. She had thought her partner was away, had seen him leave before she did. Yes, she was prepared to identify him.

Making assumptions about the reactions of people who may be in shock is unwise, but still Lisa's lack of emotion was disturbing. Kershaw hadn't wanted to go into the background in front of an audience, but Campbell had said with his usual directness, 'You don't seem too upset.'

Lisa had looked at him calmly. 'I'm not, really.' Then, as Ina hissed in delighted horror, she went on, 'I'd thrown him out. That's why I thought he wasn't there.'

It was, Kershaw thought, a chilling response, but Campbell had only said, 'Right,' as if pleased to have a logical explanation. After that no one seemed to have anything to say and it was a relief when Buchan's return broke the silence and they were able to comply with the instructions radioed to Campbell to go back to the campsite and wait for the helicopter.

'OUT ALL DAY yesterday, up tracks and ploughing through mud, and what do we find?' an indignant engineer complained to DS Andy Macdonald. 'Only that someone's had the bright idea of cutting the line to the house. You lot had better get him put behind bars, that's all.'

'Not up to me,' Macdonald said regretfully. 'I'd throw away the key.'

He would, too, when he thought about all the problems that had caused. Though, of course, if this was part of the sabotage effort that had brought the bridge down too, even the most bleeding-heart judge would have to think custodial.

That was the only interesting snippet that came his way all morning. The statements the uniforms were getting from the campers and the contractors were without exception unhelpful. No one had seen anything; few people could remember exactly where they were when, or who was with them. Half of them seemed to have been asleep in the afternoon – and probably half cut as well. 'Nothing else to do,' one had said bitterly.

If there was any action, it certainly wasn't here and Macdonald was bored. If being a sergeant meant you got lumbered with organising while the others went off and did the interesting jobs, it wasn't worth all the studying and the courses and the exams. His one hope was that when Big Marge came to be airlifted out, she'd decide she couldn't do without him back at headquarters.

Still, at least the news coming in about the replacement bridge was good. The campers were packing up their cars, with the promise of getting off the headland in a couple of hours.

Suddenly Macdonald noticed that up at the top of the hill, just by the police tape surrounding the crime scene, there was a child – a boy, didn't look more than seven or eight. He was talking to PC Langlands, the uniform on duty at the site, but this was no place for a kid! Macdonald started up towards them.

Langlands, a pleasant-faced young man celebrated for his sympathetic way with children and those of a nervous disposition, started pulling agitated faces over the boy's head as Macdonald approached.

'This is Nico, Sarge,' he said. 'Nico's, well, wanting to know about his granddad.'

'Right.' Macdonald looked down at the child, a little uncertainly, but Nico's blue eyes met his with total confidence.

'My granddad was killed in there, right?' He pointed to the clump of trees. 'Can I see?'

Langlands cravenly retreated. Macdonald said firmly, 'Sorry, no. It's a crime scene. No one's allowed in there.'

Nico scowled. 'But I'm family. I have a right to see him. I'll speak to Marjory – she'll give you a row.'

Macdonald blinked. '*DI Fleming* will tell you the same. Whoever you are, you can't go in.'

The boy's face became stormy and for a moment Macdonald thought he was about to throw a tantrum. Then with startling suddenness he smiled. 'You can tell me, then – did someone hit him and hit him with a stone until he was dead? Was there lots of blood?'

Macdonald heard a choking sound from Langlands and felt slightly queasy himself. Of course kids were ghouls, but this was going over the score.

'I think you should go back to the house,' he said firmly. 'No one's going to tell you anything and nothing's going to happen for a long, long time. Your mum's probably looking for you.'

'Her?' Nico said scornfully. 'She's so fried she wouldn't know if I was there or not. But I'll go back and ask Cris. He'll have to tell me because he's my servant now my granddad's dead.'

He swaggered off, leaving Langlands and Macdonald staring after him with dropped jaws.

'WELL, LOOK AT YOU!' Joss Hepburn said with his lazy smile as he came into the conference room. 'Could catch on – rainbow make-up!'

Her nerves taut as piano strings. Fleming said in her coolest, most professional voice, 'Morning, Joss. Would you like to sit down?'

His lips twitched as he stood surveying her teasingly from his considerable height. 'Why, thank you, Madge. Or should I call you Inspector Madge?' He sat down.

She mustn't smile. 'I have to ask you, please, what your movements were yesterday afternoon.'

'Of course. Easier if I demonstrate, perhaps.' Disconcertingly, he swung his long legs on to the chairs to his left, then lay down on his right side across the chairs to his right. His voice came from below the level of the table.

'I lay down on my bed. That was my first movement. My next movement – can you see? – was on to my back, like this. I lay that way for a bit, contemplating the ceiling and the ineffable tedium of being stuck here indefinitely. Then –' he appeared again – 'I guess I sat up and smoked, using this movement –' he mimed puffing at a cigarette – 'several cigarettes. Could be I dozed, briefly.' He put his head down on the table and made small, comic snoring snuffles, then sat up looking at her hopefully.

It was funny, but she remained stone-faced. 'Then?'

'Then I most likely got out my gui-tar,' Hepburn put on a Texan drawl, 'and just strummed awhile. I guess my only hope of an alibi, Inspector—' He broke off, laughing. 'No, I definitely can't. Inspector Madge is positively my best offer.'

'No need to call me anything,' Fleming said crisply. 'Since we're the only people in the room, I can make a guess that you're talking to me. Your only hope of an alibi . . . ?'

'Is if someone heard me. That's it. Otherwise, I could have popped up the hill and bashed Gillis's head in. Except, of course, that I didn't. Why should I? He was a mate, a professional contact. I'd nothing against the guy, except his tendency to want to tell me his problems. You may remember I was never much interested in other people's problems.'

Hepburn looked at her quizzically and Fleming heard herself say, with feeling, 'Oh, yes, I remember,' then had to make a swift retreat to safely professional territory. Recalling his earlier reaction to the question, she asked, 'Crozier's business – you were a bit vague about it when I asked you before. Were you involved in it?'

'Involved? No.' Again she sensed tension in the flat denial, as he went rapidly on, 'Gillis fixed up a lot of gigs for me, here and in

Europe, so he called in a favour to get me here to headline the pop festival. Bi-ig mistake, even before all this. I should never have agreed. Boredom ought to be on the proscribed list as a form of torture.'

Ignoring his attempt at distraction, Fleming asked if he had a key to Crozier's study.

'Of course not. Why should I?'

'Or see anyone going in there last night?'

'Afraid not.'

He hadn't asked why she wanted to know. Perhaps he was simply assuming she wouldn't tell him. Or perhaps—

The sound of the helicopter low overhead interrupted them. Feeling anyway that there was little more progress to be made and relieved to have kept control of the interview, more or less, Fleming got up and walked round the table to the door. 'I'll have to go. That's all I need to know for the moment. You're not intending to go back to the States immediately, are you?'

He joined her. 'Planning to confiscate my passport, Madge? No need – I'd welcome a chance to hang about and renew auld acquaintance. It's sort of an obligation on us Scots, isn't it – dear old Rabbie Burns!'

She held open the door for him. 'We would just prefer you didn't leave for the next few days, that's all. Someone will take contact details later.'

'But I would so much prefer to see you than someone,' Hepburn protested. 'I might have to pretend that I have important information I will only disclose to you personally.'

'It's called wasting police time.' She added deliberately a distancing, 'Sir. And we always ask for prosecution.'

Hepburn's laugh was one of unaffected amusement. He looked down at her, then very gently cupped her injured cheek. 'You put up a great front. But she's still there, you know, under the tidy hair and the smart professional clothes – my crazy Madge. If you ever want to let her out again, I'm sure one of your officers will know where to find me. OK?'

He left, and she shut the door and slumped against it. For a moment she had thought he was going to kiss her and she honestly didn't know how she would have reacted.

The wild, self-destructive girl she had once been was long gone, but as she stood there trying to calm her racing pulse, she felt all of a sudden bereft.

THERE WAS STILL one more check Fleming had to make before she left. She went through the under-stairs door at the back of the hall, hoping to find Pilapil in the kitchen. He wasn't there, but when she called his name, he appeared from a door off the corridor beyond it.

'Just one thing I wanted to ask you, Cris,' she said. 'Did anyone go into Mr Crozier's study last night?'

'I locked it and gave you the key.'

'That wasn't what I asked you. I guess there may have been other keys – who had them?'

'I'm not sure.'

He was looking everywhere except straight at her. Fleming was disappointed in him: she'd had him marked down as one of the good guys.

'I'm not going to let you get out of it by evasion, Cris. If you're not going to tell me the truth, it's going to have to be a direct, straightforward lie. I think you know that someone went into the study last night and removed a lot of papers. Who was it?'

Pilapil raised his head and looked her straight in the eye. 'I don't know anything about it, Inspector Fleming.'

She had invited him to do it, and he had. 'I'm sorry you said that. Very sorry. Are you sure you don't want to change your mind?'

His head went down but he said nothing. She had no alternative but to leave.

Chapter Eleven

LISA STEWART LOOKED at herself in the mirror above the basin in the ladies'. At the parting, her roots were beginning to show, sort of like her old self was creepily emerging again. Hastily, she fished out the comb from her jacket pocket to try to cover up the tell-tale red, though there wasn't much point, when the policewoman who had brought her here to the mortuary had seen through that slight disguise straight away.

Her mobile was in her pocket too, along with her purse, and she took it out, holding it away from her as if afraid it might bite. It must be all right now, surely . . . But so strong were its connections with distress that she had to take a deep, calming breath to steady her hands before she could switch it on.

Her eyes widened as the text message came up. It wasn't what she had feared it might be, but it wasn't what she was expecting either and she certainly wasn't ready to deal with it. She had to do some more deep breathing before she felt calm enough to emerge.

DC KERSHAW LED the way to the small waiting room. As they sat down, she explained the procedure, then added, 'And we'll need the name of someone else who knew your partner. In Scotland there has to be a second witness, you see, but it doesn't matter who – a relative, a friend, anyone who knew him.'

It was the first time Kershaw had escorted someone to perform an identification, but she had imagined they would be, if not invariably distraught, then certainly nervous. Perhaps Lisa was just very good at concealing her emotions, but she seemed disconcertingly self-possessed.

'I can't think of anyone.'

Kershaw was taken aback. 'No one who could identify him?'

'No.' Lisa, sitting with her hands clasped loosely in her lap, didn't seem to think this was odd.

'What about his family?'

'Don't think he had any. None he mentioned, at any rate.'

'It doesn't have to be someone close to him, just someone who could recognise him – a friend, a neighbour, even,' Kershaw suggested.

'We moved around a lot, and I didn't know any of his friends.'

Kershaw tried again. 'Where did he work, for instance?'

'He didn't, not when we were together.'

This really wasn't normal. 'Was he on the dole? Where did he go to sign on?'

Lisa looked completely blank. 'He never said. I paid for most things. I'd a bit of money from selling my flat.'

'Right. How long were you together, then?'

'A few months – I can't remember, exactly.'

Eventually Kershaw elicited the information that Lisa thought he'd done something with sound systems before, but had no luck with where he had lived before moving in with her.

What on earth had they talked about, Kershaw wondered, or was the girl being deliberately obstructive? And no friends, no acquaintances, even if they had been moving about? There was something very strange about Lisa Stewart.

A mortuary assistant came to summon them and they followed her through swing doors to a bare side room with a glass wall through which they could see a trolley covered by a sheet with a woman in white coveralls waiting beside it.

There was a strong smell of chemicals in this area; that was what hit you first. Kershaw, concentrating on Lisa's reaction, hadn't considered what her own might be. She rapidly had to switch to breathing through her mouth and she braced herself as the woman by the trolley, with a sympathetic look towards Lisa, folded back the sheet.

He had been quite a tall man, and older than Kershaw had expected – early forties, probably. The top of his head was covered by a white cloth, presumably to conceal an injury, but a lock of dark hair lay across his brow. His eyes were closed, and on the cold, waxy skin a shadow of stubble was visible. She had read somewhere that it went on growing after death and this, more even than the smell, made her feel squeamish. She looked away hastily.

Lisa was standing very still, staring at the body. Then she turned to Kershaw. 'Who is this?'

'Isn't it your partner?'

'Of course not! Lee's not as tall as this, and he's got short, spiked hair. And Lee's twenty-four – this man's old!'

Oh God, it was the wrong body! Kershaw shot an accusing look at the assistant, but the woman shook her head. 'I was there when the tag was checked. This is definitely the body that was found at 2 Rosscarron Cottages.'

'So it's not Lee Morrissey? You're sure?' Even as she spoke, Kershaw was aware it was an idiotic question.

'Of course I'm bloody sure!' Lisa's irritation was understandable. 'And before you ask me, I don't know who it is. It's nothing to do with me. You've made me go through this when I didn't need to – I told you my partner wasn't at the house. So can I go now?'

She shouldered her way past Kershaw and walked out, leaving the two women looking at each other, perplexed.

'So who is this, then?' the assistant asked.

Kershaw groaned. 'Blessed if I know. And what was he doing there? I can only tell you it's going to cause all sorts of trouble. They'll want top priority on the autopsy – can you pass on the message?'

ALICK BUCHAN LOOKED small and shrivelled, sitting there in the interview room. He eyed DI Fleming and DS Macdonald like some cornered animal waiting for the spade to come down and split its head.

As the helicopter brought them back, Fleming had watched him fidget, pick at his nails, sigh and cast hunted glances around him, looking as if he was feeling queasy – in stark contrast to Lisa Stewart, who had sat still as a waxwork model throughout. Buchan appeared still to be suffering the after-effects of his drinking bout: he stumbled coming out of the helicopter, and when Fleming shot out a hand to stop him falling, she could feel him shaking.

She had warned Macdonald not to go in hard, and indeed the man was such a pitiful object that it looked as if he'd crack at the first question. Buchan didn't even wait for that to come. With the recording formalities complete, he launched in before Fleming had finished saying, 'Now, Mr Buchan—'

'I ken it looks bad. I lost my temper, I'll give you that, and I'd had a wee drink. But I never done this – couldn't of! If you'd seen what I seen in the army . . . That was what set me going – the body.'

'Crozier's body?' Fleming asked, startled.

'No, no! I've telt you, I never done that. The body in the cottage – it was me was sent in. Not Crozier, oh, no! He doesn't soil his hands – still the officer, him, and I'm just the poor bloody infantry. Brought everything back, that woman in Ballymena – I was in the army then, just a lad. It was her head too.' He gave a shudder. 'Then I went away home to have a dram – you can't blame me. But I got angry, after. I went to the big house, I mind that, and I mind shouting at him. Then I lost my keys somehow and went to walk home, but I was that tired! Up half the night too. No wonder I was needing a wee rest, and it was raining, so I looked for a bit shelter. Nothing wrong with that, is there?'

Buchan's tone had become self-pitying and even slightly aggressive. Fleming suspected that when he wasn't scared, he might have quite a nasty streak. She decided to push him a little.

'So just by chance, you happened to fall asleep in the copse where Mr Crozier's body was found later?'

'I didn't know that, did I?' That was definitely aggression now. 'I went to sleep, woke up, walked home. That's the whole story. I never seen him. I never touched him.'

At a nod from Fleming, Macdonald took him minutely through the story again, but it was still the same in every essential, right down to the hint of resentment that Crozier had been inconsiderate enough to go and get himself killed just where Buchan was enjoying a refreshing nap. He was more than willing to have the clothes he had been wearing forensically examined, and even seemed disappointed to discover that taking a lie-detector test wasn't standard practice in a Galloway police investigation.

The news that he was free to go, for the present, he received with incredulous relief.

'Obviously thought we were going to throw him in the slammer straight away,' Macdonald said to Fleming, as they walked back from the interview room.

'To tell you the truth, I thought he'd make a confession on the spot. It's disappointing – there he was with the classic means, motive and opportunity, but the terrible thing is, I can't convince myself he was lying.'

'Maybe he did it when he was completely fou and he can't remember. Thinks he's telling the truth.' Macdonald's attempt at optimism was only half-hearted, and he added, 'Though he'd be clumsy, and surely there'd be traces on his clothes.'

'I'm not saying I'm ruling him out. He's got a massive chip on his shoulder and a grudge against the boss. But think about it – he's very drunk, he staggers up behind Crozier, armed with a stone, and the man doesn't hear him coming?'

'Throws it, maybe? Knocks the man out – a lucky shot? Then gives another couple of bashes to make sure?'

Fleming gave him a cynical look. 'It would have to be. Trying to throw anything in the state he was in would more likely pitch him forward on his nose. And if he had seen Crozier there, which would be more likely – that he'd sneak up behind him or confront him with some more abuse?'

Macdonald pulled a face. 'Put like that . . .'

They reached the foot of the stairs. 'We may have to think about Jamieson – pull out the stops to track him down,' Fleming said. 'Now, the briefing's at six, but I'd better see you and Ewan before that – say half five. And I think Kim should join the team too – I'm quite impressed with what I've seen.'

'Tam might be back by then. He said he'd just have a quick kip.' Macdonald grinned. 'Can't bear the thought of missing anything.'

'That would figure.' Fleming turned to go upstairs, then turned back. 'Andy, do you know what's wrong with Tam? There's something eating him, but he won't tell me what it is.'

Macdonald frowned. 'He's not been himself for a while. He's – he's sour, somehow. He's always had a sharp tongue, but he was never nasty. But now he's . . .' Macdonald stopped.

'It's unofficial,' Fleming said quickly. 'I'm worried about him.'

'He's got a real pick against Kim Kershaw – don't know why. OK, she didn't like Glasgow, but I've made the odd joke about the place myself, plenty times, and he just gives as good as he gets – better, usually.'

'I got the impression he resented her sending her daughter to boarding school, thinks it shows she doesn't care about her, and of course he's ultra-sensitive because it's always been a tragedy for him and Bunty that they couldn't have children. But for a working mother with crazy hours, it's actually a good solution.'

'Ewan thinks the kid's got problems,' Macdonald said. 'Don't know why – he's never forthcoming – but he's usually right.'

'He is, isn't he?' Fleming was thoughtful. 'Kim certainly didn't say that, but maybe she doesn't like talking about it. I'll put out feelers. Thanks, Andy.'

'It can't wait, you know that,' Cara Ryan was saying as Cris Pilapil opened the sitting-room door. She was standing looking down at her husband, who was slumped on a sofa with a half-full tumbler of whisky at his elbow, but now she broke off and left the room, looking through Pilapil as if he weren't there.

Glancing over his shoulder, Ryan scowled. 'Yes? What is it?'

Pilapil didn't come further into the room, as if he were reluctant to breathe the same air. 'I thought you'd like to know. Alex has vanished.'

'What did you want with my father-in-law's lawyer anyway?' Ryan's tone was sharp. 'And what do you mean, *vanished*? Do you mean you've been trying to contact him and failed?'

'No,' he said coldly. 'I mean, his girlfriend has been on the phone demanding to know where he is. He was meant to be here by now and she can't raise him on his mobile.'

'You may not have thought to tell her we've been cut off from the outside world, so he couldn't be here. And that beyond Watford there are plenty of dead spots. She probably doesn't know that.'

'I told her, yes. But it also seemed to me that since he wasn't here, *cut off from the outside world*,' Pilapil mimicked him, 'it was odd he couldn't find a phone to call his girlfriend. She's getting hysterical.'

'I didn't know Alex had a girlfriend. Must be a recent acquisition, and if she's the possessive type, he may well be trying to dump her. Quite a good method – come up to the wilds of Scotland and vanish.'

'He's *vanished*, yes. That's what I said. And she's talking about the police.'

Galvanised, Ryan sat up. 'Oh for God's sake! The police?'

Pilapil gave a thin smile. 'Yes, I thought you'd want to know that.'

'The last thing we need is the police mucking around at that end too. Stall her. Tell her he just phoned and he's gone on to do some business in Glasgow – no, better still, Inverness. I bet there are dead spots around Inverness – or at least she'll think there are.'

'I suppose we'll have to. But—'

Joss Hepburn appeared behind Pilapil, who stood aside to allow him into the room. He looked from one to the other. 'High-level conference?'

'Problems,' Ryan said grimly.

'Do I want to know?' Hepburn, pulling a face, went to sit down and noticed Ryan's whisky. 'That looks good. Fix me one of those, Cris.'

Pilapil snarled, 'I don't take orders from you, or anyone. Gillis was my boss and he's dead, though that doesn't seem to have bothered any of you much. I'm keeping things going for his sake, but for something like a drink, you can damn well get it yourself.'

Hepburn stared. 'Hey, hey! Whoa, man! It was a casual request, not an invitation to start World War III. Just tell me where to find it, and I'll bring you one too. You sound like you need it.'

Abashed, Pilapil bit his lip. 'Sorry. Sorry, Joss. I overreacted. I just get tired of being treated like a slave. But I'll get it – Scotch?'

He went out, and Hepburn turned to Ryan. 'Have you been winding him up? At a time like this it's really not smart to alienate one of the key players.'

Ryan brushed that aside. 'We can buy him. But we could have problems. Alex has disappeared.'

'Alex? He was meant to be coming here – doing a job for him, Gillis said.'

'Whatever it was, he's gone off the radar. And he seems to have picked up a neurotic girlfriend who's talking about getting in the police to look for him.'

'She can't,' Hepburn said flatly. 'Until we get that end tidied up it would be a disaster. We've got to find Alex before the cops start taking an interest there too.'

'Can't you take care of that? Persuade your Madge to lay off? Charm's your stock-in-trade, after all.'

Hepburn looked at him with dislike. 'I know this will take you totally out of your comfort zone, but she's straight.'

'Still got a soft spot for her? How touching. So if you can't hack it with charm, what about blackmail? Surely there must be one or two stories you could threaten to feed to the tabloids? "DI's Past as a Swinging Groupie"?'

'She'd probably tell me to publish and be damned. But if the worst came to the worst . . .' His mouth twisted in distaste as he looked at Ryan. 'You have no idea how much I regret having to associate with someone like you.'

Ryan gave his sneering smile. 'That's only because you tell yourself pretty stories about the kind of person you are and I rub your nose in reality. OK, you want to hit me – shooting the messenger, that would be.'

'I wouldn't. You probably carry a knife.' Hepburn stood up and moved away, though, as if despite what he said, the temptation was there. 'Anyway, I take it you've told all the others what's happened?'

'I told them we have this end covered, but they're not pleased.'

'They'll be even less pleased when they hear this about Alex. I hope to hell he decides to turn up soon.'

Pilapil came in, carrying a tumbler of whisky. He held it out to Hepburn.

'Thanks, Cris. But do you mind if I take it in the kitchen? I'd enjoy it more with better company.'

Ryan watched him go with an indifferent air, but once the door shut, he picked up his own glass and downed what was in it. The pulse in his temple was throbbing again.

'But it's my account, isn't it? Surely I can close it if I want to?'

'Sorry, Miss Stewart.' The young bank clerk ran a finger nervously round the inside of his shirt collar, which seemed unaccountably tighter than it had been when this interview had started. 'I've explained, it's a joint account, and to close it you need the signature of the other party.'

The woman was finding it hard to sound reasonable. He was afraid she'd lose it altogether.

'Look, it was my account originally. You can check back over your records and you'll see. I only put my boyfriend's name on it because we were living together, but now I've thrown him out and I don't want him to get my money.'

The words, 'More fool you,' suggested themselves, but he reverted instead to the formula: 'Sorry, but you need the other signature. He has to agree, you see.'

'But he won't, will he? He's going to go on drawing out money and spend it on the woman he's taken up with.'

She was definitely losing it now. The clerk's neck was sticky with sweat; he undid his tie a little, and suddenly inspiration struck. 'Your account allows money to be withdrawn on a single signature. You can't close the account, but you can withdraw the money yourself, before he does. You have another small savings account with us – you could pay it in there.'

For a terrible moment, he thought she was going to kiss him.

Lisa was relieved she had got to the bank before Lee had. Finding her money was still there, and putting it safely out of his reach, was security. Far too much had gone already, but there was enough so that Lisa wouldn't have to go to some well-meaning but interfering organisation for a hand-out. She'd had time to buy toilet things and a tote bag before the shops closed, and now she was in this cheap room in a small guest house in a Kirkluce backstreet.

It wasn't great. The skimpy curtains, wavy around the hem, were a depressing oatmeal, the bedcover was brown with orange stripes and the carpet was thin, synthetic and stained. There was no en suite, and the washbasin had been installed by someone who had mastered only the most basic principles of plumbing and joinery, but there was a little tub chair to sit on and she could lock the door and be on her own. Compared to her recent accommodation alongside the feed sacks, with every breath of dusty air she took begrudged, it was luxury enough.

Lisa was still trapped, though – trapped and exposed and vulnerable. The police knew where she was and had told her to stay there; if she disappeared, it would look suspicious, but she wouldn't feel safe until she could slip on her cloak of anonymity and vanish again. Though she'd always been traced before, now it was different. Gillis Crozier was dead. She only hoped that was enough to liberate her.

She sat down and took out the thought to have a look at it. She didn't contemplate the reality of bloody death; she had a talent for withdrawing from unpleasantness, honed in her childhood. It had been developed for self-preservation when, aged six, she'd found out from a helpful neighbour that her estranged father hadn't, as her mother had told her, died in a car accident, but in a brawl in prison. It came in handy later too, when her mother suffered her long, harrowing terminal illness. Lisa thought of it sometimes as having an armoured shell she could get inside, like a tortoise.

It hadn't protected her from the poison of Crozier's messages, but it had worked all right this morning, when she'd gone in to see the body. She'd been able to do what she had to do, untouched, and her thoughts now of Crozier, dead, were framed only in terms of her freedom. But she couldn't be sure – there were others who hated her as well. Could she only stop being afraid after they too were dead?

Lisa could hardly remember not being afraid.

It had been all right at first when they arrived at Rosscarron Cottages. That night there had been a beautiful sunset over the Solway Firth and they'd brought a wine box with them and drunk too much and got giggly and made love. It had almost been like the first days all over again.

But in the morning they woke to rain and after that it never seemed to stop. The windows of the cottage were small and it was dark and depressing. Then there were people close by to be avoided, renting the holiday cottage at the farther end. One week there were small children, and as they played on the shore she'd watch from the window with tears in her eyes. She loved tiny kids. They didn't judge you, reject you, lie to you.

She and Lee were getting on each other's nerves. The dream was disintegrating into permanent bickering.

The only good thing was, there were no messages. Crozier hadn't found her, hadn't thought to look so close at hand, most likely. Maybe Lee was right – this was the way to handle it. And supposing Crozier managed to kill her here, without leaving a trace – it would be over then, wouldn't it? Sometimes she thought that would be better than having to live in permanent fear.

Then Crozier at last arrived at Rosscarron House. There were posters everywhere for the Rosscarron Festival the following week.

She'd wanted to go and confront him immediately. Lee wouldn't. She could tell he was making excuses; she didn't know why, and he wouldn't admit that he was. They had one of their worst ever rows, with her screaming and throwing things. If he hadn't dodged her granny's cast-iron frying pan, Lee would have been on a trolley in the mortuary too.

All he would say was that the guy would be busy, wouldn't want to be bothered at the moment. 'You want to get him in a good mood, don't you? Talk him round?' It sounded reasonable enough, but somehow she knew he'd some sort of plan he wouldn't tell her about. He denied it and got angrier than ever when she asked.

He went off in the car most days – for a bit of personal space, he said. Which left nothing for her to do but walk, walk and think, and when it was even briefly dry, go up to the seat on the bluff above the cottages and try to tell herself that one day it would be all right.

She'd slept badly ever since Crozier arrived. Then came the night when she hardly slept at all, sitting downstairs in the little sitting room, wrapped in a comforter that had belonged to her grandmother.

What did Lee do when he drove away from the cottage? He wasn't going to the pub – she would have smelled beer on his breath. He couldn't be meeting anyone – he didn't know anyone around here.

At last it came to her. You couldn't email from here. She knew there was an Internet café in Kirkcudbright.

It was Thursday morning. Lee had gone off in the car, and when he came back, she was ready for him. 'There's a couple of things I need in town,' she said, and used his own excuse about personal space when he offered to come with her, as he usually did when they went shopping.

It wasn't hard to find out what was going on. He had an email account under the name Jazza, for some reason, and he didn't know

she'd happened to see him keying in the password once. She remembered it, and keyed it in now.

And there it was, the evidence of her own folly. She spooled back
through all the emails sent to 'Tanya' – dozens of them, over these
last few months – and opened some at random. He was working
abroad, was he, but would be coming back soon? It hurt that Lee –
Jazza! – was writing words of love he'd never used to her, but what
stabbed her to the heart was his cruel description of the 'colleague'
he was always complaining about, a stupid, ugly, neurotic woman,
pop-eyed and overweight.

She opened the most recent one. 'Not long now,' it finished.
What did that mean? Maybe it just meant once he had sorted out
Lisa's problem with Crozier, but somehow it didn't sound like that.
It sounded as if he had a job to do and it gave her a sick, terrified
feeling inside.

She was so angry she didn't bother to read Tanya's responses, or
any of the other emails, and she had worked herself up into a furious rage by the time she got back to Rosscarron. Better to rage than
to give way to panic and despair.

But fear lurked, like a rat gnawing away in the corner of her
mind. Why had he persuaded her to come here, and what was he
going to do?

And Lisa still didn't know the answer, still felt she was blun-
dering about in the dark. And the text – what was that about? She
fished out the phone, read it again and sat considering it for a long
time. At last, very deliberately, she pressed 'Delete', followed by
'Compose.'

FROWNING AT HER computer screen in concentration and tapping
her finger on her front teeth, Fleming was reading the reports that

had come in when there was a knock on the door and DC Kershaw appeared, standing on the threshold as if uncertain of her welcome.

'Sorry to bother you, boss, but I wanted a word ahead of the meeting, if that's OK?'

'Fine. Take a seat.' Fleming shut down the program and swung her chair round to face Kershaw. 'Was Lisa Stewart all right about making the identification?'

'She didn't, I'm afraid.'

'Oh dear.' Fleming pulled a face. 'Still, can't blame her for getting cold feet, I suppose. Not easy, to do that.'

'Sorry, no. She didn't get cold feet – just the opposite, in fact. She was so calm it was weird. She just went in, looked at the body and said it wasn't her boyfriend.'

'*Wasn't?* Who was it, then?'

Kershaw shrugged. 'No idea. She said she didn't know, had never seen him before, couldn't think why he should have been in her house. Absolutely flat – that was all there was to it. Nothing to do with her.'

'I'm struggling to get a handle on this,' Fleming said. 'A completely unconnected man somehow found his way into her house and managed to get himself caught up in a landslide which killed him – that's the story?'

'As far as there is one. I talked to Lisa afterwards and she was adamant. She'd told us her boyfriend wasn't there, that he'd been two-timing her and she'd thrown him out. He wasn't there, just as she said, and because we didn't believe her, we'd put her through an unnecessary ordeal – though I have to say she didn't show much sign of being upset. Quite aggressive, to be honest. After the trial there were claims she had issues with anger management and I'd believe that.'

'I don't remember a lot about that case, except that when she was acquitted, there was a fuss because if it wasn't her, it had to be the baby's brother,' Fleming said. 'And to tell you the truth, having observed Nico Ryan at close quarters, I wouldn't find it hard to believe.'

Kershaw was unconvinced. 'There's something weird about her,' she insisted. 'Very stand-offish. I asked her if she needed somewhere to stay, and told her Dr Forbes, her neighbour, had suggested she went to the hotel she's staying in herself – even offered to pay for her, if that was a problem – but she turned that down flat. Didn't even seem grateful. She's booked herself into a guest house in Kirkluce.

'Anyway, I told them at the mortuary that the autopsy should be high priority and I just wanted to clear that with you.'

'Of course. We'll need every scrap of information as soon as possible to try to establish identity. I wonder if there's a report in on the clothes already? Hang on . . .' Fleming turned to the computer again. 'Here we are.' She read the list, then looked up, frowning. 'That's an odd thing. He was wearing a casual shirt and trousers. Nothing in the pockets – nothing at all. If he wasn't wearing a jacket, on a day when it was coming down stair-rods, he must have driven there. So where are his car keys?'

'He could have put them down on a table when he came in,' Kershaw suggested.

'Yes, but no money, no wallet? You don't go into someone's house and empty out your pockets, even if you're a regular visitor, which allegedly he wasn't.'

'His car would be there too, presumably,' Kershaw pointed out.

'Yes, but under a few tons of rubble from the cliff face. Remote rural areas are way down the priority list for the council, so it'll probably be weeks before they get round to clearing it. I think I might give the mortuary a call, find out when we can expect a full report.'

Kershaw waited as Fleming was put through, then heard her say, 'Oh, better still. I'll hold.' She mouthed, 'The pathologist wants to speak to me himself. Hello? Yes, Marjory Fleming here.'

She listened intently, her face registering shock. Then she said, 'I – I see. Yes, the report just as soon as you can. Thanks.'

She put the phone down and stared at it for a second. 'I'm feeling a bit stunned. He did say after a cursory examination at the site that the fatal injury wasn't from a falling beam and now he's had a better look. He hasn't had time to complete the autopsy, but the cause of death was definitely a blow to the base of the skull with some heavy object, about an inch and a half deep. Mr X was murdered.'

Kershaw's eyes narrowed. 'Was he indeed,' she said slowly. 'Look, I know this is going to sound crazy, but . . . No jacket, no wallet, no keys. That would only be normal for someone living in the house.

'It seemed really strange that when I asked Lisa Stewart for a contact to do the second ID, she said she couldn't think of anyone – didn't know his family, didn't know his friends or where he worked, hadn't any neighbours because they'd moved about. I'm just beginning to wonder about Lisa Stewart. Suppose she was lying. Suppose it had been her boyfriend, murdered – who would be our prime suspect?'

Fleming looked thoughtful. 'When you put it like that . . . I was going to tell you all at the meeting that after the interview with

Buchan I seriously doubt if he's our man. And what was Lisa Stewart doing, hanging around in the vicinity of a family she would have had every reason to avoid?'

'Gillis Crozier made a death threat after she was acquitted,' Kershaw said. 'The bereaved grandfather – no one thought a lot about it, really. But if she believed she was in danger, it wouldn't be a bad motive for killing him.'

'I think,' Fleming said grimly, 'we need to take a much closer look at Miss Lisa Stewart.'

Chapter Twelve

PERCHED ON THE edge of the table at the back of DI Fleming's office, behind the chairs where his three colleagues were seated, Tam MacNee listened to DC Kershaw expounding her theory, his lip curling but only inwardly. He'd no appetite for another run-in with Big Marge.

The others might be impressed, but he wasn't. Kershaw had maybe shown that Stewart had a motive for killing Crozier, right enough, but in his view the rest of it was far-fetched, and not worth the effort of dragging it along to the party.

He'd no time for Kershaw anyway, snotty cow! Glasgow wasn't good enough for her and neither, obviously, was he – and her poor kid, bundled off to strangers! That told you all you needed to know.

MacNee was in kind of a black mood anyway. To add to his troubles, he was suffering the after-effects of his exertions in cold water as well as lack of sleep. Being indestructible was one of his small vanities, but today he was just feeling wabbit. It was a sign of age, probably, to be so wiped out, and that didn't cheer him either.

At least his worrying yesterday had been unnecessary. The animals were fine: his neighbour had done the needful, noticing that his car wasn't back. She was a treasure, that woman, neighbourly without being nebby. When she asked how Bunty was and he said, 'Fine,' she'd left it at that.

Kershaw was getting a lot of support now. There was Campbell, even, usually the voice of common sense, piping up with, 'If she could murder a wee baby, her ex would hardly be a problem.'

'If !' MacNee said. It came out more aggressively than he had meant it to and the three heads turned.

Across the desk, Fleming frowned. 'Yes, Tam?'

'Stewart got acquitted, right? Or doesn't that count any more, if someone's got a hunch she was guilty after all? I've seen enough of Nico Ryan to put money on him being happy to take his wee sister outside and leave her there, just for a laugh. That one's a bawbee short of a shilling.'

'I'll give you that,' Fleming acknowledged, and Macdonald chimed in with an account of his macabre conversation with the child.

'There you are,' MacNee said triumphantly. Without realising he was doing it, he shifted on the table to move closer to the group.

Kershaw's lips tightened. 'You're not actually suggesting that the kid went out and bludgeoned his grandfather to death? For heaven's sake—'

'Never said that, did I?' MacNee could feel his hackles rising. 'All I'm suggesting is that you're making a lot out of there being no car keys or wallet on the body in the cottage. Like if you killed someone you'd leave ID to help us out? And no jacket's the giveaway – you wouldn't have walked even a hundred yards on Wednesday without a jacket.

'We're not needing fancy theories when there's an obvious suspect – the man who nearly killed the both of us.' He gestured towards himself and Fleming.

'Jamieson, assuming he sabotaged the bridge,' she said slowly. 'Certainly . . .'

'Well, let's put it this way.' MacNee was leaning forward now as he urged his point. 'Whoever did cut through the supports of that bridge was prepared to take lives and I'm saying I doubt if Lisa Stewart just happened to be carrying a chainsaw when she escaped the landslide.

'And the man they found in her house – she said from the start it wasn't her boyfriend, because he'd left. Your report' – he nodded towards Kershaw – 'even said the neighbour saw him leave with a suitcase. So when Stewart looks at the body and says it isn't the boyfriend, suddenly she's lying? If you hadn't chosen to believe the jury got it wrong – after listening to the whole case, remember – she wouldn't be in the frame at all, would she?'

Kershaw's face crimsoned. 'Look, MacNee—'

'Hold it right there,' Fleming said. 'Both of you.'

Kershaw looked down at her lap. MacNee held the inspector's gaze defiantly for a moment, but then his eyes dropped too.

'Correct me if I'm wrong,' she said coldly, 'but I was under the impression this was a team and that discussions like this are a chance to throw around ideas, not a competition to see who's got the best one and to hack down anyone who thinks differently. If anyone starts getting possessive about a theory, the whole thing's pointless. Maybe it's Stewart's partner, maybe it isn't, but—'

'If it's not, he's got to be somewhere else,' Campbell put in.

'Good point. Of course he does. We can post an alert and appeal for him to get in touch, and that would settle it. You deal with that,

Ewan.' Fleming glanced at her watch and got up. 'Time we went down for the briefing. But I'm tasking you two now. Kim, I want you to take on tracking down Jamieson. Tam, you can check out Lisa Stewart – get the number of Morrissey's car while you're at it. And both of you can grow up.' She swept out.

In an awkward silence, Campbell looked from one to the other sardonically. 'That's you telt, eh?' he said, as he and Macdonald followed Big Marge out.

MacNee didn't look at Kershaw, but he suspected that, like him, she was grinding her teeth.

NICO RYAN WAS jumping on and off one of the sofas in the sitting room. U2's *Rattle and Hum* was playing over the speakers and Nico was singing tunelessly along to 'Helter Skelter' now. He must, his father decided irritably, be tone deaf.

Cara was sitting beside Declan on a sofa at the other end of the room with a half-smile on her face, apparently oblivious. She could sit like that for hours, which was beginning to get on Declan's nerves too.

'Cara!' he said loudly. She didn't respond and he tugged at her hand. 'Hello-o? Anybody there?'

She turned her head slowly. 'Of course I am.'

'Can't you find something for Nico to do? He's driving me crazy.'

'He's got something to do.' She gestured to the child, now dancing to the music with extravagant abandon. 'He likes it.'

Declan drew a deep breath. 'I don't. Look, we've got a problem here. He's had his medication but he's still going wild because he's bored out of his skull. You know I need a clear head just now – how can I think with that going on all the time? If you won't make an effort to occupy him, why don't we get in a local girl, or a boy, better still, who could take him out, play football, tire him out—'

'No!' Suddenly the passive blue eyes were blazing. 'No! How could you even say those words? You know what happened.'

Declan sighed, running his hands through his hair. 'Of course I frigging know. But he's worse up here, where there's nothing for him, no school or anything.'

'We can't leave. Not yet.'

'I know that too. Of course I do. For a start, the police want us here, and what they want, they get, right?'

'Of course,' Cara said, but he could see she had drifted away as she usually did when she had no more to say.

In sudden irritation, Declan seized the remote control and killed the music. Nico's face turned puce with rage.

'Why did you do that?' he yelled, and launched himself at his father, swearing and kicking, while Declan, grim-faced, held him off.

Cara looked at her son, raising her voice a little to be heard. 'You know Mummy doesn't like to hear swear words, darling.' Then she turned to Declan, holding out her hand. 'Give me that. Nico likes the music.'

With a helpless shrug he gave it to her and left the room.

Nico's tantrum stopped as suddenly as if a switch had been flicked. Smirking, he started dancing again as 'Van Diemen's Land' began.

THE RAIN HAD come on again. It should still have been light, but the sky was leaden grey and a heavy dusk had fallen as Marjory Fleming, feeling limp with exhaustion, turned on to the Mains of Craigie track.

The house, she always thought, looked like a child's drawing with its two windows up, two down, and the seldom-used front door in the middle. Tonight, with most of the windows lit, it looked so cosy and welcoming and, well, normal, that weak tears came to her eyes.

I must be in a bad way, she reflected, as she drove round to park in the yard by the back door. Get a grip, woman!

But as Marjory got out of the car and Bill's dear, familiar figure appeared at the back door to greet her, with Meg the collie bounding around giving welcoming barks, she had to sniff and gulp before she could greet him with a smile.

He looked at her face with dismay. 'For heaven's sake, lassie, what have they been doing to you? You're looking like the wrath of God!'

'There's nothing like a compliment to make a woman feel better – and that's nothing like a compliment,' she joked, as he hugged her cautiously. 'It's not as bad as it looks.'

'I can only hope not,' Bill said, as they walked along to the kitchen. 'Seriously, though, how are you feeling?'

Awful, was the honest reply. 'I've – I've felt better,' she said.

'I see. Awful,' Bill said. 'You're going straight to your bed. Have you seen a doctor?'

'No need, honestly. It was just a bash on the head and now I'm shattered. It's been a tough couple of days.'

'You said you were snowed under when you phoned, and it's on the news this evening. What's—'

Cat appeared from the hall as he spoke. 'You're late, Mum. Wow! You look terrible!'

'Gee, thanks!' Marjory said.

'I'm sending Mum to bed,' Bill said. 'There's soup left, isn't there, Cat? Just heat it up and put it on a tray. I'll bring her a dram – she's looking as if she needs it.'

'You could say,' Marjory said with feeling. 'Is Cammie in his room? I'll look in on my way to bed.'

He hadn't come down to see her, as Cat had. As Marjory climbed the stairs, which seemed much steeper than usual tonight, she told herself not to be oversensitive, but their relationship had been dented earlier this year when Cameron had felt she put her work before her family. With a certain justice, she sometimes thought guiltily.

However, when she opened his door, Cammie – a big lad now, with his father's build and his mother's dark colouring – was lying on his bed, plugged into an iPod and reading a rugby magazine. He looked up with a grin, which changed to concern as he saw her technicolour face.

Warmed, she reassured him, said goodnight, then dragged herself to bed, sighing with satisfaction as she lay down. It was wonderful to be back in her own room, with the photos of her children on the dressing table and the curtains that were a little faded and the bedside light with the cut paper shade that fell off every so often but which she refused to replace because it was so pretty, and her own bed – not even the expensive mattress at Rosscarron House was as comfortable as her own bed, which had just the slightest hollow where she always lay. And she was safely distanced from the investigation; she wouldn't have to lock the door and lie wondering who might be prowling in the corridor outside.

Marjory thrust the thought from her mind as Cat came in and set a tray on her knees. She realised she was very hungry indeed. When had she last eaten? She couldn't remember.

'Granny's been here, obviously,' she said, spooning up the thick Scotch broth. 'How is she?'

'Oh, she's having a fine time,' Cat assured her. 'Karolina keeps trying to do the housework and stuff that she's paid to do, but Gran keeps clucking over her – forcing her to go and rest, though it's months till the baby's due. Just an excuse to take over, I reckon.'

Marjory shook her head. 'She's an awful woman. Still, if it makes her happy and it isn't driving Karolina mad . . . Oh, that looks good too, Bill!'

Bill smiled down at her, setting two glasses and a bottle of Bladnoch on the bedside table. 'So, tell us what's been going on.'

'Wait!' Cat interrupted. 'I've got to know. Did you get to meet Joshua?'

A mouthful of soup went down the wrong way and Marjory spluttered. Damn! She should have been prepared for that question.

'Well, yes,' she said, as lightly as she could. 'The weirdest thing, Bill – you know who this "Joshua" turned out to be? None other than Joss Hepburn!'

Bill, unscrewing the cap on the whisky bottle, froze. 'Joss Hepburn?'

'Yes. Extraordinary, or what?'

Oblivious to the atmosphere, Cat stared at her mother. 'You mean, you know *Joshua*?'

'Knew,' Marjory said, too hastily. 'We both knew him when we were young.'

'Why didn't you tell me?' Cat demanded. 'And how come you knew him, anyway?'

'I'd no idea he was your Joshua. He came from round here. He had a band called Electric Earthquake and we all used to go to the gigs.'

'Oh wow!' Cat said reverently.

Bill's voice was carefully neutral. 'And how is he?'

'Oh, much the same. Still got a crooked nose.' Marjory hoped this might raise a smile, but Bill only nodded.

'Tell me what he's really like,' Cat begged.

Marjory simply didn't feel strong enough for the sort of careful weighing of every word that this conversation would need. She had finished her soup; she gave a huge yawn.

'Quite honestly, I don't want to go through it all tonight. I'm shattered, and I have to be in early tomorrow. I'm not sure I even want a drink after all, if you don't mind.'

'Of course not.' Bill collected up the unused glasses. 'You get some sleep. I'll try not to wake you when I come up.'

Cat looked wistful. 'OK. But you promise you'll tell me all about him tomorrow?'

'Mmm,' Marjory said. 'Just put the light off, will you?'

As they left the room, Marjory heard Cat say to her father, 'You and Mum had some well cool friends, didn't you?' and winced.

Despite her tiredness, she didn't sleep immediately. There had been so much else going on that she'd given very little thought to Bill's reaction to her meeting Joss again, except to reflect fleetingly that, while he might still be sensitive, surely after all these years of happy marriage he could hardly doubt her enduring love. It had occurred to her it might be wise to plan how to present this, but with one thing and another she'd forgotten.

But she hadn't forgotten how it had been after that horrible night when Joss showed clearly what he was and when Bill, playing knight in shining armour, had felled him: how she had felt revulsion for Joss and everything he represented, how she had felt almost physically sickened by the squalor of it all. How badly it had hurt.

'Stay me with flagons, comfort me with apples.' She remembered romantically quoting the Song of Solomon to Bill some time later, in her longing for something cleaner, more wholesome, to use that old-fashioned word. He had smiled quietly, and on their next date had brought her the biggest red apple she had ever seen, polished to a brilliant shine.

'But I hope,' he said, completing the quotation, 'that you're not altogether "sick of love". It would be very disappointing.'

Marjory had laughed and kissed him, though there was a misunderstanding there. 'Of', in the phrase, meant 'from'; her love for Joss was a malady from which she had not then recovered. But afterwards she did. Of course she did. She had loved Bill ever since then. She had loved him because—

Should you love someone *because*? Or was it more in the nature of love to love *despite*? The rebel thought made her shudder.

But then, *because* Joss was a total bastard, being 'in love' with him hadn't been enough – not nearly. And she loved Bill, with all his virtues, *despite* Joss's mockery of them, then and now.

Marjory was into her forties. Her hair, which had once had a riotous life of its own, had long ago been tamed. She wore neat, well-cut trouser suits to work. She wore jeans and sweaters when she was off duty. She couldn't remember the last time she had done something wild and irresponsible.

Grown-ups didn't. But she wasn't entirely sure she wanted to be grown up. Not yet.

Marjory heard Bill's footsteps on the stairs, the cautious way he opened the door. The cautious, *loving* way he was trying not to wake her. She shut her eyes and pretended to be asleep.

Saturday, 22 July

THE SMELL IN the Balmoral Guest House lounge almost made DS MacNee gag: a smell compounded of stale air, dust and, he suspected, mice. The beady eyes of Mrs Wishart the proprietor were out on stalks, and though she had left after fetching Lisa Stewart from her room, MacNee suspected she was next door with a glass pressed to the wall.

'This is just a wee informal chat,' he said to Lisa, smiling at her, though not too broadly, MacNee's gap-toothed grin having been known to have a less than reassuring effect. He had to show her he was on her side, which was, of course, on the basis of his dispassionate analysis of the facts and nothing at all to do with DC Kershaw. He could only hope that in going after Jamieson, Kershaw was being equally scrupulous.

Lisa didn't smile back. She sat on the fake leather sofa, just looking at him with those funny, round eyes, which didn't give any hint of what she was feeling. MacNee began to see what Kershaw meant about the girl being odd.

He elicited that Lisa was feeling all right, that she'd bought some T-shirts and stuff, and that she didn't know if her cottage was insured. She gave him the number of Lee Morrissey's car. She volunteered nothing, only waiting calmly for the next question.

They could go through the facts again, but MacNee hadn't time to waste on a repetition of what he knew already. He stood up.

'Is there a garden or anything? The sun's out for the moment at least, and this room stinks.'

For the first time, Lisa responded. 'The whole place stinks, but it's cheap. There's a yard out the back – it's car parking mostly, but there's a couple of seats and a bit of grass.'

'That'll do me.'

As they walked out of the front door and through the passageway at the side of the house, MacNee reviewed his tactics. He needed a story from her, not a statement, but the bleak yard at the back wasn't conducive either to a cosy chat. There were a couple of cars parked there, and another half dismantled, being repaired, but judging from the rusted parts and tools scattered about, not recently. As he sat down on a weather-stained white plastic chair on the scrubby strip of grass, kicking aside some litter blown in off the street, he said, 'I'm going to tell you something, Lisa. We're not convinced you've been telling us the truth.'

Her hands gripped at the arms of the chair. 'What about?'

'You said the body you looked at yesterday wasn't your partner. Are you sticking to that?'

Lisa looked at him in blank incomprehension. 'Sticking to it? What do you mean?'

'We've only your word that it isn't your partner.'

She burst into laughter, laughter tinged with anger. 'I can't believe you're asking me that! Lee was twenty years younger than that man, just for a start. And he wasn't tall, and he had short hair, and— Oh, this is the most stupid thing I ever heard of!'

'Have you a photo of him?'

'I don't have a camera.'

'What about your mobile?'

'I lost that as well as everything else.'

The reply came readily enough, but MacNee was almost sure Lisa was lying. Surely bloody Kershaw wasn't right after all?

'You said there wasn't anyone who could identify him. That's kind of odd – not knowing anyone.'

He sensed her relaxing. 'Oh, is that what this is about? How ridiculous! You don't understand – we didn't get to know people because we kept moving, that's all.'

'Why?'

'*Why?*' Lisa stumbled over the word, as if it was a question she hadn't thought he would ask. 'Well, we – we just didn't find the right place. If it's any business of yours.'

'Oh, it's our business, right enough.' MacNee abandoned the idea of a cosy chat. 'We're investigating the murder of two men. And one, you say, isn't your boyfriend. Let's talk about the other one, then. Gillis Crozier.'

She was pale anyway, but even the slight colour in her cheeks vanished. 'Gillis Crozier?' Her attempt to sound offhand was pathetic.

'Oh, you remember him, I'm sure. The grandfather of the baby who died. The guy who threatened to kill you too.'

His sarcasm produced a flash of temper. 'Of course I remember him!' she snapped. 'But what he said – he was just upset. It didn't mean anything.'

'That's a very mature attitude, Lisa. So all the moving wasn't an attempt to cover your tracks so he couldn't find you?'

It took her a moment to reply. 'It wasn't him – nothing to do with him. It – it was the press. And people – I wouldn't have harmed a hair on Poppy's head, but thanks to the press, and to the police, like you,' – she shot him a look of hatred – 'lots of people still think I did it. I've had to dye my hair because if I'm recognised, total strangers will come up and give me abuse. Why do you think Lee and I didn't get to know anyone? He was the one person in the world I could trust – only I couldn't trust him, after all. He was – he was using me.'

Lisa's eyes had filled with tears. MacNee never liked it when women cried. He said quickly, 'Right, right. I understand that. There's a call going out for him now, so maybe he'll contact us and we can put this one to rest.

'There's just one more thing I need to ask you. You were hiding from everyone. You were afraid people would be unkind to you. How come you decided to live here, when anytime you went out, you could bump into the family?'

She floundered. 'Well, I didn't think I would – I thought I could just avoid them. I didn't go out much. Lee did most of the shopping, you see.' Then, with more conviction, she said, 'Why shouldn't I? I had my granny's cottage and I wanted to live in it. They don't own the place, however much money they have.'

Her synthetic indignation didn't convince MacNee. She wasn't telling him the truth. 'I still have to ask you where you were on Thursday afternoon, when Gillis Crozier was murdered.'

There was a brief silence. She sat back on the grubby plastic chair, as if she were withdrawing from him mentally as well as physically. When she spoke, she sounded detached.

'I don't know when he was murdered.'

Neither did they, exactly, MacNee reflected. You'd think by now, with all their grand technology, they'd be able to say, 'Twenty past five, give or take ten minutes,' but not a chance. 'Just tell me what you did between two o'clock and eight in the evening.'

'I was at the Buchans' cottage except when I took the baby for a walk.'

'Where did you walk to?'

'You don't walk *to* anywhere, out there. You just walk about.'

'You could walk *to* Rosscarron House. To where Mr Crozier was *murdered*.' MacNee emphasised the word. It had got a definite reaction last time, but now she just looked at him with cold eyes.

'I wasn't near the house. You can't prove I was. Because I wasn't.'

MacNee got no further after that. He left Lisa sitting calmly, contemplating a couple of cars and the rubbish. To his intense irritation, he found himself in agreement with Kershaw that Lisa Stewart had only a passing acquaintance with openness and honesty.

And to quote the wise words of the Bard, 'There's none ever feared that the truth would be heard, but they whom the truth wad indict.'

So THAT WAS it, then. The end.

Douglas Jamieson looked at the hot tap on his bathroom basin, opened to its fullest extent but yielding not a drop of water. The supply from the tank, which had actually lasted longer than he expected, had run out and it was decision time.

In any case, his neighbours had started to return. From behind the curtains, he'd seen the Watsons next door come ploughing through the stinking mud left behind by the retreating waters. She was crying; he had a comforting arm round her shoulders, but he looked pale and shaken himself. A little later they had knocked on his broken front door and called his name, but Douglas had kept very still until they went.

He'd seen an official-looking young man with a clipboard at one of the other houses – an insurance assessor, no doubt. Soon the clean-up would start.

And the police would return too. He couldn't hide here for ever, not without water. Anyway, what would be the point?

Douglas had made his preparations already, against the day when he would find he had enough courage to take the only way out. Or rather, when he found he was more afraid of staying alive than of dying.

He'd reached that point. He could see what lay ahead of him with terrible clarity; to be dead would be better than that. He just didn't much fancy the process.

Throughout her agonising illness, Margaret had a shining belief that, in the end, all would be well and they would be together again. Douglas longed for that, with all his heart and soul, but he had never had her gift of faith.

Suppose she was right about the hereafter. He had been wicked, very wicked, and now he was preparing to take his own life. Suppose her God punished him with oblivion, or worse? But then, how could Margaret be happy in cold eternity without him? Her God, as she saw Him, was merciful. Perhaps . . .

Anyway, he wasn't going to huddle here to be flushed out, like a cornered rat. Whisky was an old, familiar friend, and Margaret's sleeping pills would put him out quickly. They were waiting for him, on the tray on the dressing table.

Douglas picked them up, with a glass, and went over to the bed. He straightened the covers before he lay down; he could almost hear Margaret's anxious voice, 'Did you leave everything tidy?' His eyes were wet with tears as he took the first handful of pills.

CAMPBELL HAD SAID Jamieson wasn't at his house, but DC Kershaw couldn't think where else to start. She had a search warrant in her pocket, and if he wasn't there, perhaps she could find something to suggest a follow-up.

As she parked her car, looking with disgust at the sea of mud, the revolting stench greeted her. She had heavy boots with her, but she wouldn't much enjoy sharing the car with them afterwards.

There were some signs of activity at the site: windows open at one of the houses, and a van and another couple of cars beside where she herself had parked. Once she'd had a look around Jamieson's house, at least there would be people to talk to who might know where he was likely to have gone.

Kershaw hadn't wanted to do this, but since she had no alternative she was determined to succeed. MacNee would sneer if she failed, even if there was no way he'd have been able to find the man if she couldn't. She wondered how he was getting on with his little friend Lisa: giving her the benefit of the doubt, probably, just from spite.

The door to Jamieson's house had been kicked in – by Campbell, she guessed, unless some enterprising tealeaf had thought of doing a spot of looting. For form's sake, she knocked on the door and called, but there was no answer.

Looking around what had been a trim, comfortable and cherished house, Kershaw felt a surge of pity for the man, whatever he had done. And certainly, if you believed someone's greed had done this to you – wrecked your dream home, ruined everything you had worked for all your life – you might well be angry enough to sabotage his music festival and hit him over the head. She had to be honest and admit that MacNee was right about that, at least.

Campbell had said there were signs that the man had been living in the master bedroom at one stage, anyway, so that was where she headed first.

It was a pleasant room, a bit fussy, with flowery curtains on the bay window and a dressing table with a frilly flounce. And he was there, lying on the bed with a glass at his side, which had spilled whisky on to the rose-patterned cover.

At first Kershaw thought he was dead, but when she bent over him, there was still a thready breath. She got out her mobile, looked at it, swore, then ran out of the house, back to the radio in the car.

Suicide was as good as an admission of guilt. Tam MacNee could be right after all. Damn, damn, damn!

Chapter Thirteen

AFTER DS MACNEE had left, Lisa Stewart jumped up. She was churning inside, as if the panic she had managed to control was building up and would have to burst out in a scream, like the steam from a pressure cooker. She felt as if she'd been trussed up in sticky threads, a Bilbo Baggins in a Mirkwood of her own making, caught in a web of tiny lies.

The lies about Crozier were straightforward enough. If Lisa had admitted Crozier was stalking her, that scary little man with the menacing smile would have had the handcuffs out before you could say, 'Where's the evidence?' He suspected she had killed him, she could tell.

He'd rattled her, pulled her out of her safe shell, exposing her confusion and anger. It was only with a gigantic effort of will that she had drawn herself back into the detached state where it was all happening *out there*, not *in here*. She was paying for it now with shaking hands and a pounding heart.

But the other, smaller lies – she'd have to remember precisely what she'd said – like the baby being with her that afternoon. It had sounded better, suggested improbability – who would take a baby with them if they meant to attack someone? – and it was a safe enough lie: they probably wouldn't ask Maidie, and if they did, she probably wouldn't remember.

And having lost her mobile – she fingered it now in her pocket. She almost wished that she had. Perhaps she should have ignored the message, pretended it was indeed lost. But at the moment she was stumbling around in scary darkness, and this was her only chance to make sense of what had been happening, of getting answers to the questions whirling round in her head, questions that she should have asked long ago.

She wasn't a fool. She could smell danger, but even now, she couldn't quite believe that it would come to *that*.

'So,' DI FLEMING said, 'the position is that we're looking for Jamieson, we have an APB out for Lee Morrissey, and we're keeping an open mind on everything else. It's natural that at this stage we should have to follow up several lines of enquiry.'

She sensed she wasn't taking Superintendent Bailey with her. The frown lines were running right up into his bald head.

'That's all very well, Marjory,' he was saying unhappily, 'but I told the chief constable it looked an open-and-shut.'

Fleming almost groaned aloud. It was her own fault, of course: she'd talked up the case against Buchan to give herself breathing space, and she was paying now for that short-term gain.

'We haven't ruled him out completely, of course, but after questioning him, I'm not optimistic. Obviously we're still waiting for full forensic details, but I've had an interim report saying that the SOCOs found a flattened area in the bracken right at the bottom of the spinney, consonant with someone having lain down there. There's no sign of broken vegetation leading from there up into the copse, but there are signs that someone came from the top and waited concealed close to where Crozier was attacked, though it's just flattened grass and bracken and they can't get footprints. Which bears out Buchan's story, and means that my having seen him coming out from the trees doesn't prove a thing.'

Bailey was looking distinctly uneasy. Before he could say anything, Fleming hurried on, 'I did also think we should be looking into the business Crozier was running. There seemed to be odd things going on.'

'Oh, no doubt it will be investigated in due course. But first things first.' Bailey was dismissive. 'This is all very unfortunate. The Scottish press has been having one of its periodic rants about police incompetence, and the CC was anxious to demonstrate a copybook operation. And I won't conceal from you, Marjory, that he wasn't altogether happy that you would be the senior investigating officer.'

Fleming's stomach gave a nervous lurch. 'I'm very sorry if he doesn't feel confident. We only have one other SIO available and he's caught up with a drugs operation at Stranraer. And I would claim I had a good record—'

'Yes, yes, of course you have, as I pointed out. And no one could say that it was your fault that the start of the investigation was botched. But it may mean that your problems with the last case are raked over once again, which won't do any of us any good. It's, well, unfortunate.

'It would be a very good idea, Marjory, a very good idea indeed, for your top priority to be showing significant progress – something solid and substantial.'

Good gracious, would it? Thanks for the tip – it hadn't occurred to me. I thought I would concentrate on minor irrelevancies, ignore a few obvious leads, take as long as I liked . . . Fleming did a little riff on the response she wished she could have made as she went gloomily back to her office.

The red light on her phone was winking to tell her there were messages waiting. There always were. For a moment she thought of ignoring them, of clearing space for thinking and reading through the reports that were building up, but buying time, as she had seen already this morning, sometimes came at too high a price. She picked up the phone.

Good decision! A few minutes later, after speaking to Kershaw, she was hurrying back to Bailey's office.

'Marjory?' He looked surprised, then, as he saw her face, hopeful. 'Something come in?'

'Jamieson,' Fleming said a little breathlessly. 'Kershaw went to his house – the one that was flooded – and he'd tried to kill himself. She called in the air ambulance and he's on his way to hospital now.'

Bailey's plump face brightened. 'Now, that's *really* good news!' Then, collecting himself, he added, 'Of course, very sad, very sad – a man feeling constrained to take his own life. But it's as good as a confession, isn't it?'

'No. No, Donald, it really isn't.' He mustn't be allowed to go dashing off with that idea. 'It may be the line the media will take, but he didn't leave a note of any kind, so it will depend on evidence emerging.'

Bailey's face fell. 'Oh, I suppose it will.'

'This is a man whose home has been wrecked. Kershaw has spoken to neighbours who say that he's had problems since his wife died. I agree remorse could be one interpretation, but we mustn't make assumptions, even when speaking to the CC.' Fleming couldn't resist that tiny dig. 'And we have to hope he survives and can tell us what we need to know.'

'I suppose you're right, Marjory. And supposing he doesn't – where does that leave us?'

'Just getting on with the spadework, Donald, like we were before.'

When she got back to her office, Fleming found another two messages. The first told her that Douglas Jamieson had been dead on arrival, and the second that Kershaw had just found a chainsaw in his garage.

DC KERSHAW, WEARING plastic gloves, dumped the huge chainsaw in the boot of the jeep, along with her disgusting boots, and got back in. The arrival and swift departure of the air ambulance, with all the attendant drama, had left her feeling deflated once it was no more than a speck in the sky.

She'd had a chat with a couple who were dragging spoiled furniture out of their ravaged house; the Jamiesons, they told her, had been a very ordinary, pleasant couple until Margaret's illness, but after that Douglas had been, as the wife put it, strange, or according to the husband, totally bonkers.

'The festival,' Kershaw said. 'Mr Jamieson was very keen to stop it going ahead. Was that what you all felt?'

They had looked at each other, then shrugged. 'Not really,' she said, and he added, 'The rest of us were OK with it. It was only one weekend and it's just kids, after all. We've got grandchildren ourselves. But quite honestly, I'd find it hard to blame Douglas if he took the law into his own hands and killed Crozier for what he's done to us here. I just hope it doesn't mean we can't sue him, that's all.'

Not the sort of epitaph you would choose to have, Kershaw thought, as she drove away. What sort of man had Gillis Crozier really been? A god to Cris Pilapil, a devil to Douglas Jamieson – presumably somewhere in between, like most people.

She could go back to Kirkluce now, with her limited triumph – she'd found the man, after all. But she had a nasty feeling that MacNee would claim victory for his point of view and she certainly hadn't any counter-arguments to put forward. She'd even come to believe he was probably right. But going back to be crowed over wasn't appetising.

She would have to turn left at the end of the road to reach the Bailey bridge, which seemed to be doing its job very effectively – just as well, since there was little chance of a new one until all the wrangles between the owners, the council and the insurance companies were resolved. There was an unspoken assumption that if you chose to live in the backwoods, inconvenience was only to be expected.

Instead, she turned right. She would go and have a chat with Maidie Buchan, the stoic victim of a nasty husband and of the mother-in-law of every woman's nightmares. It would be good to find out a bit more about the bizarre set-up at Rosscarron House, and Maidie had spent more time with Lisa Stewart than anyone else too. Kershaw still hadn't quite given up on that.

MacNee was definitely strutting as he came into DI Fleming's office. 'What did I say?' he gloated. 'Jamieson – there we are!'

Fleming was out of all patience with MacNee at the moment. 'Where are we?' she said coldly.

'Well . . .' MacNee gave her an uncertain look. 'It looks bad, doesn't it, in the circumstances?'

'Yes, it looks bad. But it doesn't prove anything, except that we now know Jamieson had a chainsaw and I will agree it's perfectly possible – even likely – that he used it to sabotage the bridge. But there's nothing beyond motive to connect him directly to Crozier's murder at present, far less to the murder of Mr X. I've got Macdonald and Campbell contacting the witnesses from the campsite to find out if anyone saw him in the vicinity, so until then we won't jump to any conclusions. Anyway, how did you get on with Lisa Stewart?'

MacNee hesitated, and Fleming's ears pricked up. 'Well?'

'Kershaw's got a point,' he said reluctantly. 'There's something not right there, but I can't put my finger on it. I don't believe Mr X is her boyfriend, though – I can tell you that. My guess is that he'll turn up before long. But I reckoned she was lying about almost everything else – what she was doing here, living right beside the family, why they kept moving around and where she was at the time Gillis Crozier was killed.'

'Mmm.' Fleming looked thoughtful. 'It would be convenient to get hard evidence on Jamieson, but we need to keep Stewart in the picture for the moment anyway.

'But, Tam, the other thing I want you to do sometime is to get back to your pal Sheughie in Glasgow. Remember what he said about one of the big boys hanging around?' She told him about the emptied filing cabinet.

MacNee nodded. 'Like we said, a pop festival's a gift for cash-laundering. And if there's a consortium, Rosscarron's a great meeting place too – no one to notice who's coming and going. Are we getting the Fraud Squad in on this?'

Fleming shook her head. 'Not yet. The super thinks it would be a distraction. I don't want to scare anyone off, but we could put out a few feelers here and in Glasgow among the CHISes, get the word going that it could be worth their while if they've a story to tell.'

After MacNee had gone, Fleming's thoughts ran on. There was no doubt in her mind that something was going on there that neither Declan Ryan nor Cris Pilapil wanted the police to know about. And Joss Hepburn was in on it too. Oh God, Joss Hepburn!

Why the hell did he have to cross her path? This morning Bill had got up very early and was on his way by the time she came downstairs at seven. Usually he'd have lingered to chat while he finished his tea, but she'd found his mug by the draining board, only half empty.

Surely he wasn't going to be stupid about an old boyfriend from twenty years ago – more, in fact? But Marjory knew she should have told Bill when first she spoke to him on the phone after she got back to headquarters. He would definitely believe that such a surprising encounter would be at the top of her mind – as indeed it had been – but she'd ducked it at the time, and now he was obviously reading more into it than there really was. Her meeting with Joss was just a casual, rather uncomfortable encounter – that was all.

But she would have to see him again, professionally of course. He was her best bet for finding out what was going on – the weakest link in the chain, she guessed.

Or perhaps that was Cara. Heroin addicts with no supply problems could lead lives that were relatively stable, and it was just possible she might be more with it next time Fleming spoke to her. Lack of inhibition could make her more communicative than any of the other residents of Rosscarron House seemed inclined to be.

THE CANTEEN WAS busy at one o'clock. Macdonald, sitting at a table with Campbell and their plates of bridie and baked beans, raised a hand to greet MacNee as he came in.

MacNee glanced at what they were eating. 'I could murder one of those. Keep me a seat.'

He came back from the hatch with a solitary sausage roll and a bitter expression. 'You got the last one,' he said accusingly. 'And the last of the beans. She offered me peas instead – peas!'

Macdonald cleared a space on the table for him. 'Fancy Maisie not knowing you're allergic to green vegetables. And no, however hard you stare at my beans, they won't jump off my plate and on to yours, and I'm not sharing.'

'Me neither,' Campbell said, a little indistinctly through a mouthful of greasy pastry.

'Selfish bastards!' MacNee sat down. 'How's it going, then?'

'Working through the list of witnesses from the campsite. No sightings so far,' Macdonald said. 'But I've struck one – Damien Gallagher – who gave me a false number and a fake address. My guess is, we know him under a different name and there's things we might want to discuss.'

MacNee frowned. 'What did he look like?'

Macdonald looked at Campbell. 'You spoke to him, didn't you?'

Campbell paused with the fork halfway to his mouth. 'Shortish, gelled hair in spikes, brown eyes, ten stone maybe, mid-twenties, Fat Face sweatshirt, flashy trainers – Hugo Boss orange, I think.' The fork completed its journey.

'You're good!' MacNee eyed him with respect. 'He's the one who was with a couple of girls, right?'

'Certainly was,' Macdonald said. 'I spoke to one of them, Stacey, and she'd been trying to contact him too. Bit of a lad, it seems – she hadn't met him till that day, but he'd definitely pulled.'

MacNee looked pained. 'Lassies like that should be locked up till they're twenty. Picks up a villain, the next thing you know he's beating her up and we get lumbered with sorting it out.

'But Jamieson. Just because no one saw him, doesn't mean he wasn't there. Was there no one even *thought* they might have seen him?'

Macdonald shook his head. 'Quite honestly, they were all pretty uncertain about where they were when. Drunk half the time, probably. Any half-decent brief could tie them in knots. It's been a wasted morning, frankly.'

'Story of our lives,' Campbell said, getting up. 'Anyone else fancy a doughnut?'

MAIDIE BUCHAN WAS alone in the kitchen when DC Kershaw arrived. The kennels were empty – Buchan had gone off somewhere with the dogs – and Calum was having a nap upstairs. His grandmother, Maidie explained in carefully neutral tones, had packed her bags and departed the previous night.

Kershaw accepted her offer of a cup of tea and sat down at the chipped Formica table, observing her hostess as she put the kettle on to boil on the ancient Calor gas cooker. Maidie looked as if she was painfully holding herself together, like a character in a cartoon whose whole body was a maze of cracks, needing only the tiniest tap to crumble into rubble.

Racked with pity, Kershaw said gently, 'It's really hard for you at the moment, isn't it?'

The words of kindness were the tiny tap. Maidie swung round with a wail, putting her hands to her face and bursting into sobs, which shook her slight frame. She tried to speak through them, but all Kershaw could hear was, 'So frightened . . . nowhere . . . Calum . . .'

Putting her arm round her shoulders, she helped her to a chair and Maidie collapsed over the table, crying helplessly. Kershaw looked around for tissues or a kitchen roll, but there was no sign of such luxuries and she had to scrabble in her bag for a pack of Kleenex, then stuffed some into Maidie's hand.

The kettle was dancing on the stove now, emitting a piercing whistle, and Kershaw snatched it off. She might as well make tea; there was nothing else to do until the poor woman had cried herself out.

She set down a mug beside her and took one herself, not saying anything, just waiting. It was a few minutes before Maidie sat up again, gasping as she tried to stop and scrubbing at her face with the tissues in a way that made Kershaw wince.

'Do it gently! Your cheeks are looking raw already.' Then she stopped, looking more closely. There was a dark blue shadow right down the edge of one cheek. She pointed. 'What's that?'

Colour came into Maidie's pale face. 'Oh, nothing.' She took a sip of her tea, avoiding Kershaw's eyes.

'He hit you, didn't he?'

Her shoulders slumped. 'He . . . well, he was angry Ina left. She said now he'd be losing his job she wasn't going to find herself supporting the lot of us, and anyway what she was getting from me

wasn't worth what she was paying for it. So he was . . . well, angry.'
She spoke as if that was an excuse.

'Does he get angry often?'

'Not – not that often. If he's had a few, maybe, but now, I don't
know. He's angry all the time now.'

Kershaw's ex-husband had only once laid hands on her, shaking her till her teeth rattled; that had been the end of the marriage,
which had struggled anyway after Debbie had become her first
concern. Now she was finding it difficult to control her cold rage
on Maidie's behalf. 'What are you going to do?'

'What can I do?' Maidie's face was tragic. 'I've nowhere to go.
And once Alick loses his job, we'll be out on the street anyway.'

'What about your own family?'

She gave a bitter laugh. 'My family? My father's freer with his
hands than Alick is. He'd take me back as a skivvy – my mother
died, worn out at forty.'

Looking at Maidie, Kershaw could see her destined for the
same fate, exhausted and brutalised. 'Look, there's a women's refuge I can get you into,' she said. 'They'll give you somewhere to
stay, sort out benefits, that kind of thing. No problem.'

Maidie was dubious. 'Alick wouldn't let me . . .'

'Alick wouldn't have to know. You only have to give me the
nod.'

Maidie half smiled; then the tears started again. 'I'm sorry –
this is daft! It's just the relief, knowing there's somewhere, if it
comes to that, but I'll wait for now, see if things settle down.'

Kershaw sighed inwardly. Battered women always did. They
stayed with drunken bullies, sometimes until it was too late, but
there was never any point in arguing. 'The offer's always there.
Here – that's my number.' She gave her a card.

'But I really came to ask if you could give me any background about Lisa Stewart – Beth, if you like.'

The change of subject seemed to pull Maidie together, but she had nothing to offer. Beth, it seemed, hadn't been any more communicative than Lisa was. 'I can tell you this, though,' Maidie said fiercely, 'I don't believe for one minute that she killed that poor wee mite. She was that patient with Calum – he's really missed her today.'

'She was acquitted,' Kershaw pointed out, echoing MacNee. 'But I did wonder why she would choose to be so close to the baby's family.'

'She never said. Just she was living in her granny's old house – maybe she'd nowhere else. Where's she staying now? I wish I could help her, but—'

'She's fine,' Kershaw assured her. 'Staying at the Balmoral Guest House in Kirkluce.'

She went on to her next line of questioning. 'Alick organises shoots and so on for the people who come for meetings to Ross-carron House, right? How many of them? And do you know who they are?'

'There's usually about five or six. Before Calum was born, I used to go sometimes and help Cris at the big house. There were a few foreign gentlemen – one was French, I think, and there was another one told me he was Italian. Then there's Mr Lloyd and Mr Driscoll, of course – Alick knew them from when they were in the army with Mr Crozier. The three of them played in a sort of band together, he said once. Officers, of course. Alick never had much time for officers.'

A man with a grudge might be a very useful source of information; Kershaw filed that one away to suggest to Big Marge later. 'Do you know what the business was?' she asked hopefully.

Here she drew a blank. Maidie had no idea. 'Made a lot of money, that's all I know,' she said wistfully.

Kershaw left it at that. She still had a long drive back to Kirkluce, but there was no briefing tonight with it being Saturday, when they were all on overtime. She'd have plenty of time to look in and see Debbie before she was settled down for the night.

CRIS PILAPIL CAME into the conference room, where Declan Ryan was sitting at the table with a shredder and piles of paper around him.

'Has Alex got in touch?' he said, without preamble.

Ryan didn't look up. 'Not with me.'

'It's funny.'

'Alex's a maverick. He wouldn't have been Gillis's lawyer if he wasn't.'

'I'm worried. The girlfriend's been on the phone again.' Pilapil came forward to lean on the table, and this time Ryan did look up.

'You told her he was in Inverness, didn't you?'

'Yes, but we both know he isn't.'

'We don't, actually. He might be anywhere. You know Alex. Look, Cris, I'm scared about this.' For once, Ryan was speaking without his usual sneering sarcasm. 'Alex is key to the whole thing. It couldn't be more unfortunate that he's gone AWOL like this, and if the police start sniffing around at that end, we're all up the creek.

'I can't dash off to London when the police have asked me to stay here. Lloyd and Driscoll are keeping at arm's length from the whole thing and I don't want them to find out there's a problem over Alex – they're likely to overreact.'

'Yes.' Pilapil's agreement was unhesitating.

'So . . .'

'OK, OK. If she phones again, I'll give her some story. At least he told the office he'd be away for a bit – I checked. I just wish he'd get in touch before everything falls apart.'

Pilapil saw his own anxiety, bordering on fear, replicated in the face of the other man as he turned to go.

'BILL, I WANT to talk to you about Joss Hepburn.'

There, she'd said it. They were on their own for supper: Cat was out with her boyfriend, a medical student at Glasgow University, and Cammie had been evasive about his plans, but from the smell of aftershave Marjory reckoned that her sports-mad son must have discovered girls at last. So she and Bill had only Meg for company, if you didn't count the elephant in the room, which they had studiously ignored.

Bill was concentrating on putting sugar in his coffee. 'Maybe you should wait till Cat's here. You won't want to have to go through it all twice.'

'It's not the sort of conversation I was planning to have with Cat. Bill, Joss is just someone I knew a long, long time ago. All right, someone I was in love with a long, long time ago. I found out what he was like, I ditched him, and I fell in love with you. This was a casual, unimportant encounter, that's all.'

'So unimportant that you didn't mention it until you had to?' Bill looked up and she saw hurt in his eyes. 'Do you think I don't know that you put it off because you were trying to find the best way of convincing me it was unimportant?'

'You're just proving me right, Bill!' Marjory cried. 'You're reacting as if you're jealous.'

'Yes, I suppose I am. And I can tell you why – because I know exactly what you'd have done if this meant as little as you're making out. Immediately after you'd told me about the accident, you'd have said, "Bill, the most awful thing! You'll never guess who's here – Joss Hepburn, and the last time I saw him, you'd just given him a broken nose! How embarrassing is that?" Something along those lines.'

Marjory opened her mouth to deny it, but the words wouldn't come.

'I'm not afraid you're going to run off with him. You're an honourable person and you're not stupid either. But the trouble is, there's always been something in you that could never be satisfied with life as the wife of a simple farmer – it's why you need the drama of policework. But just at the moment I think you're wondering what life would have been like if you'd walked off on the wild side with Joss and there's a part of you regrets not having had the nerve to do it. And that hurts – of course it does.

'I'll get over it. And when he's gone, the waters will close over him, and though you'll spare him a thought now and then, that will be all. I don't see much point in discussing it now when I doubt if you're being honest with yourself, let alone me.'

Bill had spoken levelly and calmly. But now, as he got up from the table, he said with a sort of anger in his voice that she had never heard before, 'Just as long as that bastard hasn't poisoned your pleasure in the life that has made us so happy up till now.'

FOR THE HUNDREDTH time, Lisa Stewart consulted her watch. It wasn't a cold night, but she was shivery with nerves and she had put on the one-bar electric fire in the dingy lounge. She was alone; she'd seen only one other guest, a dispirited-looking man in a tired suit with a battered briefcase, but he had gone to his room, as Mrs Wishart clearly hoped Lisa would. She'd come in a couple of times to check, making plain her opinion of such wanton extravagance with a grudging look at the fire. Eventually she had given up and gone upstairs, telling Lisa to be sure to put off the lights 'and the fire' before she went to bed.

Lisa wasn't intimidated. Through the small window, she could see that it was dark now and there was a smirr of light rain on the dirty pane; a wind had got up, blowing with a soft, groaning sigh. The Balmoral Guest House was in a quiet backstreet with only the occasional passer-by, whose footsteps echoed on the pavement.

There was an old, dog-eared copy of *Hello!* open on Lisa's knee, but she hadn't read a word of it. She couldn't think of anything except what lay ahead and she was feeling sick.

Why hadn't she just put her head in the sand, ignored the text message he'd sent her, hoping this would all go away? But she hadn't, and anyway she knew that wouldn't have solved anything. It was her only chance to get the answers she wanted.

Perhaps she should have insisted on meeting in a public place, but she wasn't sure whether the police were watching her, even now. Or watching him.

And now the hands of her watch had crept round to the time agreed. There was no going back. Lisa got up, put the magazine back on the pile on the rickety coffee table, switched off the fire and the lights, and let herself quietly out of the front door.

She looked carefully up and down the silent street. There was no one to be seen, and all the curtains were drawn across the lit windows in the other houses. The wind ruffled her hair, and after the stuffy atmosphere inside, the cool, damp air made a clammy film on her cheeks. She shivered again.

If he'd passed the window, she would have seen him, but of course he could have come from the opposite direction and be waiting for her. She walked towards the side of the guest house, unable to stop herself from checking over her shoulder.

Under the yellow street lights, everything looked cold and unreal, like a stage set, the deserted street heavy with undefined significance. She turned away and, with a deep, deep breath, set off down the dark alleyway that ran between the houses to the miserable garden at the back.

Chapter Fourteen

Sunday, 23 July

MOIRA WISHART PUT the greasy frying pan into the sink and ran in hot water. When she squeezed the detergent bottle, it gave only a despairing groan, so muttering under her breath, she turned off the tap, fetched a key and went out of the back door to the shed where the stores were kept.

Lisa Stewart and the other resident were sitting at their separate tables in the small dining room. They acknowledged their enforced intimacy with a polite, embarrassed greeting and were now eating their fatty bacon and frizzled egg, careful that their eyes should not meet.

When the screams came from the direction of the kitchen, the man was pouring out tea. He missed his cup and the hot liquid ran off the table and on to his knees; he jumped up, pulling the steaming cloth away from his legs. 'Oh my God, whatever's that?'

Lisa had jumped up too. She was very pale. 'Mrs Wishart. Something's happened.'

She was first through the door to the kitchen, the man hopping after her, still plucking at his trouser leg. Mrs Wishart came staggering in through the back door, wild-eyed and looking over her shoulder as she emitted scream after scream. Lisa went to her and took her by the arms, shaking her to try to stop the noise.

'What's wrong? Are you hurt?'

'She must have seen something,' the man said, going out into the yard as Moira at last quietened enough to gasp out, 'Dead – out there – man.'

'A man dead? Are you sure?' Lisa asked.

'Sure? Of course I'm sure!' Seized with indignation, Moira found her voice. 'He's had his head beaten in with a bloody great crowbar! That's why I'm sure.'

The man came back in, his face grey-green. 'Don't go out there,' he warned. 'It's ghastly.'

Lisa ignored him. As the man poured himself a glass of water with a shaking hand, she walked out past him.

Beside the dismantled car, a body was lying. The head was a bloody mess of brain, bone and tissue; beside it lay a rusty-looking iron bar. The man's eyes were shut, and on the other side of his head the short, spiky hair was caked with dried blood. He was wearing a sweatshirt and jeans, and on his feet was a pair of trainers with orange Velcro fastenings.

'Here! What's been going on?' A man was leaning over the garden wall. 'We heard screaming.'

Lisa, who had been standing impassively beside the body, looked up. 'Someone's been murdered. We'll need to get the police.'

THERE WASN'T MUCH progress to report at the morning briefing. There was plenty of housekeeping to be done, of course – routine crime didn't conveniently stop for a major investigation – but when it came to the follow-up on the killings, Fleming couldn't with any degree of honesty say that there was a clear line to follow. At the moment it was a waiting game while forensic tests were running, and the reports never came in as quickly as you hoped they would.

Lack of clarity was bad for morale. The teams always worked harder and more effectively when the dog could see the rabbit, which, Fleming reflected gloomily, was at the moment well concealed in the undergrowth.

Still, she talked positively about what they knew already, cautioned against making the sort of assumptions the media were already making about Douglas Jamieson, and tasked the various teams with searches and interviews. She was just bringing the meeting to an end, asking if there were questions and/or suggestions, when the message came through that she was needed elsewhere.

As she went out, Fleming saw glances being exchanged, heard the ripple of talk and the word 'Breakthrough?' Years of bitter experience had made her less optimistic: it was always wise to assume that an unexpected development was bad news until proved otherwise. She went off to see her uniform counterpart, Mike Wallace.

IT WAS DS MacNee she called to her office. Fleming might be out of sympathy with him, but there was no doubt that he was her most effective officer, with a knack for picking up on things that weren't in plain view – guessing what was on the other side of the hill, in Wellington's phrase.

'At least we know one thing – Jamieson didn't kill this one,' MacNee said morosely, as he came in.

'Thanks, Tam. I had just managed to work that out.' She wasn't in a cheerful mood either. A third murder, no visible progress on the other two and a chief constable with doubts about her competence left her feeling as if she were dangling above an abyss, suspended by a rope whose fibres were being severed one at a time.

'It's landed on our plate, at least meantime, and the procurator fiscal's satisfied that we can cope. Thank God Duncan Mackay made such a good recovery and got back to work – he's always been a great supporter.'

'So what's the position?'

'A man's body has been found in the backyard of the guest house where Lisa Stewart is staying.'

MacNee's ears almost visibly pricked up, and Fleming went on, 'I know, I know, but it may be completely unrelated.'

'It's related,' MacNee said. 'I feel it in my bones.'

'I'm not saying you're wrong, but Mike Wallace talked to them while the scene of crime was being secured and no one admits to knowing him.'

'Doesn't prove anything,' MacNee said stubbornly. 'It's the missing boyfriend. Bets?'

'I've given up betting with you. You're right too often, and if you're not right, trying to get you to admit it and pay up is like trying to shove an eel into a jam jar. Let's get along there and see what's happening.'

BLUE-AND-WHITE TAPE WAS draped round the entrance to the passage down the side of the Balmoral and a small crowd had gathered, though not, thankfully, the media as yet. The sergeant on duty logged their names and they went along to the garden at the back.

It had been efficiently set up by the crime-scene manager, and Fleming and MacNee stood on the concrete beside the cordon; at a nod from Fleming, an officer in white coveralls went forward to lift a covering off the body.

She looked at the horribly bloodied young face – so pathetically young! – with a faint prickle of recognition, but as she struggled to pin down the memory, MacNee exclaimed, 'I know who that is! You mind we saw him up at the campsite, and Campbell gave me his description yesterday – he gave false information when they took his statement. He's Damien Gallagher – or more likely he isn't.'

'I KNOW WHAT you're thinking,' Lisa Stewart said, with surprising calm. 'You think I killed him. I didn't. I've no idea who he is.'

It was the first time Fleming had spoken to her. She had seen her, of course, on the helicopter bringing them back from Ross-carron, but at the time her attention had been focused on Alick Buchan. What she had heard from MacNee and Kershaw had made her curious, and now she sat slightly behind Lisa on one of the worn chairs in the stale-smelling lounge, while MacNee dealt with the routine stuff.

Lisa's naturally pale skin was a dirty grey and there were purple shadows under her eyes, but MacNee was finding her composure hard to shake. He went into some very aggressive questioning, but that didn't seem to disturb her either.

Then he said, 'I'm asking you again – did you know the man who was found dead in your cottage?'

She glanced at him scornfully. 'No. I've never seen him before in my life. That's the truth, and however often you ask the question, the answer's going to be the same.'

He went on, 'And do you know the man who's lying dead in the garden right now?' and Fleming realised what he was doing. It was an old trick – ask a question you believe will get a truthful answer, follow it up with one that may provoke a lie, and observe.

Lisa suddenly met his gaze very directly. Her voice hardened. 'No. I didn't.'

The difference was stark. The over-direct stare, the flat tone, the brief reply – they were the tell-tale signs of ineffective lying.

But whatever suggestion MacNee made – and they became blunter and blunter – her responses didn't vary: she had no idea who the man was; she had never seen him before; last night she had read magazines in the lounge and then gone to bed. That was all. She remained entirely unemotional.

Could that be the chilling indifference of the psychopath? It was possible, certainly, but observing the girl, Fleming was reminded of something she had read about detachment as a symptom of psychological distress – a learned defence against intolerable reality. Lisa's calm seemed almost trance-like, and the harder MacNee pushed, the more remote she seemed to become.

With faint stirrings of sympathy, Fleming leaned forward. She knew how to use her voice effectively and when she said, 'Lisa, you've had some dreadful experiences lately,' it was very soft and very warm. 'You must be feeling shaken.'

Lisa's head whipped round. She met the inspector's clear hazel eyes, and for a second her own filled with tears. She blinked them away, and it was as if a veil came down. 'Naturally,' was all she said, and she said it coldly, but it told Fleming that her assessment had been right.

Joss Hepburn came downstairs late. Breakfast never featured in his life, but at a certain stage coffee became essential and he headed for the kitchen. As he passed the sitting room, he heard Declan Ryan's raised voice. 'I know, I know. But we have to wait.' Hepburn went quietly on.

In the kitchen, there was no sign of Cris Pilapil, but others had breakfasted and no one had cleared afterwards. There were plates, bowls and mugs on the table, along with a pack of butter still in its wrapper and a jar of jam with a sticky knife laid beside it. There were crumbs everywhere and someone had spilled milk without wiping it up. Hepburn wrinkled his nose; he abhorred messiness of all kinds, whether physical or emotional.

Still, at least the room was empty. While the espresso machine sputtered and gurgled to produce his fix, he gathered up the debris and dumped it by the sink, then wiped the table.

He needed out. Now. Every instinct was screaming flight, but there were other pressures. Till he was sure everything had calmed down, he mustn't do anything to court attention. And Madge had been showing a thoroughly unhealthy interest in the business; until she could be distracted or diverted, they were all at risk.

It was getting to him, though, making him feel stifled. It was just like old times, before he'd escaped to the wide skies and the sunshine and the promise of the New World. He had felt cramped by the smallness and sameness of everything, the little towns where nothing had changed for a hundred years, and where they liked it that way.

And here he was back, an international star, which didn't change anything when you were stuck with this – the dismal weather, the isolation, the weirdness of a house that felt like a hotel with no staff, the other inmates.

Oh, yes, the other inmates. He had just poured his coffee into a satisfyingly thin white porcelain cup, found an ashtray and lit up a cigarette when the kitchen door opened and Nico Ryan appeared.

Hepburn sat down, eyeing him with distaste. 'Hi,' he said, as discouragingly as he could.

Nico marched over and stood in front of him, a little too close. It was a habit he had; Hepburn pushed his chair a few inches further back.

'That's going to kill you, you know.' Nico pointed at the cigarette. 'Your lungs are going black already and you'll start coughing them up in little bloody bits until you can't breathe any more. I saw a film.'

'I'll risk it. And I might even survive longer than you do, if you go around being fresh like that.' Now it had been suggested, Hepburn could feel a tickle developing, but he wasn't going to give the monster child the satisfaction of hearing him cough. He cleared his throat.

Nico was gleeful. 'There you are. It's started already. It's probably too late for you by now.'

'Haven't you got anything better to do than stand there annoying me?' Hepburn exhaled, making no attempt to divert the smoke.

'No.'

The boy's unflinching stare was becoming positively uncomfortable. 'Why don't you go and find your mum and dad? Or Cris?'

Nico still didn't move. 'Mum's going on at Dad. Dad's shouting. They put me out. And I hate Cris. He won't obey my orders, even now my granddad's dead. Anyway, why are you staying in my house? I don't like you.'

'Is it your house?' Hepburn enquired with mild interest.

'It will be. It's my mum's now, but when she's dead, it'll be mine. I'll like that.'

Presumably he didn't mean he'd like his mum being dead, though with Nico you couldn't be entirely sure. 'I promise I won't come to stay when it belongs to you. And I shall be leaving the minute I can, I assure you.'

Hepburn finished his coffee, stubbed out his cigarette and got up. Even his bedroom, which had begun to feel like a cell, would be better than this. Perhaps he could risk driving to Kirkluce and demanding to have his formal statement taken at once because he had business to do in London. That would sound reasonable enough. Indeed, it was true. He was worried about what might happen at the other end of the operation. Or at this end, come to that.

'If you're looking for something to do, you could always clear up the breakfast dishes,' he said over his shoulder as he left the room, then winced as he heard a crash behind him. Nico's favoured method of clearing up was apparently unorthodox.

KERSHAW WAS FEELING low today. She had got up early so that she'd have time to look in and see Debbie on her way to work. Debbie was at her best first thing in the morning, more alert and sometimes smiling in what her mother could convince herself was recognition. You needed these small boosts to keep positive, but today the little girl had still been asleep after a restless night.

And now, when the station was awash with stories that Lisa Stewart was involved in another murder, where was Kershaw? In front of a computer terminal, collating reports and reading through statements, that was where she was.

Who was it who had alerted the boss to Lisa in the first place? Yeah, right. But who had she taken to the crime scene with her? MacNee. It wasn't fair, but then, she couldn't claim that anything in her own experience had suggested that life would be fair. Kershaw gave a deep sigh and went back to her task.

The more she went into it, the clearer it became that Jamieson wasn't a murderer. Casual about other people's safety, yes: a report in this morning confirmed that his chainsaw had destroyed the bridge, and he'd probably severed the phone line as well, though they hadn't as yet found the cutters he would have needed, or even a ladder. But a statement from a neighbour confirmed that he had been at home on the afternoon and evening of the landslip, not along at Rosscarron Cottages killing Mr X. So unless you reckoned the murders were unrelated, he was in the clear.

Which, along with this latest development, put Lisa Stewart in the frame fair and square. When they brought her in, Kershaw decided she was going to ask Big Marge if she could be involved in the questioning. She reckoned she'd shown insight into the way the woman thought, and surely Fleming would agree it was only fair.

Fair! There she went again, still a cock-eyed optimist in spite of everything.

'SIR! COULD I have a word?' DS Macdonald stopped DI John Purves as they met in a corridor.

Purves was in his forties, a dark, thin-faced man with heavy brows, who went about his administrative responsibilities with quiet efficiency, and covered for his colleague Fleming when her duties as a senior investigating officer took her away from deskwork.

'Sure, Andy. What's the problem?'

Macdonald looked up and down the corridor. A Force civilian assistant was coming towards them and Macdonald jerked his head. 'In private, maybe?'

Purves raised his brows. 'If you say so. My office?'

As Purves shut the door and waved him to a seat, Macdonald said, 'I've got an authorised CHIS with a story to tell. I'm reporting to you as my controller.'

'Good man!' Purves was pleased. The guidelines for dealing with covert human intelligence sources were tight nowadays, with designated handlers in contact with them, controllers to ensure the contact didn't become too friendly, formal contracts, and firewalls everywhere. If there was the smallest infringement of the rules by an overenthusiastic handler, it could compromise any evidence obtained. 'So what's for sale?'

'Won't tell me. He wants to talk to DI Fleming.'

'Uh-uh.' Purves shook his head. 'We have to follow arm's-length principles. It should be filtered through you, then me, so we have a sterile corridor and neither she nor I knows who he is. Source-protection rules.'

'It's not that simple. He says he won't speak except to her. He was on a charge a while ago, and apparently she passed on to his brief something that got him off. He claims she's the only honest copper he knows.'

Purves sighed. 'We'll pass over the slur on you and me. How good is the material anyway? What level of payment will he be expecting?'

Macdonald told him and he whistled. 'That high up the scale, eh? Is he a realist?'

'I'd say so. He's got a lot of contacts with Glasgow, and he's given us useful small stuff before, but nothing on the scale he's suggesting now. And I tell you something else – he's scared this time, really scared. He needs the money – in debt to someone with unsympathetic methods of getting it back, I'd reckon – but he wants to be sure that if he needs to disappear, we'll look after him.'

Purves's beetling brows shot up. 'As hot as that?'

'He seems to think so. From his reaction there are big guys involved.'

'Hmm.' Purves thought for a moment. 'Did he just come up with this out of the blue?'

'Apparently he heard a whisper up in Glasgow that we're interested in what's been going on at Rosscarron House.'

'Gillis Crozier's place?' The brows were working overtime. 'So it's about the murders?'

'Apparently not. I asked him and what he said was that it wasn't about murder – yet. He could just be bigging it up. But he definitely won't tell anyone except DI Fleming, like I said. I don't know how we arrange that.'

'With extreme difficulty. Permissions, forms, risk assessments – you can imagine. But at least it's easier if it's about something else – if it was about these killings, as SIO she couldn't be in contact. I'll have to talk to the super.'

As Macdonald got up to go, Purves added, 'But just see you depress his expectations, Andy. We're on a budget.'

'I'M TELLING YOU this,' Moira Wishart said theatrically, 'you're not keeping me here. I'm away to Paisley to stay with my sister. I'm not spending another night in this place until you have whoever did it under lock and key. I couldn't sleep easy in my bed.'

Moira was making the most of her fifteen minutes of fame, looking from one detective to the other to judge her effect. Her hand was permanently pressed to her heaving bosom, and she would clearly be in her element once the press arrived. That could be anytime now.

'How very wise, Mrs Wishart,' Fleming said warmly. 'Indeed, provided you leave your sister's number with us, I see no reason why you shouldn't go immediately. How many guests are staying at the moment?'

'Just Miss Brown. The other gentleman's left already.'

Fleming nodded. The gentleman in question, shaken already, had become almost tearful at the notion of having to stay longer. He was driving back to Leeds, so they had interviewed him first, taken his business card and allowed him to go, since his evidence was only that he had gone to bed early, closed the curtains without looking out and slept till morning.

'We'll find somewhere else for Miss Brown,' Fleming assured her. 'But you're quite, quite certain that when you locked up at about ten o'clock last night, there was nothing in the garden?' In deference to Moira's sensibilities, she avoided the word 'body'.

'The body, you mean? Oh, no. Like I said, I went to put out some rubbish in the bin and walked right past where it would have been. But I'll tell you something.' Moira looked round conspiratorially, as if someone might have joined them in the little sitting room unnoticed. 'That girl was in here last night after I went to bed. I couldn't shift her to go to her own room so I could lock up and put off the fire – not that she was needing a fire in July. And this morning, with all that going on, she was as cool as a cucumber. Funny, I thought that was.'

LISA STEWART WAS lying on her bed with her face buried in her pillow. She wanted to scream, but all she dared do was groan out her despair and fear, trusting that it would be muffled.

Still, she had got through it somehow. She had stuck to her story, she hadn't cracked, and if she had come up here afterwards and been violently sick, they weren't to know.

She'd deleted her 'Sent' message. Could they find it again? She didn't know. They hadn't got Lee's phone, anyway: she'd taken it from him and hidden it under a loose floorboard, in case they searched her.

From somewhere she had got the strength to say steadily that she didn't know him, again and again, without a tremor in her voice. Perhaps it had helped that it was, at least in one way, true.

They'd spoken to the other guest first and he'd told Lisa when he came out that they said it was someone called Damien Gallagher. She didn't know anyone called Damien Gallagher. She knew someone called Lee Morrissey. And also Jazza, apparently.

There was a knock on her door. Lisa sat up, quivering. 'Yes?'

'May I come in?' It was the inspector's voice, and she turned the handle as she spoke.

Lisa had taken the precaution of locking the door. 'Just a minute,' she said, and went to check herself in the mirror above the washbasin. Her face was ashen but showed no other signs of her emotional turmoil. Her hair was wild, though. She combed it, splashed her face and pinched her cheeks, swilled water round her mouth and then went to the door.

DI Fleming was alone. 'I'm sorry about this, but Mrs Wishart is closing the guest house. I'm afraid you'll have to find somewhere else to stay.'

That, at least, was good news. Lisa had been afraid they would insist on her remaining here.

Fleming was going on, 'There are a few other guest houses in Kirkluce, but I have to warn you that the press will be arriving in force anytime now and it wouldn't take them long to find you. We will be asked for the names of the residents here and I'm afraid, since we know your real name, we won't be able to give them an alias.'

Without warning, it came back to Lisa: the rattle of cameras, the flickering flashes, the babble of shouted questions, the waves of hatred, which in themselves were like an assault. Her legs threatened to give way and she leaned against the doorway as she fought for control.

'I – see.' Her voice was strangled. 'So what should I do?'

That might even be pity in the inspector's face. 'Have you family you could go to? We would have to know exactly where you were.'

Lisa shook her head helplessly. And then she remembered. 'One of your officers gave me a card. It's my neighbour from the cottages, Dr Forbes – she said I could go to the hotel where she's staying if I'd nowhere else.'

She had a sudden picture of Jan Forbes, solid, kindly, reassuring. She'd only said hello to her a couple of times, but she had a smile that made you feel she was a good, honest person. Honest – oh, how tired Lisa was of lies, lies, lies!

Perhaps if no one knew where she was, she would feel safe. Perhaps she would be able to sleep if she wasn't always frightened. She was tired, so tired.

'DC Kershaw, was it? That sounds all right,' the inspector said. Then, her voice hardening, she added, 'But you must not move from that address without informing us. Is that clear?'

'Right.' Lisa nodded.

As soon as the inspector left, she collected her few belongings and put them into her tote bag. She lifted the floorboard cautiously and picked up the mobile phone, holding it between thumb and forefinger as if to distance herself from it, then dropped it into her bag with a shudder.

Once this is over, she promised herself, I shall find a hilltop where no one can hear me and scream and scream and scream.

Chapter Fifteen

'Is IT URGENT, John? As you can imagine . . .' Fleming spoke into the phone, flapping her hand at her cluttered desk as if DI Purves, at the other end, could see it, then listened to what he had to say. 'How extraordinary!' she said at last. 'I've no idea who that could be. Anyway, come on up.'

As she waited for her colleague, she mentally scanned her 'Villains I Have Known' file, but no one stood out. The principle of full disclosure of evidence to the defence might not be universally honoured by the police force, but since Fleming always tried to be scrupulous, the CHIS's compliment didn't narrow it down much. Perhaps John Purves could shed a bit more light.

Purves was a fairly recent addition to the Kirkluce CID, after the long-overdue retirement of a DI who, when it came to modern practice, had raised passive resistance to performance art. Fleming rated Purves highly: he had an impressive appetite for the administrative and organisational duties that to Fleming were the downside of the job, and he managed to be a stickler for compliance without nit-picking – not an easy balance to achieve. Though they regularly traded insults like 'stuffed shirt' and 'adrenaline junkie', it all worked very well.

Bouncing a few ideas off him when he was here anyway wouldn't do any harm. Fleming always liked to clear her mind by talking things through, but she was short of a confidant, with MacNee in his present dour mood and Bill – well, she couldn't see them sitting down for a chat over a cosy dram right at the moment.

The mysterious CHIS, however, was at the top of the agenda.

'I don't know who he is either, as yet,' Purves told her, disappointingly. 'You know the rules.'

'Of course I do. Theoretically. And of course I've had the odd tip-off, sanitised through the system, but since the new regulations came in I've had nothing to do with that area, except to say thank you when a useful snippet comes through. I know the general principle, but I didn't exactly study the fine print.'

'Tut, tut,' Purves said mildly. 'I'm a controller for several handlers – Andy Macdonald, in this instance.'

'Andy?' Fleming was surprised. 'I saw him earlier and he didn't say anything.'

'He wouldn't. We try to keep the firewalls in place. I wouldn't be telling you now if I hadn't cleared it with the super, and he had to check it with the top brass. It isn't to do with your present investigations or they'd have ruled it out completely. This does seem to be an exceptional case. The man appears to believe that if it gets out what he's doing, he'd find himself sipping sewage in the Clyde.'

Fleming blanched. 'Oh *please*! We've got enough problems already. Maybe he could be told not to risk it and we'll just muddle along ourselves.'

Purves looked at her under his brows. 'You know you don't mean that.'

'No, I suppose I don't,' Fleming said hollowly. 'All right, where do we go from here?'

'We have to talk about risk.'

'Don't we always? I know coppers who use "risk assessment" as a sweary word.'

Purves smiled. 'You look as if your last assessment wasn't that effective.'

Fleming put a hand to her face. 'Oh, this? I'd forgotten about it. Looks much worse than it feels now. Anyway, risk to our CHIS, weighed up against value of information?'

'And risk to you.'

'To me?' She was startled.

'He was very specific that it had to be you. If someone wanted you out of the way, it could be a way of drawing you into a trap.'

'That – that hadn't struck me.' It gave her a cold, nasty feeling inside.

'That's what procedure is for,' Purves said in mild triumph. 'So we can work round it.'

'So how do we do that?'

'I'll tell you nearer the time. It won't be immediately – there's a lot to put in place. It'll seem a bit elaborate, I'm afraid. You'll think we're being melodramatic, but if we're dealing with bad guys from Glasgow, we won't be playing nursery games – except, if we're not careful, the one where we all fall down at the end.'

Fleming swallowed hard. 'Suddenly, investigating three murders seems a simple, straightforward business.'

'How's it going? There's conflicting stories whizzing around.'

'We don't have any other kind of stories at the moment. Do me a favour – be a stooge, John, would you? Ask the obvious questions, while I go through it.'

'Born for the part,' Purves said easily, settling back in his chair.

'Where to start?' Fleming pondered for a moment. 'Jamieson, I suppose. He was the obvious suspect for Crozier, and he certainly sawed through the supports on the bridge and then waited for them to get destabilised. But he has an alibi for the first murder, the one at the cottages, and of course now . . .' She shrugged.

'What about the girl – the one who allegedly didn't kill Crozier's grandchild? The hot money in the canteen's on her.'

'Oh, she's involved in this somehow – if that was the bet, I'd wager my hen-money without a qualm. She's stonewalling, and she's good at it. We don't know why, and we can hardly pull her in just because she happened to be around. Maybe forensics will come up with something. If she's scared but not guilty, as I could almost believe she is, it would be in her own interests to stop lying, trust us and open up.'

'You think?' Purves was inclined to be cynical. 'Not something her brief would advise, if she had one.'

'No,' she admitted. 'And certainly, flatly denying everything puts all the onus on us to get at the truth.'

'Truth, Marjory, has nothing to do with us. It's proof we're after.'

'With three bodies, one of them completely unidentified and another with false ID? Chance would be a fine thing!'

'So, the girl's out at – what? – thirty-three to one? All right – run me through the rest of the card.'

'Take your pick. Cast of thousands, with contractors and security and pop fans – including, incidentally, the man found dead this morning. Then you have the dysfunctional family – the daughter's a junkie, the grandchild's a monster, the son-in-law, who fits the part perfectly, has an alibi for Crozier's murder from Tam MacNee, of all people. There's a Filipino houseman who seems to have been devoted to his employer but who definitely lied to me, and to add a little spice, Joshua, the pop star, who is also a stranger to the truth.'

'It occurs to me to ask whether you're sure the deaths are connected.'

'Sure? I'm not sure of anything. I wish I was. I'm beating my brains out trying to establish the connections.'

'Some common background that argued for taking them out one after another?'

'One after another.' Fleming picked up on the phrase. 'It may simply be consequential, of course – after one death, the next for some reason became necessary, and the next . . . It would be a simpler way of looking at it, but we still need a plausible motive for the first one as a starting point, and I certainly can't see it as yet.'

'Not easy.' Purves looked at his watch and got up. 'Have to go. I've a lovely policy document to work on – excellent stuff. Fancy swapping?'

Fleming looked at him, then at her desk. 'I'm snowed under, I'm confused, I'm stressed out, and I probably won't get home before ten o'clock tonight. No. Not a chance.'

PC SANDY LANGLANDS was doing door-to-doors along the streets by the Balmoral Guest House in the drizzling rain. He was in an uncharacteristically downbeat mood, bored and cold. Most people were out at work, which would mean he'd have to come back later, and even the people who happened to be at home had nothing useful to say but said it anyway.

Gloomily, he tramped along the street round the corner from where the guest house stood. There was, he noticed, rather a natty silver Lexus parked on a double yellow line. It wasn't causing an obstruction, though, and he'd better things to do at the moment.

He'd had no luck so far in the terrace of small houses that opened directly on to the pavement. Four no answers, two don't knows. He rang the bell of the house beside the parked car and waited.

The woman who opened it was more keen to bend his ear on the subject of the car – 'About time you came to do something about it!' – than to listen to his questions. She didn't hold with having strangers coming round the place late at night. 'Quarter to eleven, it was, when I heard him slamming the door. And it's been there all night. That's not right.'

There was more, quite a lot more. Eyes glazed, Langlands let it wash over him until at last she finished – 'I just hope you're going to get it towed away, right now' – and paused for breath.

'Indeed, madam,' he said gravely. 'Now, could I just ask you – we're interested in the movements of a young man, medium height, spiked hair, wearing a dark green sweatshirt and jeans?'

He liked to think that if he hadn't been bludgeoned with irrelevant information all morning, he'd have put two and two together before she squealed, 'That's him! That's the very man!'

It took him some time to extricate himself, but with the car's registration number written in his notebook, he walked back to the Kirkluce headquarters in triumph.

THERE WERE THREE or four detectives working at computers when DS MacNee got back to the CID room. One of them was Kim Kershaw, who glanced up briefly as he passed but didn't speak.

The Balmoral Guest House was now empty and locked up. He had ushered Mrs Wishart firmly to her car, ignoring the longing looks she cast over her shoulder at the gathering journalists, and watched her drive away to make sure.

Lisa Stewart had been more problematic. MacNee wasn't feeling charitably disposed towards her, but Big Marge had spelled it out that she wasn't to be thrown to the wolves. Fellow feeling, that was – there had been a couple of jeering questions shouted by the press about her last case as Fleming herself drove out.

Anyway, Lisa had no transport, so he'd had to give her a lift to Tourist Information to ask about a bus to take her to Rowantrees Hotel. He heard her gasp of fright at the camera flashes as they drove past and her thanks, given along with a surprisingly attractive smile, when he dropped her off sounded heartfelt. He found himself wondering what lay beneath the hard shell – apart from the answers he needed. He'd no doubt that Lisa knew them.

But she wasn't going to tell, was she? Back to square one, he thought grimly, and start again.

He found a terminal free and called up the Missing Persons Register. Presumably someone had checked that already, but he wanted to see it for himself. Maybe he could spot a connection they hadn't.

It wasn't a long list, and none of the names and descriptions triggered the blaze of insight he had been hoping for. If Mr X was a misper, he certainly didn't come from around here. MacNee scowled. He needed inspiration.

He hadn't been to the Rosscarron Cottages – or what was left of them. The SOCOs would have done their stuff by now, so the authorities could start clearing the site. It was all on film – he could conjure it up at the touch of a button – but he was unrepentantly old-fashioned. You couldn't get the smell of a crime scene from a screen, couldn't look around for the detail that would catch your eye or sense how people had moved about. If it was back to square one, that was where he should start – where it all began.

He should clear it with the boss, but they weren't seeing eye to eye at the moment. Fair enough, he was maybe a wee bit edgy himself, but if she knew what he was going through . . . Suddenly it all swept over him again and he bent his head over the keyboard, biting his lip.

For just a moment he thought of telling Fleming. There might be relief in that – they'd been through a lot together – but Tam MacNee didn't go around bleating about his problems, and there was a kind of shame attached to it too, somehow.

MacNee sniffed, picked his leather jacket off the back of the chair and went out.

IT WAS RAINING again. Well, not raining, exactly, just drizzling on in a grey, depressing sort of way.

'This dreich weather really gets to me,' Macdonald complained to Campbell, as yet again they drove along the A75 heading for Kirkcudbright. 'I'd rather have a downpour and clear the air.'

'It's like a kid whingeing,' Campbell said with feeling. 'Better if they just yell and get it over with.'

Macdonald agreed. 'Though mind you, if you think of the last couple of weeks, there's no guarantee that a downpour will stop it.'

'No guarantee with kids either.' Campbell lapsed into gloomy silence.

Thinking aloud, as was his habit when driving with Campbell, Macdonald said, 'I wonder if the Ryans have heard about the fate of their former camper, or if we'll be breaking the news? Always useful to get in first and see the reactions. They sound a weird lot anyway. The kid's like something out of a horror movie, and Tam says the mother's stoned most of the time.'

'Probably explains the kid,' Campbell suggested.

'Right enough. You can't blame him – no problem kids without problem parents.'

Campbell shifted uneasily in his seat. 'Not necessarily,' he said with paternal defensiveness.

Macdonald, childfree, grinned. 'Take a good look at Nico Ryan. He's a horrible warning about what happens if you get it wrong. Look, that's the turn-off. Rosscarron – fifteen minutes, say.'

'SANDY!' COMING BACK from a quick lunch in the canteen, Fleming hailed PC Langlands, walking ahead of her along the corridor. 'Well done!'

Langlands turned, beaming. 'Just luck,' he said, with perfect truth. 'Still, it's good, eh? Have they got his name now?'

'Yes. Alex Rencombe. It's a company car, registered to some solicitor's firm in London.'

'Great. Thanks, boss.' Langlands, still beaming, went on his way.

Fleming had no wish to rain on his parade, but it seemed far from certain that they had discovered the identity of the dead man. A company car, a solicitor – the spiky-haired twenty-something? It didn't fit.

At least, though, it gave them a starting point. They had contacted the office and spoken to Mr Rencombe's secretary, but purely on the basis of a traffic offence. The more important questions could wait.

Mr Rencombe, she said, was on a business trip to Scotland. With professional discretion, she was vague about where he might be but promised to try to contact him.

So was the Lexus a stolen car? It hadn't been reported, but if someone told her that 'Damien' was into that sort of racket, she wouldn't fall over backwards in surprise. They'd have his fingerprints before long anyway, and then it would be a matter of minutes to do a check for any previous.

Even if they did find out his real identity, it wouldn't necessarily solve anything. This one, she thought uncomfortably, was going to run and run.

THERE WAS A 'Road Closed' sign on a metal barricade across the access to the cottages. A huge digger was parked just short of the landfall, with a Portakabin beside it as well as three skips. There was no one about.

DS MacNee parked the car, then stepped past the barrier and, skirting the huge pile of earth and rubble, walked round to the site.

It was eerie out here. The air was clammy with a grey mist and there was no view, except of a dark, sullen sea, no sound except the relentless lapping of the waves in front of the ruined houses. Even the workmen seemed to have fled: there were some spades stuck into a pile of earth and an empty wheelbarrow abandoned beside them.

MacNee felt a cold chill run down his spine. It was as if the greyness were closing in on him, trapping him in this unchancy place where a life as well as the cottages had been destroyed. He tried to shake himself out of it: the absence of activity was no more than another example of the Great British Workman not at work, and there would be no sense of urgency about any project that wouldn't have votes in it for the councillors. It still felt creepy, though.

Number 2 Rosscarron Cottages – that was the one he was looking for, with the blue-and-white tape still round it, though a couple of strands had broken off and were hanging limp from the poles.

The house wasn't as badly damaged as the first one, which was still almost completely buried, but from the look of it if Mr X hadn't been dead before the cliff fall, it would have killed him.

Picking his way carefully, MacNee went in through the broken door, propped open with a rough plank, glancing nervously up at the hole in the roof and the huge boulder blocking the staircase. He wasn't about to try going up, but he wanted to stand in the room where the body had been found and see if it had a story to tell him. There were metal supports propping up the doorway and the ceiling; it looked safe enough.

There were signs of the SOCOs everywhere. The room was bare now; everything in it would have been removed for testing, and underfoot there was only the rubble of fallen plaster and lathes of wood. But even when it was furnished, it could never have been anything other than dark and a bit bleak, with that small window and the old-fashioned cast-iron fireplace and grate.

The chalk marks on a cleared area of floor showed him exactly where the body had lain, underneath a roof beam, which was now propped up. MacNee had seen the photos on the board in the incident room, of course, but this told him a bit more. Mr X, felled by a blow from behind, had fallen quite near the door.

He hadn't been on his guard, expecting it. He had turned his back – when he was leaving, perhaps? You didn't, in normal conversation, turn your back on the person you were speaking to.

Had there been a row? Mr X turns to walk out; on the spur of the moment his assailant seizes something – something, with any luck, that the SOCOs would identify – and strikes the back of his head.

And then what? Clears out the man's pockets, takes his car, then leaves in a panic? Hears later of the landfall with incredulous delight, hoping perhaps that no one will ever know how Mr X met his end? Then disappears completely, once the hunt is on?

Or stays around and brazens it out. Kershaw would be sure to point the finger at Lisa, especially in the light of later developments. Yet MacNee had believed the girl when she swore she hadn't known Mr X.

Why had he been there at all? He was hardly likely to have wandered into a random cottage, thoughtfully bringing his murderer with him. So the boyfriend, the so-called Lee, he was fairly sure, must have . . . must have . . . what?

He had intended to leave, witness the suitcase Jan Forbes had seen; had Mr X, perhaps, arrived unexpectedly and been taken back to the house for a talk, which had developed into a quarrel, murder and subsequent panic?

In that case, could the death at the guest house be a revenge killing? And if so, who knew all about this but was lying low?

MacNee emerged from the cottage. He'd got plenty to think about and an idea or two to follow up, but he wasn't ready to go back to headquarters yet. When he was in the area anyway, he'd go and pay another call on his old friends at Rosscarron House. There was no reason why they should have heard about the latest killing and he'd like to have the chance of judging whether it came as news to them. Or not.

LISA STEWART GOT down from the bus, waving a thank-you to the driver, who had made an unscheduled stop for her.

The road ran close to the shore here, and on the opposite side a brilliantly whitewashed house stood on its own, looking out across Wigtown Bay and encircled by a grey stone wall. A sign in the well-kept garden read, 'Rowantrees Hotel,' and by the entrance there were indeed rowans, one on either side in the traditional position for protection against witches.

Lisa stood, her eyes half closed, and breathed deeply. The drizzling rain and mist had just cleared and the fresh breeze carried the tang of salt and seaweed. It felt so . . . so *clean*!

She walked across to a gap in the golden banks of whin lining the road and then over the springy turf, which gave way to coarse sand and stones, going to stand at the water's edge. A flock of oyster-catchers further along the beach rose as one and swirled round with their piping cries, before settling back to run among the pebbles on their red, stilt-like legs.

The sea was quiet today, with only that slight breeze ruffling its surface and giving the waves white, feathery tops as they ran up almost to Lisa's feet, then retreated with a soft fizzing of foam, which left a trail of bubbles on the hard sand. She had to take a hasty step back when a wave, bolder than the others, threatened to soak her feet.

Almost mesmerised by the rhythmic sounds, she stood for a long time, gazing out to sea. The sky was overcast, but suddenly a rift in the clouds appeared and a shaft of light gilded the farther side of the bay with its direct rays. A Bible sky, Lisa's granny had called it, because it looked as if the heavens had opened. A good omen?

At last, reluctantly, she turned to go, then stopped. Reaching into her bag, Lisa took out the mobile she had hidden under the floor, then threw it as far as she could into the sea.

Walking back across the road, she felt lighter, freer already. Perhaps getting rid of the phone had begun the process of starting afresh, and at the gate of the Rowantrees Hotel she glanced up at the graceful trees as if they might, indeed, be guardians to protect her.

The lobby of the hotel was old-fashioned, with a gleaming wooden floor and dark furniture. A bowl of roses stood on the reception desk, their scent competing with the smell of furniture polish. It felt comfortable and reassuring. And *safe*. Lisa blinked away exhausted tears.

There was no one about. A little hesitantly, she pinged the glittering brass bell on the counter and a moment later a plump, cheerful-looking woman with greying hair and bright blue eyes popped out from the door under the stairs.

'Oh, you must be Lisa! I'm Susan Telford. I'm so glad you caught that bus. With the service on Sundays you'd have had a long wait if you'd missed that one.'

'I just made it. The driver let me off by the hotel.'

She nodded wisely. 'Ah, that would be Doddie. You were lucky – if it'd been Rab, he'd have gone on to the official stop and you'd have had a mile to walk. Now, let me take you to your room.'

Still chatting, she led the way up a staircase, carpeted in turkey red, then opened the door to a light, spacious bedroom to the front of the house with a shower room off it.

'I thought we'd give you a nice sea view. Jan said you were needing to be cosseted, after all that's happened, so we'll have to look after you.' Susan smiled at Lisa with great warmth. 'There's a tray there for tea, and some of my biscuits in that wee tin there. Now, you just take your time, have a nice rest. When you're ready, you'll find Jan down in the sitting room. She's looking forward to seeing you again. Anything more you're needing?'

Lisa managed to say no and thank you. When the door closed, she sat down on the bed. The white bed linen smelled faintly of lavender fabric conditioner.

It was so quiet, so peaceful! It felt – that word again – *safe*.

It was dangerous to relax, to let her guard down. There were times when she'd thought she was safe before and he'd found her. But he was dead now, wasn't he?

Chapter Sixteen

THE DOOR TO the sitting room at Rosscarron House burst open and Cris Pilapil appeared in the doorway.

'Well, it's really hit the fan now!'

Declan and Cara Ryan were sitting together on a sofa to his right. Both heads whipped round; both faces registered expressions of shock and alarm. From the other side of the room, hidden by the open door, DS Macdonald and DC Campbell were perfectly placed to observe their reaction.

Pilapil stepped fully into the room. He looked unkempt, Macdonald thought, and his face was pale and puffy around the eyes. He said, 'I've just been on the phone, and—' then stopped in consternation.

Ryan moved quickly. 'Never mind the problems with the PR firm, Cris. This is rather more serious. The officers have come to tell us that one of the fans was murdered in Kirkluce last night.'

As an exercise in damage limitation, it was impressive. Pilapil, though, was struggling to follow the lead. 'Oh – oh, really? That's – that's very sad,' he stammered. 'What happened?'

'Sounds like a brawl outside a pub,' Ryan said. 'Can't see it's anything to do with us, Sergeant, but of course if we can help in any way . . .'

'That's not quite what I said, sir,' Macdonald corrected him. 'The body was found in the garden behind a small guest house. The gentleman was someone we interviewed here yesterday, before the campers were allowed to leave. He gave his name as Damien Gallagher – does that mean anything to you?'

Pilapil said quickly, 'I have nothing to do with the campers. Sorry.' Ryan looked blank and shook his head. Cara was looking blank anyway, sitting back now on the sofa with her hands clasped in her lap.

Perhaps he shouldn't jump to conclusions – perhaps she was still just in shock after her father's death. 'Mrs Ryan?' Macdonald prompted.

Cara looked at him vaguely. 'The campers? I don't know. I didn't go up there.'

The doorbell rang. Pilapil said, 'I'll go,' and disappeared.

'Where were you last night?' Campbell said bluntly.

'We were all here. As you can imagine, there's been a hell of a lot to do, sorting things out. We want to be ready to leave here whenever you lot give the OK so we can deal with what will be waiting for us at the other end. Maybe you could get on with that, instead of asking us stupid questions.'

Ryan's petulant response seemed a little too pat, Macdonald thought. 'When you say "all"?' he probed.

'Cara, myself, Nico of course, Cris and Joss Hepburn – one of the stars of the festival. He's an old friend of my father-in-law's.'

'Perhaps we could have a word with him too,' Macdonald was saying, when the door opened and Pilapil ushered DS Tam MacNee into the room.

Seeing his fellow officers, MacNee's face fell. 'Didn't know you were here,' he grunted.

This wasn't the moment to point out the virtues of simply doing what you were tasked to do, but Macdonald promised himself that this would be a treat deferred.

'We've just been asking Mr and Mrs Ryan about last night,' he said, allowing his annoyance to show. 'Everyone was here all the time, apparently.'

Impervious, MacNee turned to Ryan. 'You'd be sorry to hear about Mr Gallagher.'

Like a dog sensing danger, Ryan stiffened. 'Sure. But I didn't know him.'

'Aye, did you!' MacNee said. 'You were having a wee crack with him the first time I saw you, on Thursday. Then again, when we were up together at the campsite later, I saw you and him having a good blether.'

There was a moment of stillness. Ryan's eyes flickered; then he said, 'I – I talked to everyone at the site. That was my job. OK, I probably talked to him. So? I didn't know his name or anything about him. What did he look like?'

Again, it was a clever reply. Macdonald had to oblige with a description and Ryan was able to say immediately, 'Oh, I know who you mean. Nice guy. That's really tragic.'

Campbell said, 'You'll have his booking form?'

'I guess. It'll probably be on the computer that your lot took away.'

Stalemate, Macdonald reckoned, but MacNee wasn't giving up.

'So, you were here together all evening, all of you, all the time? Just a cosy, domestic evening.' There was a sneer in MacNee's voice.

It was, surprisingly, Cara who rose to the bait. 'Yes, it was,' she said fiercely. 'And anyway, why are you going on at us like this? It's nothing to do with us. Surely you should be looking at the people who are staying in the guest house?'

Was that an indrawn breath from her husband? MacNee's eyes, suddenly thoughtful, fixed on her face, but before he could speak, Ryan said, 'I'm sure they'll be doing that as well, Cara. Anyway, do you want to check our story with Joss Hepburn? I'm positive he'll confirm it.'

'Oh, so am I,' MacNee said jovially. 'But one more thing – do you know someone called Alex Rencombe?'

This time, it wasn't a moment of stillness. It was the silence of utter shock.

THE DOOR HAD hardly closed behind the officers when the recriminations began.

'I was trying to warn you!' Pilapil opened his defence. 'His secretary phoned to say the police had booked Alex's car and were trying to trace him. She wanted to know where he was – you'd told me to say we were in touch.'

'Trying to warn us!' Ryan snarled. 'Dropping us in it, more like, you stupid bastard. If you thought a bit more and drank a bit less, this sort of thing wouldn't happen.'

Hepburn, sitting at the farther end of the room as if trying to distance himself, said angrily, 'Just can it, will you? Running around like headless turkeys isn't smart, and slagging off Cris won't help either.'

His eyes were cold and hard. Ryan didn't even try to meet their challenge, dropping his head and saying tiredly, 'All right, all right. Sorry. Now what?'

'Fine. Now, let's try and sort out this God-awful mess. Where is Alex, Declan?'

'How the hell would I know? You tell me. All I know is that Gillis said Alex was doing a job for him, unspecified, and since he wasn't broadcasting what it was, I assumed it was something he'd prefer the police didn't know about.'

'Gillis would have preferred the police didn't know about most of what he did. We all would.' Hepburn's languid pose had disappeared; he took a short, nervous drag at his cigarette.

There was a sudden crash overhead, a thud and then a wail. Cara, brooding in the corner of the sofa, sat up. 'That's Nico, Declan. He's hurt himself.'

'You go,' Ryan said shortly. 'I've got my hands full.'

'But he might need you,' she persisted.

Ryan's patience snapped. 'You deal with him. If he's destroyed anything, I can't guarantee not to give him something to cry about.'

Cara's eyes narrowed. 'You don't care, do you? I'll remember that.' Her pale face flushed with anger, she got up and stormed out, slamming the door.

Pilapil broke the awkward silence. 'What are we going to do, then?'

Ryan, who had turned his head to look glumly after his wife, sighed. 'We can't afford to have them digging around the business.' He looked at Hepburn. 'We talked about it before, remember? Fleming's got to drop it, before she gets anyone else interested. Call her off.'

Without waiting for a reply, he left the room. Pilapil, not looking at Hepburn, got up to follow him.

Hepburn lit up again. His face was dark, and the hand holding the cigarette was rigid with tension. As he drew the smoke deep into his lungs, he heard Cara's voice, screaming muffled abuse at her husband. He guessed she must be due her next fix.

As THE POLICE officers went back to their cars, Macdonald said, in aggrieved tones, 'I thought you were meant to be at the Balmoral, not out here, Tam. And how the hell did you know about this Alex Rencombe?'

'Ah, well, I'd had a wee idea, and then a radio message came through about his car being found,' MacNee said, sounding smug. 'The boss had asked them to contact you, but you weren't answering. I said I'd go and spring it on the Ryans since I was nearby. How did they react to the news about Gallagher?'

'Him? Cool – too cool, maybe. Her? Well.' Macdonald shrugged. 'Broke out at the end, though.'

'Yes,' MacNee said thoughtfully. 'Knew Lisa Stewart was staying there, I reckon – wonder how? But they certainly went into shock when I mentioned Rencombe's car.'

'The Filipino lad wasn't as surprised as the others – the phone call, presumably. But you certainly got your reaction,' Macdonald admitted.

'Didn't do much good, though,' Campbell pointed out with his usual bluntness. 'They clammed up.'

Indeed they had, Hepburn too when they called him in. MacNee, on the defensive, said, 'We found out he was Crozier's lawyer anyway. And that he wasn't the dead guy who'd been driving the Lexus. But it didn't take Ryan long to think of saying the car must have been stolen.'

'Couldn't explain why it wasn't reported, though,' Macdonald pointed out. 'Or tell us where Rencombe is now.'

'In the mortuary,' Campbell voiced MacNee's thought. 'He's Mr X, obviously.'

THE FINGERPRINT INFORMATION that had just reached Fleming pointed to the same conclusion. Mr X's fingerprints were all over the Lexus, though overlaid with prints taken from the body at the guest house. And those prints belonged not to a 'Damien Gallagher', but to one Jason Williams, with a conviction in London for demanding money with menaces.

Having groped in the dark for so long, it felt almost dizzying to have names and background all at once. How to deal with such riches?

It made up for the disappointing interim report from the computer analyst. It had been entirely straightforward to access the files on Crozier's PC, all of which concerned the organisation of the festival and the local housing development. There was no record of other business, and there were no personal emails or CDs with extra information. A further search would be done to make sure they hadn't missed anything, but the professional view was that this was unlikely.

Which, of course, suggested that somewhere there had been a more sensitive laptop, a laptop that had been removed along with the papers from the filing cabinet while Fleming slept the sleep of exhaustion upstairs.

Both could still be in the house, but what chance had she of a general search warrant? There was no evidence that whatever business Crozier was carrying on had any bearing on his death, and sheriffs didn't issue warrants on the basis of a DI's gut feeling that something wasn't right.

Anyway, how could she open up a new front when they were at full stretch already? She'd simply have to shelve all that meantime, and at least now there was solid progress to report, which might get the press off their backs. They were revving up already to take her apart: the details of her last case and her suspension had been rehashed with relish, and Donald Bailey was visibly twitching. She tried to put that out of her mind. After what she had suffered at their hands the last time, it made her feel sick.

Rencombe. Fleming was considering her next move on that when DS MacNee appeared, looking pleased with himself.

'Tam?' she said hopefully.

'Gillis Crozier's lawyer, that's who he is. They don't know any-thing – allegedly – except that he was doing a job for Crozier, unspecified, and that he was expected at Rosscarron House and didn't arrive. Presumably he's our—'

'Mr X,' Fleming finished for him. 'I know. His fingerprints are all over the car. I've just been working out where we go from here . . . Formal ID first. Wheel in Ryan and someone else – one of the other men, preferably. Cara would be less than ideal if she's spaced out.'

'Pilapil and Hepburn both know him,' MacNee said. 'But you'd maybe rather keep Hepburn out of it?' He gave a suggestive wink.

'Whichever,' she said coolly. 'Something in your eye, Tam? Or are you developing a twitch?'

MacNee didn't respond.

She went on, 'Right. I've another piece of good news.'

She told him about the identification of Jason Williams, aka Damien Gallagher. 'We can pretty safely work on the presump-tion that if he was driving Rencombe's car, he killed him first. So what's the connection between them? How did Williams come to be driving Rencombe's car?'

'I've a wee theory about that,' MacNee said slowly. 'I went out to Rosscarron Cottages today.'

'I did wonder when they said you were going there. Thought you were meant to be at the guest house?'

'I was, until it was locked up. Then I took that dour besom Lisa Stewart to find out about a bus to the hotel, to get her past the cameras.'

'I'm glad you did that. There'll be a frenzy when they realise she's involved in this. Anyway, you went to the cottages?'

'It's a right mess out there,' MacNee said. 'If you ask me, they'll end up levelling the lot, for the insurance. There was no one actually living there, after all – and would the owners really want to rebuild, out at the end of the road to nowhere? But in number 2 . . .' He paused. 'I know you've seen the footage, but when I was there, I could kind of see better what would have happened. And what we know now would fit with that. Mr X – Rencombe – was hit on the back of the head, near the door – leaving after a row, maybe. So then Williams panics and goes off in his Lexus.'

'You're assuming that Jason Williams, Damien Gallagher and Lee Morrissey are all the same person? That Lisa's lying about not recognising Williams's body?'

'Damn sure of it.'

Fleming was frowning. 'But what about their own car? They must have had one – where is it?'

'Ah, that I can tell you. Under a bloody great heap of rubble, where the car park was. Williams maybe couldn't resist taking the posh car instead of his own.'

'Fair enough. But Jan Forbes saw Lisa's boyfriend leave, right? Why did he go if Rencombe was coming to see him?'

'Maybe Rencombe never said. Just had the bad luck to arrive as he was leaving.'

Fleming considered that. 'OK, that works. So what had he come to see him about? That's the key point.'

MacNee shrugged. 'No idea. What I do know is that if Lisa Stewart told us all she knows, we'd be halfway there. At least.'

'I'm with you there. I might get Kim to have a go at her, see what she can do.'

MacNee said nothing in a pointed manner, but Fleming chose to ignore it. 'I want you to phone and break the news to his secretary, once we get a firm ID on Rencombe. But organise that as a matter of urgency.'

JAN FORBES, WITH her plastered foot up on a stool and her crutches at her side, was sitting in the hotel lounge knitting when Lisa Stewart came hesitantly in.

She had always been pale, but the girl was paler than ever now, with a crop of angry spots on her chin and dark rings under her eyes. Shocked by her appearance, Jan held out a welcoming hand.

'My dear, it's good to see you. Come away in and sit down. We'll have the place to ourselves. Susan's got a couple of families staying, but they're always out during the day. I'll enjoy having company – the Telfords are much too busy to waste time blethering.

'Are you all right? You've been having a dreadful time – I'm so sorry.' Behind the glasses, her grey eyes were warm with sympathy.

Lisa came forward and took her hand in a sort of awkward handshake, as if she weren't quite sure what to do with it, then sat down opposite.

'Oh, I'm all right,' she said in a flat, listless tone that gave the lie to the words. Then she added, almost grudgingly, 'Thanks for suggesting this place. It's – it's really nice.'

Her voice faltered and Jan wondered for a moment if she was going to break down, but Lisa went on, 'It was the reporters. They've probably told you – I'm Lisa Stewart. There was a trial . . .'

'I remember the trial,' Jan said gently. 'You were acquitted.'

Lisa gave a bitter laugh. 'Oh, yes, though you'd never know it. Everyone still thinks I did it. I might just as well have been found guilty.'

'I don't think you'd have enjoyed prison.'

'I suppose they'd have given me a hard time. They don't like child killers and it wouldn't have made any difference that I wasn't one.' Lisa's voice wobbled and she stopped, biting her lip. 'Sorry. I'm being stupid. Just tired, probably.'

Just on the verge of falling apart, in Jan's opinion. Always practical, she said, 'You're probably hungry too. I know Susan would heat up some soup and make a sandwich.'

'I'm all right.' Lisa's reply was brusque, as if she regretted having allowed emotion to show.

'Are you sure? It's always very good soup.' Jan hesitated, then said, as delicately as she could, 'You probably found yourself with nothing, after the landslip. If money's a problem . . .'

'No, I'm fine.' Lisa got up and went to the door. 'I'm just going up to my room for a rest.'

Jan picked up her knitting again, a red and blue sweater with an elephant on the front for the Telfords' grandson. She liked knitting; it gave you something to do with your hands while you were thinking.

The girl was farouche, certainly. It would have been gracious at least to acknowledge Jan's offer of help rather than walking out of the room.

But under her abrupt manner Jan could see a frightening level of strain. Lisa was trying desperately to keep control and Jan was afraid of what she might do when she failed, as she most certainly would.

The girl needed to talk to someone, and it looked as if Jan was the only person around. As she wove in the grey wool for the elephant's trunk, she puzzled over the problem.

LISA WAS BREATHLESS when she reached her room and locked the door behind her; she had run up the stairs as fast as she could. It felt almost like needing to reach the bathroom before you were sick. If she had stayed there, without volition, it would all have come spewing out in a messy stream: all that had happened to her, all she had done, how scared she was, how scared!

She mustn't. It was dangerous, this place: the comfort and the tranquil atmosphere made you feel that here nothing bad could happen to you. And Jan Forbes was dangerous too, with those wise eyes that seemed to see much more than you were telling her, and her lethal kindness.

Because being on your guard against aggression and cruelty and deception was easy – Lisa had learned that trick long ago. But putting up the barriers against goodness and generosity and warm concern, fighting the longing to have someone listen and care – that would be the hardest thing she had ever done.

Because she mustn't tell anyone. If she told anyone, it would be the end.

DI Fleming had been waiting for the SOCOs' report on the search at number 2 Rosscarron Cottages and she was getting impatient. She'd nudged them once already and been promised it today, but it was almost time for the afternoon briefing and there was still no sign of it. Irritably, she picked up the phone.

'I'm glad to hear it's on its way,' she said tartly in response to the excuse from the other end. 'I hope by "on its way" you mean the same as I mean.'

Muttering sceptically, she went back to preparing her briefing notes, but she was doing them an injustice. Five minutes later the report came through on her computer and she pounced on it eagerly. She would just have time to skim it before she left.

She scrolled rapidly through the background information, then coming to a paragraph headed 'Significant finding', stopped to read it more carefully. As she took in what it said, her eyebrows shot up. Breakthrough, at last!

Chapter Seventeen

'Big Marge is looking cheerful this evening,' DC Kershaw said to DS Macdonald, taking the seat beside him at the afternoon briefing. 'But what the hell is she doing with a frying pan?'

There was, indeed, a large frying pan on the table in front of her. Macdonald was intrigued. 'Going to whip up bacon butties for us, maybe,' he suggested. 'You're right, she's not looking as hodden down as she was. Has to be good news – and look at Tam. He's scented something.'

In the next row, MacNee was looking intently at Fleming as she shuffled her papers and his head was indeed up, like a dog testing the air. Officers were taking their seats and gradually the general hum of conversation died. As Fleming stepped forward, she was smiling broadly.

'There's good news tonight. We now know the identity of Mr X's killer and are in a position to lay charges, but there is a problem with that.'

There was a buzz of surprise and the talk started again; she held up her hand. 'Plenty of time to exclaim later. We've a lot to get through and I don't expect you want to be kept any longer than necessary on a Sunday night.

'We have good reason to believe Mr X's body will tomorrow be identified as that of Alex Rencombe, Gillis Crozier's solicitor. The SOCOs' report has found very promising fingerprint evidence too.

'The weapon used to kill him was a cast-iron frying pan. The handle had been wiped, but a thumbprint was overlooked and was found in a very interesting place. The canteen kindly lent me this to show you.' She held up the pan, to a ripple of amusement.

'If you are cooking with a frying pan, you hold it like this –' she demonstrated – 'and your thumb is on top of the handle. If, on the other hand, I got annoyed with Sergeant Naismith here – don't panic, Jock, I only said, "If"!'

Naismith mimed alarm.

'My, my, we *are* in a chirpy mood tonight,' Macdonald murmured to Kershaw, as Fleming grinned and carried on.

'Look.' She swung the pan in an arc. 'To get proper purchase on it, I would turn it over and my thumb would be here, on the underside of the handle. Which is exactly where the thumbprint was found – the thumbprint of Jason Williams from London who has previous. His fingerprints were all over the rooms in the cottage. He is also the man found dead this morning at the Balmoral Guest House.'

This time Fleming let the reaction go on for a little longer before calling them to order.

'The bad news is, of course, that we can't question him to find out what it was all about. We still don't know who killed Crozier, or who killed Williams himself, and we've no idea of the motive behind any of these killings. So – don't groan – we're talking old-fashioned graft.

'We know that Williams, calling himself Damien Gallagher, turned up at the campsite along with the earliest fans for the rave at Rosscarron House. We need every scrap of information we can get about him at that time, which means that everyone who was there has to be questioned again more specifically.

'It would be useful to know where Williams has been since he left the campsite. Check out the hotels, guest houses and B & Bs. He could be calling himself Gallagher, Williams or even Lee Morrissey, though that's less likely.

'Sergeant Naismith will be tasking the teams, and my own team – MacNee, Macdonald, Campbell and Kershaw – will be following up on the family and others most directly involved.' Fleming looked towards them. 'My office, after this. Right – any questions?'

A hand was raised in the front row. 'The female who was in the guest house lived in the cottage where Rencombe's body was found, didn't she? Has she identified Williams as her partner?'

'Not as yet,' Fleming said. 'Anything else?'

A very careful reply, Kershaw thought, as Fleming dealt with a couple of other routine queries, then left the room.

'I could have done without this tonight, I must say,' she said to Macdonald with a grimace. 'I'd planned to go and see my daughter before she goes to sleep.'

'Your daughter? How do you think I feel? I have a hot date – well, I *had* a hot date.'

'If she doesn't understand about the job, it hasn't got a future anyway.' Kershaw was unsympathetic.

Macdonald looked alarmed. 'Who said anything about the future? She's not exactly the sort of girl you'd take home to Mum. The future I had in mind doesn't stretch beyond tomorrow morning.'

He was texting gloomily as they went up the stairs to Fleming's office.

'WE HAVE TO get Lisa Stewart to admit she was lying. That's our first step,' Fleming said.

MacNee, she was interested to note, was today sitting on one of the chairs by her desk. It was Macdonald who, coming in behind the others, found himself offered the edge of the table.

'Shall I go and fetch another chair, boss?' he had asked.

'Just perch if you don't mind, Andy,' she said. 'I don't like getting the room too cluttered up with chairs.'

Fleming knew they thought it was odd that she was always one chair short, but she found it a useful indicator of the state of mind of her team. Deliberately choosing the table when a chair was vacant usually indicated detachment. Today, however, they were all interested and committed, and Macdonald looked quite irritated at being at one remove.

She went on, 'I can't see Lisa has any alternative. She can hardly claim not to have noticed someone whose prints were found all over her house. I'm open to suggestions here. I think I'm inclined to bring her in, do it formally, zap her with the evidence. The alternative would be to have Kim go to the hotel to talk to her there and see if she can persuade her to open up.'

'Depends if she killed him or not.' Campbell, uncharacteristically, was the first to speak.

'Killed Jason Williams, do you mean?' Fleming asked.

'Could be Crozier too. There or thereabouts each time.'

MacNee nodded. 'Right enough. Bring her in – we tried having wee chats and where did it get us?'

'I don't agree.'

Predictably, Kershaw took up the opposite position and Fleming groaned inwardly. She *really* didn't want to have to referee their silly squabbles, but it looked as if sooner or later she would have to.

Kershaw was saying, 'I understand why Tam thinks that, and it could work better – I'm not saying it won't. If I go and talk to her, though, and don't get anywhere, we have a fall-back position but if we force her into a "helping with enquiries" position, there's no way we can do the cosy-chat bit afterwards.'

That made sense, and Campbell and Macdonald were nodding. MacNee wasn't. MacNee was scowling.

'Looking for an opportunity to show that you can succeed where I failed?' he said. 'Well—'

Fleming cut him short. 'Shut it, Tam. Right, Kim, you've convinced me. You have a go, and if nothing comes of it, we can move on to the formal stuff.

'Now, I want to focus on what we know about links between our victims and the other people in the frame. Start with Lisa. Lisa knew Crozier, and she must have known Jason Williams – in her case, aka Lee Morrissey.'

'Williams, Morrissey, Gallagher,' Campbell interrupted. 'I've just realised.'

Macdonald and Kershaw were there immediately. 'Of course,' Kershaw said, and then as MacNee looked from one to the other, Macdonald explained kindly, 'All the surnames of stars from the world of popular music, Tam.'

'So, as I was saying,' Fleming said hastily, 'Lisa has links with those two, but denies any with the other victim. Rencombe has links with the family, with Pilapil and with Hepburn, though not with Lisa. But Williams – I can't find a link with either Rencombe or the family.'

'Pop stars' names as aliases? Music, that's the common thread,' MacNee said triumphantly. 'Which means there's someone else to think about whose name hasn't really featured – Joss Hepburn.' He looked very directly at Fleming.

With a sense of hurt, Fleming realised he was putting her on the spot. Punishment for having supported Kershaw? But she agreed coolly enough: 'I certainly don't trust him.' She looked past MacNee to the others. 'I knew him quite well many years ago, and I know what I'm talking about.' She hurried on in the uncomfortable silence. 'I think you're probably right to say that's how they all became involved. We need to press harder to find out the how, where, when – the standard questions.'

'Maidie Buchan told me that Crozier met his business partners when they were in the army and formed a band,' Kershaw offered. 'It could be worth talking to Alick Buchan about that – he seems to have had quite a grudge against his boss.'

'Right.' Fleming thought for a moment. 'Have you arranged for the identification of Rencombe's body, Tam?'

'Ryan and Hepburn, tomorrow morning.'

'Good. Then afterwards you and Macdonald could see what you can do to rattle them.'

'Maybe you should have a go at Hepburn,' MacNee suggested, too innocently.

She didn't even glance at him, saying flatly, 'No – too much pressure on my time tomorrow already. Kim, talk to Lisa – do that on your own. You might get further with her one to one. And take time to read up the witness statements first. Ewan, go with her, and after she's finished with Lisa, you can both go on to Rosscarron to interview Alick Buchan. He's at the bottom of the suspect list after this latest development, but it might give us a new angle if we knew more about Crozier's business interests – though if it's all as dodgy as I think it is, that'll be Fraud Squad business, not ours.

'It's getting late. We could go on discussing theories all night, but I've another couple of hours to do here and I'd like to get home before dawn. OK?'

Andy Macdonald took a quick look at his watch and was pulling out his mobile as they filed out.

Monday, 24 July

LISA HADN'T SLEPT as well on the lavender-scented linen as she had hoped she would. She had fallen straight into a deep sleep but woke, shuddering and gasping, from a nightmare in the early hours. And it was persistent: every time her heavy eyes closed it returned, in much the same form. It was dark and cold, with a chill rain falling, and she knew there was someone following her, following her so closely that she could even feel the breath on the back of her neck, though when she turned there was only empty darkness. But the breathing was still there, along with an overpowering sense of imminent disaster, and she would start awake again in a sweat of terror.

But the sun was actually shining this morning and there was a powerful shower in the little bathroom. She stood under it until she felt a bit more human, and as she went downstairs, she could smell bacon cooking.

Jan Forbes was in the cheerful dining room already and looked up with an expectant smile. Her heart sinking, Lisa realised that she would have to join her. She had always been shy, and at the moment her mind was too full of all the things she couldn't say to welcome the idea of making conversation.

She needn't have worried. Jan was happy to chatter on, with only a nod or a few words from Lisa to keep her going.

Two of the other tables were occupied by family groups: at one, middle-aged parents with a teenage daughter and son who looked as if they had been dragged out of bed unwillingly; at the other, a younger family with a girl of about five, a baby in a high chair and a toddler, who was squirming restlessly in her seat. At last, with an apologetic look around the room, the harassed young mother let her get down, with an admonition not to be a nuisance.

Watching her, Lisa's face softened as the little blonde girl, wearing tiny jeans and a frilly pink top, trotted importantly around, taking a good look at the other occupants. When she got to Lisa, though, she stopped and gazed up at her.

'Got dolly,' she announced. She was holding a fabric doll, featureless from too much loving.

'It's a lovely dolly,' Lisa said. 'What's her name?'

'Dolly.'

Lisa caught the mother's eye and smiled. 'That's a very good name for a dolly. Does she go to bed with you?'

The child nodded. Then she said hopefully, 'Sto'y?' and trotted across to fetch a book lying on her family's table.

'Rosie, you mustn't bother the lady,' her father said, but Lisa assured him she was unbothered, picked up the little girl and set her on her knee while she read a vapid tale about a rabbit. The soft, warm little body snuggled into her, and it was quite hard to keep her voice steady as she complied with two more 'Again sto'y' demands.

The family finished breakfast and Rosie's mother came over. 'Thank you so much! I don't know how you can be so patient,' she said, scooping up Rosie, who was now reluctant to be parted from her new friend.

'I'll see you later,' Lisa promised, and Rosie waved over her mother's shoulder as she was carried away.

Lisa looked down at her plate, knowing that her eyes were wet. Looking after small children was the only thing she had a gift for and she would never be able to do it again, never.

Jan had noticed, though. Her voice was very gentle as she said, 'Children mean a lot to you, obviously.'

Lisa blinked hard. 'They don't lie, do they? Everyone else lies – oh, and they will too, when they get older, but before that, they're so lovely.' Then, to her horror, she heard herself saying, 'I had a baby once, but he – he died.'

Jan reached out a hand to touch hers. 'Oh, my dear, I'm so sorry!'

Lisa hadn't meant to say that. He'd only been days old when he died, that little helpless thing, and she'd gone back to school afterwards and never talked about it. And now she'd gone and blurted it out, to a woman she hardly knew, in a public dining room with the waitress coming to offer her more coffee. She mustn't break down.

Lisa hardened her voice. 'It was a long time ago,' she said, then, 'No, thank you,' to the waitress. Saying, 'I've got some things to sort out,' she got up and left the dining room.

What was she to do? She'd known Jan Forbes was dangerous; what else might Lisa find herself giving away? She couldn't just disappear when the police had told her to stay – and anyway, where would she go? She didn't want to leave this quiet, ordinary place with these nice, normal people. And Rosie might want some more stories later on.

'WOULDN'T MIND STAYING here,' Kim Kershaw said to Ewan Campbell, as he turned into the Rowantrees Hotel car park. 'It all looks immaculate, and that's a really great view out over Wigtown Bay.'

'Mmm,' Campbell said. He hadn't said a lot else on the drive down, but Macdonald had warned Kershaw not to take it personally.

'He doesn't make conversation – only speaks when he's actually got something to say. I just blether on, say whatever comes into my head, and it works all right.'

Kershaw had adopted Campbell's attitude rather than Macdonald's and had enjoyed the quiet drive, punctuated only by the standard radio messages. It was sunny too today, and though it might not last, at the moment the lush, vivid green of the fields and the singing blues of sky and sparkling sea were colours so fresh that they might have been invented that morning.

Leaving Campbell in the car, Kershaw went into the hotel. Susan Telford, if a little stiff in her manner, cooperated to the extent of offering their own private sitting room for the interview with Lisa Stewart, though she said warningly, 'She's very tired and shaken after all that's happened, poor child. She's been under a great deal of strain.'

'I'm sure,' Kershaw said noncommittally. She had every intention of going in hard, though she felt a certain misgiving when she saw how haggard Lisa was looking. Nevertheless she had a job to do, and lying to the police was a choice with consequences.

Susan hovered protectively for a moment, then left, saying, 'I'm just next door if you need me, Lisa,' clearly making sure that Kershaw knew she was within earshot of a cry for help if they started running needles under fingernails.

Lisa hadn't spoken. She sat down, folded her hands in her lap and looked towards Kershaw with cold, expressionless eyes.

Kershaw didn't waste time on preliminaries. 'Lisa, you lied to us.'

'Oh?' She raised her brows.

'You told us you didn't recognise the body of the man found outside the guest house yesterday morning. We now know he was your partner. His fingerprints are all over your cottage, so unless you are going to tell us there was someone sharing your home whom you never noticed . . .'

She ignored Kershaw's sarcastic tone. 'You said it was someone called Damien Gallagher. My partner's name was Lee Morrissey.'

Kershaw almost gasped at her effrontery. 'But you saw the body!'

'I didn't want to look at it closely.'

Oh, she was good! Kershaw, however, had done her homework. 'We have an eyewitness who describes it differently.'

In her most dramatic reaction so far, Lisa blinked. But she went on, 'It may have looked like that. I was probably in shock. I thought at first it could have been Lee, but his head was . . . well, damaged, and when you said who it was, I thought I must be wrong.'

Kershaw had believed she held all the cards, but she wasn't winning this round. 'But you admit it was your partner?'

'If you say so. I expect you'll make me go to that place again to look at him.'

'Perhaps. Did he come to the guest house to see you?'

'If he did, I didn't see him.'

'It would be a bit of a coincidence otherwise, wouldn't it? Especially since you sat up late in the sitting room after everyone else had gone to bed – almost as if you were waiting for someone.'

'I – I wasn't sleepy. I was reading magazines.'

The hesitation was a good sign. 'But you heard nothing, saw nothing?'

'Nothing.'

Kershaw shifted the ground. 'There was a body found at your cottage too, Lisa. Just another coincidence?'

Lisa didn't reply, only stared at her with those strange round eyes.

'We have reason to believe that he was Alex Rencombe, Gillis Crozier's lawyer. Did you know him?'

'No. I told you.'

'Did your partner know him?'

Lisa shrugged. 'He might have, for all I know.'

'The thing is, it looks as if your partner killed him. With a cast-iron frying pan.'

Bizarrely enough, that was what broke her calm. 'Granny's frying pan! But we didn't use it – it just sat by the range. Kind of like decoration, you know?'

'So your partner could just have picked it up from there on the spur of the moment?'

'Yes, but Lee wasn't there! He had gone. I saw him off. Maybe Lee met him at the car park and brought him back, to talk to him or something. How would *I* know? I'd gone out by then.' Lisa was agitated now.

'Did you? In that case,' Kershaw said with deliberate malice, 'Mr Rencombe would have been dead before you left the house. Was he, Lisa?'

'No, no, of course he wasn't!' she cried frantically. 'I've told you again and again, I never saw that man before in my life.'

Kershaw allowed a pause to develop. Then she said, 'You see, Lisa, we can't trust you. We both know you were lying about your partner, so why should I believe you now? But I tell you what. Let's wipe the slate and start all over again. Did you know that was your partner when you saw the body yesterday?'

'Yes.' It was a whisper. 'I knew it was Lee.'

'Why didn't you tell us?'

'Why do you think?' That was a spark of anger. 'Because I was afraid if you knew who he was you'd think it was something to do with me. And you have.'

'And it wasn't?'

'No!'

'You're lying again.' Kershaw's tone was conversational. 'Let's go for another take. Was it something to do with you, Lisa?'

Lisa was shaking now. 'Sort of.'

'What was it about?'

'I don't know!' she cried. 'I got a text message from him, that was all. He said he had to see me about something important – he didn't say what. And we arranged to meet in the garden round the back. Then . . .' She stopped.

'Go on, Lisa,' Kershaw coaxed her. 'You're doing the right thing, I promise you.'

'I went out at the time we said and – and he was – lying there. I – I didn't know what to do.'

Next time, just call the police, Kershaw thought, but she said, 'Did you see anyone else?'

'No.' Lisa stopped again. 'But – but I thought I heard a noise, a rustle behind one of the bushes. I was really scared. I just ran back down the alleyway, into the house.'

Did she believe her? Kershaw wasn't sure, but the formal, recorded interview would be the time to apply pressure. She went on to the next big question. 'Mr Rencombe was apparently doing a job for Mr Crozier. So what was your partner's connection with him?'

It was as if Crozier's name had turned her to stone. Kershaw saw Lisa go physically rigid, and when she spoke again, it was in that cold, dispassionate voice. 'I didn't know he had one.'

Despite pushing every button she could think of, Kershaw couldn't shift her. She had to leave it there, but going back to the evening of Williams's death, she was able to tidy up some loose ends, and even came away with one particularly interesting piece of information.

Kershaw went back to the car and opened the door at the driver's side. 'Come on, out of there, Ewan. How do you fancy paddling?'

THE IDENTIFICATION THIS time was straightforward. Declan Ryan and Joss Hepburn confirmed that this was, indeed, Alex Rencombe and then, as agreed, were driven to the Galloway Constabulary Headquarters in Kirkluce and shown to a waiting room.

MacNee, when he appeared along with Macdonald, viewed them without enthusiasm. He had no doubt who had been given the plum interview to do this morning, and it wasn't either of them.

'Right,' he said brusquely. 'Who's first?'

Hepburn, sitting back in a chair with his long legs stretched out, was all in black again today – black open-necked shirt, black expensive-looking jeans and a black leather jacket which, MacNee saw with resentment, was the soft, supple kind that cost thousands, unlike the one he was wearing himself, picked up at TK Maxx in Glasgow five years ago. Black made Hepburn seem taller than ever; MacNee didn't like that either.

'You go first, Declan,' Hepburn said to his companion who, in pale chinos and a light grey zip-top sweater, looked somehow insignificant beside the other man and, MacNee noted with interest, nervous too. Maybe they might get somewhere this morning after all.

Hepburn, however, was saying, 'I need to have a word with DI Fleming first. Perhaps that could be arranged before you talk to me?'

Macdonald glanced at MacNee. 'I don't think—' he began, but MacNee cut across him.

'Fine. I tell you what, you come with me and I'll take you upstairs and see if she has time for a wee word with you.'

Macdonald registered alarm. 'I really don't think . . .' but found he was addressing MacNee's departing back.

Hepburn, following, turned at the door with a broad wink. 'It's all right – we're old friends,' he said.

As MacNee keyed in his security number, Hepburn said, 'This is great – I thought I might have problems fixing this up.'

'Aye,' MacNee said, setting off at a brisk pace up the stairs, keeping a couple of steps ahead to gain height advantage: he hated being towered over. 'I'm not guaranteeing anything, mind. She's maybe busy, but it's worth a shot.'

He knew he was heading for trouble. He was asking for it, almost as if looking for a legitimate reason for his present sense of grievance. Anyway, Fleming was letting the personal intrude on the professional, in his opinion. It should be her doing the interviews with him, not Macdonald. Her background knowledge of Hepburn might have given them some sort of edge. Even with all this rationalising, though, it was with belated misgivings that he knocked on Fleming's door.

She was at her desk. 'Tam! Come on in. I had something to ask you.'

He said, 'Mr Hepburn needed a word with you,' then stepped back to allow Hepburn to pass him.

'I hope this isn't inconvenient,' he said, smiling at her.

Fleming looked at MacNee and he saw her look of hurt betrayal before it changed to one of glacial anger.

'Since you're here,' she said to Hepburn, 'I can spare you five minutes. You can go, Sergeant.'

Perhaps that hadn't been such a good idea after all, MacNee reflected, as he went back downstairs. Fleming was dangerous when she was as angry as that, but what troubled him more was the thought of betrayal. Rabbie Burns had some hard words to say about traitors.

And he realised suddenly what Hepburn, in his 'cool dude' blacks had reminded him of: the bad guy in a western. He wondered uneasily how the gunfight was going.

Chapter Eighteen

'OH DEAR,' HEPBURN drawled, as the door closed behind Mac-Nee, 'is the poor guy in trouble?'

'Very probably,' Fleming said, tight-lipped. 'So what's this about, Joss? I really haven't time for playing games.'

'Of course not.' His tone was offensively soothing. 'I just have a couple of things I reckon we should talk about.'

Fleming ignored him. 'Since you're here, you can tell me what the "job" was that Rencombe was doing for Crozier.'

'Ve ask zee qvestions, eh?' he mocked her. 'Babe, if I could! Not the slightest idea. Maybe he told Cara or Declan – or Cris, even, though he denies it.

'Incidentally, Cara wanted to know if you'd figured out that her ex-nanny, the one who killed her baby, was calling herself Beth Brown and staying at the guest house where the camper's body was found.'

'How did she know?'

Hepburn laughed indulgently. 'There you go again, my little *Obergruppenführer*! Local gossip, I guess – the gamekeeper was at the house yesterday. And apparently Nanny was staying along at the keeper's cottage just at the time Gillis was killed. Kind of suggestive, wouldn't you say?'

'I'm always prepared to listen to opinion.' Fleming half rose. 'Thank you for yours. Now, I have a great deal to do . . .'

'Sit down, Madge.' There was a slight edge to his voice now. 'I told Cara I would get an assurance from you direct. Can I take it that Lisa Stewart is about to be arrested for murder?'

'No.'

He looked taken aback at the bluntness of her reply. 'But at the very least she has to be prime suspect?'

'She is obviously a suspect. Others are equally under suspicion. You, for instance.'

He gave a brief, humourless smile. 'You were never one to pull your punches. So you wouldn't be ready to agree we can all return to London?'

'I can't physically stop you, but just at present, that is my firm request.' Fleming hesitated, then said, 'I might be inclined to take a more favourable view if I felt you were all being open and truthful in your answers to questioning. For instance, what is the nature of Gillis Crozier's business?'

'Ah.' Hepburn shifted in his seat uncomfortably. 'That was the other thing I wanted to talk to you about.'

'Suddenly I'm interested. Go on.'

'If I give you my word that his business has nothing to do with all this, will you drop that line of enquiry?'

'*Your word!*' Disappointed, she laughed in his face. 'Joss, I've known you since you were in your twenties. Don't be silly.'

'Touché.' He was looking acutely uneasy now. 'Madge, I didn't want to do it like this. But if you don't stop snooping into what doesn't concern either you or the cases you're investigating, I'm going to go to the tabloids with some choice anecdotes about your past. You can most likely guess which these would be.'

Stricken, Fleming blanched, so that the sickly yellows and blues of the fading bruises stood out starkly.

'My God, I knew you were a bastard, Joss, but this is something else! This is disgusting! You sicken me.'

Again the small, sour smile appeared. 'Oh, I don't like myself much either. But it's been forced on me, and there it is. The choice is yours.'

'Get out of my office.' Fleming got up, walked to the door and held it open. 'I'd like to think you knew before you said that what my reply would be. Attempted blackmail of a police officer is a serious offence and what you have succeeded in doing is convincing me that my gut reaction's right – there's something very wrong about Crozier's business. And I'm going to find out what it is.'

'Are you sure you won't reconsider?' Hepburn sounded almost pleading.

'The receptionist will expect you at the door in two minutes. And don't even try to pull a stunt like this again. You won't be admitted. Goodbye.'

Hepburn got up. 'I can't tell you how sorry I am that you can't see it my way.' He walked to the door, then looked down at her. 'But in another crazy way, I'm kind of glad. You're a great lady, Madge.'

This time, he did kiss her hard on the lips. Then he was gone.

FLEMING LISTENED TO his footsteps clattering down the stairs. She phoned reception, then took a tissue and scrubbed at her lips. She had never realised that moral nausea could make you feel physic-ally sick. Oh, fear was there too, but her overwhelming feeling was one of visceral revulsion.

It shouldn't have surprised her. She herself had said to the team, only last night, that Joss Hepburn wasn't to be trusted. Her head knew all about that, but in her heart of hearts . . .

He was her glamorous past. He was powerfully attractive and she had secretly found it both exciting and flattering that he still felt a spark was there. Or had he? Was that all just part of the dirty game he was playing? What was he saying about her behind her back? Her face turned hot and red at the thought.

In a way, she acknowledged, Tam was right. She had dodged another meeting with Joss because she found it so hard to restrict the conversation to entirely professional subjects. A part of her disgust was at her own contemptible ineffectiveness.

And she was afraid too. She had suffered ordeal by media once before, and until you had been through it, you didn't understand what a terrifying experience it was. It had been unpleasant enough this week when they started rehashing the details of her last case, and she daren't think what it would be like with 'revelations' being published in the tabloids. It would, quite simply, be the end of her career.

She couldn't even charge Hepburn with the serious crime of attempting to blackmail a police officer and get an injunction. It was only her word against his, which in the Scottish legal system meant there was no case to answer. She was totally at his mercy.

Mercy? From the man she now knew Joss Hepburn to be?

It was perfectly clear what Fleming should do. She should draw a dotted line round her neck, find an axe and a block, and report to her superintendent to be officially terminated. It was a stark choice: warn Bailey what was going to happen and pull her life down in ruins on her own head, or wait for the tabloids to do it for her.

There was no one she could go to for advice. Bill, usually her first choice for support and wise counsel, would never be crass enough to show anything other than sympathy, but she couldn't bear the humiliation of watching him trying not to think, I told you so, too loudly. Tam? Well, when she'd finished with him today, he'd be disinclined to speak to her, let alone to help sort out her problem. And she had no right to involve Purves in her messy professional life.

She was on her own for this one. She tapped a fingernail on her front teeth, trying to think it through.

Joss Hepburn was holding all the cards. On the other hand, he just might be bluffing. It was years since Fleming had played poker, but this was a no-brainer: follow the rule book to certain disaster, or take the gamble that his had been an empty threat.

She made up her mind: say nothing and tough it out. And damn your black soul to hell, Joss Hepburn!

It was only then that she realised it had not crossed her mind for a second that she might capitulate.

'You're a crazy man, MacNee,' Andy Macdonald said, as they headed towards the canteen together after their interviews with Ryan and Hepburn. 'A complete bampot!'

MacNee had had time for reflection. 'Aye,' he agreed hollowly. 'You ken how it is – seemed like a good idea at the time.'

'No, frankly, I don't know how it is. I don't know how anyone would think, even for a nanosecond, that it was a good idea to break every rule in the book and take a punter in to see Big Marge without an appointment. And I *really* don't know why anyone would do it when the punter in question was an old boyfriend, unless they had a death wish.'

'Maybe I do,' MacNee grunted, and Macdonald looked at him sharply. But he was going on, 'I thought perhaps we'd manage to get something out of that pair that I could take to her.'

'Like a peace offering?'

'Kind of.'

'But there isn't anything,' Macdonald pointed out helpfully.

'No need to rub it in.'

Ryan and Hepburn had, in their separate ways, taken up two hours of the detectives' morning in adding absolutely nothing to the sum of their knowledge. Hepburn had been calm, urbane and anxious to be helpful in a totally unhelpful way. Ryan had snarled and sneered – he had taken delight in emphasising MacNee's position as his alibi for the time of his father-in-law's murder – but again had told them nothing they had not been told before.

At least this time the bridie, beans and chips were forthcoming, and MacNee and Macdonald went to sit at an empty table.

'I had a thought,' Macdonald said suddenly.

'Had to happen sometime, I suppose.'

'Very funny. Anyway, we know who killed Rencombe and we know someone else killed Williams, but all three murders were spur-of-the-moment jobs. Williams picked up the nearest thing to fell Rencombe, someone used a stone to hit Crozier, and with Williams the crowbar was presumably lying beside the car that was being repaired.'

'No,' MacNee said. 'It wasn't.'

'How do you mean?'

'I questioned Lisa Stewart in that garden. I was looking right at the broken-down car for half an hour. There was a jack, yes, a wrench, yes, a couple of rusty spanners. But take it from me – a crowbar, no.'

'Right.' Macdonald didn't argue: observation was the bed-rock of police training and MacNee was famously hawk-eyed. 'So you're saying the murderer brought it with him?'

'Aye. Unless someone took it out in the afternoon to work on the car. But if they did, they brought it out just to put it down. Nothing's been done to that car for months, if not years. There's grass growing up round the tools.'

'So we were meant to think it was lying around?'

MacNee thought about it. 'Maybe we're being a bit elaborate. It could just be the weapon of choice – simple and deadly. But of course they could have done a wee quiet recce once Lisa had told Williams where she was staying.'

'Tell Big Marge that,' Macdonald suggested. 'It's a new thought.'

'If you think I'm going to mention crowbars to Big Marge, you're daft. I'm not going to go putting ideas into her head,' Mac-Nee said, with just a flicker of a smile.

ALICK BUCHAN MADE no attempt to welcome his visitors. As Mai-die, with Calum clinging shyly to her legs, made flustered offers of hospitality, he said, 'You'll not be staying long enough to drink a cup of tea. What are you after now?'

He didn't offer Kershaw and Campbell a seat. Campbell unhes-itatingly pulled out a chair and joined Alick at the table, where he was sitting with a mug of tea and a local newspaper open at the property pages.

Kershaw sat down too, ignoring his question. 'Thinking of buying a house, Mr Buchan?'

He smirked. 'We-ell, maybe not buying just at the moment. We'll be renting meantime, to see what's available.'

'So you've found another job?'

'Not exactly.' Buchan was definitely looking pleased with himself. 'I've been under a lot of strain lately. I'll be taking a wee rest.'

'That sounds good.' Kershaw turned to smile over her shoulder at Maidie. She was holding Calum, who was looking at the strangers with his thumb in his mouth and wide, wondering eyes. Maidie smiled back uncertainly. The bruising on her cheek was just a yellow shadow now.

'Mr Buchan,' Kershaw went on, 'today I wanted to ask you a little bit about your job here. You were in the army with Mr Crozier, and when he came back to the area, he employed you, right?'

'Aye.' The surly scowl had returned.

'And you would run shoots, fishing and so on for his business colleagues who came here for meetings?'

Buchan grunted agreement.

'Now, I believe some of these men were old friends of Mr Crozier from his army days – a Mr Lloyd and a Mr Driscoll?'

Buchan sat bolt upright. 'Who the hell told you that?'

Kershaw heard Maidie's tiny gasp of fright. 'Company records,' she said smoothly. 'Can you tell me more about them?'

'No.'

'You won't, or you don't know?' Campbell asked.

'If I did, I wouldn't. But I don't.'

'You didn't get on with Mr Crozier, did you?' Kershaw had a nasty feeling that they weren't going to get anywhere on the basis of Buchan's grudges, but it was worth a try.

Buchan snorted. 'Look, I took a dram that day I had the row with him. I was out of order – said things I shouldn't of. But he was all right.'

'A good boss, then,' Campbell said. 'Looked after you pretty well, no doubt?'

For a moment Kershaw thought the fish had taken the bait. Buchan's eye kindled. 'Looked after me? Me in this hovel, him in his fine big house, nothing too good for him, nothing to do but give me orders?' Then he seemed to collect himself. 'Aye, but that was just the way of it. Gave me a roof over my head, anyway.'

'And what about the Ryans?' Kershaw asked, without much hope. 'They'll be your new bosses. Or are they selling the place?'

'Aye.'

'But they'll see you right, if you're made redundant?'

A slow smile spread across Buchan's face. 'Oh, aye, they're see-ing me right.'

They were wasting their time here. Buchan claimed to know nothing about foreign visitors, nothing about what sort of busi-ness it was.

The dogs in the kennels by the house worked themselves into a frenzy of barking as the detectives got back into the car. As they drove off, Kershaw said to Campbell, 'Bought his silence, I sup-pose. And if he's got money now, poor bloody Maidie will stay with him to get support for her child, no matter what he does to her when he's drunk. Sometimes I really hate men.'

Campbell felt it wise to remain silent. But then, he hadn't really been planning to say anything anyway.

'CARA, I MADE the point to her as forcibly as I could,' Joss Hep-burn said, not trying to conceal his irritation at the woman who had come to meet them in the hall as they arrived back from Kirkluce. 'Unfortunately, I'm not in a position to order police to do anything.'

Cara was twitching and blinking, licking her chapped lips, and she was not taking it well that Lisa Stewart was not about to be charged. 'She killed my baby! She killed my father! She blackened my son's name!' She was screaming now. 'And the police are on her side, and you don't care – or you!' She turned on her husband.

Ryan had to raise his voice to be heard. 'Cara, it's upstairs. I've put it in the dressing-table drawer for you. Go on. You'll feel better.'

She looked at him wildly, then ran upstairs as if demons were chasing her. As perhaps they were.

Ryan looked at Hepburn with a defensive shrug. 'I've tried, you know. It's impossible—'

Hepburn cut him short. 'I have obviously failed to convey to you how little your domestic problems interest me.'

'You really are an unpleasant bastard! I can't wait to get you out of my house.'

'Your house? Is it? Presumably we have to wait until one of Alex's colleagues produces the will. You never know what Cris may have persuaded him to do.'

Ryan stared at him. 'You don't think he'd leave his estate out of the family? If that little sod has got round him somehow, I'll break his neck!'

'Hey, hey! What a bloodthirsty guy you are,' Hepburn said acidly. 'I would have thought there were quite enough bodies around already. Anyway, we need Cris on our side, remember? We have to get together now and decide what the hell we're to do.'

'When are you going to phone the *Sun* about Fleming?'

'When it suits me. But I warn you, it's too late. She'll have passed on what she knows already.'

'Then the sooner the better,' Ryan said with venom. 'If I'm going down, I want to have the pleasure of seeing her tortured first.'

SHE STILL HADN'T sent for him. MacNee was under no illusion that Fleming was too busy, or had forgotten. No, she was just making him sweat – which he was doing, wishing he hadn't been so bloody stupid. He had to get a grip; he barely knew himself these days.

He gazed unseeing at the computer screen in front of him. The trouble with Big Marge was that she was unpredictable. He'd worked with her closely all these years, yet he still didn't know what she would have in mind. He didn't think she'd go down the official disciplinary route; she might, of course, but that took time and he guessed that it would be something more immediately unpleasant.

Like taking him off the case. God, he would hate that! There were so many ideas whirling round in his head, ideas that he'd have liked to throw about with Marjory, one to one, without other people to shove their oar in.

Like Kershaw. If he was out, she would be in, taking his place with the boss – all girls together! He gave a snort, startling the detective working at the next terminal in the CID room.

He could wait to be sent for, get a bollocking, hear his sentence, say nothing and leave, or he could go now, say his piece and apologise. He would feel better then. It wouldn't be enough, but it just might soften the blow and give him a way back in afterwards. Deliberately seeking out the lion to stick your head in its mouth was an uncomfortable thought, but he got up before he could change his mind.

His knock on Fleming's door was tentative, though, and when Fleming looked up, he didn't feel any better. She was frowning and her eyes were unfriendly.

'Yes, MacNee?'

'I've come to apologise, ma'am.'

'Apology accepted. I daresay you realise it doesn't make any difference?' She wasn't going to make it easy for him.

He hadn't thought she would. 'I realise it was a serious breach of security, and that I dropped you in it personally. I'm sorry.'

'I'm extremely angry,' Fleming said. 'Leaving aside the personal angle, and the breach, what you did was put me at a considerable disadvantage with a murder suspect, who now knows that one of my subordinates was deliberately trying to humiliate me. Not clever, MacNee.'

Put like that, it wasn't. 'I accept that. I thought you'd maybe get more out of him than we would, but I wish I'd never done it now.'

'You and me both.' Fleming wasn't giving him an inch.

'I can only say again that I'm sorry, ma'am, and take the consequences.'

'My first reaction was to drop you from the team, but you are professionally useful and while you have something to offer you have to stay. There are conditions, though. In the first place, you have to stop this childish sniping at Kim Kershaw. I've had more than enough of it. Secondly, I'm grounding you. Your job, until I change my orders, is sitting at a desk reviewing all the evidence that comes in. You can make a digest of anything you think significant and present it to me before the afternoon briefing each day.'

MacNee didn't even try to argue. 'Yes, ma'am.'

'That's all, Sergeant.' Fleming turned back to her computer screen.

He hesitated, about to say something, then thought better of it. He was almost at the door when there was a knock and DC Kershaw came in, looking smug.

'Hope you're not too busy, boss? I wanted to tell you myself – we've got some good new evidence. Lisa Stewart admitted Williams was her partner and claims she found him dead the night before. According to her, he'd texted her to ask her to meet him, so she took his mobile phone from his pocket to remove the link with her. She threw it into the sea after she arrived at Rowantrees Hotel, but Campbell and I went paddling and found it. I've sent it off to the labs.'

Fleming's face brightened. 'Well done, Kim. That just might be the breakthrough we need. Give me a quick rundown on your interview with Lisa Stewart.'

Kershaw sat down as MacNee left, sick at heart, with his departure unacknowledged.

LISA STEWART SAT at the window of her bedroom, looking out over the front garden and Wigtown Bay. She wasn't seeing the view, though, or even little Rosie playing with her sister in the garden below. She was trying to repair her fragmented self.

Once, she might have been angry about what had happened to her, but somehow now she hadn't the energy for anger any more. She had stayed perfectly calm at first under the detective's questioning, safe inside the shell where no one could reach her no matter what they said, but there were dangerous cracks in it now. The toddler this morning had opened up one of them, and Lisa had found herself telling – had *wanted* to tell – Jan Forbes about her own baby.

And Granny's frying pan! That had opened up another, as she remembered being a little girl, watching her grandmother make the best girdle scones in the world in the pan that had belonged to *her* mother, and her grandmother before that.

She hadn't been able to scuttle back quickly enough. She'd handed herself to the police on a plate. Oh, they hadn't done anything yet, but they would, in their own time. Lisa had been there before; she knew all too well the slow torture of the process.

She had seen the detectives down on the shore, finding the mobile, which she hadn't thrown hard enough or far enough. Even so, they wouldn't be able to read the deleted text message – and thank God, she was so hardened to thinking about Crozier that the shell wasn't threatened when they got on to that.

But it was all beginning again, the horror. The questioning, the statements, the re-questioning to try to trip you up, the relief when a day or two passed and you thought they'd believed you, then the ring at the doorbell, which set your heart thumping as you realised they were stalking you, wearing you down, until the moment when they pounced.

And now gradually, bit by bit, they would drag everything out, her shell would be shattered, and she would, quite simply, fall apart. Lisa would be back in the dock and this time there wasn't a jury in the country who would acquit her.

Supposing, just supposing, it didn't come to that. Suppose they charged someone else instead. What then?

For a long time Lisa hadn't looked to her future. Getting through each day was challenge enough. Now she looked, it was bleak indeed.

A wail from the garden below caught her attention. Rosie had fallen; her sister was picking her up now and lugging her into the hotel to find comfort.

Tears started to Lisa's eyes. She would never again be in a position to kiss it better for a crying child. And who would give her any sort of job, with a past like hers? The road ahead of her, like the one to Rosscarron Cottages, led to nowhere.

And if Gillis could always find her, the Ryans could too. The messages would start again and she would wake every morning with a sick dread of what the day might bring.

What was the point of struggling on? She just wanted it all to stop – she was tired, so tired! She hadn't the strength to go on. There was no point.

The answer was obvious, once you thought about it. All she looked for was peace, and since she hadn't found it even in this tranquil, reassuring place, there was only one way to get it. The means was right there below.

Lisa got up. She needed to act before her courage failed her, but then she hesitated. There was still unfinished business. She had lived stigmatised as a murderer; she didn't want to die with her side of the story untold. And Jan – wise, kind, Jan . . . Lisa owed her the truth.

She had a pen in her bag, but no paper. Sometimes hotels had notepaper and envelopes, so she looked in all the drawers, but there was nothing. The only paper was a sheet lying on the dressing table, detailing meal times and facilities.

It would have to do. She sat down and turned it over to the blank side. She began to write, slowly at first, then faster, writing as small as she could to get all she wanted to say on to that one sheet – her last words.

Lisa didn't read it over when she had finished. She folded it in four, wrote, 'JAN,' on the front of it on top of the hotel information and stood up. She took a deep breath, then walked out of the room.

There was no one in the hall, but she could hear Rosie's subsiding wails from the hotel lounge. Lisa propped her letter on a little table by the front door, then walked out. As the door closed, a gust of air caught the flimsy note. It wafted off the surface, landing underneath an old-fashioned hat-stand.

Lisa walked down the drive, under the rowan trees, which had not, after all, protected her from harm, then across the road and between the whin bushes on to the shore.

The sea was silky calm today, a dark greyish-blue under an overcast sky. The lapping of the waves was a soothing sound, almost like a lullaby. There was a sweet, coconut perfume in the air from the yellow flowers of the whin.

Lisa stepped into the water, gasping from shock at how cold it was. She was shivering with nerves and her heart was beating so hard that it felt as if it might leap out of her chest. Turn back now? She didn't have to do this . . .

But tomorrow would be another day of torment, and then there would be another, then another, until— They said drowning was an easy death.

She took a deep, deep breath and then another step into the water, and one more, and one more until she was walking steadily into the sea. The penetrating cold was painful at first, but as she went further and further, she began to feel a curious sort of warmth, and at last the ground dropped away from under her feet.

Chapter Nineteen

JAN FORBES SAT knitting in a chair by the window of the Row-antrees Hotel lounge, her plastered leg up on a stool in front of her. She looked over her spectacles with an indulgent smile as Rosie's mother tried to convince her daughter that the barely visible scratch on her knee was unlikely to prove fatal.

She glanced down at her pattern chart and back at the knitting, pulled a face and started picking back the previous row. The ball of elephant-grey wool slipped off her knee and she reached down awkwardly to fetch it. As she straightened up, she glanced out of the window, then stared, at first unable to take in what she was seeing.

'Oh! Oh, no, it's my friend!' She swung her leg off the stool and struggled to her feet as Rosie's father came over to see what had upset her. 'She's walking into the water – I think she's trying to drown herself?!'

Before she had finished the sentence, the man was out of the room and running down the drive.

MACNEE WENT TO make his report in some trepidation, but he'd been working hard that afternoon and there'd actually been satisfaction in getting a grip on all the evidence and knowing exactly what was happening, even if it wasn't a lot at the moment. They'd discovered the pub where Jason Williams had taken a room, but it hadn't turned up anything new.

But he'd had a wee idea that had paid off; he'd keep that till after Fleming had read right through, like the sweetie they gave you in posh restaurants with the coffee to put you in a good mood to pay the bill.

She maybe didn't greet him with a great big hug, but she was pleasant enough. She'd never been one who believed in holding grudges, right enough, and when she'd gone through the report, she said, 'That's very helpful, Tam,' then added, with what was almost a smile, 'Maybe you're wasted out on the streets.'

It wouldn't be too clever to retort, 'Away and boil your head!' just at the moment. Instead, he said, 'There's another thing I came up with. They're just starting to run through the CCTV footage for Saturday night and I thought I'd have a wee keek at it first. It only covers the High Street, mind, and there's plenty side streets you could go along instead. But there was a big silver Mercedes coming along at around nine o'clock, and when I checked the number, guess whose it was?'

'Joss Hepburn's.' Fleming's voice was very flat.

'The car-hire firm's,' MacNee corrected her. 'It's not even to say Hepburn was driving, and there's no record of the car coming back. But it shoots holes right through the alibis those bastards gave us.'

'Most likely Hepburn, though.'

'Most likely,' MacNee agreed. 'But I've been thinking . . .'

'Oh? I like it when you say that, Tam.' For the first time Fleming's voice held real warmth.

'What would Hepburn want to kill Williams for? There's maybe murky stuff we don't know about, but you see there's this idea I keep coming back to. We know Williams killed Rencombe, right? And we know Rencombe was only doing a job for Crozier, so it's a reasonable bet that Williams needed to kill Crozier too.'

Fleming nodded. 'I think that's been in all our minds. Go on, Tam.'

'Who cared most when Crozier was killed?'

'Pilapil. Of course,' Fleming said slowly.

'Me and Andy Mac were talking about the methods. The first two killings, it was something that came to hand, like it wasn't planned in advance. The third one . . .' He explained his reasons for believing that the murderer had come prepared.

'Revenge,' Fleming said, thinking about it. 'Pilapil could see it as performing a last service for his beloved boss.'

'Right. Do you reckon he maybe knows what Rencombe's business with Williams was – maybe been in touch with Williams since?'

'Otherwise how would he know where to find him? Taking it at its highest, it's possible. He looks like our only source of information on that, unless Williams's mobile gives us a few hints or we get something from the Met once they get round to checking out Rencombe's office. For some reason they're not giving it top priority.'

MacNee sniffed. 'We'll wait long enough, no doubt. Too grand for the likes of us, that lot.'

Fleming rolled her eyes, but let it pass. 'Tomorrow, then. We'll start by bringing Hepburn in again, first thing. We'll turn

Kershaw and Campbell loose on him this time and see what he has to say about the car being in Kirkluce. Once we find out about that, we can talk to Pilapil.'

She hesitated. 'I know you think I should do a formal interview with Hepburn. I'll watch through the one-way panel, and if there's anything I see they could pick up on, I'll pass it through, but I have reasons for feeling that in an interview my position would be compromised.' Her expression was rueful.

Feeling deeply uncomfortable, MacNee said, 'Aye. I'm sorry.'

Fleming went on to discuss details. She hadn't relented yet on the desk job for him, but he got up feeling that he was at least heading for forgiveness. He was on his way out when she said, 'By the way, how's Bunty? Still at her sister's?'

'That's right. Oh, she's fine,' he said, but he shut the door with an uncomfortable feeling that he hadn't sounded convincing.

WITH HER THROAT raw from vomiting sea water, Lisa Stewart was lying on her bed with her eyes closed. Jan Forbes, looking shaken, was in a chair beside her holding her hand, while Susan Telford hovered with a mug.

'Could you maybe manage a sip or two of this, dear?' she said. 'It's just hot sweet tea – very good for shock. Look, I'll put my arm behind you, like this.'

It was easier to do as she was told than to argue. Lisa sat up, and indeed the drink was soothing. It gave her something to do too, so she didn't have to see the look of pity on the other women's faces.

Her head was spinning. It was hard to think clearly when you were so buffeted by emotions – feelings like embarrassment and anger with herself. How useless did you have to be, to try to kill yourself and fail, and end up having to thank a well-meaning stranger for pulling you out and carrying you dripping and choking into the hotel, as if you were grateful? Well, she wasn't. Why couldn't they have left her to drown?

There was a doctor coming, they told her. There would be questions, follow-ups, medication even. Lisa tried to blot out the thought of it.

At last she managed to drink enough tea to satisfy Susan, but Jan didn't leave with her. Lisa lay back on her pillows and shut her eyes, but when Jan took her hand again, she didn't pull it away. The warmth of that firm grasp was comforting.

As was Jan's soothing voice, talking, not asking questions. 'You've had too much to bear, Lisa. You've been shouldering the sky, my dear, and no one can do that for long without help. I expect you're sorry you didn't succeed, just at the moment. You probably feel angry that we brought you back. But you have friends now and there's nothing so bad that we can't sort it out together.'

Lisa felt tears beginning to roll down her cheeks, silent tears, which spilled over as if her misery were welling up from inside and overflowing. She had no control over them.

The grip on her hand tightened a little. 'Tell me the worst thing,' Jan said. 'Just the worst one.'

Where to start? But the words, like the tears, came out before Lisa could control them.

'The lies,' Lisa's raw, husky voice whispered. 'It's always been lies, lies from everyone, so that I have to lie too. Not my gran, though – she never did. She was the only one I could ever trust.

'But my mother – my dad was a bad man, but she told me he was killed in a car accident when he'd actually died in a fight in prison. Then I had to lie about that too, because if the police had found out my background, they'd have been even more sure I'd killed little Poppy.

'And they all told lies, after she died. Cara told the police Nico was asleep in his room when they came back home that night, and it wasn't true. I'd heard him moving about the house all evening, but I couldn't find him. He was hiding from me – he was angry after I punished him for hitting his little sister. He came out when his parents came home and I saw there was mud on his shoes.

'I went to check on Poppy and she wasn't there. The cot . . . the cot was empty.' Lisa's breathing grew ragged in her agitation. 'I just knew what he'd done. I ran down the stairs – I fell, because I was going so fast. I scrambled up and went outside.

'It was a terrible night – wind and rain and very dark – but I could see a white bundle on the lawn and—' She choked. 'She was just lying there, like a little doll. Still and white – but so pretty, my Poppy, even then! I loved her so much! I hugged her, I tried to warm her, but she was cold, so cold . . .'

Lisa was sobbing now, and Jan's own eyes were full of tears. 'It wasn't your fault,' she said. 'You did what you could.'

Lisa grabbed a handful of tissues from the box they had put beside her and mopped her face. She swallowed her sobs, and when she went on, there was anger in her voice.

'Then there was the press, and the police too. They told lies about me, and then after the trial they said I shouldn't have been acquitted – oh, they were smart, the way they hinted, so there was nothing I could do about it. But it meant if people recognised me in the street, they shouted things, so I had to lie again – change my name and dye my hair.'

Jan gave a sympathetic grimace, but before she could say anything Lisa was going on in that brittle-sounding voice.

'And then there was Lee – Jason, I suppose he was. He started by lying even about his name. I thought he loved me and wanted to help me, but he didn't. He had another girlfriend, and he laughed about me behind my back. I don't know why he had to tell me a false name, or why he was with me at all, really. Maybe he was just after the money from selling the flat.'

'How did you meet him?' Jan asked.

'He picked me up in a shop near where I lived, not long after the trial. He was so sympathetic about what had happened to me – and then after, when the messages started—' Lisa broke off. Her eyes, which had been drooping, shot wide open and her hand went up to cover her mouth, as if the movement could recapture the words she had uttered.

'Messages?'

'I – I shouldn't have said that.'

'Maybe you said that because you needed to tell someone,' Jan said with gentle persistence.

'If I tell you, will you promise not to tell the police?'

She could see that the other woman was hesitating. Then Jan said carefully, 'If the police asked me a direct question about it, I couldn't lie, Lisa, but I certainly won't go running to them with anything you tell me – unless it's criminal.'

Lisa gave a harsh laugh. 'Oh, it's not me that's criminal! It's just I know if I told them, they'd try to stitch me up again, say I'd killed Gillis because of the messages.'

'What were they about?'

'Threats. I was going to suffer. I was going to be killed. Maybe they were only threats, meant to drive me crazy – sometimes they almost succeeded. Wherever I moved to, he'd find me. I'd changed my name and my address and my phone, but before long it would start again – "You think you can hide from me, but you can't."

'I don't know how he did it – paid spies, I suppose, he'd plenty money – and Declan and Cara could go on with it, even now Gillis is dead. I can't escape, ever.'

'You don't think,' Jan suggested shrewdly, 'that perhaps your boyfriend was telling him?'

Lisa gaped. 'What?' But even as she spoke, things began falling into place.

'Perhaps he recognised you in the shop,' Jan was saying. 'You said people did, after all the publicity. Perhaps he went to Gillis and got money for telling him where you were, what your phone number was.'

How could she have been dumb enough not to work it out? Lisa was filled with anger at her own stupidity, but compared to despair, anger was her friend.

This changed everything. She could escape, after all. Her phone could be disposed of – more carefully this time – and then she could just disappear. Back to London, perhaps – lots of people vanished in London.

That was her way out. Tomorrow.

A knock on the door heralded the arrival of the doctor. Lisa submitted to the injection that would give her the rest she knew she needed, and when he left lay with her eyes shut, planning her escape. There was an early bus . . .

It was only as she was drifting off that it came back to her – the note she had written! She struggled to rouse herself, but the weight of drowsiness made her limbs too heavy to move, and any-way, her thoughts were swirling like mist in her head as she fell into a profound sleep.

NICO RYAN SAT in his little den in the shrubbery. He liked going there: it had a good sort of creepy feeling about it, and if his dad was looking for him and couldn't find him, he always went mental, and Nico liked that too.

He was picking at a scab on his knee. He didn't want it to bleed again, but if he was careful . . . There! The last bit was off and his knee was all smooth again. He'd screamed a lot about it, not because it hurt but because it was part of him that was damaged. He hated that, but it was OK now. He rolled down the leg of his jeans.

He was bored, and being bored made him angry. He hated being at Rosscarron. There was nothing to do and he wasn't even allowed in Granddad's study, where he could play *Grand Theft Auto* on the computer. Dad had a laptop, but he just said he was using it, and when Nico screamed, his mum didn't tell Dad to let him have what he wanted, like she usually did. She was weirder than ever these days and they were always yelling at each other and paying no attention to him.

And there wasn't even anyone to make him burgers when he wanted them. Cris was never in the kitchen now, and when Nico had gone to his door and banged on it, Cris had said some really bad words and told him to go away. He hadn't, of course – he'd kicked the door and yelled for a bit, but it hadn't done any good.

He realised suddenly that the seat of his jeans was all wet from the damp earth and he got up. It was uncomfortable, but he couldn't go and put on another pair since all his clothes were in a dirty heap on the floor because Cris hadn't taken them away to be cleaned. When it was his house, he'd whip Cris and whip him till he did what Nico told him.

He was brooding on this when a pheasant came stalking past on the drive in front of the house. Stupid bird, with its silly peck-peck-pecking! If he had a gun, he could shoot it. Bang! Bang! He mimed the shots.

But there was a stone on the ground just beside him. He was quite good at throwing stones. He picked it up and hefted it in his hand, eyeing the oblivious creature. He threw it with all his force, but the bird caught the movement and with a screech of alarm flew off in a clumsy flurry of feathers.

Stupid, stupid bird! He turned away discontentedly and went back inside.

He could hear the grown-ups were talking in the sitting room as he went through the hall. He wasn't going in there. It was boring, like everything else. There wasn't even any music playing now and the house felt weird. Nico liked really loud music, played through the speakers.

He drifted upstairs to his parents' bedroom. He hadn't been allowed in there by himself since he spilled some of his father's expensive cologne on the carpet, so it was good they were out of the way. He made a picture on the mirror with his mother's make-up, then noticed a pair of scissors on the dressing table.

Snipping them together experimentally, Nico looked around. There was a soft red and blue rug with silky fringes on the floor by the bed, and he sat down, deciding to cut them off. Then he noticed something.

Under the bed, there was a laptop. If he took it to his room, he could play with it whenever he liked, even after he was sent to bed at night. He put the scissors back where he had found them and wiped off the mirror picture carefully so no one would know he had been there, then carried the laptop off in triumph to his own room.

MacNee reread the report that had just come in. It had looked the dull sort of thing he'd not have paid much attention to, if he hadn't been stuck here, but it was dynamite. Maybe there was something in doing a desk job after all – not that he was going to admit that to Fleming.

The risk was that she might decide he was more use where he was. On the other hand, she would have to know about this, and it had a lot of implications they'd need to discuss. If he went and told her face to face, it could be quite like old times.

'You again, Tam?' Fleming greeted him. 'Another useful bit of digging?'

'Bit of a strange one come in, boss,' MacNee said, sitting down. 'I thought you'd maybe like to know before the briefing tonight. Gives the whole thing a twist.'

Fleming's ears pricked up. 'Good twist? Bad twist?'

'Hard to say. You know how the phones were cut off at Rosscarron?'

'Oh, I remember, Tam. Believe me, I remember,' Fleming said with feeling.

'The linesman's report just came in. The phone line for the area goes to Rosscarron House first, right? And someone cut it. It hadn't broken.'

'We knew that. Poor Jamieson, presumably, as part of his revenge for his ruined life.'

'We thought that, aye. Seems we were wrong,' MacNee said with dramatic satisfaction.

'I don't need entertainment, just information,' Fleming said tartly. 'Take the rabbit out of the hat before it escapes.'

'The line was cut at Rosscarron House. Not just at, but where it could be reached from a window. So unless someone went and put up a ladder against the house without anyone noticing, it was an inside job. And we know that Jamieson didn't have a ladder.'

Fleming's brain was racing. 'So someone in that house wanted to cut off the phone and the Internet. Now why would they do that? To isolate them from the rest of the world? But they couldn't have known the bridge would be sabotaged. The struts were definitely sawn through with Jamieson's chainsaw.'

'Aye.' MacNee scowled in concentration. 'So was that just a wee bonus for them?'

'Or didn't it matter? What mattered was the phone being out. Was there something on the Internet that Crozier shouldn't see, for instance?'

'Something to do with that business no one wants to talk about? Stinks like a Glasgow close on a Saturday night.'

Fleming, he thought, looked uncomfortable. 'I have a nasty feeling that it does. But I can't see how to get at it.'

'We've questions we're needing to ask them, anyway. Here – say you and me go out there tomorrow?' MacNee looked at her hopefully and she laughed.

'OK, Tam. Hepburn's coming in first thing. I'll sit in on that from next door, then I'll commute the desk sentence. You're only out on licence, mind you.'

'ROWANTREES HOTEL,' SUSAN Telford said into the phone. 'Can I help you?'

'Could you put me through to Lisa Stewart, please?'

It was quite a coarse voice; some instinct made her hesitate. 'Who's speaking, please?'

'Just a friend of hers.'

That settled it. 'I'm afraid we don't have anyone of that name staying here. There's a place called the Rowans in Kirkcudbright – you could try there.'

There was a pause; then he said lightly, 'Oh, never mind. I must have made a mistake.' He rang off before she could put the phone down.

Susan went through to the lounge, where Jan Forbes was alone, sitting by the window again, knitting. She looked up when her friend came in.

'That's the elephant finished,' she said, holding up her handiwork. 'Isn't he a handsome fellow?' Then, seeing the look on Susan's face, she said, 'Oh dear! Something's happened?'

'I think so. We were expecting the press to catch up with poor Lisa, and I think they have. There was a man on the phone asking if she was staying here. Of course I said no, but I hesitated at first and I'm not sure I convinced him. I'm not a very good liar.'

'It was bound to happen,' Jan said. 'If they're on to her, they won't stop till they find her.'

'Should we warn her, do you think?'

Jan considered that. 'Do you know, I think we should leave it for the moment. She's in a very fragile state, and she has us to protect her. If they turn up here, you can always turn them away.'

Susan gave her a cynical look. 'And you expect they'll go? Still, the doctor's given her something to make her sleep and she'll be feeling stronger tomorrow, poor lamb.'

THE MAN IN the silver Ford Focus, parked in a side street in Kirkluce, switched off his mobile with a small, grim smile of satisfaction. He looked at his watch. Seven o'clock – time for a pie and a pint. Or a half-pint, anyway, since he never ran the risk of being caught by the breathalyser.

He chose one of the shabbier pubs, which was already busy. On this sort of job you never wanted to draw attention to yourself. He had to wait a few minutes at the bar to get his drink, then carried it and the wooden number for his order over to a table away from the window. You never knew who might be passing in the street.

He didn't see a slightly built man with longish brown hair and a row of steel earrings shrink back into the further corner of the bar with an expression of shock, or notice him slip out of the pub, attaching himself to a noisy group who had just got up to leave.

He didn't know that outside, tucked out of sight in an alleyway, the man was making a phone call with shaking hands.

Chapter Twenty

Tuesday, 25 July

IT WAS DRIZZLING again this morning. When Marjory Fleming had set out to feed her hens, it hadn't looked heavy enough to warrant a jacket and hood, but it was the soft, wetting stuff that soaks you through almost unnoticed. As she came back into the farmhouse kitchen carrying a bowl of eggs, she shook herself like a dog.

'I should have taken the shampoo out with me instead of washing my hair in the shower,' she complained.

Bill, just finishing his mug of tea, smiled. 'I was out earlier, but I was smart enough to put on a jacket, so I was all right, wasn't I, Meg?'

The collie, lying by the Aga, twitched her tail in response.

Marjory pulled a face. 'Smug isn't pretty, is it, Meg? We may both have got soaked but we think it's pretty pathetic of you to need a jacket for a wee bit rain like that.'

Bill smiled again, then rinsed out his mug and set it upside down on the draining board. 'I don't care what she says, Meg – only a fool doesn't know how to be comfortable.

'I'm just off, then. You'll be late again tonight, I suppose?'

'Probably. Have a good day.'

As the door shut behind her husband and Meg, Marjory sighed. That had been the familiar sort of light-hearted exchange, but she'd noticed that increasingly they were involving the dog in their conversations, almost as if it was safer to be in company than alone. They were both being very civilised, but she didn't want to have to be civilised. She wanted the old natural, loving rela-tionship back, which had seemed so easy that she'd never given much thought to how it was achieved. If Joss Hepburn carried out his threat, if the newspapers represented her youthful follies in the ugliest possible way – as they would – might the damage it caused to her career be the least of her problems? The ringing of her mobile was a welcome relief from her unhappy thoughts.

It was John Purves. She listened for a moment, her brow fur-rowed. 'What on earth for?' Then she said, 'Right. I have to moni-tor an interview first, but I can clear time after that.'

She ran upstairs. Catriona, in an early-morning trance, was on her way to the bathroom.

'Don't forget to tell Cammie to change his sheets today, will you?' her mother said. 'I'm going in now. I'll probably be late back.'

'How unusual!' Cat yawned. 'Remind me who you are again?'

Ignoring her daughter's sarcasm, Fleming went into her bed-room and opened her wardrobe door. What on earth would a woman who ran a builder's yard wear when she was checking out an applicant for casual labour?

DEBBIE HAD BEEN very sleepy this morning too. Kim Kershaw's mind was on her daughter as she drove towards work in Kirkluce from Newton Stewart. She had again looked in on her way to work and wakened her with a kiss, but Debbie's eyes had opened only briefly, then closed again.

It was early, admittedly, since Kershaw was on a seven-to-three shift, and the carer said she'd had another restless night so it wasn't surprising Debbie wanted a lie-in. And after the bad turn she'd had, it wasn't surprising either that she was taking some time to recover, but as ever fear for the child's health gripped Kershaw like an iron hand twisting her inside.

She couldn't afford to think about it. There was a busy day ahead – a challenging day too.

There'd been a lot of gossip among the lads – fairly ribald, some of it – about Big Marge's relationship with a pop star like Joshua, of all people. Kershaw wasn't a reader of celeb magazines herself, but according to those who were, he certainly wasn't the kind of guy you'd take home to meet the chief constable. Still pretty fit, though, even at his advanced age; she'd found herself looking at the boss with new respect.

Fleming was going to be watching the interview from the room next to the main interview room, with its one-way glass panel. It made Kershaw a little uneasy; she'd had superior officers do that in the past to check up on her technique, sometimes without telling her. Fleming had been open about it, though, and said she'd prompt any questions that occurred to her.

Kershaw would have said Big Marge wasn't lacking in courage, but rather than checking on her subordinates, could she be ducking out of doing the interview herself? Her reaction to Tam MacNee's extraordinary breach of procedure in springing Joss

Hepburn on her had resulted in MacNee sitting in front of a computer terminal in the CID room all day, acting like a Rottweiller with a migraine if anyone spoke to him.

Whatever you said about the job, it wasn't dull. And this morning looked like being even more interesting than usual.

MacNee was early today too. He came into the CID room with a spring in his step. There was nothing like a day stuck at a desk to make you appreciate getting out to do the hands-on job that was real policework to him. The rest of the stuff inflicted on them was just fantoosh – all the unnecessary frills and bows of form-filling and writing logs and going on diversity courses. At the thought of the last, he gave a small, involuntary shudder. Lucky Big Marge hadn't thought of that or he'd be marked down for one right now.

Fleming, unusually, was there talking to Ewan Campbell. She turned when she saw him.

'Morning, Tam. I was hoping you'd be in early. Change of plan – I've got another commitment today.'

MacNee's face fell. His 'Right, boss' was very flat.

Fleming smiled. 'Oh, don't panic. I want you to go anyway, just on your own. Do a spot of sniffing around at Rosscarron House and see what you think.

'I was so impressed with what you came up with when you went through all the reports that I'm asking Andy Mac to do a trawl this morning, but he'll be available if you need back-up. Ewan, I'll see you and Kim after the briefing to discuss the Hepburn interview. OK?'

MacNee felt a faint pang of jealousy. At least he was free to do what he did best, but that was one he'd have liked to be in on.

He was wondering, too, what it was Fleming was doing later that took precedence over driving on the inquiry. She'd normally say, 'A meeting,' or, 'A conference,' often pulling a face about the hoops she had to jump through. But 'A commitment'?

His nose told him there was something going on. She wasn't wearing one of her usual smart trouser suits this morning, and the jeans, casual shirt and zip jacket suggested she wouldn't be spending time in the office. He hated being out of the loop, but he'd only himself to blame. And he hated that too.

LISA STEWART WOKE with a start and looked at her watch.

It was just after seven o'clock. She was relieved, having feared it might be later, but then it had only been nine o'clock when sleep overcame her last night, and this morning she definitely felt more alert and refreshed. If she'd had bad dreams, Lisa couldn't remember them – or perhaps the insight Jan Forbes had given her had exorcised her demons.

But the note she had left for Jan was uppermost in her mind. Without even waiting to dress, she went out in her pyjamas and crept down the stairs.

There was no one about, but the note had gone. With a hollow feeling inside, she returned to her room. She told herself firmly that it didn't matter; she was going to disappear anyway, but now it was a matter of real urgency.

She had three-quarters of an hour to catch the early bus. Breakfast didn't start until eight and before that there would only be staff busy setting up. By the time anyone got round to missing her, Lisa would be long gone.

After a speedy shower, she crammed her few belongings into her bag and, doing a rough calculation, left some money on the bedside table. She shut the door quietly as she left the room. There were faint sounds from behind the closed doors in the corridor, but the hall below was empty.

Downstairs, Lisa could hear voices and the clatter of crockery from the breakfast room, but its window was towards the side of the house. Once she was out of the front door, she should be able to reach the road unseen.

It was a depressing day. The air was thick with water vapour, and curtains of silvery rain came sweeping across a grey, sullen sea. There was no view at all now, and even the bright gold of the gorse seemed dulled in the wet, its prickly leaves mud-splashed from the passing cars.

As she walked out between the guardian rowans, Lisa felt a twinge of fear. She was totally on her own now. Jan, the kindly Telfords – they had given her a sense of safety and she was putting herself beyond any help they could give her.

But it wasn't really safety. They wouldn't protect her from persecution by the police or the press once they had read her note. She had to vanish.

Lisa pulled up the hood of her jacket and began her trudge along the verge. She couldn't rely on the bus driver being the obliging Doddie who had stopped for her outside the hotel; she had, according to what Susan Telford said when she arrived, a mile to go to the official bus-stop.

It was a quiet road, but it wasn't pleasant walking. A car appeared round the corner ahead just as one came up behind her, a silver Ford Focus that was so close to her it actually had to swerve, and even then a fine spray of mud soiled her jeans. She glanced down irritably, but she didn't bother to brush it off. She'd still quite a bit to walk and no doubt other cars would do the same.

When Lisa reached the bus-stop, she was reassured to see that a small queue had formed already. Sometimes timetables were out of date, but it looked as if hers had been right.

Everyone looked depressed this morning, standing in silent stoicism under the rain. Lisa joined them, and a few minutes later, just as the bus appeared, a man came up to stand behind her. She noticed idly that his jacket and his hair, very dark and growing in a deep widow's peak on his forehead, looked surprisingly dry. He must live quite close by.

Lisa couldn't remember where the bus ended up. 'The terminus,' she said.

'Newton Stewart?' the driver asked, and she nodded, paid and found a seat.

The man who had got on behind her sat down at the front of the bus. He got off again at the next stop.

Newton Stewart. From there, presumably, she could get a bus to Dumfries, then a train to Glasgow. She could even go to earth there for a bit, if the police came after her when they found she'd gone. She was at ease with big cities. No one was interested in strangers, and anyway the only photos of her showed her with distinctive red hair. She'd change her name again too, then stay quietly somewhere till the fuss died down and she could take a train back to London.

ROSIE TURNED AWAY from her parents' bedroom window where she had been pressing her nose to the glass. She'd waved and waved, but the lady hadn't paid any attention.

'Rosie, come on,' her mother said in harassed tones. 'We're going down to breakfast and we're waiting for you.'

'Lady gone,' Rosie said sadly, but no one was listening.

HOW OFTEN DID people say, 'I'd love to be a fly on the wall'? Here, behind the one-way glass, DI Fleming was in that privileged position as DCs Kershaw and Campbell ushered Joss Hepburn into the interview room.

Spying, you could call it. Fleming was scrupulous about informing her officers when she was to be there, but even so she still always felt a prickle of discomfort. It was definitely useful, though: without the distraction of directing the interview, she could observe its subject minutely for body language, fleeting facial expressions and what gamblers call 'tells' – unconscious gestures showing stress. You could miss a lot when you had to concentrate on finding a killer question to ask.

Yes, detachment was useful. And of course Fleming could still have an input: Kershaw was wearing a discreet earpiece.

Hepburn noticed it immediately. Fleming saw his fractional stillness; then his eyes travelled to the blank panel on the wall opposite him. He gave a little nod and a slight, sardonic smile, as if he were looking through it straight into her eyes.

Fleming took an involuntary step backwards. He couldn't see her, of course he couldn't, but in some uncanny way he knew she was there. It shook her for a moment.

Duh! He'd really got her spooked. Of course he would guess. He was a man used to studios and to every trick of filming and production: one-way glass would hardly be an unfamiliar concept. Fleming narrowed her eyes and assessed him for signs of tension.

She couldn't see any. With that half-smile still lingering on his face, he was sitting in a relaxed position, elbows on the arms of his chair, hands hanging loose. There were no jerky movements, no tiny twitches, no protective crossing of his arms. He watched in calm silence as Campbell set up the tape.

Kershaw, on the other hand, was nervous, shuffling her papers and shifting in her seat, as if she were feeling Fleming's eyes on the back of her neck. Once, she even half turned, then turned back again, as if she'd had to fight an impulse to look over her shoulder.

Campbell returned to his seat and completed the formalities in his usual unruffled way.

'Mr Hepburn,' Kershaw began, 'you made a statement that you, the Ryans and Mr Pilapil were all together all evening on Saturday night.'

Hepburn half closed his eyes and gave a bored sigh. 'Oh dear. Yes, I guess I did.'

'So it wasn't true? Are you now withdrawing that statement?'

'We-ell . . . not exactly *withdrawing*. Kind of modifying, you could say.'

Fleming couldn't see Kershaw raising her eyebrows, but she heard it in her voice. 'Modifying?'

'Oh, come on, Officer, get real! You've seen the house.' Hepburn's tone suggested sweet reason. 'Obviously, we were hardly sitting looking at each other all evening.'

'So what were you doing?'

'Mostly sitting in my room avoiding, as far as possible, contact with the Ryans and their unspeakably obnoxious offspring. I guess Cris was doing the same.'

'Why did you lie about it, then?' Campbell was reliably blunt.

Good lad! But it hadn't rattled Hepburn – or if it had, it didn't show. Fleming couldn't see any of the signs of stress; the hands were still hanging, relaxed.

'It kind of seemed rude, to contradict my host, you know? And since I had no reason to figure it wasn't true, and since I'm not in the habit of suspecting my close contacts of murder, I guess I just went along with it.' His hands turned palm outwards in the classic gesture of openness.

Now, hit him with the CCTV stuff, Fleming urged Kershaw, though only mentally.

Kershaw needed no prompting. 'You see, Mr Hepburn,' she said sweetly, 'we have evidence that your hired car was in Kirkluce that evening.'

Hepburn raised his brows. 'Was it? Oh dear, I'm just so careless about my keys! I wonder who borrowed it?'

No indication of shock, or surprise, even. The man was a performer, of course, constantly on stage, and Fleming remembered something suddenly.

'Ask him if he takes acting lessons,' she said into the microphone. He'd gone up to Glasgow for coaching every week when she knew him.

There was a hint of surprise in Kershaw's voice as she put the question and for the first time it provoked a reaction. Hepburn sat forward in his chair. 'Well, yes, but . . .' Then he looked towards the panel with a short laugh. 'As DI Fleming knows, I always did. My job is putting on an act.'

'You're good at it.'

Ignoring Kershaw's acid tone, he went on, 'Look, this is some kind of farce. DI Fleming is behind that panel. If she wants to ask questions, why doesn't she cut the crap and ask face to face?'

'Because I'm doing it,' Kershaw said sharply. 'And I want answers. Your hire car was seen in Kirkluce on Saturday evening, as I said. Are you stating that you weren't driving it?'

'I'm stating that I'm careless with my keys.' Hepburn was getting promisingly angry now. 'And that anyone in the house could have taken them.'

'Where were the keys, then?' Campbell again.

At last, they had got to him. 'I – I can't recall.' His jaw, Fleming noticed, had tensed up and his hands had closed round the arms of the chair.

'Have you driven the car since Saturday?' Kershaw asked.

'Until this morning, no.'

'So this morning, before you drove in, where did you find the keys?'

Hepburn glared at her. Then, with a visible effort, he relaxed again. 'Hey, this is crazy! I'm an absent-minded guy and suddenly I'm being featured as a suspect for killing some kid I never even met!'

'Not suddenly. You always were,' Campbell said, and Kershaw went on, 'You see, we only have your word for it that Jason Williams was "some kid" you didn't know. And I can't see any reason why I should take it.'

Hepburn gave a dismissive shrug. 'That, I have to say, is a matter of supreme indifference to me. You have evidence that my car was in Kirkluce. I guess you've no evidence that I was driving it, or you'd have produced it. Anyway, say I was in Kirkluce? It wouldn't prove I'd killed anyone, would it?'

He was perfectly right. Kershaw tried, 'Are you admitting it, then?' and got the short answer. The interview was running into the sand.

Had he, Fleming wondered, really come in at nine o'clock to do a murder later? And been careless enough to drive along the main street, where there were likely to be cameras? But he had to have had a compelling reason to drive all the way to Kirkluce . . .

A thought struck her. 'Ask him,' Fleming said into the microphone, 'if he was visiting his drug dealer.'

It is hard to ask a prompted question as if you had thought of it yourself, and Kershaw failed. Hepburn gave her a look of contempt, got up and came across to stand in front of the panel, looking directly at the unseen Fleming.

'I'm not playing games any more, Madge. This is utterly futile. You're not going to arrest me, so I'm leaving, and if I have to come back, it will be with my lawyer.

'But I wish you'd think over very carefully what I said to you yesterday. This is important. I really, really want you to change your mind. For your own sake. I'll even say please.' He put the palms of his hands together in a supplicatory gesture. Despite the glass, his silver-grey eyes seemed to stare straight into Fleming's own.

'Once you can fake sincerity, you've got it made' had been one of Hepburn's favourite sayings, but this time, she almost believed he was genuine. Oh, not because of what he said about her, but because of what she could see in his eyes – raw, naked fear.

Hepburn turned and walked out of the room. As Campbell said, for the benefit of the tape, 'Mr Hepburn has terminated the interview,' Fleming stood with her hands to her burning cheeks.

'WHAT DID YOU make of that?' Kershaw demanded once the microphones were switched off. 'Hardly a great success, was it? We got absolutely nowhere, and I felt a right idiot. I never did see ventriloquist's dummy as a fulfilling career.'

'Hepburn's right,' Campbell said. 'We've nothing against him, except an inaccurate confirmation of someone else's informal statement.'

'He's a cold-blooded bastard. I could see him taking out any number of people without disarranging his carefully casual locks. And what was all that with the boss – *Madge*?'

Campbell was never a rewarding person to gossip to. 'No idea. Better not hang about or she'll know we're discussing her.'

YOU COULD GET tired of driving through the back of beyond in the rain, through all these wee places where only a handful of people lived. If they'd just the sense to get all together and live in a city, or even a decent-sized town, hard-working coppers could get the job done in half the time. DS MacNee looked disparagingly at the passing countryside as he drove to Rosscarron House. It had always been his opinion that when you've seen one sheep, you've seen them all.

He drove on to the Bailey bridge over the Carron with exaggerated caution. It gave him a nasty feeling in the pit of his stomach to glance down into the river, now shrunk back within its normal bounds. If he went in now, he could wade across, but he still didn't fancy it.

The army, anyway, seemed to have done a good job. There was some heavy plant working now at clearing the mess for the poor bastards whose homes had been wrecked.

There was no one around at Rosscarron House. There were two cars and the Discovery parked at the front, but somehow it seemed to MacNee to have a forlorn look about it. Maybe he was just getting imaginative in his old age. He'd have to put a stop to that.

The rain had gone off now. He walked to the side of the house, where he could see the wires of the phone line coming in, the connection just beside a window on the upper floor. Easy enough to reach out of there and cut it, certainly. He went back to the front door.

The brass handle and the bell itself were tarnished, and when MacNee rang it, there was no reply. He rang again and heard an irritable voice shouting, 'Cris, the doorbell! Where the hell are you?'

Declan Ryan flung open the door. 'Yes? Oh – it's you again. What do you want this time?' He looked dishevelled, and judging by the bags under his eyes, he wasn't sleeping well, and was probably hitting the bottle too.

MacNee smiled. There was a warm glow spreading through him, like the first sip of a good malt: it was a real bonus to see a suspect softened up before you even started.

'That's not very nice. And here's me thinking we were old pals. I'm just back for another wee crack with you.'

'I don't suppose it will do any good to tell you I've nothing to say to you?' Ryan sounded weary.

The sergeant shook his head. 'Uh-uh.'

'You'd better come in, then.'

The white hall, with its random purple wall, was just as chillingly impersonal as MacNee had remembered it. He hadn't enjoyed the music that was always playing, but in its absence the place felt colder and more unwelcoming than ever.

The sitting room, however, looked definitely lived-in, though not in a good way. There were dirty plates and glasses abandoned on the tables and floor, and it was plain that no housework had been done for days. Ryan even seemed embarrassed by the mess.

'We'd have been gone by now if it wasn't for you,' he said bitterly. 'The cleaning woman won't come back because she says she's scared and Cris seems to be on strike.' He sat down, running his fingers through his hair. 'Get on with it, then. I've too much on my hands to waste time dictating something for you to write down in your notebook.'

'I'll get straight to it, then.' MacNee took his seat immediately opposite. 'Was it you cut the phone line to the house?'

Ryan gaped, opening and shutting his mouth like a codfish. 'No, no. I – I don't know what you're talking about.'

Bull's eye! 'Aye, you do. The phone line. The line that brings the telephone connection.' MacNee spoke like a nursery teacher addressing a three-year-old with learning difficulties. 'You know, the one you leaned out the window to cut.'

The man wasn't going to boak, was he? His face had gone pale green, but he managed to say, 'I've no idea what window you mean.'

'That'll be right,' MacNee said ambiguously. 'I had a wee look as I came in so I can maybe find it.' He got up and went to the door.

Ryan jumped up, saying hastily, 'I'll come with you.'

'Second window from the front on that side, as far as I can see.' MacNee pointed as he led the way up the stairs.

'One of the guest rooms,' Ryan said. 'I don't think it's been in use.'

His voice, MacNee noticed with annoyance, had steadied. He opened the door indicated and MacNee saw a room similar to the one he'd used himself after the accident – white-painted with splashes of colour in a canvas on the wall and cushions on the bed, rust and orange this time.

Ryan went to the window and stuck his head out into the rain. 'Oh, yes, here it is. I'd never noticed before.'

'Do you tell me that?' MacNee said with polite incredulity. 'So, who would know, then?'

'Possibly my late lamented father-in-law. Or Cris, quite likely.' Perhaps it was the rain that had revived him: Ryan sounded quite perky as he threw Pilapil to the wolves. 'To be honest, I'm not sure I've ever been in this room before, but he's responsible for all the maintenance. He's the man you need to talk to.'

'Oh, I'll be doing that, right enough. Who else was here on the Wednesday night?'

Ryan had suddenly become obliging. 'Myself, Cara, Nico, of course. Gillis too, because it happened before he died. Cris, Joss Hepburn – no, I tell a lie, Joss arrived next morning. So really, you need to talk to Cris. In fact, he can tell you that I came to him at the time to ask what had happened to the line.' Ryan had started to look pleased with himself. 'And of course it could have been someone from outside.'

It had taken the man a wee while to think of that, but now Mac-Nee watched with a jaundiced eye as Ryan warmed to his theme.

'It could easily be that man who killed himself – much more likely! Nothing to stop him shinning up there at night.'

'Won't wash, Declan. We've searched his house – no ladder.'

'Maybe he borrowed one. Or dumped his somewhere.' Ryan made a passable attempt at sounding bored. 'Anyway, I'm afraid I can't help you there. Now, did you want to speak to Cris?'

Reluctantly recognising a dead end, MacNee agreed.

As SHE GOT off the Newton Stewart bus in Dumfries at last, Lisa Stewart was feeling light-headed after two journeys on an empty stomach. She'd better get something to eat before she drew attention to herself by fainting from hunger. There was a little café just across the road there; she went in, found a table by the window and ordered coffee and a bacon buttie. So far so good.

The trains to Glasgow were quite frequent, so she should be on one before anyone missed her, but she'd need to find a cash machine first and take out as much as she could on her card. There were a few things she ought to buy, like hair dye and more knickers. And jeans – she was still wearing the ones Maidie had given her. The new pair she'd bought were drying somewhere in the hotel.

Lisa felt her spirits lift. Even just sitting in this dingy little café, she had a sense of relief, of freedom. No one in the world could know she was here, now there wasn't someone at her side betraying her every move. She hadn't felt hungry for days – weeks, even – but the bacon roll tasted really good. She might even order another one.

She didn't notice the silver Ford Focus parked just across the street, or the man wearing driving gloves and reading a newspaper as he sat at the wheel, a man with dark hair that grew in a widow's peak.

Chapter Twenty-one

KERSHAW WAS BRIMMING with questions she didn't have the guts to ask, and Fleming's stony face, when she met them after the interview, wasn't encouraging. After they agreed that even if Hepburn was in Kirkluce that evening, it was basically a 'so what?' situation, she ventured to ask, 'Did we get anything out of that, boss?'

Fleming hesitated, and Kershaw had to fight the impulse to say, 'You owe us!'

Perhaps that had occurred to the inspector too. 'Just one thing,' she said, with some reluctance. 'There's a drug dealer who's been on our books for years. Small fry, done a couple of stretches when he's been more than usually careless. I happen to know that Hepburn used to buy from him, and I smelled cannabis on him when I was staying in the house. After a few days at Rosscarron he could be running short. It occurred to me he might have remembered, and paid the man a visit.'

'Right,' Kershaw said slowly. It would have to be checked out, of course, but she'd thought herself that nine o'clock was early to come into the town, if you planned to kill someone two hours later. And of course Hepburn would be evasive if he was buying drugs. Disappointing, if true.

Fleming had left almost immediately. 'Where's she going, dressed like that?' Kershaw asked Campbell, not expecting an answer.

'Under cover, maybe,' he said.

'Under cover? You're joking,' was Kershaw's immediate reaction, but maybe Campbell was right. He often was.

DI FLEMING WAS seldom a passenger in a police car, since she much preferred to drive. Today, though, she was in the hands of DI John Purves – also wearing jeans, with a thick checked shirt – and he drove as he did most things, with quiet competence. Once she realised that he was applying the brake pretty much as her own right foot touched the floor, she found it was quite relaxing.

'So, where are we headed?' she asked.

'Girvan. The Asda superstore coffee shop.'

'Girvan?' Fleming was startled. 'Into Strathclyde? Have we got permission?'

'It's not official. We had to get off our own patch. I doubt if anyone would know me, but you're quite high profile among the local villains. And our guy is nervous – very nervous. We're taking serious precautions, and I'm not even going to tell you what they are.

'I told you the story. You're Mrs Hay and you own a builder's yard in Stranraer. I'm Bob, your foreman. You're needing someone to do deliveries, collect supplies and generally shift stuff around. That envelope in the pocket beside you – there's a job description with hours and rates of pay, and a couple of brochures from suppliers to show the sort of stuff you deal with.'

Fleming took out the transparent folder and flipped through the contents. 'You've been thorough, I'll say that for you.'

'When he arrives, call him Dave, which isn't his name. We both shake hands with him, then you produce the bumf and spread it out on the table. We talk about the job until we can be quite sure no one's followed him in.'

Fleming shook her head, feeling a little dazed. 'The whole thing sounds, well, like a film script.'

Purves glanced at her. 'It's all too real, I'm afraid. This guy's taking a big risk. If we don't look after him . . .' He drew his finger across his throat.

Silenced, Fleming applied herself to memorising the details on the papers she had been given. It still felt as if she were learning her lines for a play – a play in which failure to convince would mean sudden death, not in the stagy sense but in the most literal way.

CRIS PILAPIL SEEMED to have fallen apart since MacNee saw him last. The efficient, well-groomed personal assistant was unshaven and the clothes he was wearing were crumpled and not even particularly clean. When he opened the door to MacNee, he was reeking of drink, and in the corner of his room the bed was unmade and there were piles of clothes on the floor. A TV was showing a panel game, and there was a half-full bottle of gin and an empty glass on a table in front of it. Pilapil looked at his visitor with lacklustre eyes.

MacNee walked into the room without invitation, shutting the door on Ryan hovering in the corridor behind him, and switched off the set.

'We're needing to talk, Cris. Sit down.'

Pilapil did as he was told and reached for the glass and the bottle. 'Want some? There's another glass somewhere.'

'No,' MacNee said, suppressing a shudder. 'And you'd better not either. I'm wanting to get some sense out of you.'

He removed bottle and glass from Pilapil's hands. The man blinked at him owlishly, but made no protest.

Was he too far gone already? MacNee really didn't want to have to take him in to Kirkluce to sober up in a cell; apart from anything else it was hell trying to get the smell of sick out of upholstery and he'd take a bet Pilapil would be throwing up within the hour.

'Where does the phone line come into the house, Cris?' he asked.

The young man's brow furrowed. 'Phone line? I don't know. Beside the study, probably.'

At least he had understood the question, and MacNee believed his answer. The man was too drunk to think quickly, and besides, if Ryan hadn't cut the wires himself, MacNee was as sure that the slippery sod knew who had, as if he'd confessed rather than trying to cover up.

He moved on. 'You thought Gillis Crozier was great, didn't you?'

Pilapil's eyes brimmed. 'He was my saint. I would do anything for him, anything. He is dead and now I have nothing. What am I to do? Where am I to go?' Maudlin tears began to fall.

'Whoever killed him was a total bastard,' MacNee said, his eyes fixed on the other man's face. 'Shouldn't get away with it, should he?'

'I hate him! I hate him to my very soul!' Angry colour came to Pilapil's face and he bowed his head over his clenched fists. 'If

I had him here, I would kill him now. No mercy – I would show him no mercy.'

Just drunken belligerence, or was there more to it? Carefully, MacNee said, 'You can tell me, laddie. Who was it that did it? Who killed Gillis?'

Pilapil looked up again, showing a mask of despair. 'If I knew, you think I would be sitting here, crying? I would have gone after him, found him. I'll show you what I would do.'

He got to his feet, walking unevenly, and pulled open a drawer, producing a long, pointed knife with a razor-fine edge. He stabbed and slashed at the air.

Making no sudden movements, MacNee got up, keeping a wary distance from him on the other side of the chair. The guy was very drunk, high on grief and anger, and waving one of the most businesslike shivs MacNee had been on the wrong end of for a very long time. The hairs on the back of his neck stood up.

'Now, laddie,' he said as soothingly as he could, 'no need to get upset. Just drop it and you sit down again. Here—' He grabbed the bottle, poured a couple of inches of gin into the glass and held it out, saying mendaciously, 'You take this and you'll feel better.'

Pilapil looked down at the knife in his hand as if he weren't sure how it had got there. He put it down on the table, keeping it within reach, but took the glass, sat down again and drank thirstily.

MacNee stepped forward to pick up the knife, but Pilapil's hand shot out and grasped it again. 'No! Don't take it! I need it – for protection.'

'OK, OK.' MacNee took a step backwards, his eyes never leaving the other man's face. 'Who do you need protected from, Cris?'

The young man looked around him as if he were afraid that someone else had come into the room. 'They know now, you see,' he said. 'Not happy.'

'They?' MacNee edged nearer.

'It's nothing – nothing to do with me. Don't know anything. They can't say I did. But they'll ask me. Won't be able to – to tell them. Angry, maybe.'

'They?' MacNee said again. He was only a step away now.

Pilapil seemed to realise what he was saying. 'Oh – people,' he said. 'Mustn't – mustn't talk about them.'

With a swift movement, MacNee made a snatch at the knife. Pilapil's response was surprisingly quick for someone in his condition; he tightened his hold on it and jumped to his feet, then stumbled. Even as MacNee leaped back, the arc of Pilapil's flailing arm brought the knife straight towards him, at the level of his heart.

It struck him, but there was no force behind the blow and it glanced off MacNee's jacket, leaving a neat razor cut in the leather.

His life had passed before his eyes, there. In blind rage MacNee smashed the side of his hand down on Pilapil's wrist, sending the knife spinning to the floor.

Pilapil gave a cry of pain, then stood swaying, blinking stupidly and rubbing his wrist as MacNee seized the knife. He took a couple of staggering steps and collapsed back into his chair.

As MacNee's heartbeat slowed to a healthier pace, he eyed the brainless, drunken bastard with cold fury. He could arrest him; on the other hand, he wanted to know more before the man passed out – and it was clearly a race against time.

'Look, lad,' he said, admiring his own restraint, 'you're needing to calm down. A knife's no answer to anything. You've drunk too much and you're not thinking straight. Tell me what the problem is and we'll sort it out.'

Pilapil gave a half-laugh. 'Police? Sort it out? You're – you're joking.' The last glass of gin had taken effect: he was slurring his words now and his eyes had begun to roll. 'Look, I'm tired, very tired. Got to – got to have a rest.' He fell back in his chair and his eyes closed.

Sighing, MacNee put the knife in his pocket and left Pilapil to sleep it off. He inspected his ruined jacket, assessing – not hopefully – the chances of a successful claim for a replacement. An expensive accident, that, but, as he slipped his fingers through the slit and felt the beating of his heart directly below, cheap at the price.

THE MAN WITH longish brown hair and a row of steel earrings in his left ear parked his elderly Astra in the street near Stranraer Station. He was about five foot eight, thin but wiry, with the pinched look that goes with poor nutrition in childhood. He had no strong distinguishing features, the sort of man who eludes description – a considerable professional asset in his line of work.

He didn't look over his shoulder as he walked towards the station, but stole a sideways glance behind him when he stopped to look in a shop window. There didn't seem to be anyone following him, but at the station he bought a newspaper even so. If at any stage he was uncomfortable, he was to throw it away and the eyes watching him for his own protection would know he'd pulled out. He'd just go home and try again another time. If he could get up the courage to try again.

He bought his ticket to Glasgow, as he was instructed. He had no idea what he was to do when he got there, but he had a mobile phone in his pocket. He just had to take it all on trust. But he wasn't a trusting man, though, and when he got on the train and turned to the sports pages in his *Daily Record*, they were a blur before his eyes.

As THE TRAIN pulled out, a man in jeans and a Celtic top turned away and spoke into a mobile phone. 'On his way. No problem that I could see. Over to you.'

At Girvan Station, another man, in chinos and a bomber jacket, said, 'Roger,' into his phone, and looked at his watch. Time for a cup of coffee before the train came in.

LISA STEWART WAS lingering over her breakfast. The café owner, a cheerful, wizened little man, had topped up her coffee free. At first she thought only about the day ahead, but as she sat there sipping, the question she had pushed to the back of her mind started to nag again. Why had Lee – or Jason, as she should call him – been so insistent that they came to Rosscarron?

Oh, she'd accepted his argument at the time – that it was the only way they could confront Crozier, make him see that it couldn't go on. She'd been too stressed to think straight, too desperate to do something – anything! – that would stop her living her life in fear of what the day might bring. And he'd insisted, threatened to leave her . . . She remembered the feeling of panic when he said that.

Jason liked money. If Crozier had bought him, had he given instructions that she was to be brought up to Rosscarron? Lisa had said at the start that she wouldn't go – was all the persecution just to drive her to agreement? Up here, on Crozier's own patch, an 'accident' to a city girl, unused to rough country, would be only too easy to arrange, the sort of accident that might even suggest she'd taken her own life in remorse for killing his grandchild.

But it didn't quite fit. There'd been plenty of time for Jason to take her on the walk from which she wouldn't return, but he hadn't even tried then. And, she remembered with an inward shudder, there was the dead man, the stranger she had looked at so impassively in the mortuary, but who had haunted her dreams since.

There were still things she couldn't understand going on, dark, dangerous things that Jason's death had not resolved. Fear began to seep back into her mind, and the rest of the coffee in her mug had grown cold. She must move, keep on moving, so no one could find out where she was.

That hadn't worked the last time, but as a plan it felt, well, familiar, and this time, she told herself firmly, she had reason to believe it would work. Lisa paid, thanked the owner and went out into the street.

Thinking about it all had made her feel nervous again. But there was no need, she told herself firmly. No one at all could possibly know she was here; even so, she couldn't resist looking over her shoulder to check that there wasn't someone shadowing her along the street.

There wasn't. Of course there wasn't. She was just being foolish.

THE MAN IN the silver Ford Focus had been reading his local newspaper for longer than one might think its content warranted, and the way he folded back pages from time to time suggested irritation. Wearing gloves made him awkward. Now, quite suddenly, he sat up, threw the paper impatiently down, got out of the car and set off along the street, though at a surprisingly leisurely pace.

MacNee was still feeling shaken as he put the knife away in the pocket of his jacket and opened the below-stairs door into the hall of Rosscarron House. Ryan was nowhere to be seen, and the house was silent. What now? He paused to consider his next move.

MacNee had thought he was on to something with his theory about Pilapil – the only one who'd seemed to care about Crozier. And right enough, he'd got it spot on about him wanting revenge.

The only wee snag was that Pilapil obviously hadn't done it. He'd been far too drunk to lie efficiently, and given the shenanigans with the shiv, he wasn't the crowbar type.

The crowbar. MacNee kept niggling away at the crowbar. It was pure chance he should have known it had been brought to the site, not found there. Maybe it was no more than an effective weapon, but it crossed his mind to wonder whether someone had tried to rig Williams's murder to fit with the others – a spur-of-the-moment killing, carried out with whatever came to hand, by the same person in a fit of temper? And could the someone being framed be a woman known to suffer from lack of control – Lisa Stewart? Or was he making too much of it?

'Sergeant!'

The voice behind him made him jump. The voice was no more than a whisper and he hadn't heard anyone approach, but when he turned, Cara Ryan was at the foot of the stairs.

'Oh! Mrs Ryan,' he said in surprise.

'Sssh!' She put a finger to her lips as she joined him in the hall. 'I want to speak to you. Quickly – in here.'

She moved on tiptoe and opened the door to the conference room with exaggerated care. He followed her as quietly as he could.

Cara looked nervous, but neither glazed nor manic this morning – midway between fixes, MacNee reckoned, sizing her up with an experienced eye.

'I daren't be more than a minute,' she said urgently. 'I have something to tell you, but Declan mustn't know, mustn't guess I've spoken to you.'

He felt a surge of excitement. Was this a breakthrough, at last? 'Go on,' he said.

'There was a man in the house, the night before my father was killed. I saw him. That's it.' She turned to go.

'No, no – wait. A man? What kind of a man?'

Her blue eyes were vague. 'It was just a glimpse – slim, quite short, spiky hair.'

Williams, MacNee thought exultantly.

'I saw him going into one of the spare rooms. I didn't see him after that. Now I have to go or he'll be looking for me and then . . .'

Instead of finishing the sentence, she grimaced, then slipped out of the room again before he could stop her. When MacNee went back into the hall, she was nowhere to be seen.

His mind was racing. Williams had come here – for refuge? – after he'd killed Rencombe, then got hold of a tent and gone to lose himself among the many fans at the rock concert. A bit of a blow for him, when the hoped-for camouflage didn't materialise.

Had he then killed Crozier? And why?

The first thing they needed was a search warrant, and the allegation that Williams had been at the house was good enough grounds for getting one. The rest of the questions could wait till he had time to run through them with Big Marge.

But it looked as if Cara Ryan might be the key to the whole thing. She'd lost her dad, after all, and if she believed her husband was involved, she might be persuaded to give them the information they needed, as long as she was assured of her own safety. They could easily pull Declan Ryan in for questioning, then come back with a search warrant and talk to her at the same time.

He was just getting into the car when a stone hit him on the back of the head. Swearing, he turned round and saw Nico Ryan standing grinning a few yards away.

He didn't even attempt to run away, which kind of bugged MacNee. It wasn't unknown for kids to throw stones at policemen, but they usually scarpered when you moved towards them threateningly. Nico held his ground.

'You can't touch me,' he said.

The little bugger was right. That was the problem with modern policing; even at this kid's age they knew exactly how much you couldn't do. Still, MacNee moved in close enough to make the boy take a step backwards. He smiled, not pleasantly.

'Ah, well, that's where you're wrong, you see. What age are you? Eight?'

Nico, eyeing him uncertainly, nodded.

'In Scotland, if you're eight, you're not just a child. You can go to court and they can lock you up. And you've just assaulted a police officer. Not a good idea.'

A flicker of unease crossed Nico's face – but only a flicker. 'It was an accident,' he said coolly.

Feeling grateful that he was unlikely to be in the vicinity when this one was a teenager, MacNee said, 'Like throwing stones, do you?'

'Sometimes.' It was a wary response.

'Your granddad got hit with a stone, didn't he?' He tried to make it sound like a conversational remark.

'I didn't throw stones at my granddad. I'd have got in trouble.'

Surely a kid couldn't pound a member of his own family to death, then lie with such assurance – but it was such a calm, slick reply! MacNee said carefully, 'You wouldn't, if he didn't know it was you.'

'No,' Nico agreed. 'I'd have had to hide.'

'If you were in that wood there behind him, he wouldn't notice you.' Maybe he was crazy to go on with this questioning – the rules concerning minors were strict – but if he got the truth now, he could do the compliance bit later.

'I could have hidden in the wood when he went up to the campsite,' Nico acknowledged, with what sounded almost like regret, 'but I didn't think of it.'

MacNee caught his breath. 'You – you saw your granddad going up to the campsite that day?'

'Yes. I was in there.' The child pointed to the bank of rhododendrons across the drive. 'I've got a den. *They* don't know.' He flicked a contemptuous glance towards the house.

'Can you think back, Nico? Did you see anyone going in after him?'

Nico shook his head and MacNee's sudden hope died. Then he went on, 'But there was a lady in a hood watching him from up there.'

Now he was indicating the rising ground beside the rough road leading on to Keeper's Cottage. It was flat at the top and anyone standing there could certainly be seen from Nico's position here, and could certainly see into the spinney below.

'A lady?' Lisa Stewart? She had admitted to him that she was out that afternoon, taking the Buchan child for a walk. 'A lady with a toddler in a pushchair?'

'No.' Nico was definite. 'Just a lady by herself. It was funny. She looked just like our old nanny, only our nanny had red hair and her hair was brown.'

MacNee's car had just disappeared down the drive when Cara Ryan came hurrying out of the house. 'Nico! Nico! Oh, there you are! Listen, sweetheart, this is terribly important. Did you take the computer that was in our bedroom under the bed?'

Nico's blue eyes were limpid with innocence. 'No, Mummy,' he said.

It was only after she had asked him again another couple of times, got the same answer and gone away that he glanced towards the den. He knew they would search his bedroom once they realised it had gone, but it was safe here. He always sneaked it back in when there was no one about and then he could play with it. He was getting quite good at *Grand Theft Auto* now.

Jan Forbes was working at her laptop in the Telfords' private sitting room where she could be undisturbed. She always spent a few hours in the morning keeping on top of administration, essay marking and emails, and the Telfords were meticulous about not interrupting her.

Eleven o'clock was coffee time, though, and when Susan appeared with a tray, she was looking worried.

'I gave the cleaners instructions not to go into Lisa's bedroom this morning so she could have her sleep out, but there's still no sign of her. I just wondered if I should maybe tiptoe in and see that she's – well, all right.'

Jan met her eyes with perfect understanding. 'Listen at the door, maybe,' she suggested. 'If you don't hear her moving about, you could give a wee soft tap that wouldn't wake her if she was still asleep and then just put your head round the door.'

Susan departed, and Jan waited for her return with just a little niggle of anxiety. Stupid, probably, she told herself. Though the doctor had said the sedative he had given her was very mild, it was perfectly possible that it had laid her out. And of course the young had that enviable ability to sleep in for hours that you lost as you got older.

When Susan came back, it was clear from her face that Jan's worst imaginings had been unfounded. But she was still looking concerned, and was holding a wad of notes in her hand.

'She's gone. Taken all her things and just gone. Left the money for her stay, look.'

'Very organised. That sounds as if she's all right, anyway, though I'd have liked to know where she was going. Still, if she didn't want to tell me . . .' Jan shrugged.

Susan was inclined to be indignant. 'There was no need for her to sneak off like that. We wouldn't have stopped her doing what she wanted to do. And it would have been nice if she'd thanked you. She'd have drowned if it wasn't for you.'

'Oh, that doesn't matter. I'm not entirely sure how grateful she was anyway. Lisa's had a sad, difficult life and I don't think conventional courtesy has featured in it much. She seemed very fragile last night. I just hope she knows what she's doing.'

'Should we tell the police, do you think?' Susan suggested. 'You said she told you they wanted to know exactly where she was.'

Jan considered for a moment, then said no. 'I promised her I would keep her confidence as far as possible. If the police want to speak to her, of course we must tell them what's happened, but they didn't ask either you or me to keep them informed.'

Susan, in awe of Jan's superior intellect, allowed herself to be convinced. 'And if that man from the press turns up, I'll tell him I never heard of her,' she said with a little more relish. 'Now, I'll let you get on. And drink that coffee before it gets cold.'

But after her friend had left, Jan sat staring into space for a long time, thinking about a damaged, vulnerable girl who had turned her back on the offer of friendship that might have helped her sort out her life.

LISA TOOK THE money from the ATM, then looked at her watch. She'd spent a long time over her breakfast and it was late enough now for them to realise she had left Rowantrees Hotel. They might even have phoned the police. She should get herself on a train before they started looking for her.

She'd planned to go to the High Street for her shopping, but Lisa spotted a funny, old-fashioned ladies' outfitter with cheap jeans in the window; she could get knickers there too, and it would be quicker. She crossed the road and went in.

Twenty yards behind her, a dark-haired man stopped and swore, much to the indignation of a passing Dumfries matron. He walked past on the other side, then crossed to look in the uninspiring window of the gents' outfitter next door, as if the display of socks, ties and checked flannelette shirts were of absorbing interest.

Still no sign of her. He went back to the other side of the road, parked himself beside the entrance to an office and lit up a cigarette. He smoked it as slowly as he could, but when it was right down to the filter, she still hadn't emerged. He dropped the butt and viciously ground it out with his foot.

Was she trying on clothes, maybe? The window display didn't suggest much that would detain a young woman.

A sudden cold thought gripped him. Abandoning caution, he dived across the road and looked in the window. Instead of the dingy interior he had expected, he could see right through to a street behind.

He was sure she hadn't seen him. Unintentionally, probably, his quarry had left by a door on the far side. He wasn't paid the sort of money he always demanded to make mistakes, and this one was elementary.

He swore again, this time earning a scandalised 'Well, really!' from two young mums passing with buggies. He ran back to the car.

Chapter Twenty-two

'I NEED A pot of yellow chrysanthemums,' DI Purves said, as he parked outside the superstore in Girvan.

DI Fleming smiled. 'Present for the wife?'

'Not exactly, though if I pay for it myself, she might get it in the end. No, it's so Dave can recognise us. We're meeting here because you're a busy woman who has to combine business and running the home. So you'd better buy some stuff.'

'Bread and loo rolls,' Fleming said, following him in. 'We're forever running out. Meet you in the café.'

There was a woman she recognised standing near the entrance, scanning the news-stand. She was looking towards the door, but as the two officers came in, her eyes slid away and she bent to pick up a magazine and flipped it open.

One of theirs, on duty, obviously. What was this operation doing to the budget, and what would have to be cut to pay for it, Fleming wondered, as she collected her groceries. She added milk to her short list – they were always running out of that too – then went to the checkout.

The café was fairly quiet. An elderly man and woman were sitting by the window, staring out in silence and ignoring each other as they sipped their tea and ate pastries. Two women, with piles of shopping bags on the floor beside them, were having an animated conversation, punctuated by bursts of laughter, and there was a little group of young mothers round a corner table with assorted offspring. It was hard to imagine any of them taking any interest in the elaborate charade that was about to be performed at the table where DI Purves was sitting.

He half rose as Fleming approached. 'That's what you told me to get, isn't it?' he said, indicating the pot of yellow flowers.

Entering into the spirit of the thing, Fleming sighed. 'I did say pink, but never mind.' She dumped her purchases on the floor and sat down.

There was a tray with three little pots of tea and three mugs on the table, along with a couple of packets of biscuits. 'I thought I'd take a chance on tea,' Purves said. 'OK?'

'Fine.' Fleming picked up one of the pots and filled a mug, peering dubiously at the colour of the liquid. 'I hope his won't be cold. I wonder how long he'll be.'

'Four minutes, give or take,' Purves said.

She hadn't expected so precise an answer. 'You're certainly keeping tabs on him. I saw young Thomson at the magazines on the way in.'

'We don't take chances with stuff like this. So far so good, anyway, and none of this lot look alarming. We'll just have to check on anyone who comes in afterwards. Ah! That looks like our man now.'

Fleming watched as Purves got up and walked over to a slight man with a row of earrings in one ear, looking hesitant at the entrance to the café. She heard him say, 'Dave? Ah, good. I'm Bob, Mrs Hay's foreman. You're right on time – she'll like that.'

The girl behind the counter looked at them incuriously and then went back to her conversation with the kitchen staff.

Fleming recognised the man at once. He was a petty criminal, with a minor record; the only time he had been in real trouble was when he was charged with driving the getaway car for a bank robbery. He was identified, but Fleming discovered there had been irregularities in the administration of the identity parade and, to the distinct displeasure of the arresting officer, had disclosed this to the defence. Since the man had in all probability been guilty, he certainly did have reason to be grateful to her.

By the time they reached her, she had the documents spread out on the table. She got up. 'Dave. Thanks for coming. And I need a good timekeeper, so you've made a fine start.'

If anyone was interested, it was a good cover story for the man's obvious nervousness. When Fleming shook his hand, she could feel that he was trembling, and he kept licking dry lips as she asked routine questions about his journey.

They were at a table in the far corner of the café with no one near them, and no one at any of the other tables had even turned their head. The elderly couple got up and left, still in silence, and a woman arrived with two noisy children demanding cokes and burgers.

After a couple of minutes Purves said, 'Let's not waste time. What have you got to tell us?'

Yet again Dave licked his lips. He looked towards Fleming and said, 'You'll see me right, won't you, miss? Won't let them drop me in it?'

'No, I promise they won't. They're being very careful of you – you can be sure of that.'

He gave her a long, measuring look, then sighed. 'I'd rather trust you than the rest of them. And I suppose I've done it now, anyway.'

He began his story. He had been a driver for Gillis Crozier, chauffeuring guests when he was at Rosscarron and at other times collecting goods that came in to Stranraer on the Irish ferry. They were always boxes of American DVDs, Dave said. He would be told what the name and address on the packages would be and given the appropriate documentation, but whatever the address was, he had to take the delivery to Rosscarron House if Gillis Crozier was there, or to a post office to be sent to his London office if he wasn't. Then a couple of weeks later, maybe, the same goods would go back to Ireland, but to a company with a different name from the one they had come from.

'You could maybe think it was just business,' Dave said, 'but I was aye given instructions I was not to do this and I was not to do that and I was to keep my gob shut, or else—' He looked nervously over his shoulder as he said that, as if the threatened retribution might be on hand.

'Carousel fraud?' Purves said, and Dave nodded.

'There was a big case a wee while ago and I realised.'

Carousel fraud – Fleming remembered reading about the case too, and she knew there was serious money involved, but she had only the haziest idea of how it worked. She'd have to ask Purves for elucidation on the way home.

'I was getting real scared,' Dave went on. 'Lloyd's in on this and he's one of the big bosses in Glasgow – you don't get across him. I'd driven him sometimes, and Driscoll would come on the ferry from Ireland for meetings and I'd driven him too. There were foreigners at the house sometimes, as well.

'So they all knew me, and I knew quite a wee bit about them. If you're a driver, folk just forget you're there. When I heard you lot were asking questions, I knew I'd need to get out. They'd give me a going-over just as a warning not to say anything – they're like that. They might just make sure I couldn't.

'And then yesterday I saw Badger Black in Kirkluce.' He gave an involuntary shudder.

The two officers looked at him blankly. 'The name doesn't mean anything to me,' Purves said, and Fleming shook her head.

'It wouldn't. He's the best,' Dave said. 'Hitman – never been caught or even questioned. Costs a bomb. But if he's here, he's here to do business. There's someone they're wanting rid of.'

He had no idea who it might be. Purves went on asking questions, getting details of times and places, but Fleming hardly heard another word he said. She was remembering the look of fear in Hepburn's eyes as he stood staring at the one-way panel, heard again his words to her: *I really, really want you to change your mind. For your own sake. I'll even say please.*

HE'D KNOWN ALL along that Lisa Stewart was holding out on them, that there was something important there, and maybe if they'd brought her in instead of going along with Kershaw's touchy-feely approach, they'd have got it out of her. As DS MacNee drove to the Rowantrees Hotel, he was kicking himself, too, for not going in harder right at the start.

She'd seen Gillis Crozier going into the little wood where he met his death. From the level ground on top of the rise where Nico had noticed her standing, she could even see right in among the trees – MacNee had checked it himself. So had Lisa witnessed the murder, or . . . ?

She'd been out walking, by herself, from the sound of it. Nico had been definite there had been no pushchair, and it would have been clearly visible from below. She'd told MacNee the baby had been with her, though – had she hoped this would sound less suspicious? And if she'd felt the need to lie about that, had she done more than just watch?

Nico couldn't say. He'd gone back into the house just after he'd seen her, with what he suspected was unease at the thought of encountering her. You couldn't call him a reliable witness in general, but this was convincingly circumstantial.

Then it struck him. After Crozier entered the spinney, it would have taken five minutes, maximum, to reach the field above. Lisa had been on the hill, with no time to reach him before he got to the other end. She couldn't have got into position in time to kill him herself, but she had almost certainly seen who had. And that had been the secret he had sensed – she had been scared to tell them what they needed to know, in case she herself became the prime suspect. This time MacNee wasn't going to pussyfoot around. He was going to hit her with it right away, smack between the eyes.

She'd picked a nice billet anyway. He swung the car in through the gates under the rowan trees and parked on the wide gravel expanse in front of the hotel. He noticed a grey-haired woman sitting at the window of the room to the right of the front door, who craned her neck as he approached. Was he imagining it or had his arrival somehow unsettled her?

He went into the hall and pinged the brightly polished brass bell on the reception desk. The smell of furniture polish was familiar: it was the one Bunty always used to use. His house was smelling of dust and neglect now, and he was having to clear his throat when a woman appeared, wearing an unconvincing smile.

'Can I help you?'

He produced his warrant card. 'DS MacNee. I believe you've someone called Lisa Stewart staying here?'

There was no mistaking the reaction he had provoked this time. The woman's face flared as she stammered, 'Oh – oh dear! Yes – well, I mean no, not really.'

'And you are . . . ?'

'Susan Telford. My husband and I own the hotel.'

'And Lisa Stewart's staying here – or maybe she's not?'

'Oh dear,' Susan said again. 'It's – it's a little unfortunate. I'll take you through to Dr Forbes. She'll explain.'

The name rang a bell. Lisa's neighbour, who'd been injured in the cliff fall. A sensible woman, judging by the statement he'd read.

She was the woman he had seen at the window. Her leg was in plaster and she too was looking definitely flustered. When Susan had introduced him, with a pleading look at her friend, Jan took a deep breath.

'I'm afraid you may not be very pleased with us, Sergeant. Lisa Stewart has left. We debated informing you, since she said she had instructions to stay here, but we decided not to since we had no real locus in the matter.'

MacNee could take criminals, but heaven preserve him from middle-class, middle-aged wifies who used fancy words to put him in his place! Disappointed and angry, he said stiffly, 'That's a pity. Where's she gone, then?'

'I'm sorry but we don't know. There's a bus goes past just after eight and I would guess she must have taken it.'

'I only went in to check at eleven o'clock,' Susan said, eager to be helpful. 'I just wanted to see she was all right—' She stopped suddenly.

MacNee's ears pricked up. 'Oh? Some reason why she shouldn't have been?'

There was an awkward silence. Then Jan said, 'She tried to drown herself yesterday. One of the other guests rescued her before any real harm was done, and I suspect it was just the traditional cry for help.'

'You don't maybe think that when someone's disturbed like that and wanders off, that it might just be an idea to get us to look for her before she has another go?'

Susan fluttered, 'But you see, she left payment for the room on the table . . .'

'So that was all right, then – you wouldn't be out of pocket.' His tone was hostile.

'Oh, I didn't mean . . .' Susan protested. 'I know it sounds . . . but I just meant—'

'Mrs Telford means that Lisa made an organised departure. She had taken all her belongings and paid her dues. That didn't suggest that she was in a distressed state and she's an adult, after all.' The eyes behind Jan's spectacles were cool and unyielding.

Getting aggressive had been a tactical error. Swallowing his annoyance, MacNee said, 'Then I wonder if you can help me. She's a suspect in a murder case and anything you can tell me might help us to trace her. As far as we know, she had no family?'

Describing Lisa as a suspect had the desired effect. After exchanging a worried glance with Susan, Jan was prepared to be helpful. 'She told me that, yes. And she had no settled home. She and her partner were constantly on the move in the past few months.'

'Do you know why?'

Jan did not reply immediately. Then she said, 'I think you had better sit down, Sergeant. Susan, would you be very kind and bring us some tea?'

Glad of the excuse to leave, Susan hurried out.

'I promised Lisa I wouldn't deliberately betray her confidence, but that if I were asked, I wouldn't lie. Reluctantly, I feel I have to tell you what she told me.'

Jan went on to tell him of Crozier's persecution, and of Lisa's misery about her life of lies – the ones she told and the ones told to her.

MacNee had listened in uncharacteristic silence. Then he asked, 'Did she say anything about being at the scene when Crozier's murder took place?'

Jan shook her head. 'No. I had the distinct impression, though, that she still had secrets. I hoped that over time she might trust me enough to let me try to help her. She was certainly a very troubled soul.

'I'll tell you one thing, though,' she concluded, 'I don't believe for a moment that she murdered that baby. She's a sad person, not a wicked one.'

She wasn't a bad old biddy once she unbent, MacNee reflected, as he drove back to Kirkluce. But she hadn't been able to tell him what he needed to know: where to find Lisa. Where the hell had the woman gone?

LISA WAS POSSESSED by a sense of urgency now. There was a train to Glasgow in ten minutes, and she'd taken a wrong turning on the way to the station and had to ask directions. She wasn't sure how much further she had to go.

She was still feeling nervous about the Ryans. She knew it was foolish: Jan's explanation had made total sense, but she found she wasn't quite able to shake off a fatalistic belief in their power to find her. Perhaps once she was on the train on her way to Glasgow she might recapture the sense of freedom she had felt all too briefly in the café this morning.

There was the station now, on the opposite side of the road. It wasn't busy; she took a quick glance left and right, then hurried across.

Lisa never saw the car that hit her. She felt it, though: agonising pain shot through her as she flew through the air. She heard a woman scream. Then there was a sickening crunch as her head hit the kerb. Then nothing.

It was a man who reached the pitiful, rag-doll body first. The eyes were wide open, round blue eyes like marbles, and already they were glazing over.

He took out his mobile phone. 'Ambulance,' he said, 'but I'm afraid you're not needing to hurry.'

THE SILVER FORD Focus accelerated away, overtaking the cars in front through a dangerously narrow gap. Once it was round the corner, it slowed to a more decorous pace, then took lefts and rights into a warren of little streets.

The driver was smiling, a wide, satisfied smile. His luck had held, after all. It usually did – he often joked about having sold his soul to the devil in exchange. It certainly wouldn't have done to fall down on this part of his commission; this was meant to be the easy bit, more or less a favour for a friend. The next one would be a lot more difficult.

As he turned into a quiet side road, he heard the sound of sirens and smiled again. He got out, locked the car and walked away, tucking his driving gloves into his pocket. There was a respectable householder in Glasgow who would be very surprised when the police called to question him about a hit-and-run.

Arriving for his shift at three, Andy Macdonald bumped into Kim Kershaw as she came out of the CID room.

'Just knocking off?' he asked her.

'Yes, but I'm going to the canteen first. I'm desperate for a cup of tea.'

'I'll come with you. You can fill me in on what's been happening – arrests, breakthroughs?'

Kershaw pulled a face. 'Fairly quiet today. Just the routine stuff. But I can fill you in on the Hepburn interview this morning. There was some pretty weird stuff going on with Big Marge.'

'Nothing like a bit of scandal with my jam doughnut.' Macdonald fell into step beside her.

There were half-a-dozen officers in the canteen, sitting at tables and watching TV. Sergeant Linda Bruce, holding her tray, was just finishing her chat with the woman behind the counter and she moved away smiling as they came up.

'It's all yours. And I can recommend the shortbread.'

'Sounds good,' Kershaw said. 'I'll have that, Maisie, and a tea, no milk, no sugar.'

As the woman turned away, Kershaw's mobile rang. She scrabbled in her shoulder bag, then, glancing at the number, stepped aside. 'You carry on, Andy – I'll be with you in a minute.'

'Doughnut, please, Maisie,' Macdonald said, 'and—'

From behind him, he heard a sound he had never heard before, a primitive howl like a tortured animal with a human voice. Frozen in shock, he barely heard Linda Bruce's tray fall to the ground with a crash. When he managed to turn round, Kim Kershaw was on the ground, crushed in an agony of pain. She was screaming, 'No! No!' and her clenched fists were beating on the ground.

Bruce fell to her knees beside her. 'Kim, what's wrong? What's happened?'

There was no answer, except more of those terrible cries. Macdonald bent to pick up the phone that had fallen from Kershaw's hand, his own hands shaking. 'DS Macdonald here. Who am I speaking to?'

The woman at the other end of the phone was in tears too. 'It's dreadful. It's Debbie, Mrs Kershaw's little girl. She – she took a sudden turn this afternoon and – and I'm afraid there wasn't anything we could do.'

'So, TELL ME about carousel fraud,' Fleming said to Purves, as they drove out of Girvan. She wanted something to take her mind off the fear that had possessed her since Dave's disclosure. 'Something to do with VAT, isn't it?'

'VAT and fake businesses – on an international scale here, from the looks of it. At its simplest level, you register your company for VAT, then buy goods – as it might be, DVDs – from another EU country and they'll be zero-rated. Then you add the VAT to the price when you sell them, pocket it and disappear instead of forwarding it to the taxman.

'This scam's more elaborate. They'll have some sort of syndicate. Mr A, the importer, sells to Mr B, Mr B sells to Mr C and so on, with VAT being theoretically added each time. The first company pays the tax; the rest all 'reclaim' it and finally it's exported to another EU business, zero-rated, of course. Then, having paid one lot of VAT and got all three, four, five or however many lots generously refunded by the taxman, the companies disappear and the whole merry-go-round sets off again. Multi-million-pound profits.'

Fleming pursed her lips in a silent whistle. 'We did think money-laundering had something to do with Crozier's curiously amateurish little rock festival, and the foray into building as well.

'The Ryans and Pilapil were obviously in on it, and presumably Hepburn was involved at the American end, exporting the DVDs to Ireland. He certainly knew what was going on. He was very edgy about it.' It was an understatement. 'Edgy' was not quite the word for what she had seen in Hepburn's eyes.

'With reason, I would guess,' Purves said. 'I don't know a lot about the big boys in Glasgow, but from what Dave said, getting involved wasn't a clever idea, whatever the rewards.'

It didn't help the hollow feeling in the pit of her stomach. 'What'll happen to Dave now?'

'On his way to a safe house, even as we speak. That was the final deal. We can be sure he wasn't followed, so no one will be looking for him – yet. And he's an unobtrusive sort of guy. We'll fix him up with the papers and he can find a driver's job in a city south of the border easily enough. He's got no family ties so they can't get at him that way, and we've spelled it out to him that provided he goes straight he should be able to keep out of their way.'

'Expensive way of weaning him from a life of crime, but effective, I would reckon.'

'So now we hand over to the Fraud Squad? To be honest, I can't see that this has a bearing on the murders. Indeed,' Fleming said, thinking aloud, 'with all this going on in the background, Williams killing Crozier's solicitor and bringing the police down on them must have been a disaster.'

'But the searches haven't turned anything up?' Purves asked.

'Nothing on the office computer – they've been careful, naturally enough. And of course the only areas we were allowed to search were the ones that related directly to Crozier himself – bedroom, office. The sheriffs won't grant warrants for anything that looks to them like a fishing expedition for evidence on suspects.

'Incidentally, I don't think I was here today. Even if it's not related to my investigations, it might look as if it was.'

Purves gave her a sideways look. 'Not only were you not here, I wasn't here and nor was Dave. The information he gave us will be totally sanitised and passed on to the correct quarters.

'What might become our business is the hitman he thinks is operating on our patch. That information will come through the proper channels shortly. But the big problem is, how the hell do we find out who he's targeting?'

Fleming studied her hands, tightly clasped in her lap, for a moment. She was opening her mouth to say, 'John, I think there's something I should tell you,' when her phone rang.

PARKING HIS CAR at headquarters, MacNee had spotted that Fleming's car was in her reserved space. Good! They could get things moving at once.

At the reception desk there were two of the civilian assistants talking in hushed tones, but he didn't really notice as he punched in the security number and headed up to the fourth floor. There was no answer to his knock: she must be around the building somewhere. Then he remembered that she had said she had a 'commitment', so perhaps it was just round the corner and she'd walked. Or got a lift from someone; he'd noticed Purves's car wasn't there. Some sort of special training for DIs, maybe. Bloody stupid, all this training and conferring and setting targets instead of getting on with the job.

He looked at his watch. He was entitled to knock off now, but the thought of going home wasn't very appealing. Andy Mac was on the second shift today; he might have a blether with him about the way things were shaping up.

When he went downstairs, the CID room was surprisingly full and surprisingly quiet. There were groups of detectives standing talking in low voices, and MacNee looked around with a furrowed brow.

'Dearie me,' he said to Macdonald, who was standing near the door, 'you're looking a bit glum. Who's stolen your scone?'

Macdonald grimaced. 'Tam, it's very bad news. Kim Kershaw's daughter, Debbie – she's just died.'

MacNee stared at him blankly for a second, then a red mist of unreasoning rage grew in his mind. The neglected child, fobbed off on strangers! The waste, the terrible waste! If Bunty had had a child, it would never have been out of her sight; it would have been fairly *deaved* with love and care.

He said harshly, 'I'm sorry for the woman, of course. But maybe if she'd kept her at home and looked after her instead of parcelling her off to boarding school—'

The shocked silence penetrated even his fury. He stopped.

Macdonald was looking at him with revulsion. 'For God's sake, Tam, Debbie was in a *home*! She was severely disabled and the staff told me Kim was the most devoted mother any child could have. You're sick, Tam – at least I hope you are, because if you're not, there's no excuse for one of the nastiest remarks I've ever heard.'

The anger drained out of MacNee, leaving him white and shaken. Without meeting anyone's eyes he left the room.

FLEMING LISTENED IN dismay to Macdonald's agitated voice. 'Where is she now?' she asked, then, as he went on, pulled a grimace of distress. 'For goodness' sake!' she said. 'I don't know what's got into MacNee. Leave it with me, Andy – I'm on my way back.'

'About as bad as it could be,' she said in answer to Purves's concern. 'Poor Kim Kershaw's daughter has died.'

'The handicapped one?'

'Yes. Everyone knew she was handicapped except, apparently, Tam MacNee, who made such an unfeeling remark that if he goes back into the CID room, he'll be lynched.'

Chapter Twenty-three

THE SCENE OF the accident in Station Road had been cordoned off. The body had been removed, and uniforms from the Dumfries Force were directing traffic, taking measurements and interviewing passers-by.

'The name on her bank card's Lisa Stewart,' a PC told the detective who had just arrived. 'No address or phone or anything – nothing in here except clothes and stuff.' He held up a blood-stained shoulder bag.

'No one got the car's number?' the detective asked.

'Not so far. Stolen anyway, most likely.'

'Usually are. We'll get her address from her bank. I take it she's dead?'

The constable nodded. 'Never had a chance, that poor lass.'

THE DOGS, AT least, were pleased to see Tam MacNee when he returned, the two young rescue dogs leaping around him and the elderly white one, with a rakish brown patch over its eyes and a missing leg, wagged its tail furiously instead. He ignored them and after a moment they trotted past him into the garden.

A grey cat looked up from its cushion on a kitchen chair and surveyed him with cool amber eyes, but the other cats in favourite cosy nooks paid no attention. Tam sat down at the kitchen table and put his head in his hands.

The kitchen was where he could always find Bunty when he came home, cooking or fussing with the animals or gossiping with a pal. There was always the smell of good food and cleanliness, and it was a bright and cheerful room, with the farmhouse pine units, and the flower-print curtains at the window. There were always flowers on the table too. Bunty liked flowers.

There was no scent of flowers now, just a trace on the air of rotting food from the bin he'd forgotten to empty, and the body smell of the animals. Bunty had always kept everything too clean for them to smell.

He couldn't believe what had happened to his life in these past few weeks, wouldn't have believed it was possible. He'd managed, though, to hold it together at his work, more or less, though it had cost him sometimes to go on as if nothing had happened.

Until today. He couldn't believe what he'd done today. How come he hadn't known about Kim's daughter? He knew the answer, though – he hadn't had a chat down the pub with anyone since all this happened. And Kim had got up his nose with her snippy remarks about Glasgow, and then the 'boarding school' – why hadn't she told him?

He didn't like the answer to that either. It came far too close to home.

What was he to do now? He'd felt the full force of the anger of his colleagues. How on earth was he to work with them after that? But if he didn't have the job . . .

Tam had always had a soft spot for down-and-outs. If you talked to them, they'd often a story that would get tears out a stone – the problems at home, the drinking, the loss of the job, then the house repossessed . . .

With a surge of angry despair, Tam got up and went to the cupboard where he kept a bottle of whisky. He couldn't remember the last time he'd started drinking to get drunk, but if he was going to be out on the street, he might as well take the normal road to ruin.

KIM KERSHAW WAS back in the little flat in Newton Stewart by the time Marjory Fleming rang the bell. The door was opened by Kim's mother, Dawn, a thin, wispy-looking woman who seemed out of her depth in the face of tragedy.

'Says she's cold. I've made her a cup of tea, but she's not drinking it,' she confided in a whisper. 'I don't know what else to do.'

Murmuring conventional condolences, Fleming went through the narrow hall into the sitting room. It was a small room, painted an unpromising shade of beige, with neutral furnishings – comfortable enough, but somewhere to live rather than a home. There were few personal touches apart from photographs of an unsmiling child, delicately pretty but with a blank look in the eyes that told its own story.

The electric fire was on and the room was uncomfortably hot. Kim was sitting close to it, staring straight ahead; she did not turn her head as Fleming came into the room. By her side, an untouched cup of tea had a slimy film on its surface. She gave no sign of having heard the well-worn phrases Fleming repeated, and her hands when the other woman patted them briefly were icy cold.

Fleming sat down, as Dawn drifted off to make more tea. What did you say – what could you say, when you were possessed with something like guilt about your own two healthy children who were at this moment, please God, safe and happy? An interview with a bereaved parent wasn't a new experience, but this wasn't an interview, where there were questions to be asked with a constructive purpose.

This was different. There was nothing to ask, nothing useful to say. With a friend, you would put your arms round her, cry along with her, but though Fleming knew little of Kim personally, she sensed that an emotional approach would be impertinent. Kim was a professional colleague, and this was, in a sense, a professional visit.

So keep it professional. 'Is there anything you need, that we can do for you, Kim? Of course there will be compassionate leave for as long as you need—'

'No!' For the first time, she got a response. Kim looked directly at her with tortured eyes but said perfectly calmly, 'There will be funeral arrangements, of course, but there's very little to do otherwise. I don't want to be off duty.'

Horrified, Fleming protested, 'But, Kim, you're in shock. You need time to recover—'

'Recover!' Kim gave a bitter laugh. 'You don't really think I'll *recover*, do you? When you lose a child, you only learn to live with the pain, so the sooner I get on with doing it the better. Debbie was my purpose in life and the job is going to have to take that place. Otherwise, I'd just top myself now, wouldn't I?'

She gave a bright, brittle smile and got up. 'Thank you for your support,' she said, and held out one of those cold, cold hands.

There was nothing Fleming could do but shake it and leave.

Dawn was in the hall, coming from the kitchen with yet another unwanted cup of tea. She set it down on a small table with a sigh. 'Do her good to have a wee cry,' she said, 'but she won't. I'd a bit of a cry at the home myself when I saw her, poor kiddie. But all for the best really, isn't it?'

Not knowing what to say in response to such a supremely insensitive remark, Fleming muttered something indistinguishable and left, torn between her pity for Kim's anguish and anxiety about the dreadful unwisdom of her speedy return to duty.

She had another professional problem to deal with, which she might as well tackle now.

'IT HAS TO have been him!' Declan Ryan said to his wife furiously. 'Who else could have taken it from under our bed?'

The air in the white sitting room was thick with smoke and there was a pile of stubbed-out butts in the ashtray in front of Hepburn. Cara gave a little cough, sent him a reproachful glance, then looked at her husband with dull, unfriendly eyes. 'I'm tired. You've asked him, I've asked him.'

'I know, and it's done no good. Where the hell is it? We've got to destroy it! The busies'll be all over us like a rash, with warrants and everything now for the whole house, and then it's—'

'Should have dropped it in the sea, like I said.'

Ryan turned on his wife savagely. 'And have the bosses sending messages we didn't get, and wondering why? Get real!'

'Well, they know now what's been going on – some of it, any-way,' Hepburn snapped. 'And it's getting seriously alarming.'

'You could say. But tell me about your little friend Madge.' There was an unpleasant edge to Ryan's voice. 'Has she backed off?'

There was a brief pause, then Hepburn said, 'She's thinking about it. I've given her the strongest possible warning.'

Ryan laughed. 'I never thought it would work. So, when's the news story coming out?'

Again, Hepburn hesitated. Then he said, 'The threat was what it was about. Now' – he shrugged his shoulders in a pantomime of indifference – 'not worth the hassle.' As Ryan began to protest, he went on, 'Anyway, I've made up my mind. I'm getting out. I've stayed around so the police wouldn't get too interested, but it's way beyond that now. I'm on the next plane I can get, before they block my passport. If they want me, they can extradite me.'

'Oh, nice,' Ryan sneered. 'You're going to get out, leaving us to carry the can.'

Hepburn turned on him. 'See here, my friend, there's a lot of stuff going on in this place that I don't get, and I'm not asking you to explain. It's absolutely nothing to do with me and I really, majorly, do not want to know. But Alex's murder brought the roof in, and somehow you're involved. Your problem, not mine. I'm out of here.'

Roused, Cara said, 'We – we have to stick together, Joss! Tell the same story! Please, Joss, I need you. I'm – I'm scared.'

Hepburn looked down at her from his considerable height. 'No dice, Cara. Declan's your husband – I guess you must have chosen him, though I might wonder why. Your choice, your life.'

As he shut the door behind him, Cara sagged back in her chair. Ryan went back to his theme. 'Nico's got to tell us where it is.'

'Maybe it was Cris,' Cara said. 'Maybe he thinks he can blackmail us. You'd know all about that.'

Ryan glared at her, but she had a point. 'We've searched every-where except his room. And paying up would be cheap at the price, if we could be sure it was destroyed. He was completely out of it the last time I saw him, but I'll try and get through to him – money makes sweet music where he's concerned.'

Cara nodded, but her eyes followed him as he went out of the room and she began chewing at her thumbnail without even real-ising she was doing it.

Two minutes later he returned. 'He's gone,' Ryan said. 'He's taken the runabout and cleared out.'

Before she drove away from Kershaw's flat, Fleming dialled MacNee's number. There was no point in going there if he wasn't in.

It rang several times before the phone was picked up and Mac-Nee's voice answered, a little slurred and – surely not? – heavy with tears.

'MacNee? It's Fleming,' had been on her lips, but she said, 'Tam? It's Marjory,' with real concern. 'What on earth's the matter?'

'Er . . . nothing. I'm fine.'

She could hear the effort as he tried to pull himself together. 'You're not,' she said bluntly. 'I'm on my way.'

There was a protest from the other end, but she cut him off. There was something badly wrong with Tam and she wasn't going to allow him to fob her off this time. There was a professional problem to deal with, certainly, but this was obviously personal. Unlike Kim, Tam was an old friend and on this occasion she had no doubt about what she had to do. And if he needed her to cry with him, she'd do that as well.

The villa where the MacNees lived was on the outer edge of Kirkluce, a little apart from its neighbours in a good-sized garden with fields at the back. The first thing that Marjory noticed as she came up the path was the pots of bedding plants and the hanging baskets in which Bunty, a keen gardener, produced a riot of colour throughout summer. With all the rain, they had become water-logged and were drooping, blackened and dead.

Bunty. She'd had an uneasy feeling about Bunty, from the way Tam was speaking about her – or wasn't, rather. Marjory had got the impression that she was visiting her sister, but judging by the garden, with weeds springing up everywhere, it had been more than a week or two.

Tam opened the door. He didn't meet her eyes, and she could smell whisky on his breath, but his hair was wet and the neck of his white T-shirt was damp too, as if perhaps after getting her phone call he had stuck his head in a basin of water to sober up.

'You'd better come in, I suppose,' he said ungraciously, but his speech was quite clear.

Marjory followed him in, then had to suppress a gasp of shock. She was familiar with the kitchen, the heart of the MacNee house-hold, with its red-tiled floor always shining and its air of comfort and good housekeeping.

Now that same floor was muddy with footmarks and paw prints, the surfaces were piled with dirty dishes and the wrap-pings of ready meals, and there was a sour smell of rancid milk coming from a bottle with a greenish curd in the bottom aban-doned on the draining board.

'Sit down, Tam,' she said. 'You're going to talk to me.'

Marjory had expected an argument, but Tam collapsed into the chair she had indicated as if his legs had suddenly become rubbery. She could see the mark of tears on his face; she'd never known Tam cry.

'It's Bunty, isn't it,' she said. 'Is it . . . is it cancer?'

Tam shook his head. 'Not cancer, no. But – but, Marjory, she's gone off her head!'

'Off her head? What on earth do you mean?'

Tam produced a crumpled handkerchief from his pocket and blew his nose. 'They've taken her away.'

'Sectioned her?' Marjory was horrified. Bunty MacNee had always seemed to her one of the sanest, most balanced women she knew.

'Not exactly. Just taken her away to the Crichton Royal. She's been there weeks.'

'What happened?'

An old white dog came limping in from the garden, sniffed briefly at Marjory, then went to sit down by Tam, leaning against his knee. The man's hand went out to stroke its head, as if finding comfort in the action.

'She'd to have a hysterectomy, a wee while back. It went fine, but she came home kind of down, crying a lot and that. I could see why, right enough. We'd aye wanted bairns, you know, and that was the end of that. Well, I'd known that long syne, but Bunty just kept hoping.

'And then she stopped crying and just kind of went daft – wouldn't speak, wouldn't eat, wouldn't do anything. I kept talking to her, but she didn't seem to hear me or see me. I just – wasn't there.'

Tears began to gather again in Tam's eyes. 'She's the whole world to me, Marjory. Aye, it would have been great to have bairns, but I wasn't caring as long as I had Bunty. I've never needed any-one but her.

'I thought she felt that way about me too. Oh, women mind more about having weans, maybe, but we've been that happy together all these years – you know we've been happy, Marjory. She'd the animals to pet. We'd great friends. We'd a good life. But now there was never to be kids, I was nothing to her. Nothing. She even . . .' He found it difficult to go on. 'She even – even said she was going to kill herself. It made me feel . . .' He stopped.

It wasn't a phrase Marjory had ever heard from MacNee. 'Go on, Tam,' she said softly.

'Worthless,' he managed. 'I felt worthless all my life until I met her. Just – just gutter scrapings. And now . . .'

Her heart wrung with pity, Marjory said, 'That doesn't depend on anyone else. You've shown your worth again and again. You're respected . . .' But she faltered.

'Aye, maybe. Until today.' His mouth twisted.

'Never mind that just now. I want to know about Bunty.'

Tam sighed. 'I made her see the doctor and he gave her pills, but they didn't make any difference. He said she'd gone daft and they took her away.'

'Tam!' Marjory protested. 'I'm quite sure he said no such thing.'

'Oh, he dressed it up in fancy names, but you know me – I've always been one to face facts. She wouldn't let me help her through it. She shut me out and then just – gave up. She wasn't my Bunty any more. She's gone not right in the head.'

Fleming stared at him. 'I tell you, I don't know where to start. I think it's you that's off your head, Tam. I don't know what the doctor called it, but it sounds like bad clinical depression. She'd have hormone problems after her operation, which probably triggered it, but even without that it's not uncommon. Plenty of women who have children find it hard to accept their childbearing days are over, and Bunty's such a motherly soul it was bound to hit her harder. It'll take time to get the treatment right, but she'll be fine.

'How is she now?'

'Her sister's saying she's better. But, Marjory, they're telling me I'm not to see her, that it just upsets her. So that's it – there's no point now. I've just got to find some way of coping without her. And I don't know how.' The depth of his despair was etched in lines of pain on Tam's face.

Tam wouldn't be the easiest man to live with, Tam with his insecurities and his emotional dependence. He never talked about his childhood in Glasgow, but Marjory knew there was deep damage there. Struggling to cope with the devastating turmoil of her own feelings, his wife – whose very soul was generosity – had needed to be selfish for once.

She said gently, 'You said it, Tam – Bunty wasn't herself. She was locked in with her problems and she couldn't see a way out. Now she's got medical help and she's getting better, but she probably hates you seeing her while it's still a work in progress. There's an old saying, "Fools and bairns . . ."'

'". . . should never see work half done,"' Tam finished. 'Are you saying you think she'll . . . come back, kind of?'

'I'm sure of it,' Marjory said firmly. 'You've talked yourself into this state, going over it and over it inside your head until you've got it completely out of proportion. Why on earth didn't you tell me about it?'

'I – I didn't want to let her down, telling you she was, well, you know . . .'

Marjory shook her head, suddenly feeling dispirited. 'It's nothing to be ashamed of,' she said – and yet, hadn't she herself kept quiet about her brush with mild depression? And had Kim Kershaw, perhaps, had the niggling feeling at the back of her mind that being open and matter-of-fact about her daughter's problems would, in some sense, be 'letting her down', as Tam had put it?

'Give Bunty time and space,' she went on. 'She's a great lady and she's giving herself the best chance of recovery by directing all her energies into getting better. And you know what her energy's like.'

For the first time, what was almost a smile came to Tam's face. 'Oh, aye, I ken that, right enough.'

'You'll have to be patient, Tam. That's really all I can say. OK?'

He said nothing, but gave a slight nod.

Marjory said reluctantly, 'But I'm afraid we have to talk about the other problem.'

His face darkened again. 'I'm black burning ashamed. I can't think how I said it, even if there was nothing wrong with the wee girl. It was just the waste . . .'

'Yes. The trouble is, it was said and you can't take it back. Feeling's running high, and Kim's insisting that she doesn't need time off. The only thing I can think of is that you'll have to take it off instead, until all this settles down.'

Marjory could see it was a blow, but Tam took it without protest. 'I'd apologise,' he said, 'but I think maybe Kim wouldn't want that just now.'

'No, I don't think she would. In any case, I would hope she'd never hear what you said.

'Anyway, what was the outcome of your visit to Rosscarron House today?'

Tam looked blank for a moment, then smacked his forehead with the heel of his hand. 'Oh, for God's sake! I'd been looking for you when Macdonald told me what had happened and it all went out my head. There's plenty to tell you. For a start, we need to put out an APB to get Lisa Stewart picked up. She's run for cover.'

FLEMING RETURNED TO her car, then hesitated. Perhaps she should go back to her desk, but it was almost nine o'clock. The alert for Lisa Stewart could be sent out with just a phone call, thorough searches would have to wait till the morning anyway, and now with the Fraud Squad involved, a search warrant for the whole of Rosscarron House would be their responsibility. Declan Ryan could be summoned for questioning under caution first thing tomorrow, and she'd told MacNee she'd go out to Rosscarron House then herself and see what Cara would say when her husband wasn't there.

No, she decided, she'd go home. Apart from anything else, her face was throbbing under the fading bruises and she had a splitting headache. It worried her a little: she knew enough about head injuries to be aware that recovery from the initial impact didn't mean you were safe. A clot could detach days, or even weeks, later.

But as Fleming headed for Mains of Craigie, there was a more immediate worry on her mind. Was it possible that the hitman Dave had talked about really did have her in his sights? It seemed so far-fetched now, as she drove the familiar road beside the fields and the soft hills with their green fading into grey haze under the overcast sky, past the road ends of farms whose names – Windyedge, Rathskeillour, Broadhaugh, Thirlestane – were as well known to her as the names of friends.

She had been on the point of telling John Purves and asking him what he thought. She knew what his answer would be: tell the authorities, get protection, don't take risks. He'd be right, of course, but she still didn't want to believe it. OK, Hepburn might sick the press on to her, but this was just too – well, dramatic. Criminals took out contracts on other criminals, not on police officers only peripherally involved in an inquiry. And once the Fraud Squad got involved, they would know she wasn't working alone, so killing her wouldn't stop anything – on the contrary.

Reporting her anxieties would have caused an immense amount of fuss, and she'd have looked an idiot when nothing happened. She knew all the security precautions anyway – vary your routine, check for cars following you, watch out for anyone with an odd pattern of behaviour, yadda, yadda, yadda. And formal security wasn't a safety guarantee anyway – look at what had happened to Kennedy and Reagan, or John Paul II.

That put it into perspective, somehow. Fleming grinned at the thought of bracketing herself with popes and presidents, and, with only a casual glance in the driving mirror at the empty road behind her, drove on.

She went back to the line of thought she had been pursuing in the car with Purves before the phone call about Kershaw came in. The last thing the syndicate would have wanted was to have police attention drawn to their operations. The Ryans, Hepburn and Pilapil had clearly been involved, and were equally clearly scared, so Williams's killing of Rencombe had to have been a personal initiative. Why, then, had he been given shelter and a cover story in Crozier's house?

Had Crozier known he was there? Cara, according to what she had said to Tam, had only seen him briefly, slipping into one of the bedrooms. To cut the phone wire? Again, why?

There was an obvious answer: to prevent communication with the outside world. Who was to be stopped phoning in – or phoning out?

Rencombe's killing was definitively reactive. Something happened, something that meant Williams had to stop him doing – what?

There had to have been a threat of some kind. Physical violence? Unlikely. Rencombe was only a proxy, after all. The threat must have come from Crozier: do this, or else . . . Or – and that fitted better – *don't* do this, or else. Had the situation been the other way round? Had Williams presented some sort of threat to Crozier and Rencombe had been sent to see him off?? A rich and powerful man wouldn't go himself.

Fleming warmed to the thought. Blackmail of some kind, something Crozier had done that Williams was going to expose – his persecution of Lisa Stewart, perhaps? But that was a go-ahead-and-do-what-you-damn-well-like situation – Crozier had only to say he was unbalanced by grief to get sympathy.

No, it still didn't feel quite right. She was convinced she was on to something, but there was still more to it than that.

And Crozier would reasonably be expecting a prompt report back. If it didn't come, he'd get on the phone to find out why. Unless the wires were cut.

Fleming was approaching the turn-off now, but at last she could feel the tingle of excitement that told her she was getting somewhere. She drove past the road end, barely glancing at it.

A broken phone line would be restored, though. And even if it wasn't, once Crozier became concerned at not hearing from Rencombe, he would drive off to where he could get a signal. Sooner or later he was going to find out his solicitor was dead, and he would know Williams had done it. So Crozier's fate was sealed.

Would they be able to prove Williams had killed him too? The labs would be checking all his clothes and his shoes, and analysis would show if he had been in the copse. It wouldn't show when, though, and it wouldn't, most frustratingly of all, show why.

And then, of course, who had killed Williams? The initial forensic reports had been unhelpful. A crowbar was often the weapon of choice, keeping the assailant at a distance from the victim and avoiding clothes contamination, and this one had been meticulously wiped. Fleming sighed. The strong line of thought was beginning to peter out and she was suddenly aware of her extreme tiredness.

She'd driven almost to Glenluce. She turned in to a side road and set off back, still desperately pursuing her reasoning.

Had Lisa Stewart, standing on the hill, seen her partner in the act of murder? She had little reason to trust the police, and she was unlikely to feel that Crozier had a right to justice. It would explain, too, why Williams had wanted to meet her later on.

Had she then taken her chance to kill him? Revenge for his working for Crozier, for his treacherous persecution? But no, Jan Forbes had told MacNee that the idea that her partner could have been Crozier's spy in the camp had come as a complete shock.

The argument was beginning to go round in circles. And there was Mains of Craigie now. Fleming turned in to the drive.

The house was dark, apart from the light over the back door. It felt very empty when Fleming went into the kitchen, though Meg as usual was pleased to see her. There was a note on the table; Bill and the kids had gone to see *The Da Vinci Code* and would have a pizza afterwards.

They'd all been planning to go, she recalled, before this hit her. A cheerful family outing – when was the last time she'd had one of those? Bleakly, Fleming went to the freezer. There was nothing there she fancied (why did she buy macaroni cheese, when she didn't like it?) and she couldn't be bothered to scramble eggs. Toast, Marmite, a Nurofen and a cup of tea – she daren't risk a drink with her headache.

She ate without enjoyment, had a long bath and was asleep when Bill and the children came back, and even their giggling and shushing didn't wake her.

THE CAR THAT had overtaken Fleming on the A75, a white Vauxhall Vectra, slowed down as she got near to Mains of Craigie. When her car didn't turn in, the driver, looking in his mirror, frowned. Had his information been wrong?

He kept a steady distance ahead of her on the long, straight road, and when, after a time, she went into a side road, he braked, ready to go back and follow her along it. But then he saw the lights fan across the road as she turned and drove back the way she had come.

Going home now? Odd behaviour, but he found another turning and went back himself, pressing on a little to catch up. This time, Fleming signalled and turned in to Mains of Craigie. He drove a little way past, then pulled into the side and switched off his headlights.

He saw the car arrive at the darkened house at the top of the track, and the lights go on as she entered. His big chance?

But he hadn't built his reputation on impulsive decisions. There was one way in, and one way out. A slow, narrow track, so the noise of his engine would announce his arrival and there would be no quick getaway. It looked, too, as if the family he knew she had were out; they could come back anytime and he would be trapped.

No, it was urgent but not that urgent. Later, maybe. Catch a bit of shut-eye, then go back to have a sniff around.

Chapter Twenty-four

'NAME?'

'Cris Pilapil.'

The young man looked seriously rough, unshaven and scruffy, and from the way he winced at the brusque voice of the sergeant at the charge bar he was in the grip of the mother of all hangovers. He'd certainly turned the crystals in the breathalyser an interesting shade when they'd pulled him over for erratic driving.

'Address?'

'Don't have one.'

The sergeant sighed. 'Come on, son – if you give us an address, you can probably be bailed to go and sleep it off. If not, we'll have to keep you here. Where did you spend last night?'

'Can't remember.'

Wearily, the sergeant pulled across a thick pad of forms. 'Have it your way. Let's start again. Spell your name for me.'

NICO RYAN SAT in his room playing *Grand Theft Auto*. He was in Liberty City tonight, and he'd moved up a level since he'd started.

He could get really good, now he'd enough time. He'd played for hours last night till he was too sleepy to go on. But tonight he wasn't concentrating like he should. He'd even made one or two silly mistakes.

His parents had gone on and on at him, and they'd searched his room today when he was out. It was all messy with his things out of place when he came in, which unsettled him. It had taken him ages to put everything back properly. He liked everything arranged in his own special way, and he hated broken and spoiled things.

She'd torn one of his books. She'd grabbed it in her horrid fat, pudgy hands and ripped it, but she hadn't got punished, like Nico had when he'd ripped up her pink rabbit. *She's only a baby.* That's what that nanny said, but the baby was getting bigger all the time, doing more things, and he knew what that would mean. She was messing up his life. She'd no right to do that.

Anyway, it was fine now. He didn't think about it any more, really. Except he was sure it was the nanny he'd seen that day, even if her hair was brown, and that had upset him again. She'd never liked him. She'd said . . . things. And then talking about it to that policeman made it all come back, and he didn't like that either. The policeman was a bit scary, and though Nico didn't believe him about getting locked up, he wasn't comfortable.

His parents were quarrelling again. He could hear his mother yelling at his father. She probably needed a fix and Dad was holding out on her. He didn't know why – as long as she got it, she was OK.

The yelling stopped. He went to his door and listened; he was safe enough as long as he knew where they were, but if they came upstairs, he'd have to hide the laptop. There was a little space at the back of the bed, not as safe as having it outside in his den, but it was OK while he was in the room.

A door opened and Nico heard his mother's feet clipping up the stairs. Quickly, he closed down the laptop, thrust it out of sight and was reading a comic when she came in.

She'd obviously got what she wanted. She always did in the end. She was smiling, a bit dreamy, and she gathered him to her, pushing his hair back from his face in a way he particularly detested.

'How's my precious?'

'Gerroff,' he growled, pushing her away.

Cara sighed. 'You're getting to be such a big boy now! Darling, you would tell me if you had that laptop we asked you about, wouldn't you?'

'I told you.' Nico picked up the remote control and switched on the TV. 'Don't know what you're talking about.' He became instantly immersed in *Big Brother*.

Cara sighed again. 'I know, I know, sweetheart. Daddy wanted me just to check one last time. But Cris has disappeared now, so perhaps it was him.'

Nico didn't turn his head, but he heard what she said. After a moment he said casually, 'Yeah, I saw him with a laptop yesterday. Took it to his room.'

His mother was pleased at that. 'Did you? I was sure he must have it, but Daddy didn't believe me. I'll go and tell him.' She drifted out.

Stupid woman! Nico looked without interest at *Big Brother*, but he daren't risk going back to his game. It was long past his bedtime, and if she wasn't too spaced out to care, she'd come back and fuss.

He climbed into bed without washing. Once she'd been back to check on him or else gone to bed, he could play for as long as he liked. And if they thought Cris had taken the laptop away, he wouldn't have to smuggle it in and out of the house any more.

MARJORY FLEMING HAD fallen asleep instantly. But perhaps Bill creeping into bed later had broken the pattern of her sleep waves, because she embarked on a series of vague, uncomfortable dreams, culminating in one that inspired in her such a sense of terror that she woke up gasping for breath, but with no recollection of the detail.

She sank back on her pillows and tried to drift off to sleep, lying first on one side, then on the other. That was usually enough on the few occasions when her sleep was disturbed, but it wasn't working tonight. More wide awake than ever after a quarter of an hour, she slid out of bed with an envious glance at her slumbering husband and went downstairs.

When she switched on the light in the kitchen, Meg looked up from the basket by the Aga, gave her a dirty look and went back to sleep.

Marjory laughed. 'It's all right, Meggie,' she said softly, 'I'm not going to disturb you. Unless you want a crust of my toast.'

She was hungry – that was most likely the problem, not having had a proper supper. She lifted the lid of the range, pushed across the kettle and picked up the toasting grid. Agas made the very best kind of toast.

With her snack ready, she sat down in the old chair beside it, glad of the cosiness on this cool, damp night. The light ticking of the clock on the dresser seemed loud in the quiet house; Meg was snoring gently, and from the field near the house she heard a snort from one of the beasts. Familiar, comfortable sounds. A good way to soothe yourself to be ready for sleep.

Only somehow, it wasn't. She hadn't drawn the curtains across the kitchen windows – she never bothered – and now they were great yawning squares of darkness as she sat in the lighted room, a room that had suddenly lost its cosiness. Someone could be out there, looking in at her, and she wouldn't know. She was exposed, vulnerable – what sort of security was that? And she could hear movement too.

It was the stirks, restless in the field behind the house. Marjory knew that, of course she did. But was she absolutely sure? And if it was, why were they restless? *Because they always are*, the common-sense part of her mind insisted, but there was another voice that said, *Because someone's moving among them*.

If she was going to go on sitting here, and finish her tea like a sensible person, she was going to have to close the curtains. She just didn't want to get up, walk across, exposed, a target . . .

But she was a target already, sitting where she was. Come on!

Her legs felt like jelly as she got up and walked across the room, to the switches by the door that would put out the light in the kitchen, and put on the light in the yard. If nothing happened, if there was no one there – and of course there wasn't – she could draw the curtains and be comfortable again.

Marjory had just done that and was peering fearfully out into the yard when the door behind her opened. She spun round in the darkness and screamed.

She had not seen the panicky movement outside as someone shrank into the shadows, like some creature of the dark for whom light is pain. But behind her, framed in the doorway to the lighted hall, was the burly form of her husband Bill in his pyjamas.

'Marjory, what on earth's the matter?' he said.

She had given herself too much of a fright to be calm. 'Oh, Bill, Bill,' she said, hurling herself into his arms.

'It's all right, it's all right – I've got you.' He patted her back, and Meg, who had shot out of her bed in alarm and was now looking extremely reproachful, came to push her nose against her mistress's legs.

'I woke up and realised you weren't there,' Bill said when, laughing shakily, she let him go. 'I wondered if you were all right, but I had no idea that my well-intentioned concern would provoke terror. Let's put the light on again and I'll make myself a cup of tea while you finish yours and tell me all about what's going on. And toast – toast seems a good idea. Where's the syrup?'

The normality, after her crazy imaginings, left her laughing weakly. 'It's probably not the time, the middle of the night, when we've both to be up early, but I really do need to talk.'

A certain wariness came over Bill's face. 'If you're going to talk about us, I don't care how long it takes to sort things out. If you've work problems to talk through, frankly, you'd deal with them better after a night's rest, and so would I.'

'It's only partly work. It's mainly about Joss Hepburn.'

'Then I'm all ears.' Bill spoke lightly, but his face was grave.

'It's just – I'm going to draw the curtains before I put on the light.' Marjory went across to the window.

The silent yard was empty under the lights – of course it was! She heard a sheep bleat from the lower field, then another echo it, but these were perfectly normal night sounds. She pulled the curtains across and switched the lights back on. The kitchen was homely and safe again, the threatening world of darkness and lurid imaginings banished outside.

'That's better,' she said.

Her husband raised his eyebrows at her, but didn't ask why. 'More toast?'

Marjory shook her head and sat down. 'Joss. It's difficult.'

Bill went on with what he was doing, but she could sense his tension.

'I hate getting old and boring, you know that?' she said. 'Perhaps we all see our adult selves as being clothes we put on for a marathon fancy-dress party, but underneath we're still – what, nineteen?'

Bill sat down with his toast. 'Twenty-five. Able to play a useful game of rugby, sink half-a-dozen pints and be bright-eyed for the sheep-round in the morning.'

'Nineteen for me. Nineteen, and still thinking I could break all the rules because I was immortal and nothing could go wrong. I knew what Joss was even then, really, but bad was glamorous – bad was cool.'

'I think a lot of people see it that way.' Bill's tone was dry.

'I know. And I suppose I did still see him as glamorous even now. He has charm by the bucketload.' Marjory stole an anxious glance at Bill, but he said nothing. 'He applied that charm when we met again. And I was flattered that he still felt I was worth the trouble, even though I was in a professional position and that made it very awkward.

'I wanted, I think, to believe he was still "bad" in the old, fun sense – daring, crazy, edgy, not overly concerned about breaking a few of the laws the young agree are self-evidently silly. But, Bill, he's not. He's ugly bad. I was completely wrong. There, I've said it. And if you say, "I told you so," the conversation stops here.' She half meant it.

'I don't need to.'

Marjory smiled, but she wasn't sure it was meant to be a joke. She couldn't read his expression, but she'd come this far; she had to go on. 'I thought the business Crozier was running at Rosscarron House was suspect – and I was right, though I'm not going to go into details. Joss knew what was going on, but he wouldn't tell me, and in the end he tried to blackmail me.'

That startled Bill. 'Blackmail?'

'If I wouldn't stop asking questions about the business, everything he could think of dating back to our relationship would go to the gutter press. You can imagine . . .'

'Oh, yes,' he said heavily, 'I can imagine.'

Marjory was struck with shame. She had thought about how it would affect her career and her marriage, but not how Bill would feel at having his friends read about his wife's youthful misdemeanours, courtesy of the *Sun*. 'Sorry,' she said inadequately. 'It may be bluff – it may never happen.'

Bill sighed. 'It's as well to know the worst.'

'There's something else.' At the look on his face, she said hastily, 'No, no, it's different. It's just – well, a Glasgow hitman's been seen in the area. We've no idea who the target is, but it's all linked to Crozier's business, and the last time I saw Hepburn he warned me, very seriously, to think again about pursuing my enquiries.'

'*What!* You mean that bastard's taken out a contract on you?' At Bill's roar of rage Meg started awake once more.

From the look of fear she'd seen in Joss's eyes, Marjory didn't think so, but she wasn't about to argue his cause. 'I'm probably reading far too much into what he said. It's highly unlikely that it's anything to do with me, and I'm not taking it too seriously.'

'Of course not. You're just closing curtains you haven't closed since they were put up, and screaming when I come into the room.'

'I have an overactive imagination.'

'So do I. If my wife's in any danger, I'm downright paranoid. I want her properly protected. What's being done about it?'

'Nothing, at the moment, until we see more clearly what's going on.'

Bill had his stubborn face on. 'You mean like someone takes a pot shot at you? Better hope they miss.'

'To be honest, I wouldn't feel any safer with some poor guy detailed to trail around after me. If I'm going out, I won't be out alone. And I won't go into any dark alleyways, and I'll make sure there isn't a car following me.' She felt braver as she said it, but as Bill still looked sceptical, she added, 'Anyway, over the next twenty-four hours or so the investigation's being opened up and it's going to be obvious that taking me out won't solve their problem. And dead police officers spell serious trouble.'

Marjory found she was yawning. 'Look, it's dreadfully late. We've got to get some sleep or we'll be pulp in the morning.'

'Fine.' Bill collected up the plates and mugs, and put them in the sink. Marjory glanced at his back, still unsure how things stood between them, but as she went to the door, he came to put his arm round her and turned her to face him. 'Be careful, Marjory. You're precious.'

She put up her face to be kissed. 'I will. And I love you too.'

As they went upstairs, the details she hadn't shared about her odd encounters with Joss Hepburn were on her mind, but however much she might believe in full disclosure in a professional sense, she felt strongly that in personal life you could simply give too much information. Oh, Bill wasn't a fool. He knew there were things she hadn't said and there was still constraint between them, which couldn't dissolve instantly, but at least they were on the way.

CURSING, THE MAN stumbled down the farm track in the dark, sheep bleating as he passed, making what speed he could as he headed for the car he had parked down on the main road. It had looked like all his Christmases had come at once when she appeared in the kitchen while he was doing his recce. He could have been speeding back to Glasgow by now, but he'd missed his chance, and it had looked almost as if she knew he was there. She might even have made an alarm call and police cars could be screaming this way right now.

Shaking and breathless, he needed three attempts to get the key in the lock, but at last he was on his way without any sign of danger. It was a moonless, starless night; the road stretched empty ahead, the fields on either side pitch dark under the opaque lid of the cloudy sky, the occasional house by the road lightless and blank.

How could she have known? Perhaps she had felt his eyes upon her as he assessed his shot, and would even now be dismissing it as imagination, or at worst a prowler, he told himself, but he was arguing against the nagging pain in the pit of his stomach.

Wednesday, 26 July

DECLAN RYAN PUT down the phone. He was feeling sick, as if the shock of what he'd heard had been a physical blow. What was he to do now? He was fire-fighting on every side.

He went along to the kitchen, where Cara was breakfasting on black coffee, and Nico, with his elbows on the table, was gnawing on a pizza with both hands. It disgusted him.

'Out!' Ryan said to Nico, jerking his head, and for once his son obeyed without appealing to his mother, giving a frightened look over his shoulder as he left and still clutching his unorthodox breakfast.

'That was the police in Kirkluce. They've picked up Cris for drink-driving. Traced us through the car.'

Cara gave a cry of horror. 'Oh God! The laptop?'

'I asked if there were any of our personal possessions in the car and they asked was anything missing. Couldn't say the laptop, could I, so I just said I didn't remember. They told me they hadn't found anything, but they could be lying, of course. Then they asked if Cris was staying here and had permission for the car.'

'I hope you said no.' Cara's unhealthy skin was even paler than usual and she started chewing at the loose skin on her dry lips.

Ryan felt angry frustration. Her stupid pronouncements had always irritated him, and things had gone too far now for him to defer to them. 'What would be the point? They must know already. I said he'd taken the car, though.'

'This is a disaster!' Her voice rose. 'What are we going to do? Lloyd's phoning me later today.'

'Say nothing about it,' Ryan said. 'I mean it, Cara – lie if necessary. It may blow over. We'd better hope it does. And that's the damn phone again.'

As he went to the kitchen phone to answer it, he didn't see that Cara's expression was not dutifully submissive. She was frowning, still biting at her lip; it was bleeding now.

'Yes, fine,' he said into the phone. 'Half past ten.'

As he put it down, he said to Cara with an effort at confidence, 'Interview at the police station. Knew it would come. We just have to stick together, right?'

'Right,' she said.

'Right.' He went to make himself some coffee. At least she was behind him, not like the other rats who had left – though of course his ship wasn't sinking, of course it wasn't. It was just sometimes he thought he could hear the water lapping higher and higher on the sides.

FLEMING WASN'T QUITE ready for the photograph that DS Macdonald produced when she arrived in the CID room in the morning. He had been on the early shift, and it had come in from Dumfries Constabulary in response to the APB for Lisa Stewart.

It showed a girl lying on the road, a great wound on the side of her head and those strange, round eyes wide open. Her dark hair was matted with blood; at its roots her real hair colour showed, flaming red.

Fleming gulped. This was someone she had seen, talked to, only three days ago. She had believed, rather against the run of the evidence, that she was a sad creature, a victim caught up in a web of someone else's making. Lisa was certainly a victim now.

But the victim of an accident, or of a deliberate killing? It was being presented to the press as a drunk driver with a stolen car, as accidents like these mostly were, but Fleming knew what she believed.

When Dave had talked about a target for the hitman, she had jumped to the conclusion that she herself was under threat. If she had been less self-absorbed and more analytical, would she have thought who else it might be, got Lisa some sort of protection? She felt a sense of guilt, though it had probably been too late by then anyway.

But it pointed up the terrible danger of becoming personally involved in a case; she had lost her objectivity there, and she would be on her guard against that in future.

At least Fleming's fevered imaginings had been just that, and it was a great relief to know she'd been wrong. She could really have made a fool of herself over this, and she was thankful that the only person she had told was Bill. Once she'd dealt with this, she'd phone him and put his mind at rest. He'd still been worried this morning, reminding her to be careful and kissing her goodbye less casually than usual.

Macdonald was reporting on the situation with the hit-and-run. The car had been found, stolen of course, but there were only smudges where they might have hoped for fingerprints. The driver had worn gloves.

'That makes it unusual,' Macdonald said. 'Mostly it's some lad on a bender who thinks it's all a bit of a laugh till things go wrong. What do you make of it?'

'Same as you, I guess. And I have information that there's a Glasgow hitman who's been seen in the area – there seems to be some likely association with Rosscarron. I'll be giving his description at the briefing this morning, though I won't say why as yet, just not to approach.'

'I see.'

It was clear that he did; after all, he had been Dave's handler. There was no need to discuss it.

'We have to trace who's employing him. But we'll hold back on that until we see if we can pick him up, either here or from the Glasgow end, if he makes it home. I don't want him tipped off that we're on to him.

'There's something else come in this morning,' she went on, pulling a list towards her. 'Cris Pilapil was done last night for drink-driving, in what is technically a stolen car – the Ryans have apparently said he had no authorisation to use it. We've got Declan Ryan coming in for interview later, but I want to go and talk to Cara while he's out of the way. Tam MacNee says she told him that a man – Jason Williams from the description – was in Rosscarron House just after Rencombe was killed, but she was too scared of Ryan to tell him any more.'

At the mention of Tam MacNee, Fleming saw Macdonald's mouth set in a hard, unfriendly line, but she didn't want to comment directly.

'I'm going to brief you and Ewan on the interviews with Pilapil and Williams. Tam MacNee will be off for the next few days.'

'Good,' Macdonald said, but his mouth relaxed.

'Any word of Kim this morning?'

He shook his head. 'I phoned her house, but her mother took the call. She's along at the home making arrangements.'

'Right. Maybe someone could liaise with the management there and make sure we know the time of the funeral service,' Fleming said. 'Kim's threatening to come back immediately, you know. I want to be informed at once if she does.'

Macdonald looked horrified. 'She mustn't do that! She'll still be in shock.'

'You tell her. She wouldn't take it from me. Thanks, Andy, that's all. See you at the briefing.'

She had a lot to do before that, but first she phoned Bill. She could hear the relief in his voice when she told him that she wasn't Badger Black's intended victim, though he still told her firmly to take care, before she rang off. Well, she would, but she was pretty relieved herself.

Fleming turned back to her screen. Reports, reports – but among them was one that immediately caught her eye. She clicked on it.

They had been checking on Jason Williams and had turned up his bank account. And there, among the other transactions, was a regular payment for a period of several months coming in from, surprise, surprise, one Declan Ryan.

That would be quite something to confront him with later this morning. Ruefully, she accepted that she would have to delegate it. Talking to Cara was more important, and it was likely that she would more readily confide in a woman whom she already knew.

If Tam MacNee hadn't been such a fool, Fleming would have been leaving the Ryan interview in his capable hands. But he had been a fool, so Macdonald and Campbell would just have to do the best they could.

TAM MACNEE HAD got up early. He hadn't slept well, at least partly because his bed hadn't been properly made for days, and he had risen with Fleming's parting words ringing in his ears, as she looked around his disordered house: 'You might just think how you'd feel if Bunty's better and comes back unexpectedly to give you a lovely surprise.'

So, for the first time since Bunty left, he had stripped the bed and put the sheets to wash, then set about purgation of the house. Dogs, ruthlessly bathed, wandered around, uncomfortable at this break from recent routine, and cats, deprived of their bedding, made themselves scarce. At the end of three hours the house at least looked and smelled clean, even if it looked a little like an army barracks.

MacNee made himself a mug of tea and looked around him with satisfaction. Outside, it was a filthy day, gloomy and dark, but with all this physical effort, he felt better than he had for months, more optimistic, less afraid. A clean house was a lot less depressing than a dirty one.

But when he sat down, with the rest of the day stretching ahead of him, his mood darkened. They would all be busy now; Macdonald and Campbell, no doubt, would be embarking on the interview with Ryan that he should have been doing.

And what would he have asked him? First, of course, why had he given shelter to someone he claimed not to have known.

Why, indeed. Williams had come to Rosscarron House fresh from his killing of Alex Rencombe. It had been done on impulse; he had no escape plan so he had come to Rosscarron House for shelter, and cut the phone wires once he got there.

MacNee's mind was beginning to buzz. Williams, he was ready to swear, had killed Crozier the following day, with Ryan's connivance. MacNee had seen for himself Ryan's resentment of his father-in-law; with Crozier dead, his empire would fall to his druggie daughter, and Ryan would at last have the power and the money.

Williams could have expected to carry out his second act of self-protection and then to flee. The unexpected collapse of the bridge had put paid to that idea and he'd had to lie low – very effectively, as it happened. He'd left the headland along with the other campers.

So far, so good. MacNee's tea cooled in his mug as he scowled in concentration. A fight broke out in the garden between two of the unsettled dogs, but he didn't even hear it.

Then Williams himself had turned up dead. Had Lisa Stewart lured him to the guest house to kill him? She would have seen him kill Crozier, but after what she believed the man had put her through, she probably wouldn't blame him much. Certainly that wasn't any sort of motive.

But what if Lisa had been set up for this? Williams knew where she was, and what could be more natural than sharing the knowledge with Ryan, his co-conspirator? Did Williams know too much – and this offered a chance to neutralise that threat, implicating Lisa at the same time? Everything had pointed to Ryan from the start, but it was only now MacNee was seeing past the alibi he himself had given the man.

MacNee looked at his watch. They'd most likely be in the middle of the Ryan interview by now, so he couldn't speak to Andy Mac – if he would take his call, anyway. He could phone the boss, though.

He fetched his mobile, rang her number. Infuriatingly, it was on answerphone. She must be out of range already. Out at Rosscarron House, talking to Cara. Tying up the whole thing, probably.

He put it down again, deflated. And when he thought about it, being able to construct a narrative was neither here nor there, and he still had no idea why Williams should have murdered Rencombe, or indeed what the man's business with him had been in the first place.

Yet again, he found Rabbie's words to articulate his frustration:

> 'One point must still be greatly dark
> The moving Why they do it.'

FLEMING HAD GONE back to her room after the briefing, ready to leave for Rosscarron once the word came through that Ryan had indeed arrived. When she picked the phone up, however, it wasn't the message she had expected.

It was Macdonald, in a state of agitation. 'Kim's just appeared. She's looking terrible – sort of blank and unresponsive – and we've all said she's to go home, but she won't.'

With a sinking heart, Fleming said, 'I'll be right down.'

Chapter Twenty-five

THE MAN IN the white Vauxhall Vectra, cruising past the end of the narrow street that housed the exit from the police car park, was uncharacteristically nervous. Cool calculation was his stock-in-trade: he liked time to plan, to know the ground, to assess the risks. It was why he had the reputation he did.

But the call he'd had this morning, after last night's fiasco, was piling on the pressure. He was being paid for a rush job and they thought it should have been done by now – and you didn't get across clients like that. Perhaps he'd have been smarter to take Fleming out first, but once you'd killed a cop, there'd be a roadblock on every street and he'd never have got the other one. At least that had been a neat operation, one he could take pride in.

This one was proving a bitch. The streets around here were narrow, all double yellow lines, and there were pigs coming and going all the time. He'd been cruising round and round the block, but he couldn't do that for ever; the woman might not leave the building all day, or she might leave when he was out of eyeshot.

He could feel the stress bubbling up, taste stomach acid in his mouth. If he failed, he'd lose big money. Worse, he'd earn the ill-will of some very dangerous men.

He took off a glove to fumble in his pocket for an antacid. He was getting dizzy going round and round these stupid streets, and sooner or later he'd have to come up with a better plan. It was just that for the moment he couldn't think of one.

CRIS PILAPIL'S CLOTHES were crumpled and soiled, and his stubble had begun to form a soft fringe around his face. His dark olive skin was a putty colour, and he was visibly shaking as he sat opposite DS Macdonald and DC Campbell in the interview room.

Macdonald was just about to ask the first question when, to his surprise, Campbell took the initiative. 'What're you so scared of?'

Pilapil grabbed both hands together, as if to still their shaking, but his jaw was trembling so much that Macdonald could actually hear his teeth clashing together.

He said reassuringly, 'There's no need to get in a state. You'll be appearing in court later. You'll get a fine and a six-month driving ban – no big deal.'

The look Pilapil gave him was unexpectedly contemptuous. 'You think I'm scared of you? You're the law. In this country, the law is fair, and my boss saw my papers were in order. But I need you to let me go now, before they know you are talking to me. If they find me after that, I don't know what they will do to me.'

'They?'

'The big men. It's gone wrong and they are worried. Worried and angry. Maybe there was something I failed to do. Maybe they will only think there was – I need to get away.'

'Who are they?' Macdonald demanded. 'Names, addresses – the lot. It's too late to muck about.'

'I can't, I can't.'

'Might as well,' Campbell said laconically. 'If we know who they are, we might just get to them before they get to you.'

Pilapil shot him a distrustful look. 'Maybe you are right, but mostly I don't know. They are Italian, German, French. But Gillis's two close business partners . . .' He baulked again, as if with a superstitious fear of mentioning their names.

'Spit it out,' encouraged Campbell.

'Lloyd and Driscoll.' Pilapil gave a little gasp, as if his own temerity had taken his breath away.

'Better out than in!'

Macdonald, giving Campbell a quelling glance, said, 'We'll get all the details later. What kind of business was it, then?'

Pilapil looked down. 'I don't know. It was very confusing – lots of packages, lots of forms. But Gillis dealt with it – I didn't understand.'

He wasn't a very good liar, but there was no point in challenging him on it. Fleming had warned them the Fraud Squad was taking care of that end; they'd probably be waiting for Pilapil when he came out of court this morning.

'All right, I'll accept that,' Macdonald said. 'But what did you know about the job Alex Rencombe was doing for Gillis Crozier when he was killed?'

To his surprise, Pilapil's eyes filled with tears. 'He didn't tell me. I wish he had! He was very upset, so I listened carefully, to help him, maybe. I heard him tell Alex on the phone, "I won't meet him. I won't talk to him. I don't want to know where he is, even. I suspect it's a set-up for blackmail, so I don't want any contact."

Then he said something about not allowing this man to explain what his "proposal" was, but Gillis seemed to have guessed anyway. And Alex knew too. I couldn't hear what he was saying, but he seemed to be blaming Gillis for something, because he admitted he was wrong, and something about not really being sane at the time. Maybe he meant he was around when his granddaughter died – he suffered badly, so badly.

'Then they talked a bit more, and I remember the last thing he said was, "If it's what we both think it is, Alex, there's no alternative. Tell him it's the police, straight away. It's too risky to do anything else."'

'Him?'

'*I don't know!*' It was a wail of despair. 'He killed Alex, then Gillis, then probably this other guy, and I don't know who he is! It's your job to find him. And you'd better find him before I do.'

Macdonald began on a stern warning, but Campbell said, 'Right, help us, then. Every scrap of information you can think of.'

It was quite some time before Pilapil, looking drained, was taken off for his court appearance.

The detectives took stock.

'So someone was trying to set up something he could blackmail Crozier with, but we don't know what,' Macdonald said. 'And Rencombe died because he told Williams he was going to the police, on Crozier's instructions – so from that moment on Crozier was doomed too.

'If we're to believe Pilapil – and I'd have to say that so far he's convinced me – our friend Declan insisted they lie to Rencombe's girlfriend when she wanted to know why he hadn't got in touch. That puts him in this up to his neck. How's he going to explain it when we talk to him?'

Campbell was silent for a moment. 'More interesting to know what he was paying Williams for.'

'It wasn't for killing Rencombe, that's for sure – that wasn't planned. And Crozier's death was opportunistic too.'

'Paying Williams to spy on Lisa Stewart? Not Crozier persecuting her, but Ryan?'

Macdonald looked at him. 'Father of the baby, father of the boy who ended up accused. Makes sense. And I've got this feeling that nearly all the pieces of the jigsaw are on the table and we only need to fit them together. I might just phone Big Marge before we go into the interview. She might have something to pitch in.'

He dialled, then pulled a face. 'Answerphone. Must be out of range.'

In Kirkluce the weather had been depressing, with heavy, brownish clouds low overhead and the daylight feeble and grudging. As Fleming and Kershaw went down towards Rosscarron, it deteriorated and now they were driving through fog, making poor speed on the long, twisting road.

The atmosphere inside felt almost as thick to Fleming. Beside her, Kershaw sat, still as stone, staring straight ahead, lost in her terrible thoughts. She had responded, briefly and expressionlessly, to Fleming's occasional remarks, but eventually it seemed wiser to make no attempt at engagement.

Bringing her along had been the best solution Fleming could come up with. Kershaw flatly refused to go home but was clearly unfit to work, and her sitting in the CID room in this state was disruptive and distressing for everyone else. She would probably be quite content to stay in the car while Fleming interviewed Cara.

And Hepburn again too? She had no idea whether he was still at Rosscarron House, or how she would react to him if he was. Though it still took an effort of courage to check the papers every morning, there had been nothing so far and she was starting to allow herself to believe he might have been bluffing. It would be good to think so.

The slow, silent journey was good thinking time. At least the fog surrounding the investigation was rapidly clearing, and with the evidence coming in daily, it looked as if they would be able to move against Ryan in the next couple of days, particularly if Cara was realising now that her husband had been involved in her father's death and was prepared to cooperate.

MacNee had said that she seemed afraid of her husband; she would be very vulnerable, of course. With her drug habit, Ryan could so easily push it more, and that bit more, until it got to the point where she would be too far gone in addiction to live even the sort of life she had at the moment. And she would be afraid, too, that bringing in the police would disrupt her chain of supply.

Yes, it would be a tricky interview. But back at headquarters, Macdonald and Campbell would be talking to Pilapil and then seeing what they could do with Ryan. He had been invited again, not arrested, so of course he could walk out of it anytime he liked, but arrest would mean they had only six hours to decide whether to charge him or to let him go, and they weren't quite ready yet. Not quite.

That was the turn-off now. 'Nearly there!' Fleming said in the hearty tone she might have used to a child, then was embarrassed. There was no need. Kershaw gave no sign she had even heard.

He had never been so afraid in his life. Declan Ryan got out of the Discovery he had parked in the square by the War Memorial, noticing the irony with a twisted smile. This was probably how these guys had felt before they went over the top – and look what had happened to them!

He had lived life on his wits. He'd never had great vision, or strength of character – more just an eye to the main chance – but he had a quick mind that could often dance rings round those who did. He'd proved it again and again these last few days, contemptuously seeing off the plods, who kept trying to catch him out.

They might be stupid, but there were a lot of them, and they were persistent. Now it wasn't about winning a debating match any more. It was about his freedom.

Ryan had no idea what they might have against him now. All over the country, in London, in Glasgow, here in Kirkluce, checks were being made by an invisible army and, like monkeys with typewriters, sooner or later they'd put the random fragments together to make a story.

He couldn't see a way out, unless Lloyd and Driscoll would help. And if Fleming wasn't neutralised before her persistent nosiness turned something up, there was no hope of that.

At least they hadn't arrested him. If they'd hard evidence, they'd be charging him, not asking him for another chat. As Ryan reached the headquarters of the Galloway Constabulary, he wished he'd brought a lawyer, even so.

He didn't have a lawyer, though, any more. Alex had been smart as a whip; Alex would have kept everything under control. Now, when he needed him, Alex wasn't there. And it was his own fault. He'd gone along with that stupid bastard Jason when he should have known it would backfire.

'WHY DON'T YOU wait in the car?' Fleming said, as she parked in the drive outside Rosscarron House. 'I shouldn't be long.'

Kershaw turned her head. 'No, I'll come with you. It's the job, isn't it?' She gave Fleming a smile that was only a baring of the teeth, unbuckled her seat belt and got out.

'Fine,' Fleming said hollowly, getting out herself.

The fog seemed to gather round her, damp and oppressive, until it was almost as if she had to push through it – an eerie, uncomfortable feeling. As they walked towards the house, its sandstone walls appeared out of the low mist, then disappeared into it again fifteen feet above.

It was Cara who opened the door, and Fleming saw with some relief that there was no sign of Hepburn, at the moment at least, and the silver Mercedes wasn't sitting outside. Cara looked to be on a relatively even keel at the moment; her smile was, as usual, vague, but she seemed quite pleased to see them.

'Marjory! This is a surprise,' she said, as if greeting a friend who had popped in for a coffee unexpectedly. 'Come in.'

'Just wanted a chat, Cara.' With Kershaw walking behind her like a zombie, Fleming followed her into the hall. Even with its white walls, it was dark today and the clinical perfection was marred by outdoor clothes draped over chairs and boots and trainers kicked off beside them. A tray with dirty crockery had been dumped at the foot of the stairs.

'Are you on your own?' Fleming asked, hoping that it didn't show that she was holding her breath as she waited for the reply.

'Just Nico.' Cara gestured up the stairs and Fleming saw Nico's face peering over the banister. She smiled and got a scowl in reply. The face disappeared.

'Cris and Joss have left,' Cara said. 'And Declan's . . . well, *you* know.' She opened the door to the white sitting room, also showing signs of neglect, and stood back to let them pass. 'Was it me you wanted to talk to?'

'Yes,' Fleming said. 'Cara, DS MacNee said that you told him something and you were afraid your husband would be angry if he found out. Can we talk about that, while Declan isn't here?'

Cara gave Fleming a long, calculating look. Then she said, 'Sit down. I'll fetch some coffee.'

Fleming sat down. Kershaw was still standing where she had stopped when she came into the room and was staring out of the window.

'Kim,' she said gently, 'why don't you sit down?'

Kershaw looked round as if she were surprised there was someone there, then did as she was told. Groaning inwardly, Fleming settled down to wait for Cara's return. She would need all her concentration and skill to draw Cara into confiding; she shouldn't have to worry about her constable. Still, as long as Kim sat still and said nothing, it wouldn't matter and it certainly looked as if that was what she was planning to do.

THEY'D KEPT HIM waiting quite a long time – no doubt softening him up – then they hit him with it immediately. 'What was Jason Williams, aka Damien Gallagher, doing in Rosscarron House just after he killed Alex Rencombe?' the dark one, Macdonald, asked him.

'Was he?' Ryan played for time.

'He was seen.'

Pilapil, no doubt – sneaking little sod! 'I didn't see him.'

'Who invited him in, then?'

Ryan produced a blank look. 'I've no idea. Gillis, perhaps, Cris Pilapil, Joss Hepburn.'

'Hepburn didn't arrive till next morning.'

That was the ginger, Campbell – so sharp he'd cut himself. Ryan shrugged. 'If you say so. All I can tell you is, it wasn't me.'

He felt a little better. They'd tried to rattle him and it hadn't worked. Stay chilled – that was the answer.

'The reason we thought it was likely you,' Macdonald said silkily, 'was that Mr Williams's telephone records show a lot of calls to your mobile. And from his bank records, you seem to have been paying him some sort of retainer over the past few months too.'

Ryan could only hope he hadn't gone pale. He'd forgotten that altogether. The paper trail – how many people had been caught out that way?

'Sorry?' he said. Think, man, think!

'Oh, I'm sure you heard me, Declan.'

'Of course. I just didn't realise what you were talking about for a moment. "Retainer" isn't a description I recognise. We used to be in a gambling syndicate. He placed the bets.' Not a stammer, not a hesitation. He was proud of himself.

'High rolling, obviously – £500 a month,' Macdonald said.

'On your wages, Sergeant, I suppose so.'

'And did you often win?'

'Oh, not as often as we'd have liked to.' The answers were coming pat now, but Ryan would have been happier if Ginger wasn't leafing back through a notebook in a way that suggested not so much that he was consulting it, but that he was trying to give that impression.

Like many redheads, Campbell had pale blue eyes. He suddenly looked up and transfixed Ryan with a gimlet stare.

'I've got here that you told us you didn't know who he was. Met him for the first time at the camp.'

It was a body blow. That was the other way they got you, besides the paper trail: not keeping track of the lies you told.

'Yes, I suppose I did,' he admitted, then added, 'but it wasn't under oath. I bet I'm not the first innocent man who hasn't wanted to get involved in something like this when the police come asking.'

If he'd hoped to draw them into that argument, he was disappointed. Macdonald said, with the plodding patience Ryan both despised and feared, 'Let's go back to the beginning. What was *your friend* Jason Williams doing at Rosscarron House after Alex Rencombe had been killed? And why did you give instructions that Mr Rencombe's girlfriend should be told he'd contacted you?'

This was the point at which he could get up and walk out. It wouldn't solve anything, though. They'd keep coming back, and back, and back. The alternative? Like the PR guys always told you, get your version of the story out there first.

'Look, can we scrub all this and start again?' Ryan said. 'It's complicated, and I can see why you think what you do, but if you'll hear me out, I'll explain.'

'Fine,' Macdonald said. 'Carry on.'

But Campbell was grinning broadly. 'I'm going to enjoy this,' he said.

That didn't help. Ryan's stomach was churning, and the worst of it was that he knew that if he got it right, he had a faint chance not only to get out of this mess but to cover some of the stuff that would most likely emerge later.

'First of all, the business about Alex. You have to realise that he was a bit of a maverick, and if he hadn't phoned his girlfriend, it was probably because she wasn't his girlfriend any more and just hadn't realised it yet. I didn't want to drop him in it, so I told Cris to fob her off. OK? No great sinister mystery about that.' Was he working well or what? Wonderful thing, adrenaline.

'Now, Jason. I've known him for years,' he went on. 'He was a music industry techie and did concerts Gillis promoted. We met up sometimes in a group, went clubbing or something. Celebrated our racing winnings, when we had any.' That was a nice little touch. 'Might not see him for months at a time, though – we weren't that close. Texted me to say he'd be up here for the music festival with his girlfriend.'

'Lisa Stewart,' Macdonald prompted.

That was easy. 'Beth Brown,' Ryan corrected him. 'It was only after all this happened that I found out she was actually our former nanny. She must have used him to try to get to us. A bit alarming, really. I didn't like the idea of her being so close to my surviving child – and look what happened to poor Jason.'

There was no doubt about it, he was inspired. Maybe it was true that the devil did, after all, look after his own.

'Jason did come to the house that day looking for me – I was stupid to lie about it. He was in a bit of a state, but he only said that he needed somewhere to stay – he'd quarrelled with the girlfriend. He wanted to borrow a tent if possible, so I found one for him. That was all.

'The next day everything went pear-shaped, with the bridge being down, and then Gillis was killed. It was only afterwards that we heard from the Buchans that Lisa had been on the headland. Of course it all fell into place for us then, though you lot still seem to be behind the curve even now.

'Gillis was distraught after we lost our poor Poppy, and out of his mind with rage. He'd been dumb enough to threaten Lisa, and she saw her chance that day, maybe even saw it as self-defence, and picked up a rock. Then she must have been afraid that Jason would give her away, got him to come to her hotel and you know the rest. It's obvious, if you hadn't made your mind up already. Look, give me a break. I've never killed anyone – I swear it!'

Ryan could see the dark one wavering; awed by his own cleverness, he had to try hard not to seem triumphant as he looked at Ginger.

Campbell looked back with those ice-blue eyes. 'Very neat. Don't believe a word of it.'

So, after all, Ryan maybe wasn't as clever as he thought.

He stood up abruptly. 'I've had enough. I've been more than cooperative and you just don't want to know. Can I take it I'm free to leave?'

Feeling sick, he made for the gents' toilet. He splashed his face and drank water from his cupped hands, and then on legs that felt shaky he went back to his car.

WHEN HIS MOBILE phone rang, the man with the widow's peak looked at it with distaste. He knew who it would be; there had been two previous calls, demanding reassurance he had been unable to give truthfully. He'd lied, of course, but it was stressing him out.

But when he glanced at it, it wasn't the number he was expecting. He picked it up and said hello cautiously.

The words he heard brought a smile to his face. 'I'll be there,' he said. 'Just go on as you would have done till I arrive.'

There was more, though, and he shook his head. 'No. Not two. One. That was the deal.'

He listened, unmoved. 'We'll have to renegotiate, then.' He named a price, heard the protests, then came down a little. He couldn't afford to miss this chance.

Today he had almost begun to believe he might fail, for the first time in his professional life. Mounting surveillance on the police car park had proved impossible; indeed, he had obviously missed Fleming leaving. This had delivered her to him on a plate. With chips.

Lady Luck had always been a friend of his, and today she wasn't just smiling, she was beaming and giving him a big, fat, sloppy kiss.

Chapter Twenty-six

CARA BROUGHT IN the tray and set it down on a low table. 'It's dark in here today!' she said, and went to switch on a couple of the tall steel lamps in the corners of the room. As she bent over, the light caught her forearm, highlighting the needle marks and bruising. Fleming could see bloodied marks on her lips too, where the dry skin had flaked and been torn away, and the cracking at the corners of her mouth. The woman was in a bad way and, Fleming guessed, getting worse. Now Crozier had been got rid of, would Ryan start edging her from dependency into full-blown addiction?

Fleming began while the coffee was still being poured out. She wasn't sure how long she would have; Ryan could walk out of the interview anytime and she didn't want to be still on the premises when he got back.

'Cara, this isn't official, because I know what a difficult position you're in. But my sergeant said you had told him in confidence about the man you saw in the house, and that you were scared Declan would find out you'd talked to him.'

Cara, handing round the mugs, didn't say anything for a moment. Then she said, 'Yes. Yes, I'm scared of him now. Things have been going on – he won't tell me.' She bit at the sore lip.

'What have you noticed?' Fleming had a low, attractive voice and now it was full of warmth and sympathy.

'Well, there was the man, like I said. I asked Declan who he was and he was angry, said it was nobody and I hadn't seen him. But I had. Then my father was killed, and when I heard about Alex, I was really scared.' She looked at Fleming with wide, frightened eyes. 'And then someone else died and I thought it was maybe the man I'd seen – I don't know why. But who killed him?'

'We don't know as yet,' Fleming said. 'But your husband was here all that evening?'

Cara shook her head violently. 'No, no! I said that because he said I must, but I didn't see him after about seven. I don't know where he was. He doesn't tell me what he's doing, you know.'

It was hard not to show satisfaction. This was the delicate part now, though, and Fleming said carefully, 'Do you think you would feel able to make an official statement to that effect?' As Cara hesitated, she went on, 'You know, we have reason to think that your husband was implicated in your father's murder, as perhaps you have realised?'

'Oh, my father – yes,' Cara said, but from the way she spoke Fleming guessed that this had not been, as she had been assuming, the motivating factor.

'We would only ask you for it once we were sure of our ground,' she assured her.

That worked. 'Yes,' Cara said. 'Yes, I'd do it then.'

The phone rang. 'Excuse me,' she said, and as she went out Fleming could only be thankful that it hadn't interrupted them a minute earlier. Cara could always go back on it, of course, but it was less likely once she'd made the commitment.

Time was getting on. When Cara came back, Fleming stood up.

'Thank you,' she said. 'That's been very helpful. We'll leave it there today, though. I don't want you to find yourself in difficulties if your husband comes back. Kim—'

'Oh, no, no!' Cara said. 'Don't go just yet. There's – there's other things I want to talk to you about.'

She was looking definitely jumpy. Starting to need another fix, or just nervous about something? Intrigued, Fleming sat down again. Kershaw hadn't moved anyway.

HE TOOK BACK all he had said about Lady Luck. She was a bitch, after all. The moronic old bat who had pulled out from a side road straight into his path just might have buggered the whole thing.

The Vectra could be on the stolen-cars list by now, and he'd have been in even worse shtuck if she hadn't taken so long to struggle out after the collision and get her addled brain round what had happened. By then he was three streets away, strolling along.

Now he had to find another car to nick. He'd have to rely on Cara to keep them there a bit longer, though he didn't like it. She'd been nervy already and with the problems he'd been warned she had, she could go flaky on him at any time.

Grimly, he assessed the cars in the quiet side street. There was an old black Toyota Corolla, parked in front of an empty shop and opposite a blank wall – no prying eyes. That would do.

'YOU SEE,' CARA said, 'I was scared. I found out that the woman who killed my baby was right here, on the headland.'

Suddenly Kershaw looked up. 'Of course,' she said. 'You lost your child. I lost mine, my daughter. She died yesterday.'

Fleming closed her eyes in dismay. There was nothing she could do about it.

Kershaw was going on, 'Debbie was her name. I'm trying to learn what you do, after your child dies. You need lessons, but they can't tell you. Can you help me? What did you do?'

Naturally enough, Cara was taken aback. She ground her teeth on her lower lip. Then suddenly it started pouring out. 'I – I was angry, very, very angry. That bitch of a nanny killed her. How do you cope with that? And she said my son – my little boy! – had done this terrible thing. And they believed her. She was evil, evil! She should fry in hell.'

Her voice had risen almost to a scream and there was spittle flecking the corner of her mouth. 'And you know who I blame? I blame my father, that's who! Him and his lover – her grand-mother. He believed all she said, put a woman with a violent temper in my children's nursery. I could never forgive him, never!'

Just how wrong could you be about a person's reactions? Fleming asked herself. Cara hadn't grieved for her father at all – on the contrary – but there wasn't time to pursue that thought now. She had to calm the woman down: Kershaw seemed bewildered by what she had provoked.

'It's been hard for you, Cara, very hard,' Fleming said. 'And you haven't been happy either about what has been going on in the house here, have you?'

Cara's eyes had been looking almost unfocused, but she stopped and took a deep, shuddering breath. Then she shook her head as if to clear it and said, 'Sorry. I'm sorry. I didn't mean . . .' Her voice trailed off.

At the same time Fleming saw that silent tears were starting to spill down Kershaw's cheeks. She needed to cry, but not here! Fleming picked up her shoulder bag and got to her feet again. 'We really have to go. As you can see, my colleague is under a great deal of strain.'

Cara got up too. 'No, no, just a minute.'

'I don't think—' Fleming began, but when Cara said suddenly, 'There's a laptop,' her ears pricked up. She had always been convinced there was one.

'The laptop? One that belonged to your father?'

'That's – that's right. I think Declan must have hidden it. I'll show you where it is.'

Fleming gave Kershaw a doubtful look, but this was a lead she couldn't afford to ignore. She put down her bag again and with Kershaw at her heels she followed Cara across the hall and into the passage that ran under the stairs.

Cara stopped and unlocked a door. As she opened it on to a deep, walk-in cupboard, Kershaw said in a voice thick with tears, 'It was worse for you. Your baby didn't have to die. Someone killed her.'

'Below that shelf,' Cara said to Fleming, switching on the light. Then, as Fleming bent to look, she heard Cara say, 'But it's all right. She's paid for it now. She's dead too,' and froze.

Cara shouldn't know that – and suddenly Kershaw was pushed on top of her and Fleming fell under her weight, hitting the injured side of her head on a stone shelf. She saw stars, cried out and then everything went black.

DECLAN RYAN WALKED back to the Memorial Square, still feeling shaky. He wasn't sure how much harm he'd done by walking out, but he couldn't have taken much more of it.

At least Macdonald had seemed to take some interest in what he said about Lisa Stewart. God knew they'd been given enough hints before to look in that direction, which they'd ignored. Now he'd spelled it out for them, maybe they'd go after her at last, no matter what Ginger thought.

Or maybe she'd escape yet again. Charmed life that woman led! If all had gone well, she'd have been dead by now. If!

If only they hadn't all made such a shocking miscalculation about his father-in-law's desire for vengeance, Jason would have done his pushing-off-a-cliff-to-order service by now, and with a hold like that over him, Gillis would have had no alternative but to let his son-in-law into proper partnership in the business. As was only fair – and Declan had no problem about the woman who'd murdered his daughter getting what she deserved.

Gillis had no right to the high moral tone he'd taken. Apart altogether from his business morals – or lack of them – he was the one who'd started it by issuing bloodthirsty threats.

He'd been beside himself that day, when they'd brought in the verdict. Oh, they'd all been angry, disbelieving, Cara hysterical, of course, but Declan had honestly thought Gillis would have a stroke. He'd been on every news bulletin in the country, eyes bulging, veins on his neck standing out, as he roared that she would pay in blood. He'd even been given a formal warning by the police.

For Jason, bumping into the girl in a corner shop had been like finding a pot of gold. All he'd wanted was a simple payoff for a favour done, but he couldn't persuade Gillis to meet him to discuss it.

Declan was the obvious middleman. Jason was reluctant to cut anyone else in on the deal – he'd be doing the dirty work, taking the risks, after all – but he needed cash up front to make it work, and Declan had the money.

Or rather Cara did – the money, and the desire for revenge. Where Declan might have baulked, she had driven it on, with the scary ruthlessness she showed about anything she wanted.

But it was Declan who had added a bit of finesse, with the blackmail idea, and Cara had seized on it. She resented Gillis preaching to her about drugs anyway, and after Poppy died he had definitely become the enemy. Declan had been quite shaken by her glee at the thought of making her father squirm.

Only, of course, it had all gone hideously wrong. But how were they to know that Gillis hadn't meant what he said? Mucking Jason about had just looked like distrust and the idea had been to engineer a meeting up here, so Declan could lay out the plan and assure his father-in-law that Jason was a man he could rely on.

Declan had felt sadistic enjoyment in sending the melodramatic texts. They'd worked too: the little bitch had really suffered. Hadn't they all? And once they'd manipulated her into proximity with Gillis, the trap was ready to spring. There was no shortage of convenient rocky paths to push her off – tragic accident, a girl called Beth Brown with a sorrowing partner. And of course, once all the fuss was over, there would be the real, serious, permanent payoff – a dripping roast.

That was one thing. Killing the man in cold blood was another. Though he'd never liked Gillis, he was Cara's father, for God's sake! But Jason was hyperventilating in panic at having killed Alex, Cara was showing the sort of cold excitement he didn't like to think about, and they were both insisting it was the only way out. He'd buckled under their certainty and now he was in it up to his neck. He'd set it up, even, telling Jason when Gillis would be coming up the path – and right under the nose of the snooping MacNee.

Declan felt just a faint flicker of pride at outwitting him. And after all, by bringing the police into it Gillis had signed his own death warrant – and Alex's too, selfish bugger. Alex had been a great bloke, and Ryan felt sick all over again at the thought of what would happen when the police focused on the files he'd been holding.

Of course, they'd only found out who he was because that greedy bastard Jason had nicked Alex's car, which should have been safely under a few tons of earth and rubble. He tried to tell himself that now they'd proof of Jason's guilt, they wouldn't bother with too much digging – they were always on about manpower shortages. Just as long as Fleming had been choked off before she brought in the serious fraud guys. If she hadn't been . . .

He knew Hugh Lloyd and Paddy Driscoll blamed him already. And if they found out what by the law of unintended consequences had led to Alex's death, God help him! Though admittedly there wasn't much reason why He should.

TAM MACNEE WAS restless. It would have helped to get out for a long walk, but with the weather bad and deteriorating, even the dogs were affected by the gloom, huddled in their beds and showing no enthusiasm.

He found his mind turning, yet again, to the case. Fleming should have finished her interview with Cara by now and he was consumed with curiosity to know what had emerged from it. He wished she would call him and tell him how it had gone – after all, he'd been the one Cara had talked to first – but it didn't look as if she was going to. Part of his punishment, perhaps.

Cara was a strange woman. Perhaps it was the drugs, but he'd been struck by her lack of emotion when she heard about her father's death. It could have been shock too, of course, but Pilapil had said bitterly that Cara didn't care about him anyway. And according to Kershaw, who'd read all the trial reports, the nanny had been Crozier's old girlfriend's granddaughter. Maybe Cara blamed him for introducing her into the house. Maybe she saw her father's death as rough justice.

So how aware was she of what had been going on? It was, MacNee remembered, Cara who had talked about the people staying in the guest house when they broke the news of Jason Williams's death. Had she been part of an exercise to frame Lisa?

If so, why had she spoken to him yesterday? Ryan must have told her what MacNee had been asking him and she'd then made a point of seeking him out to drop her husband in it. In a situation like that, when you had cooperative evidence from an unexpected source, you always asked yourself what was in it for them.

Had she, he wondered, realised that the net around Ryan was closing tighter and tighter, and been sharp enough to seize the opportunity to put herself in the clear, innocent and ignorant? You tended to think of her as a junkie crippled by her habit, but many people who were heroin-dependent could live all but normal lives with careful management.

That gave him an excuse to phone Fleming. She couldn't complain if he was alerting her to a new idea. He picked up his mobile and dialled. Still on answerphone.

He looked at the kitchen clock. It was almost one – she'd been there a long time. Maybe Cara was singing like a canary and they would be arresting Ryan even while he sat here, missing the fun.

WHEN FLEMING OPENED her eyes, everything was swimming in front of her and the light from the bare bulb overhead made her screw them up again. Her head was spinning so that she thought she might pass out again if she tried to lift it. She was lying on a flagged floor, and she could hear someone crying.

The waves of dizziness subsided a little and she risked turning her head. Kim Kershaw was sitting on the floor, slumped like a puppet whose strings have been cut, with her head on her knees, making sobbing wails.

'Kim!' Fleming croaked, but either she wasn't speaking loudly enough or Kim was so lost in her anguish that she was unaware of anything else; certainly, there was no response.

Fleming put a hand to her head gingerly and it came away sticky with blood. Sticky – that meant a lapse of time. How long? She had no idea. She lifted her arm to look at her watch, but the face had smashed in her fall. Was it minutes? Hours?

Her mouth was parched, and the cold from the stone floor was seeping into her. Not good, if she'd been unconscious for any length of time, with another injury to her head. She could wiggle her fingers and toes – good. She pulled her dry tongue away from the roof of her mouth and licked at her cracking lips.

'Kim!' Fleming managed to speak more loudly and Kershaw raised her swollen, blubbered face and looked at Fleming on the floor with what seemed like surprise.

'Boss,' she said, frowning. Then, 'Are you all right?' Her speech was slow and she looked almost as if she was having difficulty focusing, but at least this was some sort of response.

'I hit my head. Could you help me sit up?'

Fleming was lying half under a stone shelf; she hadn't the strength to crawl out. For a moment Kershaw only looked at her with a dazed expression, then said uncertainly, 'Yes, of course.'

The cramped space made it hard for her to get close enough, but at last she had a hold on Fleming's arm and pulled her sideways. Wincing at the pain, Fleming forced herself into an upright position against the back wall. The room spun round her and her stomach heaved; she shut her eyes, which helped, and when she felt steadier, she opened them and took stock of her surroundings.

They were in an old-fashioned larder, much like the one in Mains of Craigie, with the stone shelves that kept things cool in the days before refrigerators. Now it was acting as a storeroom with stacks of tins and paper goods. What the hell were they doing here? Her brain still felt fuzzy and unclear.

Kershaw had said nothing else. She had stopped crying; she had sat down again and was looking straight ahead with a blank expression.

Delayed reaction – she'd gone into shock. With a sense of desperation, Fleming said, speaking slowly, as if to a child, 'Kim! Kim, can you hear me? Can you tell me exactly what happened? I blacked out.'

Her head turned, and she frowned again. 'I – I was crying. I don't know. Perhaps I tripped, and then the door shut.'

It started coming back to Fleming. 'Of course! I was in here, looking for the laptop Cara mentioned. Then you lurched on top of me and I fell.'

There was certainly no laptop here – and then Fleming remembered, with hideous clarity, the other thing. 'Cara knew that Lisa Stewart was dead. She couldn't know that unless . . .'

Unless whoever killed Lisa had told her. She didn't say it aloud, but at last she had a terrifying insight into Cara's reason for stopping them from leaving.

Joss Hepburn had tried to warn her, but she had convinced herself that it was another empty threat. And now they were being held until the man they called Badger Black arrived to carry out their execution.

'Whose car is that out there?' Ryan said as he came in.

Cara was waiting for him in the hall, an unusual act of wifely devotion, and he looked at her with some suspicion. There was usually only one reason why she sought him out, but she'd had enough this morning not to be desperate yet, unless she'd really overdone it.

Hiding the stuff and rationing it was the only way he had kept her functioning. She ordered him to restrain her but then resented it, and he was never sure that she wouldn't do something spiteful like changing her will to cut him out – if there was anything to leave, but he couldn't afford to think like that.

He was tired of the whole mess, so tired. He'd been kicked around by the woman for years, because he had let himself be bought and she was like her father when it came to getting value for money. Maybe he wasn't a very strong character, but then Gillis too had been helpless against her iron will. Once all this was over and he had worked his way into the business, he decided, he wasn't going to lift a finger to stop her killing herself with an overdose.

Whatever. Right now he was going to take a stand. Cara would have to listen to him for once, instead of giving him instructions, and he'd dope her to the eyeballs to get her to toe his line if necessary.

But Cara wasn't twitching. Indeed, she looked as if she was on a high, and he said warily, 'So, what have you been up to?'

It was only then he became aware of a banging sound, and a voice shouting, and frowned. 'What's that? Nico mucking about again?'

Cara smiled. 'No, that's Marjory Fleming and her constable. Poor sad creature – she's just lost her daughter. I felt quite sorry for her.'

'What the hell are you talking about?'

'In the cupboard at the back. I'm keeping them until Badger Black arrives.'

Ryan gaped at her. 'Have you lost it completely? Who's Badger Black?'

'Friend of Hugh and Paddy's. Well, more an employee, really.' Cara gave a little giggle.

Ryan felt he was losing his grip on reality. 'Wait a minute,' he said. 'Are you telling me that you have locked up two police officers – two police officers! – because you're waiting for someone Lloyd and Driscoll are sending? What's he going to do?'

Cara giggled again. 'Kill them. He's a hitman. That's his job. He's good too. Hugh got him to do a little favour for me yesterday. He's been like a father to me, you know, better than the one I had.'

'What "favour"? No, don't tell me – I need a drink.'

Ryan headed for the sitting room and Cara followed him. 'I told you we should just have dealt with Lisa Stewart right at the start, but you wanted to do it differently and look what a mess you've got us all into! It was time someone sorted everything out, and that's just what Hugh and Paddy have done. They're *real* men.'

She looked contemptuously at her husband as he filled a tumbler with vodka, drank half of it, then sank down on one of the sofas.

'I – I don't know what to do,' Ryan said helplessly. 'You can't get away with it.'

'Oh, I couldn't possibly! But Badger's a serious professional – the best in the business, Hugh says. He'll take care of everything.'

'They'll come looking for them.'

'No they won't. Someone phoned and I said they'd left an hour ago.' Cara sat down and folded her hands in her lap.

Ryan's mind, the quick mind he was so proud of, was racing round and round like an animal frantic with fear. Supposing he went and let them out. Cara couldn't stop him, but he knew what would happen then. The person on the hit list wouldn't be Marjory Fleming; it would be him. And even if what he'd been accustomed to thinking of as the worst happened, they'd be waiting for him in prison too.

He looked at the glass in his hand. Might as well blot it out. There was nothing else he could do.

FLEMING TURNED AWAY from the door she had been banging, trying not to feel crushed by the disappointment. She had heard the voices in the hall and reasoned that the Fraud Squad ought by now to have sworn out a warrant. Clearly they hadn't. It was just Ryan coming home, presumably, and of course he would be in on this as well.

Kershaw was still slumped on the floor in her fugue of grief. Fleming had, in the least alarmist terms possible, explained the situation, but she wasn't sure how much had sunk in. She wasn't even sure that in Kim's condition the idea of sudden death mightn't be appealing. She was on her own – battered, terrified and on her own.

There was a current of air coming through a grid on the back wall, providing cool ventilation for the larder – and indeed it was cool, not to say cold, with the dank air seeping through it. The grid was small, but not, she thought, impossibly small; if it could be dislodged, she with her larger frame might have difficulty but Kershaw, who was slight, should be able to get through – though the question remained, how much use would she be once she got to the other side?

Fleming checked it out, but it had been embedded in cement round the aperture by workmen who intended it to remain in place for the next few hundred years, but if she used the penknife she always carried in her bag, she just might be able to loosen the mortar. It would take time, though, and she had no idea how much time they might have. Not much, probably – and now she remembered that she had left her bag in the sitting room.

Don't panic. Face facts. Decide what you do when that door opens and a man is there who has come to kill you. Two of you could overpower him, but it was hard to believe that Kershaw could react. No back-up, then, and the added problem of protecting a helpless colleague.

Fleming was seriously chilled already. There was a damp film on the stone floor and she had to chafe her hands to try to get more feeling into them. Kershaw was shivering – Fleming really needed to get them both moving or their limbs would stiffen up.

She didn't hear voices or footsteps. Suddenly the door opened and she was taken by surprise, completely unprepared.

Chapter Twenty-seven

TAM MACNEE'S SPIRITS rose when his phone rang and he saw the number. The boss must be at home; she'd taken her time to phone him, but he'd forgive her.

When he answered it, though, it was Bill Fleming's voice at the other end. He liked Bill; they didn't meet often enough. It crossed his mind, as Bill made the usual polite enquiries, that Marjory might have mentioned his enforced time off and this was a kindly gesture. Well, he was always on for a pint.

But Bill didn't sound like a man making a social call. He sounded concerned as he asked whether Tam knew where Marjory was today.

MacNee looked at his watch. 'I know where she'll have been,' he said. 'She said she'd be going to Rosscarron House in the morning, but she'd be back by now.'

'That's just the thing. She isn't. I've been trying to get through on her mobile, but she's not answering, so I phoned the station, but she wasn't there. They even tried Rosscarron House for me, but they said she'd left.'

It wasn't like Bill to get worked up about his wife's whereabouts. 'There's lots of places where there's no signal,' MacNee said soothingly. 'She'll likely be back for the briefing at six.'

'Yes,' Bill said, but he sounded unconvinced. MacNee thought he was going to ring off, but then he said, 'Tam, I know she would kill me if I made any sort of fuss, but you know this Glasgow hitman that's been seen in the area – Badger, she said they called him?'

Suddenly MacNee went very still. 'Hitman? No.'

'Oh, perhaps I shouldn't . . .'

'Go on, Bill. You can't stop there.'

'That girl, Lisa Stewart. She was killed yesterday in a hit-and-run – you knew about that maybe? Well, Marjory had been a bit worried before because that Hepburn creature had threatened her to try to make her drop some enquiry she was making about Crozier's business, and she was scared they might have taken out a contract on her. But she told me this morning the girl seemed to have been the target after all and it was nothing to do with her. She was embarrassed, said she'd been overreacting, but it struck me—'

'I can guess. There might be more than one target.' MacNee's face was grim. 'I'll get right on to that.'

THE LARDER DOOR didn't open fully. Before Fleming could launch herself at it, Nico's face appeared round the corner.

'What are you doing?' he said, with curiosity rather than surprise. 'I heard you banging on the door.'

Fleming drew a deep breath, trying to slow her thumping heart. 'Just waiting for you to let us out,' she said. 'There's a sort of prize for doing that, if you do it the right way.'

Nico's eyes narrowed. 'What?' he said.

Her mind went blank. 'What do you like to do best?'

'Play computer games. They're cool.'

'If you don't tell anyone you've let us out, you can choose the best computer game you can think of and I'll give it to you.'

'How do I know you will?'

Despite the cold, Fleming could feel sweat beginning to bead on her brow. 'I promise. I'm a police officer, and if we don't tell the truth, we get put in jail.' And how overcrowded would the prisons be if *that* passed into law?

He still looked unconvinced. She tried again. 'So if you don't get it, you can go to see my superintendent and he'll arrest me.'

Nico smiled. 'That'll be good. All right.'

He stood aside. Grabbing Kershaw's arm and pulling her to her feet, Fleming walked out of their prison. 'Where are your mum and dad?' she asked.

'In the sitting room. I heard them talking.'

'The deal is that you don't tell them you saw us.' Fleming closed the door and turned the key in the lock again. 'OK?'

Nico nodded. 'OK. They're stupid, anyway.'

'Is there a back door?'

He pointed, and still holding Kershaw's arm to propel her along, Fleming hurried along the passageway and opened the door on fog and blessed freedom. Now all they had to do was work their way round the house unseen and back to the car. If they met Black on the way down to the bridge, they'd just have to—

Using what for car keys? Fleming stopped in dismay. They were in the shoulder bag she had left in the sitting room where Cara and her husband would be sitting even now.

As the black Toyota took the twisting road towards Kirkcud-bright and Rosscarron, the fog grew thicker and thicker. It was low cloud now, really, implacably thick and on this windless day not even swirling into occasional clear patches so you could see to overtake. Black was prepared to take risks, but when you came up behind an elderly Allegro with what looked like an equally elderly driver, you were trapped. You couldn't overtake unless you had a death wish.

He was beginning to have a bad feeling about this one. It was as if someone was trying to tell him something, and if it had just been the money, he'd have bailed out, but it wasn't. You didn't tell men like his paymasters that you'd changed your mind, especially when he knew from the money they were paying him, and the target, that this was serious stuff.

Time was passing. If Cara got it wrong, if she hadn't managed to keep Fleming there until he arrived . . . He swore impotently, then started banging on his horn to force the driver in front to make way.

Deaf as well? He came up close, nudged the bumper once, twice – at last the car pulled in and he swept on, ignoring the shaken fist and the angry tooting.

After that he made better time. That was Kirkcudbright now. About ten minutes to the turn, Cara said.

A quarter of an hour later Black began to wonder if he'd missed it. Twenty minutes later he stopped and looked at the map. Swearing violently, he turned and retraced his route.

Fleming had never been round the back of the house before and it took her a moment to orientate herself. They were in a sort of sunken yard, an area of a few square feet between the house and the hill behind. The house itself blocked them to the left; if they followed the path to the right, it would take them past the sitting-room window.

They would have to scramble up the hill. Kershaw was staring around her. 'What – what's happening?'

'No time to explain. Up here.' Fleming grasped Kershaw's hand and started dragging her across the yard.

The slope was steep but with plenty of footholds and Kershaw, Fleming saw with relief, was climbing mechanically. With the short perspective near the house, the fog had seemed thinner, but at the top, they emerged into a sea of white.

The fresh air seemed to be clearing her head and fog could be their friend, as long as they watched where they put their feet. It would give them cover to go down through the camping field and access the road to the bridge, but to take the road was danger. That was the way Black would come – if he hadn't arrived already. Fleming's heart lurched at the thought.

Every instinct was screaming to get as far away from the house as fast as possible, but that was what they would assume she would do. She had to out-think them to survive.

To her left and below, she could dimly see the shapes of the straggly trees in the little wood where Crozier had died. From its cover, she could check whether there was another car outside the house, in which case the hunt would be on immediately. If not, they would have an indeterminate period of grace before it started. And then what? Fleming didn't know yet, and she hadn't time to think now.

'This way,' she said, heading down the hill, struggling to keep her balance on the slippery, muddy path, with Kershaw behind her.

It was weirdly silent, in among the trees and bushes. The fog blanketed sound and distorted direction, so that a twig that snapped under Kershaw's feet had Fleming peering all about her in alarm for a moment. She turned her eyes away from the flattened area, where blue-and-white tape still hung, and tried not to feel that the chill was even deeper here.

'Cold – I'm very cold,' Kershaw said, through chattering teeth.

'Sssh!' Fleming hissed, then realised that she too was soaked to the skin. Neither had an outdoor jacket and the air was saturated with water particles. 'We'll have to keep moving,' she whispered.

They reached the bottom, where the track led across to Keeper's Cottage. With a pang, Fleming saw her own car, locked and useless, and the Discovery, but the executioner didn't seem to have arrived.

The shrubbery began directly opposite, but as a precaution Fleming headed a little way up before running across the track, keeping low, then into the bushes from there. She checked anxiously over her shoulder for Kershaw, but she was keeping up.

The towering rhododendron bushes with their branches thickened with age formed vast banks here, a barrier to progress. They had to force their way round them; the great leathery leaves spilled water on them from above, icy cold, and Fleming felt a jutting twig catch at the sleeve of her jacket. It tore, and when Fleming looked down, there was a streak of bright blood welling up along the scratch. But gradually, through a maze of small gaps, they worked their way along until they were past the house and a little way down the road.

There was still no sign of Black's car, or sound of it either, though in these conditions you might not get warning until it was right on top of you. Fleming paused to take breath, and to think.

Her first objective must be to get across the bridge as quickly as possible. Once they discovered their captives had fled, they would block it to trap her on the headland. She couldn't risk the road, though; she'd have to get to the bridge by way of the rugged headland behind her – rough terrain, which would be slow going through heather and bracken and gorse, and over boggy, uneven ground, especially when you couldn't see more than a few feet in front of you. And there would be sudden drops – into the sea, even – if they got lost and disorientated. She realised that even through the fog she was hearing it now, a low moaning sound off to her left.

They wouldn't get disorientated. And they would be very cautious. And quick too, in her court shoes and Kershaw's – she glanced – smart flats, while not, of course, panicking. And any minute now a pig would fly down and rescue them.

'Come on, Kim,' she said, as if she felt confident about what she was doing, and with her constable silent and shivering behind her, she set off on to the moorland veiled in its pale shroud of mist.

TAM MACNEE TOO was suffering from frustration as he drove down to Rosscarron. Even the wipers on their highest speed weren't keeping the windscreen clear and visibility just got worse and worse; he knew the road, and there were sharp corners and unexpected cambers, which meant that only a daftie would try to speed in these conditions. Most of the drivers ahead of him obviously weren't dafties, but of course their cautious driving irritated him too.

With anxiety churning inside him, MacNee was drumming his fingers on the steering wheel and muttering under his breath.

He was wrestling too with the decision whether or not to press the panic button. Suppose the boss had gone from Rosscarron to do follow-up interviews in yet another of the areas around here with no mobile coverage – what would she say then, after she had specifically said to Bill that she'd been wrong in thinking she was threatened?

She wasn't responding to radio messages either, though. He'd got them to check that. It was certainly odd – not just odd, worrying.

And Lisa Stewart was dead, it seemed. Poor bloody kid! He remembered the tense, brittle woman whose resistance to questioning had left him grinding his teeth in frustration – and remembered, too, the brief pretty smile she had given him once. Yes, poor bloody kid. Never had a chance.

He had decided the best thing to do would be to go to Rosscarron House, where Fleming had been this morning, and check it out for himself. They might know where she had been headed.

He was through Kirkcudbright now, and there was the turn-off. MacNee was just signalling to turn on to the coast road when he saw in his mirror a black Toyota come up behind him. It overtook dangerously, forcing him to brake, and swung in left on to the road ahead of him. If MacNee hadn't had other things on his mind, he'd have gone after him for that. Some folks had no sense at all when it came to fog.

THE MAN IN the black Toyota didn't like it. He didn't like it at all, and when he got to the small, narrow road signalled Rosscarron he liked it even less. A single track – a serious threat to the 'quick in, quick out again' rule. And the Bailey bridge was the last straw. No one had told him about the Bailey bridge.

The road he was on went up past the bridge, along the bank of the river, though he had no way of knowing if there was a way out at the other end. It looked as if it could peter out in some farm-yard miles on. He drove a little further, then found an open area to draw the car off the road, turning and parking it so that it was facing back down the hill. He'd go the rest of the way on foot. If there was trouble, you could easily vanish in these conditions, and the car wouldn't be blocked in.

THERE WAS A sense of unreality about all this, Fleming thought, as she struggled through heather and bracken. Perhaps this was just another nightmare – the wet cold, the roots that snatched at her ill-shod feet, the hidden rocks that could trip you, the grazes and scratches and bruises, the light-headedness and pain persist-ing after her head injury. She was gasping with effort, and she could hear Kershaw's uneven breathing behind her too. Once or twice, when she looked over her shoulder, she knew a moment's fear when she didn't see Kershaw, but then she would appear, having fallen perhaps, or gone a long way round an outcrop. She wasn't crying now, just huddled with her arms wrapped round her body for warmth and tramping with an expressionless face.

Fleming was used to hill walking, but not in conditions like these. You would have to be insane to go out in weather like this, because in featureless hill country it was so easy to walk in a circle when you believed you were walking straight.

Was that what they were doing now? It had been all right at first, keeping a straight path somewhere parallel to the road, but you couldn't walk straight when rocks rose in your path, or when the ground fell sharply away. She had hoped she would be able to keep the sound of the sea to her left, but with the effects of the blanket of fog, the monotonous sound seemed to be all around her.

She was having to fight debilitating panic. It was hard to know how much ground you were covering, but how far could it be to the bridge from the house? A mile at most. Surely, if she had been going in anything like a straight line, they would be heading steeply downhill, approaching the Carron? They weren't. Not that their problems would be over when they reached it; it was fifteen miles to the police station at Kirkcudbright and she was beginning to worry about exposure. She had no feeling in her hands and feet any more, and the stiffness in her limbs was slowing her down. And she mustn't think that behind her someone could be stealthily tracking their every movement.

She hadn't heard Black's car arriving and surely, even in this situation, she would have heard the engine? That was good, that had to be good, she told herself. And he could have been coming from a distance; they could be safely away before he reached Rosscarron and the Ryans found that the cupboard was bare. She just had to shut her mind to any other possibility, or she wouldn't be able to think straight. If she was thinking straight anyway.

MacNee was still fuming at being carved up as he drove on towards Rosscarron. The man hadn't been some young tearaway; he'd seen him in the rear-view mirror, a middle-aged man, pale-faced with black hair in a deep widow's peak. Should have known better—

Suddenly it triggered a picture: the night he'd kept watch by Gillis Crozier's body, the face that had appeared from the undergrowth, the badger out hunting . . .

Badger. He felt cold and sick. He accelerated, and his mind raced too, as he focused on keeping the car on the road round the unseen corners.

He should have thought of this whenever Bill told him: if Lisa Stewart had been killed to order, the Ryans had ordered it. The information MacNee had given Fleming yesterday had sent her straight into a trap.

Without hesitation this time, he called in immediate assistance, top priority. But Kirkcudbright was the nearest station: he knew how long it would take them to reach here, in weather like this. It was up to him.

WHEN BLACK REACHED Rosscarron House, he was in an evil mood. The walk from the bridge to the house had been longer than he had thought it would be, and his light jacket was little protection in this sort of weather. He hated the country anyway, and this whole operation was freaking him out. He'd taken more antacids in the last two days than in the previous three months.

The gun in the special interior pocket in his jacket, his familiar Glock 19.9, was a heavy, reassuring weight. He checked that it was half cocked before he rang the bell.

It was Cara Ryan, he presumed, who opened the door, all bright and chatty and offering coffee, for God's sake.

'Where are they?' he snarled. 'Show me, then get out of the way.'

The woman gave a nervous giggle. He had the gun in his hand as he followed her through the hall. Her shoes were clicking; he grabbed her arm as she went to open the door below the stairs.

'Tell me where to find them and stay here,' he said under his breath.

He saw her eyes widen at the sight of the gun, though in excitement rather than alarm. 'I'll be quiet,' she whispered, as she opened the door quietly and pointed to the cupboard.

Black gestured. 'Bugger off.' He didn't wait to check on her obedience, pulling the door to behind him and moving on the balls of his feet as he went towards the cupboard. Another check on the gun, then he turned the key and the handle.

He kicked open the door and for a moment couldn't take in what he was seeing – an empty larder. He slammed the door back until it banged on a shelf – no one behind it, then. No one above, lying on a shelf. Empty. Had the silly cow told him the wrong cupboard?

But when Black came out again, she was still standing by the door to the hall, and the expression on her face told him that there was no other cupboard.

He strode up to her. 'What – has – happened?' he bellowed. 'Where are they?'

'I – I don't know! They were there, secure,' Cara bleated.

'Not exactly,' Black said grimly. 'Right. How much do they know about me?'

'Nothing, nothing!' Cara began to cry. 'Let me go! I just—' She stopped.

'You just *what*?'

'It slipped out. I said I knew about Lisa being killed – they probably didn't even notice. Don't hurt me!'

Black would have liked to smash in her stupid face, but there was no time. He went icy calm. 'Then we have to find them. Where could they have gone?'

THEY WERE DEFINITELY lost, moving in some sort of circle. Fleming recognised the rock configuration in front of her, though she couldn't remember how long ago it was that she had seen it. The cold was getting to her brain and she was so tired she was reaching the stage where just lying down would be worth it even if she didn't get up again.

She mustn't, she mustn't. Then she heard a sound behind her and turned. Kershaw had fallen and was making no attempt to rise. Fleming came back and shook her. The woman was icy cold, but it seemed as if she had stopped shivering – a serious sign of hypothermia.

She lay down beside her, trying to share their body heat, rubbing her with her own numb hands, trying to generate some sort of warming friction, and felt with relief the shivering start again.

'Get up, Kim,' she urged. 'You can't lie here. We must be nearly there.'

'You don't – don't understand,' Kershaw said through her cold-stiffened lips. 'I don't care. Go on, leave me.'

At that moment Fleming heard the sound of a car engine, coming closer. They must be near the road after all, and when she turned to look over her shoulder, she could dimly see it passing. It was the Discovery, and it was heading downhill at a steep angle. The steep part of the drive was only a couple of hundred yards short of the bridge.

She stood up. 'We're all right, Kim. I know where we are.' For what good that was, since they would be going down to block the bridge! Then suddenly she remembered the houses in the flooded development – deserted, probably, since no construction would be going on in this weather, but at least offering shelter and a hiding place. She said urgently, 'Look, I know where we can get shelter. There are houses just down here. It won't take long. Get up, Kim.' Then, 'Constable, that's an order. Get up.'

She wasn't sure it would work, but it did. Kershaw got slowly to her feet. Slipping an arm behind her for support, Fleming set a course parallel to the drive, at a distance where they would reach the little road that served the estate.

And there it was just below them, a thin ribbon in the mist, which was slightly less dense here at the lower level. Breathing a prayer of thankfulness, Fleming helped Kershaw down the last slope.

It would be safer to stick to the rough ground instead of the metalled surface, but by now they were so exhausted that she had to take that risk. They would hear the engine of the Discovery anyway and could take cover if necessary.

She was fairly sure now she would have been bound to hear the sound of another car arriving. Perhaps, after all, there wasn't a professional out there looking for them. Or not yet, at any rate.

HE HAD TO stay calm. Giving way to temper and taking out the two drooling retards who had got him into this situation wouldn't help anyone. With the pistol still in his hand, Black walked down the road, listening and looking, though there wasn't a lot of point in that, when you couldn't see five feet to either side. He wasn't going to take to the hills either, though doubtless that was where they'd gone. He wasn't the outdoor type and you could make a serious fool of yourself, stumbling along after an unseen quarry and probably breaking your ankle in the process.

If the Ryans could be trusted – if! – the women hadn't been gone long enough to get off the headland. With Ryan dispatched to block the bridge, it would just be a waiting game.

They couldn't explain how the pigs had escaped and it seemed to have been pure chance that they hadn't been able to drive away and alert the entire police force. Save him from amateurs! He'd never before relied on anyone else for one of these jobs, and this was why.

Black walked on down the hill, brooding. How long would it be before someone started asking questions about where the inspector was? How long before he decided that whatever the consequences, he'd simply have to abort the mission?

He was soaked through, cold and afraid now too. Afraid not just of the police, but of his clients.

The men who had commissioned him were dangerous – that went without saying. All his professional dealings were with dangerous men. Who else could afford what he charged? But Lloyd and Driscoll were not only dangerous, they were desperate this time, and Lloyd's cold eyes when he briefed Black had spelled out the price of failure.

It hadn't bothered him much. Dealing with hicks from the sticks, and good money – seriously good money. Piece of cake! Except it wasn't.

He was torn with indecision. Lloyd and Driscoll would be vindictive enemies; on the other hand, it was looking bad and putting his head in a noose wasn't smart either. Very not smart, if he wanted a chance to look at the sky anytime these next twenty years.

He had to play the percentages. When he reached the bottom, he'd tell Ryan he was on his own, pick up the car and head back to the safe anonymity of Glasgow. Unless a miracle happened between here and there.

And then it did. He heard a woman's voice, from somewhere on the rough ground up to his left, saying, 'Look, I know where we can get shelter. There are houses just down here. It won't take long. Get up, Kim.' Then, 'Constable, that's an order. Get up.'

Black smiled. He took back all he'd said about Lady Luck.

Chapter Twenty-eight

DS MacNee reached the Bailey bridge, then hesitated. He could drive up to Rosscarron House, US Cavalry to the rescue, guns blazing. Then what?

He knew fine what they were up against. Down here, when you were dealing with local crime, you could maybe forget that Glasgow, the murder capital of Europe, was just two or three hours away. But he'd lived long enough in the more squalid parts of that city to know that if one of the pros was on this patch, he'd have a gun and wouldn't hesitate to use it.

Fleming, he believed, was in deadly and immediate danger, but getting himself shot in a full-on approach wouldn't help her. MacNee knew precisely what the official position was: he would be guilty of misconduct if he did anything other than wait for the back-up he had summoned, and even then if there was reason to believe guns were involved, their instructions would be to wait for an armed-response unit.

And how long would that take? Long enough for the shooting and the escape – after which, of course, stable doors would be shut and bolted with a great stushie about lessons being learned and there'd be a fine funeral with all the top brass in their Sunday-best uniforms.

Or he could just take it quickly and quietly, get himself up there unnoticed, see what was going on and take his chances. MacNee might be too late already, but whatever happened to him, at least he'd know he'd tried.

With any luck, the lads from Kirkcudbright would be well on their way by now. He'd better keep their path clear; he drove further on, up round a corner. There, off the road on a piece of rough ground under some scrubby trees was a black Toyota. He parked his own car nearby and jumped out.

MacNee was rarely without his Swiss Army knife, and it was the work of a moment to slash all four tyres. If it turned out that he'd jumped to the wrong conclusion, he'd pay the outraged owner out of his own pocket. Then he turned his car and drove back round the corner again.

He shrugged on his heavy waterproof jacket, took a telescopic baton from the glove compartment and stowed it away. He got out and took a deep breath. 'May coward shame disdain his name, The wretch that dares not die!'

For speed, he'd have to take the metalled road up to the house until he reached the gate towards the top of it, which led into the camping field. That was the risky bit. After that he could get down to the house from behind, unseen.

It was uphill and MacNee maybe wasn't quite as fit as he should be, but he could still cover the ground. He had already reached the field where the fog would conceal him when he heard the voices outside the house.

Declan Ryan was saying in a tone that suggested panic, 'I don't know! I came back to the house about half an hour ago and they were there then. They must have picked the lock. But they won't have got far in this weather – they wouldn't risk going down on the road.'

Another voice with a strong Glasgow accent gave him his character with an impressive flow of invective. 'Get down and block the sodding bridge,' it finished. 'I'll check around here.'

The car door slammed and a minute later the Discovery came barrelling past.

So Marjory was still alive, anyway. She'd got away from them, was out there, somewhere in the fog, alone and aware that she was being hunted. She must be scared, and wet, and very, very cold; MacNee, in his police-issue jacket, was cold enough. How could he find her?

He couldn't. But at least he had found her pursuer. MacNee concealed himself behind the wide gatepost at the entrance to the field and waited.

It was two minutes later that he came past, only feet away on the road, looking round about him – the badger man Mac-Nee had seen in the rear-view mirror. He was carrying a gun, a semi-automatic pistol from the look of it. MacNee held his breath; the effects of a fog blanket were strange, muffling some sounds and amplifying others. He could hear the man's own laboured breathing, so he was stressed, then. Good! Stress led to error.

Not that MacNee was feeling calm himself, but his presence being unknown and unsuspected gave him a feeling of power that buoyed him up as he set off, walking silently on the grass verge trailing his quarry.

He was almost at the bottom when he too heard Fleming's voice, and his heart gave a massive *thunk!* in his chest. Ahead of him, the footsteps had stopped: the other man was listening too.

MacNee could, of course, launch an attack now and hope with the element of surprise to seize the gun. But gunshots could go anywhere, and Fleming – and apparently Kershaw too, for God's sake! – were nearby.

He looked at his watch. In another fifteen minutes back-up should be arriving, and he'd specified blues and twos. Hearing that approaching, any professional with half a brain would chuck it and run. Fleming only needed to evade him for ten minutes more.

He daren't follow the man down the road. With deep distaste, MacNee scrambled up on to the moorland and began taking a downward path at breakneck speed. And he probably would break his neck, if he fell. Banks and bloody braes, eh? If he'd his way, he'd concrete over the countryside. All of it.

'HAVE YOU SEEN Big Marge?' DS Macdonald said, coming into the CID room. 'It's almost time for the briefing and there's no sign of her and there's been no message.'

Campbell, working at one of the desks, looked up. 'Don't know where she is, but MacNee's just declared some sort of emergency at Rosscarron House.'

'What's he done now?' Macdonald said acidly. 'I understood he was off at the moment.'

'The boss went out there this morning. With Kim.'

'So she did.' Macdonald frowned. 'I'm edgy about this. I happen to know there's been a tip-off that a professional from Glasgow's in the area – you know, the guy we've been told to look out for but not to approach. There are some of the Glasgow bosses who might be taking an interest, pals of Crozier's.'

'Right.' Campbell was frowning too. 'So we think he took out Lisa Stewart? But why would they want Lisa Stewart killed?'

Macdonald absorbed that, then said slowly, 'They wouldn't, as far as I can see. If Ryan paid Williams to persecute the girl, he could have paid someone to rub her out, and the boss was last known to be going to see Cara Ryan. Has she walked into something?' He was sounding alarmed. 'What do we do?'

'Sounds as if Tam's doing it,' Campbell pointed out.

'If it's what I think, it should be armed response. I'd better talk to Bailey.' With considerable reluctance Macdonald went along to Superintendent Bailey's office, with not much more than a gut feeling to back up his request.

Donald Bailey was inclined at first to be sceptical, but Macdonald found himself becoming more convinced as he argued the case and eventually had Bailey almost as concerned as he was himself. After a phone call to the assistant chief constable, the immediate mobilisation of armed response was authorised.

'There may be no point,' Bailey said heavily at the end of the interview. 'If you're right, she could be dead long before they get anywhere near her. We can only hope you're entirely wrong – though of course that would make it a shocking waste of money, Macdonald.' He shook his head.

With one more worry to add to his concerns about his colleagues, Macdonald went gloomily back to the CID room.

THEY WERE BOTH limping badly – Fleming's shoes were heelless and all but destroyed; Kershaw's were little better – but they were reaching the houses now. There was no one working there today; JCBs and concrete mixers were still, shrouded shapes.

The worst of the mud had been removed and the houses nearest looked to have been cleared, with doors and windows repaired. As

Fleming picked up a stone to break a pane in the back door of the first one they came to, she felt a pang of guilt, but she didn't think she had the strength to go further to one still awaiting attention, and she was quite sure Kershaw didn't. Slipping her hand through the hole, she found the key in the lock inside and opened the door.

By then Kim had slumped on the doorstep. Fleming hauled her in, locked it again on the inside and removed the key. No point in making it easier for anyone who might come looking, though she had no illusions about what would happen if Black worked out where they were.

It was a relief, though, to have shelter from the cold and penetrating wet, and wonderful to sink down on the stairs in the internal hall, which was lit only by a small staircase window; once she had shut all the doors, they would be invisible from outside. There was even a telephone there, though when she tried it, the line was dead. Well, she hadn't expected anything else.

Kershaw seemed alarmingly cold. Might there still be furnishings, or even clothes, upstairs? Fleming didn't know how she would find the energy to climb the stairs, but hauling on the banister, she made it and in the first room found blankets still on the bed, and some towels in the bathroom. She carried them to the stairs, though her feet were so numb she didn't trust herself to walk down; she bumped and slid to the bottom, then swaddled Kim in blankets, pulled one round herself and started to rub Kim's arms and legs with the towels.

Her own numb extremities began to thaw out painfully. Her feet, she noticed with a sort of abstract interest, were badly bruised and lacerated and blistered, and on the injured side of her face, the gash had stiffened and started to throb.

Kershaw was at least opening and closing her hands and moving her feet, and showing signs of being more aware of her surroundings. She looked sideways at Fleming. 'Thanks. I'm sorry.'

'No need. Just rest – we're all right here for the moment.'

But were they? As the immediate physical problem receded, the other worries rushed in. The trouble was, she had no idea what was happening out there, and until she did it was difficult, if not impossible, to have any sort of coherent plan.

Just stay in here, perhaps. Sooner or later – indeed, round about now – they would start wondering at headquarters why she hadn't returned for the briefing and wasn't in contact. Macdonald certainly knew where she had been, and he knew enough to check up on the Ryans.

They should be safe enough meantime; Ryan would assume that they were out there somewhere in the mist, trying to work their way down to the road.

Anyway, she wasn't at all sure if there was much else she could hope to do, in their present state. Kershaw, with her head on her knees, had actually fallen asleep.

It terrified her to be sitting blind in this shadowy hall. Suppose Black was even now prowling around outside? She itched to go to a window to look, but she had to fight the suicidal impulse, waiting with her skin crawling with nerves, listening for a sound that would announce his arrival.

But she mustn't think like that. There was no reason why anyone would suspect they might be here. They just had to wait, and wait.

MacNee was on the slope just above the bridge. A faint breeze was stirring and in places the fog was starting to thin out; below him, he could see Ryan and badger man in conversation. At one point he could even hear the angry Glasgow voice, could even place the accent to within a few streets of his own birthplace. A bred-in-the-bone hard man.

He was turning away from Ryan now – leaving him to block the bridge, just in case, no doubt, while he headed down the short road to the houses, where, MacNee hoped to God, Marjory and Kim had concealed themselves effectively enough to be safe until the lads arrived – or even till they announced their arrival and the man scarpered. The fog could be slowing the cars, of course, but still, the women would be fine. Of course they would.

He'd have to tail badger man, though, just in case, and he drew out the telescopic baton, looped it over his wrist and extended it. He didn't want to take on a professional with a gun – he wasn't daft – but he'd been in plenty Glasgow street fights where there was some bam with a chib and he knew the principle: never mind the knife, play the moron. It was a bit different with guns, but here at least he'd the element of surprise.

As long as badger man didn't decide to take a quick look back. The fog was thinning all the time. Reluctantly, MacNee climbed a little up the slope behind the houses, dodging from one clump of whin to another, ducking down as the misty veil lifted. He felt a right idiot, playing hide-and-seek. And where were those buggers from Kirkcudbright? Didn't they know what that pedal on the right was for?

AT FIRST FLEMING had thought the tiny sound she heard was imagined, born of her fears. But then there was another sound, and another: sinister, stealthy movements outside. Her eyes widened, following them along the side of the house as if she could see through the walls between them. They had been tracked down, then, after all. Black, the hired killer, arrived at last? Cold terror constricted her throat; she couldn't move, couldn't think, even.

Fear – that was as much her enemy as the man outside. She had to do something – anything! – rather than huddling here, a sacrificial victim to her own cowardice. She jumped to her feet.

Kershaw was still asleep; she shook her awake, putting a hand over her mouth.

'Sssh! We're going to go upstairs and lock ourselves in the bathroom.' It was all Fleming could think of. 'There's someone after us who probably has a gun and he's going to break in.'

And how long would it take him to shoot out the lock on the bathroom door? Their only realistic chance had been if no one thought to look for them here. There was nowhere to run, nowhere to hide. They were cornered, here in this pleasant, domestic death-trap.

Kim, though, was getting up obediently, looking bewildered and moving stiffly.

'Come on,' Fleming said. 'Quick as you can.'

And then she heard it – the beautiful, amazing sound of police sirens, approaching fast. With new energy she urged Kershaw towards the stairs, then heard the even more wonderful sound of pounding footsteps, running away.

She dashed into the front room and caught just a glimpse of him before he was swallowed up in the fog as if he had only ever been a figment of her imagination. She sagged in relief as she turned to Kim.

'He's gone. And the lads will be here any moment now – listen.' There was a siren very loud and close. 'They'll have stopped at the bridge, probably. I want to see where that man's gone so I can tell them.'

Fleming opened the front door and stepped outside.

WHERE THE HELL was badger man? The wind had dropped and the fog had settled again; MacNee had lost him. But what he could hear was the blessed sound of sirens and he knew the man would be doing what any professional would do in those circumstances. He'd be trying to reach his car to make a quick getaway, and, Mac-Nee thought with grim satisfaction, would be in for a nasty shock when he found it.

He set off back along the road he had taken, and with a lift of satisfaction felt the wind pick up again, more strongly this time. Fog was a fugitive's friend, and now it was personal. MacNee was going to nail the bastard.

He glanced over his shoulder as he ran and saw Fleming coming out of the house with Kershaw behind her. They'd have been better to wait till the boys had things tidied up, but the boss had never been what you'd call patient. And then his blood ran cold.

MACNEE? FLEMING STARED. He was sprinting up the road towards the bridge. What the hell was he doing here? Had she him to thank—

From a space between the first and second houses on the side of the road backing on to the river a man stepped out, a man with a pale complexion and black hair that grew in a widow's peak on his forehead, a man with a gun in his hand.

Something strange happened to time. He seemed to be rais-ing it in slow motion, levelling it at Fleming as she stood there, presenting a target as wide as a barn door. She tried to turn, but her movements seemed slow, almost balletic.

And then Kim Kershaw was in front of her, moving between Fleming and the gun to take her solo part in the dance of death. The gun cracked and the bullet found her.

Fleming caught her as she crumpled, slowly, slowly, then lowered her to the ground. She looked at the blood on her hands, feeling only an odd detachment as she waited for execution. The gun fired again.

MacNee had launched himself at Black, but just failed to reach him before he got in that first deadly shot. Then he was on him, knocking him to the ground.

The second shot went wide, as MacNee struck the gun from his hand with his baton, sending it spinning down the road. He got in a glancing blow to the back of Black's head and, as the man scrambled to get away, flung himself on top of him, trying to pin him down. But Black was bigger, stronger and frenzied in his efforts to escape; a moment later MacNee was winded on the ground and Black vanished again, up the road and into the mist.

Fleming, ashen-faced, was kneeling beside the crumpled figure. She looked half dazed and helpless; she was staring at her hands, red with blood, held out in front of her. As MacNee reached them, he saw the dark, spreading patch on Kershaw's sweater. Her eyes were closed.

'Oh dear God!' he said, 'Is she . . . ?'

Through numbed lips Fleming said, 'It's bad.'

He could see that. He knelt down, checking for a pulse.

'She's breathing, at least.' He stood up again, looking around impatiently. 'Where the hell are the uniforms? A chest wound – we need to get it sealed and keep her warm till the ambulance gets here.'

There were shouts and the sound of running feet as the first men arrived from the patrol cars. MacNee had his jacket off and was spreading it over Kershaw; one of the others did the same, then sprinted back for first-aid supplies and survival blankets.

Another said urgently, 'Where did he go?' and MacNee pointed. 'The gun's on the ground there, though he might have another one.'

The man nodded, then set off in pursuit, yelling instructions.

MacNee turned to Fleming. She was looking ghastly, with a fresh bruise on her temple, and her body was racked by violent shuddering. 'You're needing a blanket too. You're in a bad way,' he said gruffly.

Fleming didn't seem to hear him. 'She took the bullet for me,' she said, her voice quavering. 'She pushed me aside, Tam. I – I think she wanted to die.'

Watching, that had been his reading of it too, but he said robustly, 'Well, she maybe won't. Look, the fog's definitely lifting and they could get the air ambulance here in twenty minutes. And afterwards we'll all just have to give Kim something to live for.'

HE'D BEEN A fool to take the time to get in the shot, but Black had simply lost it, furious at the bungling that had landed him in this situation, desperate to retrieve his position. It was all to play for: when he saw the door opening and the women coming out, he couldn't resist. And then he hadn't even got the right one.

Now he was cowering on a hillside in mist that was lifting by the minute, with God knows how many policemen on his heels.

He was following the course of the river, upstream of the bridge. He'd have to ford it somewhere, then come down on the other side to his car.

They'd have had no reason to suspect it would be up beyond the turn to Rosscarron House. Once he reached it, he could put his foot down and blast his way through whatever was down there. At least it was a chance.

He could hear them shouting to each other, behind him and lower down. The water was a bit shallower here – and anyway, what alternative did he have? Making as little noise as possible and grimacing, he scrambled down the bank and struggled across.

At least he was on the right side now, and though he could see maybe twenty, thirty feet in either direction, there was nothing alarming. For speed, he must risk taking the road down, though he hugged the edge where a scrubby hedgerow of bushes might give him cover. He could hear a chopper overhead; he might need to disappear.

There was his car now. Maybe there was, after all, a chance to escape disaster. With a prayer to his patroness, Lady Luck, he reached it and opened the driver's door.

It was only then he noticed a slashed tyre. A second later the door slammed over, pinning him painfully against the car, and holding it in place was a small man with an unpleasant, gap-toothed smile. It sent cold chills down his spine, that smile – that, and the three uniformed officers standing behind.

'You and me's got a wee bit of unfinished business, pal,' the small man said. 'Maybe you'd like to try resisting arrest?' He smiled again. 'We'll all have a fine time subduing you, you dirty bastard.'

And suddenly no one was smiling any more.

'I'M SURE I don't need a CAT scan,' Marjory Fleming protested. 'It was only a slight knock.'

'That's what they all say,' the young houseman said cheerfully. 'And then there's a brain clot and they drop dead without warning two days later.'

'Did anyone ever tell you that you had a wonderful bedside manner? No, I thought not,' Marjory said, with forced cheerfulness.

It was a huge effort to act normally, but it was the only way she could get through all this without disintegrating. She daren't let herself think about the woman in the operating theatre who was, in the conventional phrase, fighting for her life. Particularly since Marjory was fairly sure she wasn't.

But certainly, once she'd had the scan, it was a relief to know that there had been no lasting harm. Bill, looking shaken, had arrived just as she got the verdict.

'I'm fine,' she said. 'Surface damage only.'

'The surface is pretty bad,' he said with husbandly candour. 'They've said I can take you home – probably afraid you'll scare the other patients.'

Marjory managed to smile. 'Good. Lucky the hens are made of sterner stuff.' But when Bill went to take her in his arms, she said quickly, 'Don't, Bill. I want to get home before I go to pieces. Make another joke – that might help.'

She hobbled out of the cubicle on her bandaged feet. Behind her, Bill said, 'Not sure I can make a joke to order, but I could repeat the one Hamish Raeburn told me about a farmer, a lady vet and a farrowing sow—'

'Anything but that,' Marjory groaned, but it got her out to the car before the tears came.

Thursday, 27 July

'A GOOD, THOROUGH go to the hall this morning, Hayley,' Susan Telford admonished the young woman in a pink nylon overall. 'There's the brass to do, and it's time the floor was polished again.'

'Yes, Mrs Telford,' Hayley said meekly, only pulling a face when her employer's back was turned. Fussy old bat! But she switched on the hoover and got on with it. If it wasn't properly done, she'd only end up having to do it again.

She poked the hoover under the hat-stand. A piece of paper stuck to the nozzle; she picked it up and glanced at it incuriously – just a copy of the sheet they put in all the bedrooms. She binned it and went back to her task.

BAILEY THOUGHT HE was doing Fleming a favour by ordering her to take time off, and it was true that she was still feeling ill with shock. But she would so much have preferred to be in the thick of it all, to have an inquiry that was rapidly gathering pace to occupy her mind. She had phoned Andy Macdonald, who had told her briefly that the Fraud Squad had gone in to Rosscarron House and a very promising laptop computer had been found in the kid's bedroom. They'd sworn out warrants for Lloyd and Driscoll, and both Ryans were in custody.

He added, with obvious relief, that they'd been able to stand down the armed-response unit before it dented the budget, and that Bailey was taking all the credit going for exposing the fraud and condescending to Glasgow about having rounded up one of their serious villains. Macdonald hadn't time to chat, though, and while she was grateful for these crumbs of information, it only made her hungry for more detail.

The house was empty. Bill was away today at a sale, the kids were at school, and though her mother, Janet, clucking her distress, had said she'd be out to see her, she'd a friend to take for a hospital appointment first, so Fleming was delighted when she saw Tam MacNee's car pulling up in the yard and hobbled out on her bandaged feet into the drizzle to greet him.

Meg, bored by inactivity, bounded out too and MacNee looked gratified by the welcome. 'Oh, it's great to be bonny and well liked, as they say. How are you feeling?'

'Fine. Come on in – I'll put the kettle on. Everyone else is too busy to talk to me. I'm glad to have a companion in ignorance.'

'Who says?' MacNee said cockily, and she turned from the range to look at him.

'What do you know? Oh, have you heard anything about Kim? I phoned this morning, but they wouldn't tell me because I'm not a relation.'

'The word is, she came through the op, but she's critical.'

They were silent for a moment and then MacNee went on, 'Cara Ryan's got herself one of the Glasgow lawyers who knows every trick in the book and has a few wee wrinkles of his own, and she's ready to say she knew nothing about it and lay all the blame on her husband. And Ryan's claiming he didn't do anything except keep quiet about what she and Jason Williams were up to.'

'Where are you getting all this from?' Fleming demanded, pushing a mug of coffee across the table. Then, when MacNee winked and tapped the side of his nose, she said, 'And you're not getting any of my mother's baking if you don't tell me.'

MacNee caved in at once. 'Jock Naismith and I are old pals, and nothing goes on that he doesn't know about. He's agreed to keep me posted.'

'Right. So what about – Black?' She couldn't control a shudder as she said the name.

'He'll appear on petition this morning and they'll remand him, of course. There's a lot of interest in the gun. The lads up in Glasgow seemingly think it might clear up one or two outstanding murder cases for them. He's looking at thirty years, and that's if the judge is in a sunny mood.'

Fleming had been eating a flapjack, but she put it down again, feeling queasy. 'I couldn't really take it seriously, you know, before. I couldn't quite believe it. I mean, look at this.' She gestured around the farmhouse kitchen – the cheerful curtains, the Aga, the dog asleep beside it, the dresser with the unmatched china and the holiday postcards and the photos of the family. 'This is real – the other's fantasy. Only it isn't.'

'No, it isn't,' MacNee agreed. 'I've known that since I was just a wee boy. But anyway, we got him.'

'*You* got him.' Fleming crumbled her flapjack. 'The next bullet would have been for me. You and Kim between you – you saved my life. You're making a habit of it.'

'Och, haud your wheesht!' MacNee looked embarrassed. 'And Kim'll be all right, you'll see. She'll have to be, to corroborate your allegations about Cara Ryan or they'll be claiming she's no case to answer. A good lawyer would say your fingerprints in the larder were just the result of a search and it would be your word against hers. I'll tell Kim she's needed, if they'll let me in to see her. It'll give her something to fight for.'

'I suppose you're right,' Fleming said gloomily. 'Oh, it's all such a mess and a muddle – I'm not sure I've got it clear even now.'

'It's looking as if it was Cara who was pulling the strings all along,' MacNee said. 'She wanted to punish Lisa Stewart.'

'And she wanted to punish her father for bringing Lisa into their lives,' Fleming added. 'She said as much. And we saw for ourselves how little she minded his death.'

'Here – she maybe even set it up. Come to think of it, she gave Ryan his orders right under my nose, that day at lunch after the accident, and I was standing beside Ryan when he told Jason that Crozier would be coming up through the wood to see the caterers. Cara was Ryan's meal ticket, so he did as he was told.'

'They can't have planned that all along, though,' Fleming argued. 'It only became necessary after Rencombe was killed. I worked out that he must somehow have put Williams under threat.'

'Jock said that Pilapil more or less told Andy and Ewan there was a plan to blackmail Crozier, and he'd guessed what they were up to – if Rencombe was sent to find out the details, then threatened to expose them, that would do it. Of course, if they'd got him to commission Lisa's death – well, they'd have him over a barrel, wouldn't they?'

'Then Cara saw the chance to frame Lisa for Crozier and Williams – after all, as she saw it, Lisa had got off with her first killing.'

'And had she?'

Fleming shook her head. 'No, I simply can't see it. Nico, jealous, uncontrolled – it's far more likely. Oh goodness, I've got to buy him a computer game. He helped us escape, you know.' Then she stopped. 'What's going to happen to the poor kid now?'

'You know as well as I do. He'll go into care and it'll be a downward spiral. I just hope we're not looking for him for murder in another ten years. He's a right little psychopath, if you ask me.'

'I can't bear to think about it.'

'Forget it, then. There's nothing you can do.' MacNee was pragmatic as always. 'Try working out how we're going to nail Ryan for Williams's murder. Last time I looked, Forensics hadn't come up with anything useful at all.'

'It's an odd one, that,' Fleming said slowly. 'An incredible risk to take, just to set Lisa up to take the rap. Elaborate – a lot could have gone wrong, for a revenge that might not even work. You'd be better just paying Williams to kill her too.'

'Maybe Ryan was scared of blackmail. Williams knew too much, and that was the way his mind worked, after all. And with Crozier out of the way, Ryan would be in the money and Williams would be expecting to take his cut . . .' He hesitated.

Fleming looked at him, then said flatly, 'I don't buy it. Not convincing.'

'OK, OK, but what, then? It wasn't Black, that's for sure – too messy.'

She was tapping her finger on her front teeth. 'You know what Bailey would say, Tam?'

'Occam's razor,' MacNee said slowly. 'Cut through all the fussy fantoosh – if there's a simple explanation, it's the right one.'

'There's a simple explanation. Lisa Stewart was there, on the spot, with every reason to hate Williams. We know she couldn't have killed Crozier, so we've been looking to the others involved in his killing. But where did she get the weapon? You said it wasn't lying around.'

'It wasn't.' MacNee was confident. 'But if Williams knew Lisa had seen him kill Crozier – he'd killed twice already – taking her out would be the obvious thing to do.'

'And somehow the tables were turned on him when he produced the crowbar,' Fleming said thoughtfully. 'He was slight, and she's probably quite strong.'

MacNee nodded, then said, 'But hang on – Cara did her best to dump Lisa in it that morning when we told them about Williams. How did she know Lisa was even at the guest house?'

'Williams knew, of course. And if he was planning to kill her, Cara would have been cheering him on, and they'd be expecting to hear the news that Lisa was dead,' Fleming suggested. 'When they couldn't contact him, they'd be worried – worried enough for Ryan to go and see what had happened, maybe. And then he couldn't raise the alarm because there would be too many awkward questions to answer. They were probably hoping no one would be able to establish who Williams was.'

'And once we did, it was the ideal opportunity to claim that Lisa killed Crozier too.'

'It hangs together,' Fleming said, then sighed. 'I hate these situations – where you have a plausible theory that you can't put to the test. Unless there's new evidence of some sort, which is getting more unlikely, we won't be able to prove who murdered Williams. Then there will have to be a case review, to point out all the ways we've failed.' She groaned.

'It was probably self-defence,' MacNee argued. 'And whatever Lisa might have done, she's more than paid for it now, poor lassie.'

'But it's looking like the most they'll be able to pin on Ryan is conspiracy to murder, and if we can't make your imprisonment stick against Cara, she'll probably walk free.'

'At least when it comes to Black they'll throw away the key,' Fleming said. 'Do you think Cara paid him to kill Lisa herself, or was it just a little present from Crozier's pals?'

'She'd be their next partner. Probably their idea of a wee welcome gesture. Or it was something to keep her sweet, so's they could deal with Ryan instead of someone who's likely to be high one minute and spaced out the next. But I tell you one thing – we'll get nothing out of Black. A stint in Barlinnie is just a wee walk in the park compared with a swim in the Clyde in concrete boots.

'Look, the rain's gone off.' MacNee got up. 'I'd better go and give the dogs their walk. They're going stir crazy. Thanks for the coffee.'

At the door, he turned. 'By the way, I sent a bunch of flowers and a wee note to Bunty. I thought I'd maybe do that for a while, till she's ready to see me.'

'How ARE YOU getting on, Hayley?' Susan Telford looked critically around the hall. 'The floor's looking nice.'

'I've just got the brasses to do and then I'm finished,' Hayley said.

'Thanks very much, Hayley. See you tomorrow. Is that rubbish? I'll take it through to the back for you.'

Susan picked up the waste basket and went out to the garden. Most of it seemed to be paper for recycling. She was just about to tip it into the appropriate bin when something caught her eye.

On a folded sheet the word 'JAN' was written in block letters on top of some typescript. She picked it up, frowning.

Could it be a goodbye note from Lisa? Forgetting the rest of the rubbish, she hurried through to the lounge.

'Jan, I've just found this,' she said, holding it out.

Jan Forbes raised her eyebrows, then unfolded it.

'Oh! It's from Lisa!' she exclaimed. She read it in silence, her brows knitting together. Then she put it down and said, her voice shaking, 'Oh dear. I think we'd better get this to the police.'

THAT NIGHT MARJORY and Bill sat in the familiar sitting room in their comfortable, slightly shabby chairs with the familiar pale-gold Bladnoch in the crystal tumblers and Meg in her familiar position between them. It was a chilly night and the fire was dancing in the grate, the logs scenting the air with pine resin.

The room was just as it always had been, humdrum and comfortable, a place where you were secure and cosy and safe. Only you weren't. There was a cold, evil world out there that could break in at any time and the haven they had created was no more than a terrifyingly fragile illusion. Marjory stared sombrely into the flickering flames.

At last Bill said, 'What's happened to your friend? Is he caught up in this?'

Marjory shrugged. 'He's gone back to the States. There's no suggestion that he's implicated in the murders. He and Cris Pilapil were obstructive because they were party to a serious fraud – the authorities may even try to extradite him. Mercifully it's nothing to do with me.'

He nodded. There was a crackle from the fire as a spark flew out and Meg sat up with a jump and looked accusingly around her.

Without warning, Bill said, 'Have you ever wished you'd chosen the other path, Marjory? The walk on the wild side, where you could always be nineteen instead of having a boring farmer for a husband?'

'Oh, Bill!' Marjory looked at him, hesitating. Then she said, 'Yes, if I'm honest, occasionally, when I'm in a rebellious mood. And then I look at you and the kids and I wouldn't change a thing. I was wise enough to recognise real, lasting love when it came, Bill – you have to believe that. We've had years and years and years of happiness. And more ahead, thanks to Tam and poor Kim.' She bit her lip.

'I owe them,' he said, coming across to cradle her bruised face and kiss her gently. 'And don't think you're alone in your rebellious moments. I had my dreams too, you know. Professional rugby – I wonder how far I might have got if the farm and a family hadn't come first. In fact, I still play an occasional game for the British Lions before I drop off to sleep at night.'

Majory pulled a sceptical face. 'You must be substituted pretty early on, then. I've never known you take longer than five minutes before you're snoring.

'Anyway, right at the moment I have to tell you that a seriously boring life looks amazingly attractive.'

They both laughed. Later, when Bill went out with Meg to shut in the hens, Marjory raked out the fire and straightened the cushions. She couldn't bring herself to open the curtains for the morning before she left the room, though, as she usually did, even if her panic in the kitchen that night had been no more than paranoia. Probably.

Oh, she would get over it, put it all behind her, but it would still be there, at her shoulder, ready to whisper that happy confidence was laughable naïvety. She had been haunted lately by lines from a poem she had studied at school:

> *Like one that on a lonesome road*
> *Doth walk in fear and dread,*
> *And having once turn'd round, walks on*
> *And turns no more his head;*
> *Because he knows a frightful fiend*
> *Doth close behind him tread.*

Friday, 28 July

'Marjory!' Superintendent Bailey said, as DI Fleming limped into his office. 'I thought I told you to take time off.'

'I did, Donald. Yesterday.' She sat down without waiting for an invitation, though: her feet still felt as if someone was playing about with red-hot needles.

'Dear me! Is this a sense of duty or just rampant curiosity?' he demanded jovially. He was looking particularly pleased with himself this morning.

'Mostly curiosity,' she admitted. 'Any developments?'

Bailey chuckled. 'Oh, I think you could say that.' He reached into a tray on his desk and took out a sheet of paper. 'They brought this in to me yesterday. I was going to give you a call today before we released it to the press, but better that you can read it for yourself.' He handed it over.

Fleming glanced at the typewritten side, headed 'Welcome to the Rowantrees Hotel', with 'JAN' written across it. Then she turned it over.

The writing was careless and childishly ill formed, and it began abruptly.

Ive had to tell a lot of lies in my life but Im going to kill myself and this is Gods truth.

I never killed Poppy. I loved her. Somethings wrong with Nico, could kill again – not his fault poor little bugger.

Alex Rencombe – never knew about this Jason must have gone back to the house after I left. And I never killed Gillis Crozier either I saw who did, though.

Lee – Jason was hiding in the wood I was up above then Crozier came up the path and he hit him again and again. A lot of blood.

He must of seen me. I didnt tell the police I dont trust them they did me over.

I got back to Kirkluce and he texted me there was money in it for me. I didn't trust him Im not stupid. So I said the hotel garden so I could scream if I was scared but it was dark he came from behind put his hand across my mouth hed an iron bar in his hand I just grabbed it threw all my weight on it. Then he stumbled and I swung it at him he tried to get away and I went after and hit him on the head he fell I wiped the bar on my jacket and threw it down.

I knew Id killed him I didnt care. He would of killed me.

Thats all. I just want people to know I never killed Poppy, like they said I did. I loved her.

Lisa.

Then there was a brief postscript: 'You were kind to me no one else was. Thank you goodbye.'

Fleming finished it and laid it down. 'That's so pathetic! Poor, sad girl,' she said. 'Never had a chance, did she?'

'Oh, absolutely, absolutely,' Bailey said heartily, clearly not wanting to sound unfeeling.

Fleming went on, 'It's more or less exactly what MacNee and I worked out – applying Occam's razor, Donald, you'll be pleased to hear.'

Bailey smirked. 'Can't go wrong. But this wraps it up, Marjory. A truly positive result – and we don't need to waste resources on further investigation into either Crozier's death or Williams's.'

'We've got to go all out to nail the Ryans for conspiracy to murder, though,' Fleming pointed out. 'We should be able to get fingerprint evidence that Williams was in the house, and MacNee can state he heard Ryan telling Williams Crozier would be coming up the path.'

'And we have evidence already of money from the Ryans' bank account going to Williams,' Bailey went on, 'so I have every confidence we have a case.'

'That's good. But Cara . . .' Fleming shook her head. 'She lined us up for the hitman and presumably she was behind poor Lisa's death too. But Tam says she's got a good brief and certainly at the moment it's only my word against hers – no case to answer.'

'Ah, that's where I have some more excellent news to give you. Declan Ryan is falling over himself to give evidence against his wife. He's stated that he heard you battering on the door of the cupboard, that he saw your car at the door and that Cara told him you and Kim were locked up there to be killed by Black. Her saying to him you were there isn't proof that you were, of course, but taking it in conjunction with your evidence, the procurator fiscal has agreed to charge her.'

Fleming stared at him. 'That's fantastic news! No wonder you're looking smug, Donald!'

'Not smug,' he protested. 'Surely you can tell the difference between being smug and taking pleasure in justice being done.' But he was smiling, and Fleming grinned back.

She got to her feet, wincing. 'I'd better return to the paperwork.' Then she hesitated. 'Er . . . I assume you'd have told me if there was any news of Kim?'

'Critical but stable – that's all they'll say,' Bailey said heavily.

Fleming nodded and hobbled out. Her buoyant mood had disappeared.

THE AUXILIARY NURSE came into the high-dependency unit's nursing station. 'There's a funny wee guy outside wanting to see Kim Kershaw. Says he's a detective – he's got ID and the constable on guard duty knows him. He says he needs to ask her some questions – I've told him there's no point, but he's insisting.'

The staff nurse looked up from the notes she was writing and shrugged. 'There isn't, but I don't suppose he can do much harm. Tell him he's got ten minutes – he'll probably give up before that.'

'Fine.' She returned to the man sitting in the waiting area. 'That's OK. No more than ten minutes, though.'

'Thanks, Nurse,' he said, getting up.

She smiled because he had smiled at her – at least she thought it was a smile, though she wasn't quite sure.

KIM KERSHAW WAS lying on a high hospital bed, ghostly pale and gaunt, with her eyes closed. She was wired up to a machine, and there were drip stands and tubes and things . . .

Tam MacNee averted his eyes. He wasn't good in hospitals. Even visiting made him feel faintly queasy. Still, he hadn't much time for what he wanted to do.

'Hello, Kim,' he said awkwardly. 'It's Tam MacNee.'

She could almost be dead, except that he could see the faint movement of her breathing. She certainly wasn't responding, but he'd read somewhere that even deeply unconscious patients could hear what was said to them. Hearing was the last sense to go.

Her hands were lying on top of the sheet. She had slim, fine-boned hands and he took the one not connected up to the drips and focused on it – easier than looking at that lifeless face. It felt limp and cool in his warm one.

'I'm here to say sorry,' MacNee began. 'I didn't realise about your poor wee girl. I was jealous, I suppose, because you had a bairn when my wife was desperate for kids and we could never have them, and I was too wrapped up in my own problems to think about anyone else's. I'm sorry, Kim. It's easy to say the word, but I mean it, right from the heart.'

He felt kind of daft, talking to himself, but he went on anyway, 'You're a brave lassie. When you come back, I'll say sorry again, in front of everyone, and we'll get on fine, you and me. We'll be pals – I'll make it up to you.

'Tell you what – I'll take you to a Rangers game in Glasgow, pies and Bovril on me, and you can laugh when the other side scores and I'll not say cheep – only you better laugh quietly, maybe, because there's other fans not as tolerant as me.'

She hadn't moved. The hand still lay limp, but somehow he'd a funny feeling she'd heard that. He went on, 'I'll tell you what's happened with the cases. We've it all sewn up. The Ryans have been charged . . .'

He gave her a brief outline and he could swear that she was listening. There was no actual sign, none at all – his imagination, perhaps – but it still encouraged him to go on.

'The thing is, we're needing you to work hard at getting better. You're important, Kim – we need you on the team. You've got a good brain there – not a lot of that in Kirkluce CID, except you and me, eh?'

Was she still listening? MacNee had been holding her hand like a fragile piece of china; now he gripped it harder. 'Come on, lass! You've shown me you're a bonny fighter – get cracking!'

She wasn't with him any more. She had switched off, gone back into her twilight world where he couldn't reach her. Slowly he released her hand and laid it gently back on the covers.

He was making it up, MacNee told himself firmly as he went out. He'd been imagining it all along, Kim's interest and then her disengagement. He was a practical man who had no truck with all the touchy-feely nonsense and there'd been too many occasions lately when he'd let himself get spooked. He was needing to get a grip.

It was early in the day for it, but maybe a wee dram might stop him feeling quite so cold and bleak.

Epilogue

THEY WERE GOING to bulldoze Rosscarron Cottages. The remaining owners were happy to settle for the insurance money, it would save the council expensive repairs to the utilities, and there wouldn't be political trouble about the work that should have been done to prevent the landslide in the first place.

It seemed to Fleming a fitting outcome. The road to nowhere would now lead to nothing, just as Lisa Stewart's short life had done. The sea, over the years and the winter storms, would gradually claim its new territory, and with its salt cleansing, the passions and hatreds and terrible deeds would be swept away and forgotten.

With a sigh she turned back to her desk. You couldn't clean up people's lives in the same way. There in front of her, in the files and on the screen, were the records of more pain and suffering and corruption.

And Kim Kershaw had not recovered. She was buried with the damaged daughter, who, if you believed in a heaven, was whole and happy now, reunited with the mother who had loved her more than life itself.

Acknowledgements

My thanks go as always to my agent Teresa Chris, Carolyn Mays and all at Hodder, but especially to Kate Howard who has been such a wonderful and supportive editor.

About the Author

ALINE TEMPLETON has worked in education and broadcasting. She is the author of five more Marjory Fleming thrillers, all available from Witness Impulse. She grew up in Scotland, read English at Girton College, Cambridge, and now lives in Edinburgh. She has a grown-up son and daughter.

www.alinetempleton.co.uk

Visit www.AuthorTracker.com for exclusive information on your favorite HarperCollins authors.